TO KISS A ROGUE

Taking advantage of her good humor, Nathaniel stopped abruptly, turning her until her back was against the wall. She inhaled sharply, but made no move to escape his embrace. Encouraged, he moved closer.

When Mr. Wainwright took her chin in his hand and tilted her head slightly, Harriet's breathing came fast. But when he bent his head and placed his mouth on her lips, the dim, gloomy hallway was suddenly whirling with color.

He brought his mouth down softly at first. A taste, a tease, a nibble. Harriet was surprised by this gentle exploration that made her senses swim. Lust always held a titillating, secret interest in her mind, yet she had never completely experienced it.

Until now. And it was impossible to resist the raw longing and emotions this magical kiss brought forth. She responded in a wholly inappropriate manner by clutching his lapels and pulling him closer. He deepened the kiss, coaxing her mouth open. His tongue thrust at hers and she answered with her own, amazed at the depth of feeling and passion he could arouse . . .

Books by Adrienne Basso

HIS WICKED EMBRACE

HIS NOBLE PROMISE

TO WED A VISCOUNT

TO PROTECT AN HEIRESS

TO TEMPT A ROGUE

Published by Zebra Books

TO TEMPT A ROGUE

Adrienne Basso

ZEBRA BOOKS
KENSINGTON PUBLISHING CORP.
http://www.kensingtonbooks.com

ZEBRA BOOKS are published by

Kensington Publishing Corp.
850 Third Avenue
New York, NY 10022

All Kensington titles, imprints and distributed lines are available at special quantity discounts for bulk purchases for sales promotion, premiums, fund-raising, educational or institutional use.

Special book excerpts or customized printings can also be created to fit specific needs. For details, write or phone the office of the Kensington Special Sales Manager: Kensington Publishing Corp., 850 Third Avenue, New York, NY 10022. Attn. Special Sales Department. Phone: 1-800-221-2647.

Zebra and the Z logo Reg. U.S. Pat. & TM Off.

First Printing: July 2004
10 9 8 7 6 5 4 3 2 1

Printed in the United States of America

For my husband, Rudy, who after twenty years is still my very favorite tall, dark, and handsome hero.

Chapter One

London, 1811
Early January

A stillness hung upon the dull, gray afternoon as Nathaniel Bennet, Baron of Avery, and second son of the sixth Duke of Claridge stood before his family's ancestral London mansion. The black ribbons covering the massive brass door knocker had been removed, yet the sleeping mansion still held an aura of mourning, almost as though the sorrow and pain of its occupants had somehow become part of the stone and mortar of the structure.

Though he was already late, Lord Avery made no move to climb the steps. He waited silently, attempting to clear his mind and control his emotions. A drink would taste splendid right now, he thought. A few gulps of strong whiskey or a fine snifter filled with brandy would warm and numb, serving a two-fold purpose.

Ashamed at the direction of his thoughts, Nathaniel let out a long sigh. His breath misted in the cold air, puffing about him like a cloud. Shrugging, the handsome lord shoved his gloved hands deeper into the pockets of his greatcoat to ward off the chill. Yet he knew it wasn't the lowering temperature that brought a shivering frigidity to the depths of his bones.

These daily visits should be getting easier, not harder, he reasoned. But they never did. He arrived a bit later and left a bit earlier each day and still there was no relief. The passage of time was said to heal all wounds, yet his pain still felt raw and deep and real.

Knowing there was no possible way to delay the inevitable any longer, Nathaniel plastered a determined grimace on his face and moved forward, deliberately ignoring how the classic Greek simplicity of the building resembled a mausoleum.

His insistent knock was soon answered by a slender young footman with pale skin and light hair.

"The family is not receiving callers this afternoon. Would you care to leave your card, sir?" The footman held out a silver platter expectantly.

Nathaniel frowned. Apparently the servant was new, for he had no idea to whom he was speaking. "I am a member of the family." Lord Avery removed his greatcoat and lightly fingered the black armband on his jacket. "There is no need to announce me."

"But sir—"

Nathaniel tossed his outer wear in the general direction of the servant and turned away.

"His lordship is in the drawing room," the footman called out nervously as he lunged forward in a feeble attempt to catch the heavy garment before it hit the polished marble floor.

"I am not here to see his lordship," Nathaniel muttered under his breath.

"Ah, there you are, my lord." Mrs. Hutchinson, the housekeeper, puffed her way down the staircase, her large chin quivering. "His grace has been asking after you. He's a mite fretful, but I told him, and the ladies, that you would be arriving at any moment. They count on you so, and I knew you would never shirk such an important duty."

Lord Avery flinched, knowing he did not deserve such praise. It was his brother Robert who had always taken his responsibilities to heart.

"Have they had tea?" Nathaniel asked as he climbed the staircase.

"They were waiting for you," Mrs. Hutchinson replied. The heavy set of keys at her waist jangled loudly as she struggled valiantly to keep pace with him. "I'll have a fresh pot fetched immediately. The one in the nursery is no doubt cold by now."

"Very good."

Nathaniel continued his climb alone to the third floor, barely hesitating as he walked past the many doors lining the hallway. He knew the way well, for he had walked these very floors countless times in his youth.

He never broke stride until he reached the correct door, fearing if he slowed his movements his courage would fail. The moment the latch clicked open, Nathaniel steeled his emotions and pasted a pleasant expression on his face. Then he stepped through the doorway.

"Good afternoon."

The maid who had been sitting quietly in the corner, jumped to her feet and dipped a hasty curtsey. The mending she had been diligently attending to spilled onto the floor and she dropped to her knees to gather it. Nathaniel moved forward to assist her with this task, but she stammered and blushed so awkwardly at his attention that he backed away.

His gaze reluctantly shifted to the center of the room where three young children were huddled together around a wooden table, whispering.

The roaring fire made the room warm, the pale walls, brightly colored quilts, and toys scattered about should have made it cheerful and inviting. Yet it felt more like a stuffy, formal drawing room than a carefree, happy nursery.

"Splendid. You waited tea for me. That was most considerate. Thank you."

Nathaniel cast the group an engaging smile, hardly daring to hope for a reaction. There was none. He contained a sigh, pulled out a chair at the table where the tea had been set and sat down.

The furnishings were designed for a child's size, but he had discovered on prior visits that the sturdy wooden chairs could support his weight. Though it was awkward and uncomfortable to be seated with his knees well above the edge of the table, Lord Avery contorted his long legs into a manageable position.

After all, the children's father had done it nearly every afternoon. Until his fatal illness had struck.

"Sh-shall I pour the tea, Uncle Nathaniel?"

Lord Avery's head snapped up in amazement. Nine-year-old Phoebe's voice was soft and hesitant. He regarded his eldest niece hopefully. This was the first time she had initiated any conversation with him. During his daily visits she always spoke politely and minimally, with a shy insecurity that tore at his heart.

"If everyone else is agreeable." He smiled encouragingly at all three of the children.

Seven-year-old Jeanne Marie returned his grin

briefly. She was tiny, with silky blond ringlets falling over her shoulders, and thickly lashed blue eyes.

"Can Lady Julienne come to tea?" Jeanne Marie asked.

"Lady Julienne?" Nathaniel's brow wrinkled in confusion.

"Her doll," Phoebe whispered.

Lord Avery noted the ragged doll Jeanne Marie held tightly in her arms. Clearly it was well loved for it was missing an eye, several fingers from the left hand and was dressed in a torn and grimy blue gown.

"We would be honored. Set a place for Lady Julienne, please, Phoebe."

Lord Avery detected the slightest flicker of relief in his older niece's face. She took a slow breath and carefully slid another china tea cup next to Jeanne Marie's.

"Will you be joining us, Your Grace?" Nathaniel asked.

Gregory Quincy Reginald Bennet, eighth Duke of Claridge, turned away, crossed his arms determinedly over his chest and buried his face inside them. Plump and rosy cheeked, he was a sturdy lad, large for his four years. There had been only a passing resemblance between Nathaniel and his older brother Robert, yet by some ironic twist of fate, young Gregory was nearly an exact replica of his uncle Nathaniel at the same age, as the family portrait in the long gallery could attest.

He had apparently also inherited his uncle's stubborn, defiant will.

"Stop being such a baby, Gregory," Jeanne Marie said as she jabbed her brother in the ribs.

The little boy yelped and fell forward, stumbling on the fringe of the carpet. Nathaniel caught the boy's arm and steadied him, saving him from landing on the floor. He felt the child's body stiffen for an instant as his eyes focused on Nathaniel with unwavering regard.

"When is Papa coming?" Gregory asked sharply.

"Hush, Gregory," Phoebe admonished. "I have told you again and again that Papa cannot come to see us. He is in Heaven."

"With Mama," Jeanne Marie added helpfully.

Round-eyed with dismay, Gregory stamped his foot. "I don't want Papa to be in Heaven! I want him here! Now!"

Jeanne Marie's lip suddenly began to wobble. "And Mama, too."

Uncomfortable, Nathaniel looked from side to side, in a quandary. It was probably best if the children released some of their pent-up grief, but Lord Avery felt ill-equipped to handle such a situation entirely on his own.

At that moment Mrs. Hutchinson burst into the room, followed by a footman carrying a tray with a fresh pot of tea and additional sweet treats.

"Goodness gracious, what's all of this?" Mrs. Hutchinson cried in alarm. She knelt down and opened her arms wide. Tearfully, Gregory and Jeanne Marie rushed forward to be enfolded in the housekeeper's comforting embrace.

"They were thinking of Mama and Papa," Phoebe replied stoically. "It made them cry."

"Oh, my poor lambs!" Mrs. Hutchinson hugged tighter and the children buried their heads in her shoulders and wailed louder.

Nathaniel cast a glance at Phoebe. She was biting her lip furiously and her hands were bunched together so tightly that her knuckles had turned white. He suspected she wished to be comforted as her brother and sister but perhaps felt she was too old for such an emotional display.

Yet clearly her need was just as great. Lord Avery

shifted his chair unobtrusively and inched his way closer to his niece. He placed his hand beneath the table, near her side, though it was hardly necessary to conceal the gesture for the sake of Phoebe's pride. The drama Gregory and Jeanne Marie had created had drawn the servant's eyes and complete attention.

It must be horrifying to lose not one but both beloved parents in a single blow. As children, their understanding of the event was limited, and mixed within the grief they felt was confusion as well as fear.

A hesitant, soft brush of a fingertip against his wrist distracted Lord Avery's despondent thoughts as he felt Phoebe slip her small, delicate hand into his palm. Nathaniel squeezed her fingers gently, hoping the simple gesture would convey his support and offer her some strength. She, in turn, clasped his hand tighter.

"Your father was not only my brother, but my closest friend," Nathaniel said softly. "As his children, I hold you all dear to my heart. I shall do everything within my power to keep you from harm, protect you from danger and shield you from suffering."

"Truly?" she whispered.

"Always," he responded solemnly.

Phoebe shivered convulsively, but maintained her poise.

"There, there, now dry your tears," Mrs. Hutchinson said. "Cook has made your favorite scones as well as cream cakes. You need to eat them very soon, or else it will be too late and the treats will spoil your dinner."

Mrs. Hutchinson pulled a clean linen handkerchief from her pocket and dried Jeanne Marie's face. Gregory refused the housekeeper's assistance, wiping his nose on his sleeve before joining his sisters and uncle at the table.

Tea was generally served in most households after dinner, but since Nathaniel felt uncomfortable partaking of strong spirits in front of his young nieces and nephew, they had begun the ritual of serving the restorative hot beverage in the early afternoon, during his daily visits. At the very least, it gave them all something to do.

It was a quiet group gathered around the table, but miraculously the display of emotion had eased the thick air of tension. Still, the anxious looks in the children's eyes barely faltered as Phoebe carefully filled the china tea cups.

"If you need anything else, just ring and Sanders will bring it straightaway," Mrs. Hutchinson instructed. The housekeeper beamed pleasantly, then left.

Once alone with his nieces and nephew, Lord Avery struggled to make conversation. Jeanne Marie's doll, Lady Julienne, proved a godsend, for he could address questions and comments to it without any expectation of a response. Plus, the children thought it a great game and soon began to smile at his antics and play along.

With a half-smile and a deprecating shrug, Nathaniel took a sip of his weak, lukewarm tea and conceded that the members of his club would think him a total lackwit if they saw him at this moment, conversing with a ratty doll and three infants in the nursery.

But if this brought even a few moments of peace to the children, his foolishness would be well worth it.

Finally, it was time for him to leave. The muscles in his thighs cramped as he stood upright, but he hid his discomfort. The room became eerily silent at his impending departure. He leaned over and kissed Phoebe and Jeanne Marie on the top of their heads, then turned to Gregory.

Somehow a kiss did not seem appropriate for his rambunctious nephew, yet Lord Avery felt he could not leave without showing the child some form of affection. Motivated purely by instinct, he ruffled the boy's hair lightly, then chucked him under the chin. Gregory smiled approvingly.

The air rushed out of his lungs in a great sigh of relief the moment Nathaniel quit the nursery. For a long minute he waited outside the closed door, staring blindly down the hallway. He took a few steps, then rubbed his neck wearily. Spending just two hours with the children was as exhausting as going ten rounds in Gentleman Jack's boxing salon.

As much as he craved some fresh air and strong whiskey, Lord Avery knew his afternoon's responsibilities were not yet ended. He wanted a word with the children's governess, Miss Reynolds, to solicit her opinion of the children's well-being.

In fact, it was odd that Miss Reynolds was not in attendance as usual in the nursery this afternoon. Perhaps today was her half-day off?

But when he inquired after the calm, kind middle-aged governess, Mrs. Hutchinson clasped her hands together and shook her head. "Miss Reynolds left two days ago, my lord," the housekeeper reported. "I thought you knew."

Lord Avery frowned. "I was unaware of her departure. I thought the children got on very well with her. Were they upset when she left?"

"Terribly." Mrs. Hutchinson nodded her head vigorously. "Thankfully they still have their nursemaids to care and fuss over them. But such an upheaval in their routine cannot be good after all they have suffered. They fairly doted on Miss Reynolds and she took excellent care of them. 'Tis heart wrenching for these children to be losing so many familiar faces. Why, it has been only a month since they lost their dear mother and father."

"I assume this is my uncle's doing?"

"Oh, my yes. Lord Bridwell has made lots of changes around here since he's moved in," Mrs. Hutchinson retorted. "And not all of them good." The housekeeper lowered her head and blushed as if she suddenly remembered to whom she was speaking. "Forgive my bold tongue. I meant no disrespect to his lordship."

"Of course." Nathaniel clenched his jaw. "What exactly happened to Miss Reynolds?"

"I'm not one to tell tales, mind you, but I believe Lord Bridwell did not like Miss Reynolds insisting upon certain considerations for the children. He claimed there was some dispute with the governess over her wages, but I find that difficult to swallow." Mrs. Hutchinson clucked her tongue. "I heard the true disagreement was over the money she was spending on dresses for the girls, shoes for the boy, supplies for the schoolroom and the amount of coal she was burning in the nursery.

"We were all shocked when he sacked her, with no prior warning. Poor thing left without a reference, too. I hope she'll be able to find another position. She has an ailing mother to support, you know."

A shadow crossed Nathaniel's face. Three days after Robert and Bernadette's funeral Lord Bridwell had arrived in town and taken up residence in the family's London home. It was a bold initiative, even for the oldest male relative of the family, but Nathaniel had been too immersed in his own grief and pain to give it much thought.

Nathaniel knew that once Robert's will had

been read and enacted, the financial responsibilities of the estate and the children, would fall to him. Yet the settling of his brother's affairs had turned out to be a rather complex matter. Feeling too physically and emotionally spent to actively investigate, Nathaniel had decided instead to let the various solicitors involved sort out all the legalities.

He was now very concerned that his initial lack of interest had put him at a grave disadvantage. Though he had asked his uncle repeatedly, Lord Bridwell did not seem at all inclined to relinquish the control he had established. In fact, actions such as dismissing the children's governess illustrated that he was more secure in his position and doing everything possible to make it even stronger.

Nathaniel had hoped to avoid seeing his uncle today, but it looked as if he must. It was imperative that the older man be reminded of Nathaniel's keen interest in the welfare of Robert's children and his determination to stay involved in their lives.

"Do you know where Lord Bridwell is this afternoon?"

Mrs. Hutchinson furrowed her brow. "He never leaves the house this time of day. After we delivered the tea to the nursery, Sanders brought a fresh decanter of whiskey to the study. I suspect his lordship is in there right now, enjoying it."

"Then I shall go to the study and have a word with my uncle," Nathaniel replied grimly.

Mrs. Hutchinson turned a questioning gaze on Lord Avery. "I was wondering . . . I mean . . . well, I had hoped that you, not Lord Bridwell, would take on the children."

Her comment brought a flush of guilt to Nathaniel's face. As Robert had hovered near death, he had promised his brother he would care for them. "My uncle and I have not yet reached an agreement on the guardianship of the children, but I fully intend to pursue the matter."

"All I know is that those three little souls need you," Mrs. Hutchinson declared solemnly.

"That fact has become more evident each day, Mrs. Hutchinson, even though I'll own that I know very little about raising children."

"You'll manage it a lot better than Lord Bridwell," Mrs. Hutchinson declared loyally. She patted his forearm reassuringly. "All you can do is your best, my lord."

She was right, of course. He would be a far preferable guardian than his uncle. Though nagging at Lord Avery's brain was the ever-present worry. The children had suffered so much. Would his best be enough?

He crossed the foyer and turned past the red drawing room, the gold sitting room, and the wood paneled library. Though it felt utterly ridiculous to be announced in one of his childhood homes, Nathaniel allowed the footman to call out his name before he entered the study.

He found Lord Bridwell lounging in a large leather chair set by the fireplace, his cheek resting on his fist, his elbow propped on the chair arm. In his other hand he held a half empty whiskey glass and a smoldering cigarillo.

He offered no greeting to his guest. Nathaniel ignored the slight and strode casually to the chair opposite his uncle's. Lord Avery's senses were on full alert. Growing up, he had seen very little of his father's only brother, and what he had learned of his uncle's character these past few weeks made the man even more of a mystery. And a danger.

Nathaniel was aware that Lord Bridwell had been married, was childless and became a widower at a fairly early age. He had an eye for race horses, a nose for gambling, and a reputation as a first-class gentleman. Nearing sixty, he had retained his striking looks along with a trim build and a thick head of gray hair that gave him a distinguished, worldly air.

"Good afternoon, sir." Nathaniel broke the silence as he settled himself in the chair.

"Avery." Lord Bridwell eyed him critically. "What brings you here today?"

"I've been visiting the children. As I do each afternoon."

Lord Bridwell made a sound of disgust. "There are clean glasses and whiskey on the sideboard. Help yourself. I suspect you could use a stiff drink."

"Thank you, no." Though the idea of a strong whiskey sounded most appealing, Nathaniel refused to give his uncle the satisfaction. "I would like to discuss Miss Reynolds."

"Miss Reynolds? The pesky governess?" Lord Bridwell took a long pull of his cigarillo and blew a cloud of the pungent smoke in his nephew's direction. "Her work was unsatisfactory. I dismissed her a few days ago."

Nathaniel lifted his brow. "It was my understanding that she took excellent care of her charges. Besides, the children were very fond of her."

"Well, I found her to be rude and untrustworthy." Lord Bridwell shut his eyes briefly and pinched the bridge of his nose in irritation. "The household is running more smoothly without her."

"If you find caring for the children too taxing, uncle, I would be pleased to relieve you of that burden," Nathaniel said casually.

Lord Bridwell slowly lowered his arm and cast his nephew a veiled look of warning. "I thought we had finally settled this, Avery. You have no legal claim to their guardianship."

"My brother—"

"I don't give a damn about your brother or what he may or may not have said on his deathbed." Lord Bridwell flung the cigarillo into the fireplace. "He was dying, out of his mind, delirious with fever. You cannot put stock in the ranting of a man overcome with such a dreadful illness. I am the eldest male relative. It is my duty to see to the welfare of this family."

With effort Nathaniel contained his furious roar of frustration. How dare his uncle speak of his brother in such cold, callous terms! "I too know of my duties, my responsibilities, and obligations to the family. Robert wanted me to care for his children."

"Then he should have stated his wishes in his last will and testament."

He did! Nathaniel knew a solicitor had been summoned and he knew changes had been made to Robert's will, specifically to the guardianship of the children. Yet somehow this document could not be found.

"We are reasonable men, uncle. I feel certain if we work together a reasonable solution can be found."

"There's no need to play the gallant, unselfish gentleman with me, my boy." Lord Bridwell leaned closer and lowered his voice to a conspiratorial tone. "You forget, I too am a second-born son. I know precisely how it feels to be left with little more than a minor title, a pitiful excuse for an estate, and a miserable allowance.

"I am willing to be generous with the funds that are now at my disposal by doubling your current allowance. But only if you agree to cease interfering in matters that are none of your concern."

"The estate is to be held in trust until Gregory comes of age," Nathaniel protested hotly.

"Exactly." Lord Bridwell took a long swallow of whiskey. "The substantial income and investments are the responsibility of whoever takes care of the brats."

"I do not want the money, uncle," Nathaniel said rashly. "Just the care of the children."

Lord Bridwell stared at him in perplexity. "Well, you can take the girls if you are so hell-bent on playing the role of knight errant." He took a final sip of his drink and regarded his nephew shrewdly over the rim of his whiskey glass. "But I'll not relinquish the boy. He stays with me."

A wave of uncertainty flooded through Nathaniel. This was by far the most his uncle had ever offered. For a moment he was tempted to agree, yet he could not bring himself to separate Gregory from his sisters. It would be too cruel a blow to the young boy.

"I shall consider the offer most carefully."

Lord Bridwell laughed mildly. "I thought you might. Especially the part about a doubled allowance."

Nathaniel tensed, feeling his temper climb. By sheer will he restrained his reactions, deflecting his uncle's mocking laugh with his most arrogant smile.

Then he rose slowly to his feet, straightened to his full, impressive height, gave his uncle a curt nod of farewell, along with a deliberate, disparaging look and walked away.

The cold, biting air had a restorative effect on Nathaniel's battered mind. Hatless, he stood on the front steps of the mansion, gulping in several deep breaths. After a few moments he dragged his hand through his hair and turned towards the street.

It was time for that drink. Lord knows, he had more than earned it.

Chapter Two

The sound of footsteps rumbling overhead began as a small patter, then increased in volume to a dull roar. Miss Harriet Sainthill, comfortably ensconced in a large chair set before a cheerfully crackling fire, glanced up from the exceedingly dull book she was reading, half-expecting to see pieces of the plaster ceiling descend upon the spotless carpet.

The footsteps moved away, then sounded in the hallway directly outside the drawing room doors. Harriet closed her book and clutched it to her chest in an unconscious, protective gesture. Suddenly, without any additional warning, the doors burst open and smacked the wall.

The intruder entered the room with all the energy and enthusiasm of a charging bull. In a blur of color, the small figure flew across the room and crouched behind the gold brocade sofa.

Harriet set the book down on the small table beside her, but before she could rise and investigate, a second intruder entered. He stood mutely in the doorway—tall, broad-shouldered and imposing. His strong features and handsome face were contorted in an odd expression of equal parts anger and distress.

"Griffin!" Harriet called out in surprise as she watched her brother advance purposefully into the room. "Is something wrong?"

Viscount Dewhurst grunted a garbled response. He swept the room with his gaze, stopping to regard the brocade sofa with a lingering inquiry.

"Have you seen Georgie recently?" the viscount asked. "I seem to have misplaced my son."

Harriet cleared her throat. Before she could formulate a reply, the sound of a soft whimper echoed through the room.

The noise startled both Harriet and her brother. "What is wrong?" she asked in a horrified whisper.

The viscount's jaw clenched. "That is between Georgie and me. Have you seen him?"

Over the past two years Harriet had come to respect her brother's ability as a parent and his authority as a father. Though she occasionally disagreed with the decisions the viscount made regarding his son, she never doubted the strong bond of love that existed between the two.

Yet her instinct to protect her five-year-old nephew from his father's most uncharacteristic wrath prevailed.

"I have not actually *spoken* with Georgie since breakfast," Harriet said slowly.

The viscount crossed his arms over his chest and looked down at her with a frown. "That is not what I asked."

" 'Tis all right, Aunt Harriet," a small voice said shakily. "There is no need for you to lie. I am here, Father."

Harriet looked from her brother to the little

boy who slowly rose to his feet and stood behind
the barrier of the sofa. Georgie's normally rosy
cheeks were pale, his narrow face shadowed and
instead of the usual dancing merriment in his gray
eyes, which were the exact replica of his imposing
father's, there was anxiety.

His obvious distress tore at Harriet's heart, until
she noticed the little boy's chin was set with a pug-
nacious tilt.

"Oh, Georgie, you silly lad, there you are," Harriet
said brightly. "Were you playing a game, perchance?
Is that why you were hiding?"

Harriet smiled and moved across the room to
stand beside her nephew. The viscount dogged her
heels.

"Stop circling him like a mother wolf protecting
one of her cubs," Griffin whispered in her ear. "I'm
not going to devour him."

"I never thought that you would." Harriet retorted. "Nevertheless, I'm staying right here."

She noticed her brother's mouth quiver for a
moment in what might be considered amusement.
Then the viscount turned his full attention to his
son.

"Well, what do you have to say for yourself, young
man? The nursery is at sixes and sevens and I have
been told that you are the reason for all the may-
hem."

"I didn't do anything wrong." Georgie pulled a
long face. "Emma Kate was quiet until that mean
Mrs. Simms came in and started yelling."

"Mrs. Simms said she caught you with your hands
in Emma Kate's cradle," the viscount reported solemnly. "I know that you are curious about your
new sister and are anxious to cuddle her, but you
have been told repeatedly that you may not lift the
baby from her cradle. It just isn't safe."

"I was not being a bad boy and I was not trying to pick Emma Kate up," Georgie insisted. "The baby only started crying when she heard Mrs. Simms being mean to me."

The viscount looked doubtful. "What were you doing in the nursery?"

"I was visiting the baby."

"That's all you were doing? Visiting?"

"Well, there was one other thing." Georgie gave a slight sniff. "I was trying to taste Emma Kate's toes."

"What?" Harriet and the viscount both exclaimed.

Georgie shrugged. "I heard Aunt Elizabeth tell Mama that the baby's toes were sweet, tender nibbles so I wanted to taste them."

"You bit the baby's toes?" Griffin asked incredulously. "Is that why she started crying?"

"No! I lifted the blanket and tried to find her foot. She kicks and squirms a lot, you know. Then Mrs. Simms came in and she started yelling at me and Emma Kate began to cry."

"It certainly sounds as if Mrs. Simms is equally to blame for the incident," Harriet said as she patted Georgie's shoulder in a comforting gesture. "After all, it was the nursemaid's loud voice that woke the infant."

"Harriet." Viscount Dewhurst cast his sister a hard, steely glance. "Stop interfering."

Harriet returned the glare with a quelling look of her own. "I am not interfering. I am merely pointing out the salient facts of the incident."

"Georgie knows he is not to enter the nursery unless he has been given permission," Griffin said. "Isn't that true, son?"

Georgie shrugged noncommittally.

The viscount rested his hands on his lean waist and glanced down at his son, but the boy remained stoic and silent.

Seeing that this approach was making no impact on the child's stony will, Harriet said, "I am certain Georgie never meant to be deliberately disobedient."

"It was my room first," the boy uttered mutinously. " 'Tis unfair to get hollered at for going into my own room."

Harriet met Griffin's gaze meaningfully. As she had suspected, this incident was about far more than the baby.

"Oh, son." The viscount slowly lowered himself to a crouched position. "That section of the nursery is only meant for babies. Your new room is much bigger and much better suited for the needs of a growing boy."

Georgie shifted his weight from one foot to the other. His mulish expression told them he was not entirely convinced.

"I think that Georgie needs a few moments to consider how he feels about all of this," Harriet said.

The viscount tilted his head and sent another ominous look of warning her way. Harriet ignored it.

"I don't like having Emma Kate in my old room," Georgie declared boldly. "Not one little bit."

"Like it or not, that is how things are going to be, young man." The viscount blew out an exasperated sigh and raked a hand through his dark hair.

Georgie hunched his shoulders and stomped to the corner of the room. Harriet made a move to follow him, but her brother grabbed her arm. "Let him sulk a few minutes. Once his emotions settle he will see reason."

"Children are difficult to reason with at the best of times," Harriet said. "I doubt you will get a wounded five-year-old to act with great logic."

Griffin rubbed his face wearily. "I don't understand this behavior. Yesterday he threw a tantrum when it was time for bed, two days before he refused to eat his dinner. He has always been such a sensible, affable child."

"That was before he had a sister that everyone else fusses and coos over." Harriet set her mouth firmly. "Georgie is frightened and feeling neglected. He is hurt, worried. So he is doing everything he can to garner your attention."

"How can you be so certain?"

"You forget, I know all too well how it feels to have a parent who treats you as if you barely exist," Harriet said flatly.

"Bloody hell! I am nothing like our father, who cared only for our brother Neville, because he was the eldest son and heir. You know how much I dote on Georgie. How dare you make such a remark?"

"I was not referring to you, Griffin." Harriet tilted her stubborn chin to a more obstinate angle. "I know that Faith has had a difficult time recovering from childbirth and is physically unable to devote a great deal of time to Georgie.

"But he does not understand. What he has finally realized is that he is different from Emma Kate. He asked me three times this week if I had ever met his mother. His *real* mother."

"My God." Griffin's voice was a harsh whisper. "He was so young when she died. I doubted he had any memories of her."

"Nor do you," Harriet said tartly.

The moment the words left her mouth, Harriet knew she had gone too far. *Curse her devilish tongue.* Young Georgie was the result of a brief, indiscreet relationship her brother had engaged in while living in the Colonies, years before his marriage. In fact, he had not even known of the child's existence until a servant had brought the boy to Griffin's ship. But Griffin had worked hard to make up for his early neglect, even bringing the boy home to England when he discovered he had most unexpectedly become the new viscount.

Only the immediate family knew of the true circumstances of Georgie's birth, but they all were very much aware that secrets of this nature were eventually revealed, especially in a small country hamlet like Harrowby.

"Griffin, I am—"

The viscount held up a staying hand. He pivoted on his heel and strode several paces away from her, then turned back and glowered. Harriet could see his shoulders rising and falling as he struggled to place his temper under control.

"Faith and I have been greatly blessed by the arrival of our daughter. Yet that does not in any way jeopardize Georgie's position in this family. He is my son. And Faith's son. You remember how thrilled she was when he at last began to address her as Mama? How can you possibly doubt Faith's love for this child?"

"I apologize for my hasty tongue." Harriet bowed her head briefly. "I know how important he is to her and how much she loves him. However, I am very much a realist. There are now two children in this household and Faith will no longer be able to lavish so much of her time and attention on Georgie. She has Emma Kate to think of, too."

"There is enough love in Faith's heart for ten children," Griffin insisted. "Twenty!"

"Yes, yes." Harriet glanced to the far corner where her nephew stood with his face pressed against the wall, then lowered her voice. "I am only saying it would be understandable for Faith to favor her natural child."

The hint of guilt on her brother's face told Harriet her comment had clearly struck a nerve. "Do you think that is what has happened?"

Harriet shrugged. She had not been particularly fond of Faith before her brother married her and had voiced her objections loud and clear. Yet the marriage had occurred and it had been an exceedingly difficult adjustment for Harriet to accept that Faith now ruled a household that had once been Harriet's sole domain.

The two women had reached an uneasy truce and had tried to stay out of each other's way, discovering that was truly the best way to keep peace. Of course Harriet had not expected to linger long under her brother's roof. She had been engaged to be married, and anticipated with great joy establishing a home of her own, with a man she loved most dearly. Yet all of that had changed in an instant in the past Season in London.

Her throat tightened at the memory of all she had lost, of all the hopes and dreams of her future. But Harriet ruthlessly shook off the memory.

"I know that Georgie is unhappy and having a difficult time adjusting," Harriet said. "I am sure that Faith is doing her best, yet there must be more we can do to ease his hurt and confusion."

Her brother gazed at her expectantly and Harriet sighed. Being outspoken and opinionated did have its disadvantages. Griffin expected her to have more to say on this matter, but in this case Harriet had little to offer in way of a solution.

She was struggling to think of some sage advice when the door opened and their youngest sister, Elizabeth, entered. Dressed in a simple day gown of blue muslin, her luscious blond hair pulled back and tied with a matching bow, the younger girl's youthful beauty shone.

"Oh, there you are, Georgie. I've been searching all over the house for you." Oblivious to the tension in the room, the warm smile on Elizabeth's face brightened. "Your mother has been asking for you. Will you come and visit her, please?"

"Mama wants to see me?" Georgie immediately abandoned his post in the corner and rushed towards his aunt.

"She certainly does," Elizabeth replied. "She gave me strict instructions to find you at once and bring you to her room."

"Is she mad at me?"

Elizabeth furrowed her brow. "She did not say. Have you done something to cause your Mama's anger?"

Georgie bowed his head sheepishly. "I went into Emma Kate's room. I made her cry." He lifted his chin suddenly. "But I didn't mean to. Truly."

"Then you have no cause for worry."

Georgie's face split into a wide grin. Then he sobered and looked up dolefully at his father. "May I go? Mama is asking for me."

"I expect you to offer your sincere apologies to Mrs. Simms the moment you are finished with your visit," Griffin instructed.

"I will." The boy's eyes narrowed slightly as he added, "If I can find her."

"Georgie! I want your word. As a gentleman."

This request most definitely got the child's attention. Thanks to his father's guidance, young Georgie took his role as a protective male and gentleman very seriously.

"I *promise*, on my honor, that I will apologize," Georgie conceded reluctantly.

The viscount nodded with approval. "Then off with you. Quickly, before I change my mind."

Harriet smiled briefly at the satisfactory result.

Though she did wonder if Faith would eventually begin to favor her natural child, she did not question that her sister-in-law loved her base-born stepson and she was pleased that Faith was making an effort to spend time with the boy.

Harriet reached for her nephew, but before she could lean forward and kiss his brow, Georgie gave a shout of triumph and raced from the room. She expected her sister to follow the child, but instead Elizabeth began searching the library's bookshelves.

"Can you help me locate a book, Harriet?" Elizabeth asked. "Faith is feeling tired, but she thought a quiet activity of reading to Georgie for the afternoon would not be too taxing. She feels she needs to spend more time with him."

Harriet nodded her head approvingly. Perhaps she had underestimated her sister-in-law's understanding of Georgie's difficulties. Lord knows, it would hardly be the first time Faith had surprised them all.

Feeling more at ease with the situation, Harriet ran her fingers gently over the numerous leather bound books. The estate had suffered from neglect for many years, due to their father's selfish lack of interest, but Griffin had worked hard to reverse the wrongs of the past when he became viscount.

Thanks to his efforts, this beautiful room was once again a luxuriously appointed library, filled with fascinating volumes, comfortable furnishings, and several strategically placed lamps to make reading easy on the eyes.

"This is one of Georgie's favorites." Harriet lifted a thick book from a lower shelf. " 'Tis filled with a rather gruesome collection of fairy tales where the evil witches, goblins, and spirits meet a most untimely end."

Elizabeth blanched, but moved forward gamely.

"Faith doesn't like those stories," Griffin interjected, taking the book from Harriet's hand.

"That's of no consequence," Elizabeth declared, surprising them all as she reached for the volume. "Faith specifically told me to select a book that would hold Georgie's attention. She wants to make him happy."

"Those stories will give him nightmares," the viscount muttered.

"They will?" Elizabeth turned to her sister, an anxious expression on her lovely face.

Harriet's heart softened. Dear, sweet Elizabeth was such an innocent, uncomplicated young woman. The ordeal in London had left her even more vulnerable, more sensitive to the feelings of others. How ironic that the edginess in these stories which would eagerly capture the imagination of a five-year-old boy would no doubt frighten an almost nineteen-year-old young woman.

"Georgie has been savoring these tales for several months," Harriet said confidently. "He is constantly begging me to read them to him. I think he will be quite pleased if Faith shares a few of them with him today. Especially since he has had such a trying morning."

Elizabeth's face contorted into a worried frown. "Maybe it would be best if I deliver two volumes," she said meekly. "Then Faith can decide for herself which story is more appropriate."

"An admirable idea," Griffin said. "I shall assist you in making a second selection."

Harriet struggled to conceal her sigh. There were times when Elizabeth's unwillingness to face any potential conflict worried her. It was not as if her sister were easily swayed in matters, instead she seemed to lack the confidence to make any decision or take any position where she might need to defend her choice.

Harriet firmly believed it was dangerous to go through life with such an outlook. Especially if you were a woman. Yet she had been unable to impart this insight to her younger sister.

Of course, their brother further complicated the problem by encouraging this helpless, indecisive attitude in Elizabeth. Which was odd, since his wife was hardly one to contain her opinion, especially when it differed from her husband's. After dealing with a strong-willed wife and an equally determined sister, Harriet supposed the viscount felt relieved to have at least one woman under his roof who epitomized a weak feminine spirit.

"Oh, and I forgot to mention at dinner last evening," the viscount said as he scanned a row of books. "Faith received a letter from Meredith yesterday. If the weather holds, the marchioness and her husband will be coming for a visit early next week."

Harriet raised a disapproving brow. " 'Tis rather soon to be having visitors, is it not? Emma Kate is only a few weeks old and by her own admission Faith is hardly recovered from childbirth."

"Meredith is family," Griffin replied. "And even though they are in truth only cousins, she is like a sister to Faith."

"Well, sister or not, Faith is in no condition to entertain noble guests," Harriet insisted.

"Which is precisely why I will require your assistance." The viscount turned and faced his younger sister. "And yours, too, Elizabeth."

She blushed prettily. "I will be pleased to offer any help that I can. I like Lady Meredith very much and find the marquess to be a pleasant gentleman."

A pang of guilt sliced through Harriet. Elizabeth's gracious offer of assistance made Harriet's objections seem even more petty. Yet she could not help but feel a sense of distress over the thought of seeing the incredibly beautiful Lady Meredith again.

The animosity that existed between the two women was of long standing and though it had softened considerably, due to the fantastic events of the past Season, Harriet had not been able to completely exorcise her negative feelings for the marchioness. Even more irksome was the knowledge that Meredith did not hold a similar grudge.

"I suppose they will be bringing a horde of servants with them," Harriet grumbled. "The Marquess of Dardington is fabulously wealthy as well as the heir to a dukedom. He is used to the very best of everything."

"Though I have never met the man, I am sure our hospitality will not disappoint Lady Meredith's husband," Griffin said. "They are coming to Hawthorne Castle to visit Faith and meet Emma Kate, not for lively entertainment. 'Tis a sad state of affairs indeed if we cannot make welcome three noble guests."

"Three?" Harriet questioned.

"Yes." The viscount rubbed his chin thoughtfully. "Did I neglect to mention that Lady Meredith's brother will be joining them?"

The dull sound of a heavy book hitting the floor echoed through the room. "Which brother?" Elizabeth whispered in alarm.

"There is more than one?" Griffin asked. He bent and picked up the book Elizabeth had dropped.

"Lady Meredith has two younger brothers," Harriet answered. "They are twins, identical in appearance, though not in nature. Yet it is hardly difficult to ascertain which one will accompany his sister to Hawthorne Castle."

Griffin's gaze lifted in surprise. "Why is that?"

" 'Twas more than obvious to everyone this Season that Mr. Jason Barrington was quite smitten with our dear Elizabeth. I imagine he will be arriving with hot-house roses and boxes of sweet confections as well as original sonnets he has composed glorifying Elizabeth's beauty."

Harriet smiled teasingly at her younger sister, but Elizabeth did not answer in kind. In fact, she looked slightly ill at the notion of once again seeing her admirer.

"I have never done anything to encourage his attention." Elizabeth took a step back and pressed herself against a large bookcase. "Truly."

"I know." Harriet blew out an exasperated breath. "I was only jesting."

"Jason Barrington." Griffin repeated the name slowly. "Wasn't he the gentleman who saved you from that madman?"

"Yes." The muscles around Elizabeth's lips tightened.

"Then we must do all that we can to make him welcome," Griffin declared. "I, for one, am most grateful for his chivalrous act of bravery."

"But what if Harriet is right? What if he is coming here to court me?" The color washed out of Elizabeth's face. "What shall you say if he asks for my hand in marriage? You would not agree, would you, Griffin?"

The viscount stepped in front of his sister. "I thought you would be pleased to have such a fine young man show an interest in you."

"You do not understand," Elizabeth cried. "He might have been the man who saved my life, yet Jason Barrington is a constant reminder of everything I am struggling so hard to forget. The feelings of terror, of despair and utter helplessness. The horror at being kidnapped. Bound and gagged. A sharp, cold knife blade pressed against my throat." The lovely blonde squeezed her eyes shut. "Please, oh, please, do not force me to play hostess to him. I could not bear it."

The heartsick tone of fear in Elizabeth's voice took Harriet aback. She had known her sister occasionally suffered from nightmares as a result of the tortuous events in London, but she did not realize the pain was so deep.

Harriet instinctively moved forward to offer comfort, but Elizabeth instead turned to her brother, hugging him tightly around the neck.

"Hush, now, Elizabeth. There is no need for tears." The viscount's arms encircled his sister's shoulders. "We shall figure out a way to diplomatically cool Mr. Barrington's ardor. I promise."

Elizabeth made a choking sound. She pulled back and lowered her head. Harriet felt her own throat tighten. Elizabeth appeared very young and very defenseless.

The viscount gently ran his thumb down the line of Elizabeth's face, brushing away a tear. "You had better run along. Faith and Georgie are no doubt wondering why it is taking so long for you to bring them a book."

"Yes." Elizabeth nodded her head, but her voice held a note of uncertainty. She gathered the two books in her arms, leaned up and placed a small kiss on the viscount's cheek. "Thank you."

Silence reigned for a long moment after Elizabeth left. Harriet struggled to harness her own emotions. Their mother had died when Elizabeth was barely a year old. It had therefore fallen to Harriet to see to her sister's welfare. It was a duty she had taken on without complaint, a duty that through the years had given her a sense of purpose and importance.

The realization that Elizabeth now placed Griffin in the role of protector was painful and yet another reminder of how little Harriet seemed to be needed in her own family.

"I know Elizabeth suffers from nightmares, but I was unaware she associated her rescuer so strongly with the events," Harriet said. "I should have realized Elizabeth's fragile state by her emotional reactions to the letters she received from Mr. Barrington."

"I too believed she was starting to recover," Griffin replied. "Perhaps she will show improvement when we go to Town in the spring for the new Season."

Harriet widened her eyes. "You cannot be serious! Elizabeth is in tears at the notion of meeting the man who saved her. How can you possibly expect her to journey to London, the place where all her misery began, and begin a round of social engagements as if nothing had happened?"

Griffin looked uncomfortable. "Well, she is young, barely nineteen. There will be other Seasons if Elizabeth prefers to remain at home this year. However, I assume you will want another crack at the marriage mart."

Harriet's breath came to a sudden halt. For an instant she thought her brother's words a cruel joke, but his expression was all innocent sincerity. "I am long beyond the age of London Season. Besides, the scandal of being jilted by a fiancé who is now in total disgrace has tainted me beyond the pale. No man of decent family would have me for a wife."

A pang of loneliness struck Harriet. The words were harsh, yet undeniably true. She had given her heart to Julian Wingate and it had cost her dearly. Though she had very much wanted one, there would be no husband for her.

"Not all men are like Wingate," Griffin insisted.

"Thank heavens," Harriet said with a bitter laugh.

She closed her eyes briefly as the familiar pain washed over her. The scandal had revealed the truth—her fiancé's feelings for her had been only an illusion, but Harriet had loved him truly. And in the end, he had betrayed her.

"I do not wish to speak of such unpleasant matters." She didn't wait for her brother's acquiescence and quickly changed the subject. "I have been doing a great deal of thinking and reflecting over these last few months and have made some important decisions about my future that I need to discuss with you."

The line of Griffin's mouth lifted in a slight smile. "Strange, it sounds as though you are about to tell me what you intend to do, rather than ask for my advice or approval."

Harriet couldn't control the blush that spread to her cheeks. "Ah, how well you know me, dear brother."

"Not nearly enough to save you from tragedy."

Harriet placed her hand on Griffin's arm. "You must not blame yourself. No one suspected Julian's true nature until it was too late." It eased some of the tightness in her chest, knowing that her brother was so concerned about her. "Julian is in my past and I am determined to look ahead. While I have very much appreciated your generosity in allowing me to live here with your family, it was only intended to be a temporary arrangement, until I married and set up a household of my own. Since I will not marry, I must look to my own future."

"You are my sister, Harriet, and therefore it is my responsibility to see to your welfare. Yours and Elizabeth's."

"Oh, I fully intend to hold you to that responsibility, never fear." Harriet smiled briefly. "However,

I have decided 'tis time for me to do as I wish, not as everyone else expects."

"And what is it you wish?"

"I wish to experience life beyond this simple village. I wish to feel as though I have some purpose, some direction to my life." Harriet took a deep breath and let it out slowly. "I believe I can accomplish these goals by working. So I have decided to seek a position as governess."

"You cannot possibly wish to be a governess," the viscount said with great surprise in his voice. "'Tis a life of drudgery."

Harriet frowned. Leave it to her brother to immediately identify and express her biggest fear. "I know this is a risky endeavor, but I feel I have no choice. I want my independence, I want to taste some freedom."

"A governess is little more than a servant. You have far more freedom in my household."

"As what? A spinster? A maiden aunt who tries to stay quietly in the background, offering no opinions, causing no disharmony among the family?" Harriet shuddered. "We both know I can not possibly exist in that role."

When her brother did not refute her argument, Harriet pressed on.

"When I am no longer interested in working, I will ask you to set me up in a small, independent household on this estate, so I may live quietly and autonomously. Until then, I would very much like to try and earn my own way."

"By taking care of a parcel of noble brats?"

"No. Even if a household could be found that would employ me, I want nothing at all to do with the nobility. A wealthy merchant class family will do just fine."

The viscount was obviously leery, but Harriet could sense her brother had no logical arguments to offer.

"If you insist on going, I cannot stop you," he said with a sigh. "However, *I* must insist that you take a position only with a decent, Christian family. In this case, it shall be the employer who will need to provide references."

Harriet nodded. She had already anticipated this requirement and was prepared. "I have spoken with the vicar and he has kindly agreed to inquire among his many relations, friends, and colleagues in hopes of finding me a suitable position. I assume if our local clergyman can vouch for the family, you will have no objection?"

Griffin gave her a rueful smile, then tilted his head, assessing her closely. "You are well prepared to refute any objection I can think to offer."

"I tried to anticipate your reaction." Harriet chanced a confident grin, then sobered. " 'Tis a lesson I learned about my character, from my former fiancé. I find that I do not like surprises very much."

Chapter Three

The noise from a large, boisterous party gathered somewhere in the house was an unwelcome, persistent intrusion. It tugged relentlessly at Lord Avery's slumber, pulling him from the brief moment of peace that an unconscious mind afforded.

Nathaniel dragged opened his eyes, struggling to regain his senses. The bold splash of red velvet bed curtains revealed he was not in his own bedchamber. And the cloying, floral scent of thick perfume revealed he was not alone in the large fourposter bed. Ever so slowly he tilted his head.

"Ah, you are awake," a sultry female voice declared. "At last."

The mattress dipped as the lush, unclothed woman pushed up on one elbow, then leaned closer. Nathaniel stared up at her for a long moment. She was very pretty. Her features were dainty and soft, her eyes dark and sparkling. Shiny sable hair cascaded down her shoulders, contrasting starkly with her fair creamy skin. Her lips were full and ruby red, her breasts abundant and luscious.

An elusive memory took shape in his mind. Dinner out with an old Scottish friend, Duncan McTate, then a jaunt to a new gaming club in an attempt to cheer his dismal mood. There had been the usual assortment of women making the rounds at the tables, high-priced courtesans and unclaimed mistresses seeking new protectors, along with a few of society's females whose reputations skirted the edge of respectability.

Temptations abounded. Nathaniel had never been one to deny himself when it came to carnal matters. Thanks to his handsome face and impressive lineage, he had always had his pick of women, be they of noble or common birth.

But who exactly was this sumptuous brunette who was eyeing him like a tasty morsel? Nathaniel was unsure. Not that it really mattered. Somehow he had ended up alone in an upstairs private chamber with this entrancing creature and had used her luscious body shamelessly in an attempt to forget his mounting woes.

Trouble was, it hadn't worked.

"Yvonne?" he ventured.

"Darling," she smiled broadly, then leapt onto all fours.

Her large breasts dangled precariously close to his chin. She made a deep, guttural sound in the back of her throat and leaned forward, her lovely face alive with wanton interest.

Lord Avery hissed out a curse. He had not meant to incite her passion, yet hunger radiated from her very pores as she pressed closer to his naked flesh. Nathaniel could not recall in full detail their earlier coupling, but obviously he had left her in need.

Her fingers began to stroke his chest. A part of

him wanted nothing more than to rise from the bed and walk away. But his pride would not let him leave a woman unsatisfied, even if she was practically a stranger.

He pushed her firmly onto her back. Her legs fell open at a touch and he moved between them. He adjusted her body and entered in one long smooth stroke. Yvonne gasped, and her body tightened around him.

He stopped for an instant to savor the slick warmth, but a shout of male laughter from downstairs caught his attention. How odd to feel so completely unattached to a person while performing the most intimate of acts. Here he was, embedded inside her warmth to the hilt, distracted and aroused at the same time.

Yvonne apparently did not suffer the same difficulty. She wiggled her hips against him, then pressed her fingers painfully into his upper arms. Nathaniel shuddered.

"Harder," she gasped, as she tightened her legs and pushed at him.

Nathaniel drew out of her warmth, then slid in again, quickening his pace with each thrust. At her urging he continued pumping into her, hard and fast. Within moments Yvonne's body quivered and arched in the throes of climax.

It was over. Thank goodness. He went still inside her and realized he was still hard. Yet he felt strangely disinclined to do anything about it.

Nathaniel rolled over, attempting to withdraw and distance himself. Yvonne clung tightly, giving him no choice but to bring her with him. With a slight grimace, he moved his palms up Yvonne's firm, bare thighs, then deliberately separated their bodies. Misunderstanding, the sultry brunette arched her back, showcasing her luscious body, obviously waiting to hear him praise her many attributes.

Lord Avery remained silent.

"Gracious, you are stiff as a board," Yvonne exclaimed with obvious delight.

Nathaniel tipped his chin and glanced at his groin, which indeed was hard and stiff. Yvonne squealed again and reached for him like a greedy child. Her fingertips circled the tip of his penis and glided down the shaft, swirling lightly. Nathaniel stretched his back, attempting to evade those questing fingers.

But they were skillful. And most persistent. His mind drifted as she began rubbing and stroking, then wrapping her fingers around him.

He closed his eyes tightly, trying desperately to shut his mind off from everything but the pleasure. It was difficult. Yet his breathing deepened when she raked his stomach with her nails, then angled her head downward. Finally, the touch of her lips drove all thoughts from his mind.

Two hours later, Lord Avery left Yvonne in an exhausted, satisfied slumber and made his way to the main parlor. It was well past midnight and the gaming house was crowded with gentlemen seeking to fill their purses. Being unfamiliar with this particular establishment, since it was so very new, Nathaniel sought the aid of a liveried servant in locating his companion, Duncan McTate.

After giving the man a rather detailed description of the burly Scotsman, the footman pointed a white-gloved finger toward the gold salon. Nathaniel made his way through the throng of people, his hard stare softening in amusement when he spotted his friend.

He surmised the Scotsman was enjoying himself at the gaming tables, for there were impressive piles of coins stacked in front of him. And a strong hint of amusement in his blue eyes. Though his face was flushed and his cravat askew, Nathaniel knew McTate was still very much in command of his wits.

"Have you come to join the game, Lord Avery?" Mr. Kenyon inquired. "We could use some fresh blood. McTate's practically cleaned us all out. His winning streak remains unbroken. Perhaps a new player will foil his luck."

"I must warn you, Mr. Kenyon, 'tis nearly impossible to separate a Scot from his coin," Nathaniel replied with a smile. "I know better than to play against one who is riding a streak of good luck."

The rest of the players laughed, including McTate, and a slight flush stained Kenyon's face. With his ruddy features and close-set eyes, Nathaniel thought the man resembled an overly large rodent. Planting his palms on the table, Kenyon glared with open hostility at McTate, who was seated to his left.

Nathaniel knew that many in society thought McTate remote and notorious, for he was a man who showed little deference to their silly rules. Yet Nathaniel knew him to be a man of honor. He had come to town too late to attend Robert and Bernadette's funeral, but Nathaniel had been touched that his friend had traveled such a distance, at the height of winter, to pay his respects and offer his support.

If only there were some way he could help solve this current legal dilemma, Nathaniel thought gloomily.

McTate clasped his shoulder and leaned forward. "I'm ahead four hundred guineas. 'Twould be a shame to leave with my luck running so high, but if you feel the need to depart, I'll come along."

"And deprive you of a chance to double your

winnings?" Nathaniel cocked an eyebrow. "Do I look like a man with no regard for his life?"

McTate threw back his head and laughed appreciatively. The infectious sound of mirth brought smiles to the faces of the other gentlemen seated around the table. All save one.

Nathaniel reasoned that Duncan must have surely felt Kenyon's stare boring into him, but the Scotsman chose to ignore it. Which apparently increased Kenyon's ire. Nathaniel flashed a warning frown at Kenyon, which the other man foolishly ignored.

"I suppose, to a Scot, cheating can also be considered a form of luck," Kenyon grumbled softly. "Or skill."

In a blur of motion, McTate sprang from his chair. He caught Kenyon by the lapels of his coat and hauled him into the air.

"Now, laddie, would you care to repeat that statement to my face, instead of mumbling under your breath like a coward?"

Kenyon's face flushed a deep shade of red as he struggled ineffectively to remove himself from McTate's clutches.

Cards slapped the table and chairs scraped the floor as the other four players leapt to their feet. Mr. Kenyon was no great favorite, with his sharp tongue and superior attitude, yet it was a rare treat to see him actually step over the line into real danger.

"I am sure Mr. Kenyon meant no disrespect," Nathaniel said calmly. He stepped beside his friend and glanced up at Kenyon's quarrelsome face. "But it would probably be best if you apologized, Kenyon. Immediately."

"You must have misheard my remarks," Mr. Kenyon said stiffly.

The Scotsman tightened his grip and miraculously lifted his adversary higher. Kenyon's eyes bulged. "I meant no offense," he choked out. "Please, forgive my hasty tongue."

There were several seconds of taut silence as everyone waited to see if McTate would accept the apology. True gentlemen demanded satisfaction on the dueling field, but an uncivilized Scot might take it into his head to start a common brawl. Though he stood to inherit an English earldom one day, thanks to his noble mother, there was little evidence of his aristocratic bloodlines at this moment.

Without warning, Duncan suddenly released his hostage. Kenyon stumbled to regain his footing, clutching the table for support. His breath came in panting gasps, as if he had only just realized how narrowly he had avoided great peril. The other players wisely offered no assistance.

McTate straightened. He scooped the large pile of coins off the table in a fluid motion and stuffed his winnings in his pockets. Then he brushed off an imaginary speck of lint from his dark evening coat and with a final contemptuous glare at the quivering Mr. Kenyon, left the table.

Searching for the exit, the two friends soon became lost in the maze of unfamiliar rooms. By pure chance, they stumbled upon a small paneled room that resembled a library. The room was done in rich dark tones and the walls were covered with bookshelves packed with books, the furnishings were large, overstuffed, and decidedly decadent. A fire in the hearth crackled loudly, casting both light and warmth.

" 'Tis probably cold as a witch's tit outside," McTate said. "I think we could do with a bit of warming up, first. Do you fancy a drink before we brave the chill?"

Nathaniel nodded in agreement. A dose of strong spirits might relax him. McTate flagged down a footman. "Bring us two glasses and a bottle of your best port."

The door remained open as the servant fetched the requested refreshment. Duncan moved to the center of the room, seeking the warmth of the fire, but a shadow looming in the doorway attracted Nathaniel's attention.

For an instant he thought it might be Kenyon seeking revenge for his earlier humiliation, but it was a woman. Tall, lush, and blond. Her gold silk gown, with its tiny cap sleeves and plunging neckline, flattered her coloring and figure. Though hardly in the first blush of youth, she was nevertheless most handsome.

She shot him an assessing glance and he watched the flow of interest cross her features. Lord Avery's jaw hardened. The mysterious female was clearly looking for some excitement. Deciding he had had more than enough womanly companionship for the evening, Nathaniel met her jaded eyes squarely and shook his head.

The blonde shrugged her shoulders and entered the room anyway, sashaying toward McTate. With cat-like grace, she slid her arms around his waist. The Scotsman's head turned. His gaze traveled up and down her revealing gown, lingering for several seconds at her impressive bosom.

The blonde pressed herself against the Scotsman, parting her lips in sensual invitation. Her lashes lowered to half-mast as she tilted her head back, exposing the elegant column of her neck. McTate's blue eyes twinkled at her, then he gave an exaggerated sigh.

"Oh, lass, I only wish I had the time to properly indulge you," he said with obvious regret. "But I have important business to discuss with my friend. Perhaps we will meet at another time."

With a playful slap to her rump, McTate sent the lovely woman on her way. She passed the footman carrying in a tray on her way out. McTate insisted on using some of his winnings to pay for the refreshments and tipped the servant handsomely. Drinks in hand, the two men found a quiet corner near the fireplace, away from the gamblers and prowling females.

As they settled into two comfortable chairs, Nathaniel could feel McTate's wily eyes assessing him.

"So, have these few hours of immoral pleasures lifted your mood at all, my friend?" McTate asked.

"Not really." The ghost of a smile flitted across Nathaniel's face. "Despite all my best efforts, I find I am rather poor spirited these days."

"Poor spirited!" McTate scoffed. "I fully expected to find you grieving, for I knew how close you were to your brother and how much you admired his kind wife. Yet I never thought to see you so downhearted."

"It's all this damn court nonsense." Just voicing his concerns out loud made Lord Avery feel edgy. He stood, and began pacing. "This morning I suffered a major setback at the hands of a magistrate who is clearly lining his pockets with bribes from both sides in this case. I had been hoping to be appointed temporary guardian for my nieces and nephew, but my petition was denied flat-out."

Nathaniel drained his wine goblet, welcoming the spreading warmth that relaxed the tight knots in his muscles, then held out his glass to be replenished. Wordlessly, McTate complied.

"I've hired the best solicitor and barrister in London, paid them a small fortune, plus a bit more to cover the bribes needed to win my case and still I am denied custody of Robert's children," Nathaniel continued. "The lawyers keep telling me to be patient, but that becomes more difficult each day. Especially when I see how neglected and despondent the children have become."

McTate's face lit with concern. "Is your uncle mistreating them?"

"Worse. He is completely indifferent to them. To their needs, to their grief, to their feelings. I believe that eventually his neglect will cause them all actual harm."

Duncan McTate let out a long, low whistle. "Saints preserve us, laddie, you sound like an old woman, worrying about the *feelings* of a bunch of children."

"They are not just a bunch of children. They are Robert's son and two daughters. My brother's dying wish was that I care for them, and so help me I shall do everything within my power to fulfill that promise."

Nathaniel stared hard at the Scotsman and felt his stomach plummet with frustration. If he could not make a friend like McTate understand how important this was, what chance did he have of convincing a magistrate?

Lord Avery's stare turned to one of exasperation. "You aren't saying anything."

Duncan stroked his chiseled jaw. "I'm just trying to imagine you caring for a trio of children. Two of them *female*, no less."

The quip brought a smile to Nathaniel's face and the tension drained from the room. Lord Avery picked up the wine bottle and refilled both goblets.

"Is your uncle keeping you from seeing the wee ones?" McTate asked as he shifted to expose more of his body to the warm fire.

"No. I visit them every afternoon in their nursery. It is hardly an ideal situation, but when the weather improves I plan on taking them on outings to the park and around town. Perhaps such adventures will put small smiles back on their faces."

"It doesn't sound so dire." Duncan idly swirled his glass. "Visiting them most days and bringing a bit of cheer and caring into their young hearts. If you want my opinion, I think you are making too much of who has legal custody. Let them remain Bridwell's problem. 'Tis more important for you to be a presence in their lives. And if your uncle knows you are keeping a close watch on him, he might be forced to act in a manner more appropriate for a guardian."

Nathaniel took a long moment to think hard upon the words. Why not just let things stand as they were? His uncle would not be so foolish as to physically harm the children. Thus far Lord Bridwell had voiced no objections to Nathaniel's daily visits and if he kept a close eye on the estate finances, Nathaniel could ensure that the money would be there when the children came of age.

This court battle was proving to be a far more lengthy and costly endeavor than Lord Avery anticipated. And the outcome of a victory was far from assured, especially without the will that supported his claim of guardianship. McTate's advice was sound, yet the idea of abandoning those three helpless souls to Lord Bridwell's care did not sit well.

Nathaniel's throat tightened. If the situation were reversed, if it were his children who were suddenly orphans that were under the protection of a guardian who cared so little for them, what would his brother have done?

Nathaniel shook his head slowly, knowing in his

heart the answer. Robert would have intervened. Without hesitation, he would have taken the children into his home and nurtured them as his own.

Could he do no less for Robert's progeny?

"Letting Bridwell remain in control is the coward's way out," Nathaniel insisted. "Besides, he might one day take it into his head to deny me access to the children and I'll have no way of stopping him. I believe the only way to secure their future is to establish myself as the legal guardian as soon as possible."

McTate frowned. "If your uncle has no real regard or feeling for the children, why does he want them so badly? What's he really after?"

"Their money," Nathaniel said bluntly. "Along with the power and prestige of being in control of the Claridge fortune. As a second son myself, I can honestly say I never gave my position much thought since I had been given the lesser family title of Baron Avery as a young boy, just as my uncle had been made Lord Bridwell when he was a lad. Both titles come with generous incomes and more noble prestige than either of us probably deserve. It was therefore doubly shocking for me to discover how deeply my uncle resents being a second son."

Suddenly alert, McTate sat up in his chair. "Could your nephew, young Gregory, be in any danger?"

Lord Avery paused. "Physical danger?"

"You said your uncle resents being a second son. What lengths do you think he is willing to go to become Duke of Claridge?"

Nathaniel swore loudly. "Good God, I never even thought of the title. If Robert died without an heir, then I would have become duke. I assume if Robert's heir dies without issue the title reverts to me. Though I suppose my uncle could try to lay claim to it."

"Yet another reason for your uncle to see you as an obstacle he needs to remove," McTate retorted. "Of course, if he is as enterprising as he seems, and truly does covet the title, he would need to dispose of both you and your nephew."

Nathaniel's heart pounded in his chest. "Bloody hell, McTate, now you've given me a new worry."

The Scotsman shrugged. "I am merely watching your back, my friend. 'Tis a farfetched idea that Lord Bridwell would go to such lengths, then again, who can say with certainty what lies in a man's heart? Especially an Englishman. History is filled with examples of familial genocide. That rascal King Richard came to the throne only after imprisoning his two nephews, Prince Edward and the Duke of York, in the Garden Tower.

"Richard was too clever to kill them outright, so at first the lads were seen from time to time playing together through the bars and windows of the tower. Gradually they appeared less and less, and within a few weeks disappeared forever. Though many suspected what had occurred, no one challenged the king. The truth was not revealed until two hundred years later when the bones of two young boys were found buried at the foot of the tower stairs, under a great heap of stones."

"Richard murdered those children so he could become king," Nathaniel said wryly. "There is great wealth in my family estate, but it is hardly the crown of England."

The Scotsman blinked. "Perhaps my imagination has gotten the better of me. Yet I would be a poor friend indeed if I did not advise you to be extra vigilant."

Nathaniel knew McTate was offering sincere and prudent advice, but he wished the subject had never been broached, for it merely added to his growing list of concerns. "Once I win my case, all these problems will simply vanish," Lord Avery said with a confidence he did not truly feel.

"Aye, now, that might be your biggest mistake of all. Placing your faith in English law." McTate let out a huge, exaggerated sigh. "If you're as smart as I think you are, you'll take some advice from a Scot. Don't be waiting around for the courts to hand those children over to you, all neat and pretty and tied with a big bow. Go out and take them."

Lord Avery gasped. "What?"

"You heard me. Take them. Steal them. Right out from under Lord Bridwell's nose."

"Are you out of your mind? Or just drunk?"

McTate furrowed his brow as though he was giving the questions serious thought. "I suppose I'm a bit of both, but that doesn't make it a poor idea."

" 'Tis a wholly ludicrous notion."

"Why? My people are raiders and reivers. We have lived that way, successfully, for generations. If a neighboring clan has something that is rightfully yours and they refuse to return it, you steal it back."

Nathaniel put down his half-full wine goblet, deciding he had already had more than enough to drink. He was tempted to reach over and remove the glass from Duncan's strong hands, but decided that would not be a prudent move. "We are talking about three young children, McTate, not cattle."

The Scotsman looked startled. "I don't see all that much difference."

Lord Avery began pacing, his long legs taking lengthy strides back and forth across the carpet. "Let us say that for a moment, a very brief moment, I am considering this plan. What then am I supposed to do when my uncle shows up on my doorstep demanding that I return his wards? Or worse, what if he brings a constable and insists that I am arrested and hauled off to Newgate? Even if I manage to circumvent the full force of the law, I will never be seen as a fit guardian if I pull such an outrageous stunt."

"Aye, it's a risky move, there's no getting around it. But I believe if the courts thought you a fit guardian in the first place, your petition would have been considered more seriously. You said yourself that even with bribes you were unable to gain temporary custody." McTate's eyes narrowed as a crafty expression illuminated his handsome features. "And your uncle can hardly have you arrested or get the children back if he can't find them."

Nathaniel halted suddenly and pivoted around on his heel. "Are you suggesting we go into hiding? Like criminals?"

McTate leaned back in his chair. "I am suggesting that once you take matters into your own hands you must make certain to keep all the advantages on your side. Lord Bridwell will most likely not raise a hue and cry if you take the children from him because it will make him appear a weak and incompetent guardian.

"Hell, if he is as neglectful of the children as you say, he might not even notice they are gone from the mansion for several days. Especially if we can devise and execute a well thought out plan that will ensure the silence of several key members of the household staff."

Nathaniel's mouth tightened. Though he spoke in a calm, casual tone, Lord Avery knew McTate was completely serious. But could such a drastic plan really succeed?

"The children would be terrified if a stranger snatched them away," Nathaniel said slowly.

"I agree. That is why you must be the one to take them from the house. They know and trust you and will come without any fuss or bother."

"So I am to be the kidnapper?"

"It makes the most sense."

Conversely, it did. The knot in Nathaniel's stomach doubled in size. He would far prefer to do things in a legal, civilized manner, but if the courts ruled against him, there would be few choices left.

"Once I have the children in hand, where would we go?"

McTate's smile flashed white against his bronzed, weathered face. "I have a small, little-used property in the Highlands that will be the perfect place for all of you to reside. I guarantee that neither Bridwell, nor anyone he hires, will find you there. I'll even provide the servants, and a skilled governess, to care for the children."

"Then what?"

"After the dust settles a bit, you strike a bargain with your uncle. I suspect once he realizes you have the upper hand, he will be far more inclined to listen to reason." McTate flashed another devilish, dangerous smile. " 'Tis all very simple. Just say the word and I'll help you set everything in motion."

Simple? McTate's plan was convoluted, dangerous, and diabolically clever. Nathaniel's often sleeping conscience balked at the idea of employing such drastic, underhanded methods to obtain his goal. Yet he admitted that deep down, a small, mad part of him was seriously considering it.

Chapter Four

In addition to the family, it seemed as though every servant, including the butler, housekeeper, a host of maids, footmen, and grooms, were present in the front courtyard of Hawthorne Castle to see Miss Harriet off and wish her well on her journey. The sky was cloudless, the sun was shining, the air felt brisk and invigorating. It was a good day for traveling.

Harriet shook hands with each servant, accepting their good wishes with a gracious smile. Pulling on her gloves, she then headed toward the carriage where the family had gathered to say their goodbyes.

"I still cannot believe you are really leaving," Elizabeth said in a small voice. "And going all the way to northern Scotland. Gracious, 'tis practically on the edge of the world."

"It could have been worse, dear sister," Harriet said as she smoothed a stray blond curl from Elizabeth's cheek. "I might be bound for Ireland."

Elizabeth's eyes widened in horror. "I do not understand how you can be so glib about this, Harriet. I would be filled with utter terror at the thought of leaving home and taking up employment in an unknown household."

"I know." Harriet rested her hands gently on Elizabeth's fragile shoulders. "But I am excited about this chance to experience life beyond our small village. Please, you must remember this was my choice."

Elizabeth lowered her chin. "I shall miss you very much," she said, her voice tight with emotion. "Promise me you will not stay away too long?"

"I shall be back before you even realize I have been gone," Harriet replied. "Now, don't get sloppy and sentimental, dear sister, or else Griffin will start blubbering in front of the servants."

The corner of the viscount's eyes crinkled as he forced a smile. He leaned over and caught Harriet in a large brotherly hug. "You have no earthly idea how difficult it is for me to let you go," he whispered in her ear. "I have been persuaded to allow this tomfoolery only because you insist it will bring you a measure of contentment. But you must give me your oath that you will return immediately if you experience any problems.

"Though you are loath to admit it, there are some difficulties that cannot be overcome by sheer effort of will, even with such a strong will as yours."

"I shall be prudent and cautious as I undertake this new venture," Harriet replied, frowning at the slight trembling of fear she felt in her chest.

Two days ago she had felt exhilarated and optimistic as she packed her bags. Yet as she stood in the courtyard, surrounded by all those who were familiar and dear to her, Harriet's heart began to thump. She had never expected it would be so difficult to say her good-byes.

Except for a brief and most unhappy few months in London, she had never lived anywhere else. Was she being foolhardy to undertake such a drastic change in her life? Harriet clutched the reticule that held the letter offering her the job of governess to the three wards of Mr. Wainwright and wrestled with her doubts.

Thanks to the efforts of the local vicar, this position was found, and accepted, in short order. The vicar had kindly and generously spread the word among his many friends and relatives and his efforts were rewarded with a letter from a distant cousin in Scotland who knew of a wealthy merchant class family in desperate need of a qualified governess. Harriet could hardly believe her good fortune when she heard the details, for this was precisely the sort of opportunity she had been hoping to find.

Away from England, away from society, away from the nobility. She could make a fresh start, where no one knew of her past, where she need not fear being laughed at, or scorned, or worst of all pitied because of a broken engagement and a disreputable ex-fiancé.

There were other benefits as well. Harriet very much liked the fact that she would have several charges to care for, specifically two girls and younger boy. Her experience with her nephew Georgie made her comfortable with the notion of coping with little boys, since she felt she understood them. Certainly far more than she understood grown-up boys.

Having girls to guide would bring balance and variety to her days. And best of all, they were Mr. Wainwright's wards, not his natural children, so his interest in their welfare should be limited. That would leave Harriet in nearly complete charge, a position she felt suited her best.

Two girls and a boy. A long time ago, in what now seemed like a different life, she had yearned to have four children of her own. She had dared to dream of raising two boys and two girls, if the Lord. had seen fit to bless her.

The begetting of those children had also been something to look forward to with excitement and curiosity. Her ex-fiancé Julian had been very miserly with his kisses, yet Harriet had remembered, and cherished, each and every one with nearly reverent clarity.

The soft brush of his gentle lips against her own on the afternoon when she agreed to be his wife; the desperate, almost frantic pressing of lips and dueling of tongues on the eve of his departure to Spain, when he left to join Wellington's staff as a junior officer.

The intervening weeks and months and years had been long and lonely, yet Harriet greeted Julian with open arms and a loving heart upon his unexpected return. She would never forget the thrill of finally being alone with him. Of winding her arms around his shoulder and neck, rising on her toes to embrace his fit form, pressing her body snug against his. The movement of his breath against her cheek, the heat of his body so near to her own.

They had shared several deep, slow, erotic kisses that made her knees turn to rubber with a mindless pleasure that had stunned her. It was those kisses Harriet remembered so vividly for they had promised such glory but led to only sorrow.

She believed they would marry within a few weeks and begin their life together. A home, children, a place in society, a place among the community where they lived. It never happened. Instead there had been scandal, disgrace, and abandonment.

Given no other choice, Harriet had made the best of it. And now somewhere in the wilds of northern Scotland, two little girls and their younger brother awaited her arrival.

"Will you miss me, Aunt Harriet?"

Harriet gazed down at her nephew with a pained expression. She would indeed miss Georgie, probably more than anyone else in the household. She had loved, protected and fought over this child from the moment he entered her life. It was difficult to accept that his need for her as a champion had lessened considerably over the last year and was part of the reason she felt it was time to break away from the household.

Very much aware of the fickle nature and memories of children, Harriet feared he would soon forget her. Burying that gloomy thought deep in her heart, she bent down and scooped the child up in her arms. "You are a special, wonderful lad," she whispered in his ear. "Always remember how much I love you."

Georgie suffered his aunt's embrace with good humor, planting several sloppy kisses on her cheek before pulling away. Harriet collected herself and straightened. With brisk efficiency she embraced her sister-in-law, Faith, kissed the sleeping infant Emma Kate's cheek, and gave Elizabeth one final hug.

Harriet turned, hearing her sister's soft, gentle sobs. Feeling unsettled by the emotions that were crowding her, she brushed at the tears brimming in her eyes and focused her attention on the cumbersome coach in order to keep from crying.

The moment the steps were pulled down, Harriet held up her skirts and climbed into the coach. She settled into place with a minimum amount of fuss, deliberately facing forward. Towards her future. Amid shouts of farewell and good luck, the coach lunged forward.

"Though I am glad to be of service on this journey, Miss Harriet, I fear I will be feeling quite homesick," a female voice declared.

Harriet heaved a deep sigh and tried to shut out the soft sniffles of the maid who accompanied her on the journey. Her own emotions were just below the surface, threatening to overtake her. Yet as the carriage turned the corner and headed down the road Harriet made no sound.

"Did you see that imposing looking bear, Kate?" Harriet asked. "He was drinking from the stream, but stood his ground boldly even though the carriage passed within a few feet of him as we clattered over the wooden bridge. He must be very brave, for the noise did not seem to even startle him."

Kate lifted her head and gave a cursory, uninterested glance out the window. "The mangy creature must have just finished his last meal," the maid stated with a sniff. "If he was hungry, he'd come slinking along beside us and then attack."

"Us?" Harriet asked with disbelieved amusement. "Do bears often attack people?"

"Oh, no, Miss Harriet. Not you and me. He'd go right for the horses. They're the easy target. I imagine a bear that fierce could tear a horse to pieces within minutes. He'd go directly for the throat, I'd wager."

"I thought he seemed majestic and bold," Harriet muttered as she turned her head to catch a final glimpse of the animal.

"He's a killer," Kate declared with a knowing nod.

Harriet took a deep sigh and pressed her fingertips to her brow. Unfortunately Kate had turned out to be a rather trying traveling companion. Harriet had not spent much time in the maid's company prior to this journey and was therefore surprised to discover the older woman had a somewhat gloomy, bloodthirsty outlook on life. An outlook that she was more than willing to share.

She also had an uncanny knack for taking any situation and seeing only the negative aspects of it. Given the distance of their trip, the time of year and weather conditions, there had been a great deal for Kate to expound upon.

Fortunately the maid would be returning to Harrowby and Griffin's household soon after they reached Mr. Wainwright's home, Hillsdale Castle. Harriet had agreed to allow Kate on the journey because her brother had insisted an unmarried gentlewoman could not travel such a great distance completely on her own, even if she was taking up a position as a governess.

Harriet privately speculated she would most likely be the first governess to arrive at her post with a maid in tow, but hoped her employer would find this an amusement or just accept it as an eccentricity of the nobility.

"Will we be stopping for luncheon soon, Miss Harriet?" Kate asked. "That meager breakfast of cheese and stale bread would hardly keep a mouse alive."

"I'm sure John Coachman will pull in to the first appropriate establishment we find," Harriet replied. "As always."

Though some of the meals they had eaten over

the past few weeks were hardly memorable, they at least offered a break from the road. Harriet could understand Kate's boredom. Even if the light were sufficient, the constant sway of the coach made reading or light sewing an impossible task.

At first both women had been more than content to watch the ever-changing countryside roll by out the carriage window. When that novelty wore off, they tried to engage in conversation. It seemed to help pass the time for Kate, but it gave Harriet a headache.

However, once they crossed the border into Scotland, the view changed to snow capped hills and Harriet's interest in the surrounding landscape was renewed. She was soon in awe of the unexpected majesty, and the raw, untamed beauty of the land.

The landscape was soaring and austere. Due to the season, there was only the barest hint of green to be seen. It was as if the land had survived, even triumphed, despite the harsh obstacles Mother Nature had tossed in its path. Kate declared the terrain bleak and unwelcoming and whined for the flat roads and warmer temperatures of home.

Yet even though she had to constantly tighten the lap rug spread across her knees to find more warmth, Harriet found this rugged country strangely moving. She did however feel sorry for the coachman and footman who rode outside the carriage, exposed to the harsh elements.

Kate often remarked at the amount of drink the men consumed at each stop, but Harriet did not begrudge them their warmed cider and mugs of ale. They must be nearly frozen from the cold.

"Well, 'tis not the most respectable place I've ever seen, but I imagine it's the best one we'll find."

Harriet caught sight of the small inn they were approaching and silently agreed with Kate's assessment. The establishment looked little more than a large hut, with a thatched roof, a small orchard, and several chickens running about loose in the yard.

It was nestled in a small valley, surrounded by much larger mountains and as she stepped down from the coach, Harriet was glad those granite boulders protected them from the relentless cold winds. There were no other guests inside the common room and for a brief moment Harriet worried that they had stumbled upon a private home.

But the suspicious, cold reception from the surly innkeeper changed the moment he saw the color of the coin John Coachman flashed as he made arrangements for the care of the horses and a meal for the travelers. They dined on thick slices of hot shepherd's pie and mugs of home-brewed ale. Inquiries about the specific location of Hillsdale Castle brought more good news. It was no more than fifteen miles away.

After leaving the inn they at last began traveling in the highest mountains that days ago had appeared so far and distant. Harriet re-entered the coach in good spirits, buoyed with the knowledge that this long journey was finally nearing an end. However, her good mood was sorely tested within the hour as Kate gave several drawn-out bored sighs and began picking at a thread on the index finger of her wool gloves.

Harriet bit her bottom lip hard to keep silent. She had been lecturing the maid for days to cease this most annoying habit, but had been unsuccessful in making her stop. Once again she recited a silent prayer, asking Providence to deliver her to the castle before Kate's dreary conversation and endless fidgeting drove her mad.

Realizing it was fruitless to waste her breath on

another lecture, Harriet leaned back, wedged her head comfortably in the corner of the coach and closed her eyes. She drifted in a trance-like state between sleep and wakefulness for most of the afternoon.

A sudden, sharp jolt of the coach brought Harriet fully to her senses. She could feel the team of horses strain and stumble on the slick, winding road. She sat anxiously forward in her seat, steadying herself with a tight grip on the leather hand loop. Glancing out the window, Harriet watched the light from the sinking sun begin to fade.

The poor conditions of the road had slowed their progress once they had left the inn. Hopefully there would be a bright full moon appearing soon, for if they did not reach their destination before nightfall, they would surely become lost in this desolate land.

The increasingly steep climbs and lowering dips of the hills and valleys had brought the coach's progress to barely a crawl. The cold also contributed to the difficulty, freezing sections of the gravel road, making it treacherous going for the horses.

The deep ruts were another worry, especially when following the winding path. On the left side stood a solid wall of rock, with soil and bare tree limbs dotting the higher elevation while on the right was a dizzying drop into a rocky, jagged ravine.

Perhaps the only odd comfort was a feeling of safety from highwaymen, for no thief or brigand would venture to this remote, uncivilized area in search of prey.

Thankfully the coachman was an expert driver. Griffin would only have his best, most experienced servant undertake this challenging journey and Harriet was grateful her brother had ignored her protests and insisted on this escort.

"The horses have slowed," Harriet declared. "We must be getting closer."

"Or climbing another hill," Kate grumbled. "We should have stayed the night at that small inn where we stopped for luncheon. 'Tis pure folly to have continued on this late in the afternoon."

Harriet ignored the remarks. Traveling shut up in the coach for so many long days had blurred the lines between mistress and servant, and Harriet would allow that the journey had not always been comfortable or pleasant. Exceptions must be made.

While the maid sulked in the corner, Harriet leaned forward and pressed her nose against the cold glass of the carriage window. In the distance she could see the crest of an approaching mountain, but there was something slightly different about the outline. She squinted and saw shrouded in the clouds and impending darkness a structure perched at the very top, seemingly rising out of the land.

Though it was barely visible through the mist, Harriet saw dark stone drum towers and turrets straining towards the blackening sky. The granite battlements and ancient design made it appear more fortress than home, but Harriet somehow knew this was their destination.

"I believe we are nearly there," Harriet whispered.

The statement brought Kate out of her slump. She too pressed forward and turned her attention out the window.

"Where is it?" the maid asked anxiously.

"There, on the crest of the mountain." Harriet pointed.

Kate moved closer, her eyes eagerly following the line of Harriet's arm. There were a few moments of silence, and then the maid exclaimed, "I still don't see it. All that rests atop the mountain is a crumbling, abandoned keep. I'd never set foot inside such a terrible place. I'd wager the ghostly spirit of some long-dead Scottish warrior haunts those stone walls."

Harriet cleared her throat. "That is Hillsdale Castle," she said. "I feel certain of it."

"What?" Harriet felt the older woman shudder. "You must be mistaken, Miss. That can't be it. It's old and decayed, with nary a light burning in a window nor a fire smoking from a chimney. 'Tis a grand place for the devil himself to live, not a decent, Christian family in need of a governess."

"Nonsense," Harriet replied, although she was forced to agree that on initial impression it was a rather daunting place. " 'Tis a medieval structure that still retains its proud history. I bet it is fascinating inside, filled with authentic antiques and huge fireplaces giving off lots of warmth. And the family has most likely done extensive remodeling to make it a more comfortable establishment, yet they have cleverly preserved the rich heritage and classic lines of the castle."

The maid shot her a disbelieving look, but said no more. As they made the approach to the steep entrance drive, the fine mist of falling frozen rain grew heavier. The steady, hammering tattoo of the hard pellets on the roof of the coach seemed to intensify the women's nervous energy, and the howling wind jostled the vehicle roughly.

Harriet gripped the edge of her velvet seat tightly to keep from being thrown to the floor. Kate did the same. Though it was gloomy in the carriage, Harriet could clearly see the panic in the maid's eyes. She only hoped her own hazel orbs did not reveal the depths of misgiving she was suddenly feeling.

'Tis just the excitement and relief of the journey finally coming to an end, Harriet told herself. *And a natural*

uncertainty over beginning my new life in such a strange, forboding place.

Kate's prediction that the castle was abandoned took on greater merit as the coach rumbled over an ancient drawbridge and came to rest in an open courtyard. There was not a soul in sight, but Harriet reasoned the dreadful weather would keep anyone with good sense warmly tucked inside.

Since she had been unable to give a specific day or time for her arrival, Harriet knew she had no cause to be concerned over a lack of greeting. Yet one would think at least one person in the household would be aware of the sudden appearance of a strange coach and come to investigate. With its remote location, it was doubtful there were many unexpected visitors to this castle.

Harriet lowered the glass on the window, thrust her head partly out and yelled up to the coachman. "Kate and I will go in the front door. You and Rogers bring the carriage around back. Those poor horses are so tired they will most likely lead you to the stable on their own."

Though she would have preferred the groom to knock at the door and announce their presence, Harriet decided she needed to be practical. She reasoned her driver would require assistance with the weary team and, given the lack of activity or sign of any servants, the man would probably be left to perform these tasks himself.

The coachman edged the bulky carriage as close to the front entrance as space would allow. Harriet hastily buttoned her pelisse all the way to her throat, then with a commanding nod at Kate and an admonishment to follow closely, Harriet stepped down from the carriage.

The biting wind and pelting rain hit her full force, nearly knocking her to the ground. Harriet took a deep breath, her nostrils filling with the heavy scent of cold and rain. She forced herself to ignore the discomfort she felt at the high-pitched keening screech the wind made as it whistled around the stonework of the castle, as she prepared to make a dash for the entrance.

Dragging the edges of her woolen cloak more tightly around her, Harriet dipped her head, shielded her eyes and raced toward the curving stone stairs that swept up to the imposing front door. Behind her, she heard Kate squeal and felt the older woman grasp on to her cloak, as if fearing she would be lost. Dragging the maid along behind her, Harriet pushed and fought her way through the forceful wind gusts, eventually reaching the top of the stairs.

There was no protective portico or overhang to shield them from the elements. Torrents of freezing rain poured mercilessly over the brims of their quickly soaked bonnets. Harriet could feel the cold, wet raindrops slide beneath her collar and run down the back of her neck.

Never in her life had she longed so much to be warm and dry. A quick glance at Kate's sour expression confirmed that the maid shared the feeling. With an impatient huff Harriet lifted the heavy iron ring and banged it loudly against the door.

The dull sound echoed through the stone walls on the other side. It was an eerie, empty noise that triggered a shiver down Harriet's spine. Then all went still and silent.

"I told you it was abandoned," Kate shouted miserably. "We'd best go around back and try to find the others. If the coachman's found a stable we can take shelter there until morning. If we stand out in the cold any longer, we'll catch our deaths."

"This castle is not abandoned," Harriet insisted. Wet, frustrated and more than a bit annoyed, she wrapped each of her stiff gloved fingers around the icy cold ring, lifted it high above her head and brought it down six times in rapid succession.

This time her knocking was greeted with a furious barking that began in the distant recesses of the manor, but grew ominously closer with each low howl. Though protected by a solid wooden door, both women instinctively took a step back as the ferocious noise drew closer.

No longer caring about how cold and wet she felt, Harriet started to calculate how quickly she and Kate could run back down the stairs without slipping. But even if they managed to reach the open courtyard, where could they hide from this growling beast?

There was however, no opportunity to put any plan in motion. The labored screech of a rusty, seldom used hinge was the only warning given as one of the heavy wooden doors slowly cracked open.

Kate's dire predications and gloomy warnings had sparked Harriet's imagination. She was unsure exactly what she was expecting to see awaiting them on the other side, but the apparition that appeared made the breath catch in her throat.

It was a man. A young, extraordinarily handsome man. He was tall, well over six feet, with broad shoulders and a solid, muscular build. She judged his age to be near her own, twenty-eight. He had an iron jaw, bold cheekbones, full sculpted lips, and strongly marked eyebrows that were the same raven black color as his hair.

In one hand he held a huge torch high above his head. It gave off great plumes of black smoke that puffed and billowed and encircled him like a devilish halo. The uneven glow of the flickering flame gave his features a mysterious, almost sinister look.

He was wearing nothing but black trousers, black knee high boots and a floor length dressing gown of brilliant red silk. It was fastened at the waist, yet hung open down to his bare chest. Harriet felt her cheeks grow warm as she stared at the shapely muscles that were covered with a filigree of fine dark hair.

She opened her mouth to speak, then gulped, trying to force the air into her lungs. Recovering slightly from her initial shock, Harriet lifted her gaze. It was a mistake. Their stares locked and her heart skipped a beat. Those dark eyes seemed to be mocking her, as they studied her face and form with a thoughtful intensity Harriet found decidedly uncomfortable.

The cold, wet flesh on her neck shivered and she had a sudden understanding of how a defenseless animal felt when confronting danger.

Steady, Harriet told herself. She had barely managed to get her nerves under control when out of the corner of her eye she saw a whirl of black fur charging towards them. Without any warning, the animal snarled, then lunged forward. Harriet braced herself for the impact, but miraculously the beast stopped. She glanced down and saw the man held the animal by the scruff of its neck.

The man looked at her for a long moment, bleary-eyed and angry. He braced himself against the wall as he struggled to keep the barking dog under control. "Get inside. Quickly. If he gets out there is no telling when he'll return or where he will run."

"We can't go in there!" Kate said desperately.

"We must," Harriet insisted, though she was far from eager to step closer to the man or his dog.

"I can't." Kate made an odd, choking noise and Harriet glanced nervously towards the maid. She panted and shook like a terrified hare desperately struggling to outrun a ravenous wolf. What small stain of color that had remained in the older woman's face washed from her cheeks.

" 'Tis Lucifer himself," Kate whispered. "Lord Jesus, save us all." Then her eyes rolled up, her lashes fluttered wildly and she crumpled to the ground.

"Kate!" Harriet caught the maid with a startled cry. She swayed back and forth, trying to plant her feet more firmly in a desperate attempt to support Kate's weight before they both tumbled to the ground.

"What did she mutter?" the stranger asked.

Harriet's head snapped up. "How can that possibly matter? For pity's sake sir, I need your help, or else I'm going to drop her on this hard, filthy floor."

"In case you failed to notice, I only possess two arms."

"And very little common sense." Harriet's desperation and anger suppressed any of her remaining fear. "What is the dog's name?"

"Pardon?"

"The dog's name. What is it?"

"Brutus. Yet, I hardly see how that can have any—"

"Brutus! Sit!" Harriet commanded in her deepest tone.

The dog's ears perked at the sound of his name and he took on a far less menacing demeanor. "Brutus, sit," Harriet repeated.

The animal gradually sank back on his haunches and the man slowly released his hold on the dog's neck. Amazingly, the animal stayed in place.

"Hurry, before your dog decides to bolt."

The sharpness of her tone seemed to spur the man into action. He reached out, and swept Kate up in his one free arm. "She's not as light as she looks," he grunted.

Thinking fast, Harriet pulled the lit torch out of his hand. With both arms available, the man was better able to balance his burden. Kate's head lolled against his shoulder as he shifted her inert body, exposing her face to the freezing rain. Within minutes the maid was stirring and sputtering.

Harriet's arm fell back to her side, aching from the strain of trying to hold Kate. The man crossed the threshold. Harriet followed. Once inside, he gently set Kate on her feet, propping her against the door. Then he relieved Harriet of the torch. Harriet found Kate's hand and clasped it, trying to help the frightened woman regain her equilibrium.

Fortunately the maid was too befuddled to realize she had been briefly held in the stranger's arms. Harriet was quite certain the older woman would faint anew if she were aware of that odd fact.

"Are you all right, Kate?"

The maid nodded her head briefly and clutched the door for support.

Seeming to lose interest in them, the man stalked a few steps away, turned and shouted. "Mrs. Mullins! Mrs. Mullins! Get down here at once."

The great black, furry beast who had remained quiet during this drama awakened at the sound. Its upper lip started to curl into a snarl.

"Brutus, stay." This time it was the man who issued the command.

The animal sat back on its haunches. Harriet eyed it warily as she stepped farther into the entrance. She turned to question the stranger and request that Mr. Wainwright be informed of her arrival, but was unable to stop herself from glancing at his naked chest.

Her experience at viewing unclothed male flesh was extremely limited, yet Harriet knew she was seeing a fine specimen. He was curved with muscle, pulsing with life and heat. There was a curious constriction of her lungs at the sight of that hard plane that made it difficult to speak with the authority and propriety she felt was essential in this situation.

Having at last regained her senses, Kate stood in wide-eyed silence, shivering and dripping water on the stone floor. No one seemed to notice, or care, until the dog inched forward and began to lick at the puddle. Kate shrieked loudly, then pressed her hand to her mouth in an attempt to stifle her screams.

"Brutus, go." The animal looked up at his master and then slowly slunk away. "I realize the animal can be a frightening presence, but your shrieks only increase his interest in you."

"He's terrifying," Kate squeaked.

"He is a watchdog and therefore protective of the members of the household. Brutus regards any stranger as a threat," the man huffed with obvious impatience.

"We hardly pose a threat, sir," Harriet insisted.

The stranger did not reply, but instead gazed at them with deep suspicion as if he expected Harriet to pull a pistol out from beneath her sodden cloak and shoot him.

The hairs on her neck prickled with unease, but Harriet forced her voice to remain strong and steady. "I am Miss Harriet Sainthill. I've come to Hillsdale Castle to assume my position as governess to Mr. Wainwright's children. Would you kindly inform him that I have arrived?"

"You are the new governess?"

"I am," Harriet bristled at his astonished tone and expression.

His dark eyes closed in on Kate. "And who is this?"

"Kate is my maid and traveling companion," Harriet replied, as the older woman quivered under the scrutiny.

The stranger's mouth quirked into a grimace of amusement. "Your maid? You have brought your maid with you? Remarkable. Am I expected to pay her wages also?"

The indignity that was seething just below the surface ceased when Harriet heard the most important word he uttered: *"I."*

"Mr. Wainwright?"

There was a moment's hesitation. "Yes?"

"Och, ye've called me outa a warm bed fer this, laddie?" A slight, white haired woman ambled toward them, her lower lip jutting out in annoyance.

Mr. Wainwright turned toward the newcomer. "Mrs. Mullins, at last. We have unexpected guests. This is Miss Sainthill and her maid, Kate. I expect you will have no difficulty finding them a chamber for the night?"

Mrs. Mullins arched a skeptical brow and pulled the plaid wool shawl tighter around her shoulders. "I canna find a bit o' supper, 'cause my lasses are not 'ere to help."

Harriet strained forward. The housekeeper had the thickest brogue she had ever heard, making it difficult to comprehend more than a few words, especially since she spoke so rapidly.

"They don't need to eat, Mrs. Mullins. A clean room and a warm fire will suffice." Mr. Wainwright blew out a gust of breath and turned back to Harriet. "I assume your coach and driver have already found their way to my stable. I'll send a servant to assist them and show them where they may bed down.

Mrs. Mullins will escort you to your chamber. Good-night."

Kate peered at the darkness that loomed in front of them, then took a step closer to Harriet. "We're likely to break our necks if we go there," the maid declared. " 'Tis dark as a tomb."

Harriet silently agreed, but a quick glance at the housekeeper and Mr. Wainwright confirmed this was not the time to show any trepidation. "I am sure Mrs. Mullins can supply us with candles to help illuminate the way," Harriet said.

The housekeeper's face split into a disapproving glare. She muttered something low and unintelligible, but after a few more grunts of displeasure, she reached into the pocket of her voluminous apron and pulled out two candle stubs. Mr. Wainwright lit them.

"We can discuss your situation in the morning, Miss Sainthill," he said. "I breakfast at eight. Sharp."

More than anything Harriet wanted to tell Mr. Wainwright exactly where he and his eight o'clock sharp breakfast could go, but she successfully held her tongue and tussled with her temper. Her new employer was not at all what she expected and given this unpredictable reception by this rather peculiar household it seemed perfectly reasonable to assume she and her servants would be tossed out in the storm if she angered him.

Knowing she had no other choice, Harriet pasted a neutral expression on her face. "Good night, Mr. Wainwright. I shall see you at breakfast."

He nodded and turned away. Shielding their candles from any stray drafts, Harriet and Kate sloshed cautiously along behind the housekeeper. Finally Mrs. Mullins halted before a formidable oak door.

Harriet entered the chamber, with Kate close

on her heels. It was large, with mullioned windows on two walls. Yet even in the semi-darkness, Harriet could see that nearly everything was coated in a fine layer of dust.

Harriet walked past a small looking glass placed in a roughly constructed frame, ignoring her disheveled reflection. With a thoughtful eye she took note of the oddly arranged furniture, mismatched chairs and chests. The fire-blackened hearth was cold but it was not just a lack of fire that made the room barren of any warmth.

As if sensing Harriet's disapproval, the housekeeper spoke up. "D'ye expect somethin' grand? Aye, ye'll 'ave tae ask hisself fer better quarters. Fer yerself an' yer maid."

Harriet sighed. It would do no good to ask the woman to repeat herself, for Harriet had *heard* every word. *"D'ye expect somethin' grand? Aye, ye'll 'ave tae ask hisself fer better quarters. Fer yerself an' yer maid."*

The problem was that Harriet could only comprehend a smattering of them. But the housekeeper's sullen expression and her pointed, distasteful gaze at Kate gave Harriet a fairly good idea of the gist of what she said.

"Kate will sleep in here with me, Mrs. Mullins. If you would kindly supply a pallet, clean sheets and some fuel for the fireplace, I'm certain we shall be very comfortable."

Harriet kept her expression forceful as the housekeeper shuffled away, then grimaced as she recalled her remarks about being very comfortable. Harriet could not remember when she had ever before told such a deliberate and outrageous lie.

Chapter Five

Nathaniel shut the door to his bedchamber and took a moment to enjoy the blissful quiet and solitude. Though obscenely early to be retiring for the night, even when residing in the country, Lord Avery nevertheless escaped to this chamber each evening directly after dinner. Except for the sound of the rain pelting the windows and roof and the comforting breathing of the dog who seemed to be constantly at his heels, there was no noise to distract or intrude upon his thoughts.

If he leaned back and closed his eyes, Nathaniel could almost imagine he was back in London, comfortably ensconced in his bachelor rooms on St. James's Street. Yet when he opened his lids and gazed vacantly at the meager fire in the vast stone hearth, he knew he was far, far away from the creature comforts he had always taken for granted.

Ever since he had set foot in Scotland it had rained. Hard, heavy, and frozen most days. There had been snow, too. And cold. Bitter, biting, relentless. He had never thought of himself as a weak or pampered man, but the reality of a harsh environment had humbled him.

Especially when McTate's servants had made it abundantly clear they felt that nothing good ever came from England. Including the Sassenach Laird whom McTate had insisted they make welcome.

Tonight marked the end of his second week in exile at the castle and Lord Avery intended to celebrate. By soaking in a bath filled to overflowing with hot, steamy water, set before a roaring fire big enough to roast a pair of oxen and emptying a bottle of fine Scotch whiskey to warm anything else that needed it.

He had stocked enough wood to burn a witch and he had every intention of burning it all, down to the last twig. At least for tonight, he would find some warmth in these cold, northern Scottish mountains.

As he started to remove his clothing, Nathaniel caught a glimpse of his reflection in the small mirror that rested on top of the dresser. He expelled a deep sigh, glad that common sense had prevailed and he had left his valet in London. The priggish servant would no doubt be moved to tears over the state of his master's clothes and appearance.

He needed a haircut and a good, close shave. His garments needed attention also. They were incorrectly pressed, haphazardly folded, and therefore hopelessly creased. Yesterday he had noticed a button missing from his favorite shirt. Clearly his clothes had not fared well in the household laundry.

But Nathaniel had other, more important thoughts to occupy his mind. The welfare of his two nieces and young nephew was the impetus that drove him each day and from which he drew his strength. Even though a month had passed, it was still amazing to think that all had gone according to McTate's outrageous plan.

Thanks to the willing assistance of the family housekeeper, Mrs. Hutchinson, the children had been spirited away with no fuss. Indeed, they had thought it all a grand adventure. Nathaniel could not recall ever seeing such smiles of delight and excitement on their young faces.

If the information McTate had managed to obtain was correct, there had been no outcry at their sudden disappearance. Nathaniel wondered wryly if his uncle even knew they no longer slept beneath his roof since they had been missing from London for nearly four weeks.

Though he cautioned himself continually that the day was far from won, Nathaniel had begun to believe that success was within his grasp. All he needed to do now was to keep the children safe and hidden until the time was right to approach his uncle with negotiations for their guardianship.

Anticipating the warm comfort of his bath, Lord Avery removed his jacket, waistcoat, and shirt. Barechested, he stoked the fire, watching the progress of the huge kettle of hot water hanging in the hearth with great interest. As it started to bubble and boil he carefully ladled out several pails and poured them into the copper tub that was placed in a corner of the room, presumably away from any drafts.

A sudden noise drew his attention. The castle watchdog, a fierce, almost other-worldly looking beast of undeterminable breed, lifted his large head in curiosity. He cocked it to one side and waited, but after a few moments remained silent.

Taking his cue from the animal, Nathaniel continued with his task and emptied another bucket of steaming water into the tub. Suddenly, the beast leapt to his feet and raced towards the bedchamber door. Nathaniel was nearly knocked to the ground, only managing to keep his balance by dropping the empty pail and clutching the wooden bedpost.

The dog's nails tapped a staccato rhythm on the stone floor as he built up a good head of steam, then struck the door with such velocity and force that it flung open. What had begun as a low growl rose to a series of sharp barks the moment the dog was free. Ears flapping, tongue lolling, the animal galloped down the hall.

"Bloody hell!" Nathaniel swore loudly, threw on his favorite red silk dressing gown, and followed after the beast. The stone hallway was dark and shadowed. Weeks of bumping into things and bruising his lower extremities forced Nathaniel to grab the first source of light he came upon.

It was a large, wooden handled torch, better suited for lighting a bonfire. Lord Avery felt ridiculous carrying such an oversized, crude light, certain he resembled a demented medieval warrior. Yet if he wished to reach the front door quickly, there was no time to find something more appropriate.

The dog was pacing impatiently when Nathaniel arrived, stopping every few seconds to scratch at the solid wood door, whimper, then lower his head to sniff suspiciously. Fortunately one sharp look had the hound quiet and cowering respectfully behind him in the shadows.

The door creaked and groaned as Nathaniel struggled to open it. He fully expected to find a relative of one of the servants waiting on the other side, for it seemed the staff employed at the castle possessed enough family members to inhabit a small country.

Instead, Nathaniel encountered two rain-soaked women, shivering and speechless. Their faces were pale and drawn and they looked frightened, as though they had run a good part of their journey pursued by a pack of wolves. He could tell by the cut and quality of their garments that they were not locals. So who were they?

Mutes, perhaps, for they didn't speak. They merely stared. The older woman was dressed as a servant and in her manner deferred to the younger, taller woman. Nathaniel's gaze honed in on the features of the younger woman and he felt a smile bubble beneath the surface of his surprise. The little minx was staring rather pointedly at his chest. His naked chest.

There was no time to ponder that interesting observation, because Brutus chose that moment to lunge forward. Nathaniel expected screams of horror, cries of outrage, tears of terror, but still the women kept silent.

Most likely they were speechless with fright. Quick reflexes enabled Nathaniel to grab the dog by the scruff of its neck just before he landed on one of the hapless woman. Using every ounce of his upper body strength, he struggled to keep the beast at bay while this mysterious duo stared at him like a pair of witless fools.

Shrugging off his irritation, Nathaniel spoke. "Get inside. Quickly. If he gets out there is no telling when he'll return or where he will run."

"We can't go in there!" the older woman cried.

"We must," the younger woman insisted.

"I can't."

Nathaniel watched the ensuing battle of wills with a jaundiced eye, for some reason having little doubt the younger woman would prevail. Then suddenly, the servant mumbled a few words too low for him to hear, crossed herself piously and shivered. Her eyes rolled up, her lashes fluttered wildly and she crumpled to the ground.

Instinctively Nathaniel reached out, wanting to catch the poor woman, but he held the torch in one hand and a growling dog in the other. Miraculously the younger woman somehow managed to capture the servant in her arms and prevented her from hitting the stone floor and cracking her skull.

"What did she mutter?" Lord Avery asked.

The younger woman's eyes narrowed, then blazed at him with fury. "How can that possibly matter? For pity's sake sir, I need your help or else I'm going to drop her on this hard, filthy floor."

"In case you failed to notice, I only possess two arms."

"And very little common sense. What is the dog's name?"

Nathaniel nearly burst out laughing. They were in the midst of a crisis and this daft woman wanted to know his dog's name. "Pardon?"

"The dog's name. What is it?"

"Brutus. Yet, I hardly see how that can have any—"

"Brutus! Sit!" The dog's ears perked at the sound of his name. "Brutus, sit."

Nathaniel watched with no small measure of disgust as the traitorous dog sat obediently back on its haunches.

"Hurry, before your dog decides to bolt."

With one arm free, Nathaniel was able to relieve the woman of her limp burden. "She's not as light as she looks," he grunted.

Demonstrating a practical nature he hardly expected, the younger woman reached out and pulled the torch from his hand. Nathaniel adjusted his grip, thankful he wouldn't disgrace himself by dropping the unconscious woman in his arms. Deciding this bitter icy rain should serve some useful purpose, he shifted the older woman's inert body, exposing her face to it. Within minutes she was stirring and sputtering.

When the women were finally inside the castle, Nathaniel burst into motion. He stalked past the suits of dull armor standing sentry in the old hall and summoned the housekeeper who also served as the castle's cook. "Mrs. Mullins! Mrs. Mullins! Get down here at once."

The activity roused the sitting dog. He stood up and began to growl.

"Brutus, stay." Nathaniel warned.

The dog obeyed, keeping a respectable distance from the women. But something must have drawn his attention, for the older woman let out an earth-shattering scream.

"Brutus, go." Nathaniel ordered impatiently. "I realize the animal can be a frightening presence, but your shrieks only increase his interest in you."

"He's terrifying," the older woman squeaked.

"He is a watchdog and therefore protective of the members of the household. Brutus regards any stranger as a threat."

"We hardly pose a threat, sir," the younger woman insisted.

Nathaniel turned his full attention toward her. Though the light in the foyer was not overly bright, it did succeed in illuminating her face. Her wet bonnet sagged noticeably to one side, but her features were not obscured. She had lovely fair skin, high cheek bones, a pert nose with an upturn at the end and shrewd intelligent eyes, a pretty shade of hazel.

He stared at her for several moments, a nagging memory stabbing at his brain, then a choked gasp escaped his throat as Nathaniel felt a shock of recognition. He knew this woman.

She had been at the center of the scandal of the Season last spring. The jilted bride of a disreputable

fiancé, who was somehow mixed up with a madman who stalked and murdered innocent women.
The rumors that had circulated among the *ton*
were too impossible to fathom, yet even if only half
of what was repeated was true it was a shocking tale.

What in God's name could have brought her to
this remote corner of Scotland at this precise moment in time? Suspicion and questions crowded
his mind, but he waited, balling his hand into such
a tight fist his fingers tingled.

"I am Miss Harriet Sainthill. I've come to Hillsdale
Castle to assume my position as governess to Mr.
Wainwright's children. Would you kindly inform
him that I have arrived?"

For a second Nathaniel was unsure this was the
same woman. He had only seen her from afar, they
had never been formally introduced. He remembered a friend identifying her at the theater one
evening, just before a riot broke out. She was a member of the nobility, the sister of a viscount, which
made it rather unlikely that she was now forced to
earn a living. Unless her family had disowned her?

"You are the new governess?" he asked.

"I am."

"And who is this?"

"Kate is my maid and traveling companion."

Nathaniel nearly groaned out loud. There could
be no mistake. Only a noblewoman would travel to
a post with a maid. Miss Harriet Sainthill was *the*
woman. *Damn!* It seemed unbelievable that after
doing such a competent job on this delicate mis-
sion McTate had managed to make such a colossal
blunder by engaging the single most inappropriate person to care for the children.

"Your maid?" Nathaniel could barely contain a
grimace. "You have brought your maid with you?
Remarkable. Am I expected to pay her wages also?"

"Mr. Wainwright?"

He stared at her blankly for a moment, belatedly realizing she was addressing him. McTate's caution in keeping his whereabouts a secret included assuming a false identity that Lord Avery was unaccustomed answering to. "Yes."

"Och, ye've called me outa a warm bed fer this, laddie?"

Nathaniel turned and smiled, never believing he could feel so relieved at seeing those white corkscrew curls peeking out from an oversized mobcap and the surly person beneath them.

"Mrs. Mullins, at last. We have unexpected guests. This is Miss Sainthill and her maid, Kate. I expect you will have no difficulty finding them a chamber for the night?"

The housekeeper's sour expression was precisely the reaction he had expected. He had deliberately neglected to mention Miss Sainthill was the new governess, since he had no intention of allowing her to take up that position. But that precaution was unnecessary—Mrs. Mullins was clearly not in the mood to make anyone feel welcome at this hour of the evening.

He almost felt sorry for Miss Sainthill as she strained forward, obviously struggling to comprehend the housekeeper's thick brogue. It was at its worst when she was in a temper, as was the case tonight. He surmised the governess could not comment since she most likely had not understood Mrs. Mullins. For a few long moments they were trapped in an awkward silence during which no one had anything to say.

"They don't need to eat, Mrs. Mullins. A clean room and a warm fire will suffice." Nathaniel nearly choked on those final words, knowing full well the women would find neither in this castle. "I assume

your coach and driver have already found their way
to my stable. I'll send a servant to assist them and
show them where they may bed down. Mrs. Mullins
will escort you to your chamber. Good night."

"We're likely to break our necks if we go there,"
the maid declared. " 'Tis dark as a tomb."

Nathaniel felt a spark of encouragement light
his chest. Maybe this would all end far easier than
he imagined and the women's brave façade would
crumble. It was dark and foreboding in the arched
stone hallway, seemingly steeped in mystery. Perhaps
the new governess would make the prudent and
wise decision to leave at once.

"I am sure Mrs. Mullins can supply us with candles to help illuminate the way," Miss Sainthill said
stubbornly.

Nathaniel compressed his lips in an amused sneer.
He could not help but admire her spirit. She looked
wilted, unhappy and a bit scared, yet she did not
want for courage. She and her maid had been
treated appallingly, as if they both carried a rank
odor, yet Miss Sainthill had kept her temper and
her dignity. She would not be put out, no matter
how rudely treated.

"We can discuss your situation in the morning,
Miss Sainthill. I breakfast at eight. Sharp."

Her hazel eyes glinted at him in irritation and
Nathaniel waited for the explosion, anticipating
the ensuing burst of temper with far more delight
than was proper. But she disappointed him by uttering a chilly, polite, "Good night, Mr. Wainwright.
I shall see you at breakfast."

Whipping about, Nathaniel deliberately stalked
away in the opposite direction, which he seldom
used. It was probably crawling with spiders and
other vermin, but it afforded him the type of dismissive exit he needed.

The moment he was alone, Nathaniel expelled a deep sigh. After living in the castle for a few weeks he realized it was essential that he have assistance in caring for the children. From what little he had seen of her character and demeanor, a woman like Harriet Sainthill was an excellent choice for the job. Yet he knew it would be foolhardy to let her remain.

He had recognized her and while he strongly doubted she had done the same, perhaps in time she would discern his true identity. Secrecy was the key to making this plan succeed. He could ill afford to have someone with Miss Sainthill's keen eye around.

Relieved to have found a familiar staircase, Nathaniel climbed it slowly, pondering how he would get rid of the new governess without arousing undue suspicion. Then he smiled. Once she learned that the children were not in residence, it would take very little encouragement to get her to pack her bags and set off for England. Without any delay.

Harriet suspected she would get a small measure of sleep and when the dull glow of morning light crept through the chink in the shutters directly into her eyes she knew she was right. Her head felt heavy and dull from lack of proper rest, her mouth and throat parched. It was difficult to sleep in strange surroundings under the best of circumstances and the accommodations at Hillsdale Castle hardly qualified as the best.

She had forgone all of her usual bedtime rituals, one hundred brush strokes to her hair before braiding it, a favorite passage read from one of her beloved books while she snuggled beneath the covers. The moment her battered portmanteau had appeared in the bedchamber Harriet had donned her nightgown and leapt into bed, trying not to reflect upon the events of the day or think about her plans for the morning.

And now morning had arrived. Harriet sat up, clutching the covers to her chest to ward off the chill in the room. She glanced over to the corner where Kate lay, and listened with envy to the heavy regular breathing of deep sleep. At least it was no longer the loud, thundering snores that had echoed off the stone walls throughout the long night. Though claiming to be frightened and unsettled, the maid had apparently experienced no trouble sleeping.

Harriet did not bother to wake Kate, deciding it was easier to dress for breakfast without listening to the maid's usual patter of doom and gloom. She was perfectly capable of preparing herself for breakfast. Besides, Kate would be returning to England in a day or two. It was imperative that Harriet learn to care for herself and that included getting dressed each morning and undressed each evening. Unassisted.

With a gentle sigh she rose from the bed and went through her luggage. It was not difficult to find an appropriate outfit, since she had purposely taken her dullest and most serviceable gowns. At her sister Elizabeth's insistence she had also included two of her most flattering evening dresses, since it was not unheard of that a governess be asked, on occasion, to join the family for a social evening. Especially if an extra female was needed to make up the numbers at a dinner party or a card game.

Of course, those instances occurred in a normal household. Harriet nearly laughed out loud, trying to imagine it happening in this strange, remote place. When pigs fly, perhaps.

Wrinkling her nose with distaste, Harriet dipped

her fingers gingerly into the cold water that remained in the porcelain basin from last night and washed her hands and face. With nimble movements she deftly pulled her hair into a tight, proper knot and secured it with several hairpins.

There. She was ready. Yet as Harriet checked her reflection in the dull mirror, she felt suddenly overcome with a sense of melancholy. She had never been a beauty, nor professed any aspirations to become one. Yet the woman who looked back from the mirror seemed old beyond her years—severe, restrained, dull. In short, a governess.

Was this truly the type of life she sought? She had felt so sure of her decision when it had been made months ago, but the reality of the situation was far from her imaginings. She was not surrounded by sweet, modest, easy to manage children. Instead there was a grumbling employer, surly servants, and accommodations that left much to be desired.

Granted, they had hardly arrived under the best of circumstances, catching the household unaware, late in the evening, in dreadful weather. And she had not met the children, so it really was far too early to pass judgment.

Comforted by this notion, Harriet picked up her warmest shawl and quietly left the bedchamber. Knowing better than to expect a servant to be available to lead her to the dining room, she gamely set out on her own. The rain that had started earlier in the morning was now a full-blown storm. Lightning flashed through the windows, illuminating the shadowed hall with eerie, uneven bursts of light.

Harriet stole a nervous glance over her shoulder and for an instant considered returning to her room. But a quick look at the timepiece pinned to her gown confirmed she would be late if she did not move ahead. Imagining the smug, disapproving expression on Mr. Wainwright's face spurred her onward.

She turned another corner and her stomach gave a little twitch. Was this wing of the castle completely uninhabited? She had been walking, fairly rapidly, for nearly ten minutes and had encountered no one. Even the surly, disapproving features of the housekeeper, Mrs. Mullins, would be a welcome sight.

At last Harriet came to a staircase. She was uncertain if this was the one she had used last night, but she knew the dining room would be located downstairs, so she descended, clutching the banister tightly to keep her footing. Once she gained the landing, Harriet compressed her lips, unsure of which direction to turn.

A movement caught her eye, the flutter of a figure garbed in a simple mud-brown dress that nearly blended into the stone walls. Finally, a servant was found!

"Hello," Harriet called out. "Good morning. I am the new governess, Miss Sainthill. I was wondering if you would be so kind as to show me to the dining room? Mr. Wainwright is expecting me to join him for breakfast."

Harriet moved forward quickly as she spoke, hoping to gain an answer, but as she drew near the candle placed in the wall sconce flickered as though caught by the wind, the light went out and the servant in the mud-brown garment simply disappeared.

Harriet stood rooted to the spot, squinting into the dull light, uncertain if it was her eyes, her imagination or her lack of sleep playing tricks on her mind. Yet she was certain she had seen *something*.

A sudden, exploding crack of thunder reverberated through her very bones, sending a shiver up her spine. Streaks of color lit up the hallway and for an instant she saw a Scottish warrior, fierce, bloodied and wild, with his sword raised high.

Her mouth fell open in horror, but the scream died within her throat when she realized she was staring at a portrait, an image captured on canvas yet so real and lifelike it could strike terror upon any unsuspecting fool. Harriet winced, then shook her head, scolding herself for allowing her imagination such free, lurid rein. She was by nature a reasonable and logical woman, yet the eerie atmosphere of this strange castle was addling her wits.

Her heart continued to pound in an unnatural, rapid rhythm, but she was unable to resist moving closer to the portrait, searching among the proud, handsome features of the subject for a family resemblance to her new employer. She could see none in coloring, stature or physical characteristics, yet this noble warrior and Mr. Wainwright shared one rather striking similarity.

They were the kind of man that caught a woman's eye.

An odd noise behind her distracted her study. She tilted her head to one side and listened intently, but did not turn around. She heard it again. Was that the creak of a footstep?

"Good morning, Miss Sainthill."

Harriet gasped, then brought her hand to cover her mouth. She swung around. "Ahh, s . . . shirh."

She had lost control of her voice, her words were garbled. She sniffed, hiccupped then with sheer force of will slowed her breathing to normal.

"Mr. Wainwright. You startled me. Good morning."

She caught herself before dipping into a curtsey, remembering he was a mister and not a lord. His dark eyes gleamed like the blade of a sword, but hidden beneath their depths she saw the hint of amusement.

He had deliberately set out to frighten her! Harriet felt certain of it. But why? Did he enjoy tormenting his employees, or had he already taken a specific dislike to her?

"You are already five minutes late, Miss Sainthill, and instead of rushing to the dining room I find you dallying in my portrait gallery," Mr. Wainwright said, clasping his hands behind his back with an air of authority. "You'll have to do much better in future. I abhor tardiness."

Harriet nodded stiffly, lowering her eyes in a docile, submissive gesture. Inside she was seething, with indignation and annoyance, but it would be neither prudent nor proper to show her true feelings.

"If you would lead the way, Mr. Wainwright, your breakfast will not be delayed any longer," she said. And then, finding it utterly impossible to bear the brunt of his censure when she was so unjustly accused, Harriet could not stop herself from adding, "Unfortunately I was not supplied with a map last night and consequently have no idea where the dining room is located."

He angled his head back slightly and smiled. She could not tell if he was annoyed or amused by her comments, but his direct gaze never wavered. The moment became oddly intimate. Harriet felt the uncomfortable heat of a blush spread up her neck to her cheeks and she fervently hoped the dull light would hide her reaction.

"This way," he said curtly.

He did not offer his arm to escort her, as a proper gentleman should, yet Harriet could not fault his actions. She was the governess, not a guest, and Mr. Wainwright was far from a proper gentleman.

There was no further conversation between them and Harriet used the respite to compose herself. When they reached the wide stone archway that led into the long, narrow dining hall, Mr. Wainwright paused and indicated she should precede him.

As she brushed past him, Harriet could not help but breathe in the scent of him—musky and male. Up close, she could see that he was lean, sinewy, and well-muscled. His clothes were of the highest quality, obviously fashioned by an expert London tailor, yet there was an unkempt, uncared for look about them that was puzzling. Why would a man spend so much coin on such fine garments and then neglect to pay a servant to properly care for them?

Aside from the merchants in the village of Harrowby where she had grown up, Harriet had little direct experience with men of business. Yet Mr. Wainwright was unlike any man she had ever known, noble or common.

She seated herself in the chair he offered and watched him closely as he took the seat directly to her left. The room was long and narrow, with a set of mullioned windows running along one side allowing in the natural light. Hung high in the rafters of the soaring ceiling were several faded banners and a tapestry depicting an ancient war scene.

The furnishings were dark, heavy, and at least two centuries old. Time had not interrupted this place. Harriet could easily imagine rushes strewn on the floor, dogs roaming about searching for scraps of food, and men-at-arms throwing dice and drinking in the corner.

There was no sideboard laden with the morning's offerings, but she did not have to wait long for her meal. A servant entered the room, bearing two covered dishes. He placed one in front of each of them, then left the room and returned with two large tankards of ale.

Harriet gave a small start when the beverage was plunked down on the table, sloshing over the side onto the wood. Perhaps that was the reason no tablecloth was used?

Deciding she needed to gain at least one ally in the household, Harriet turned to thank the man who had brought the food. His thin chest puffed out with pride and she tried not to stare at his odd appearance. He was a grizzled old man with nary a hair on his shiny bald head, a gap-toothed grin and a pair of white, bushy eyebrows that seemed to swallow up his forehead. He was dressed in coarse rustic clothing, and his worn and muddy boots seemed more suited for outdoor work.

Harriet was vastly relieved to see that his hands and fingernails were clean. Given the overall condition of the castle she hardly expected liveried servants, but this roughly dressed individual was a surprise.

"If yer wantin' more, just holler fer Mrs. Mullins. She's in the kitchen."

Harriet nodded her thanks, while Mr. Wainwright ignored both the man and his comments, turning his attention to his tankard of ale. Harriet reached for the cover on her dish, then hesitated. Since she had gone to bed without any supper, she was especially hungry, but she was also very cautious. There were no aromas wafting up to give her a hint of what lay beneath the silver dome. Who knew what sort of bizarre and exotic items a household this unusual might serve for a meal?

Copying her employer, Harriet lifted the tankard of ale and took a long swallow. The potent brew sent a rush of heat through her veins—hardly what she needed at the moment. Not daring to consume any more liquid on an empty stomach, Harriet hastily set the ale down, then lifted the cover from her dish and gazed mutely at the unappetizing mixture of food, cold and congealed on the plate.

Some of the items were burnt, others appeared under-cooked, many had an off-putting odor and nearly all were unrecognizable. But in one corner of the dish there was a gray, fluid mound of cooked grains that bore a small resemblance to oatmeal. Perhaps.

Harriet took a tentative taste and then another. It was sticky, nearly flavorless and sank to her empty stomach like a stone. After three bites Harriet gently set her spoon on the edge of the dish and folded her hands in her lap. She noticed Mr. Wainwright had ignored the gruel and was making short work of the stack of oatcakes.

"You have a rather puzzled expression on your face, Miss Sainthill. Is there something about me you find confusing?"

Where do I begin? she thought wryly, wishing she had the freedom to be completely honest. "I was wondering about my charges, Mr. Wainwright. I assume they take their meals in the nursery?"

Mr. Wainwright shrugged his shoulders, but Harriet could tell that for some unknown reason the question had set his back up.

"What time do the children usually begin their daily activities?" Harriet continued. "I realize since they are being cared for by nursemaids they are on a far more relaxed schedule. While I would like to establish a routine as soon as possible, I do not want to implement anything that will be too drastic a change.

"Oh, and I need to know if there are any areas of the castle where we should not venture. I am of the strong opinion that children grow and flourish much faster when they are not always confined to the nursery, yet in a dwelling of this age I would not be surprised to find structurally unsound sections."

Mr. Wainwright's brows lowered and his eyes hardened. "Have you had a great deal of experience as a governess, Miss Sainthill?"

Harriet's mouth quivered. What sort of ridiculous question was that to ask? She had never misrepresented her qualifications. "As I stated in my letter, this is my first position, although I have considerable experience with children of various ages."

"You sound very sure of yourself, yet I feel compelled to remind you that I shall be the one who judges your competence."

He was insufferable! If she had a fan in her hand she would have shut it tight and rapped his knuckles with the edge of it. Hard. Harriet raised her chin and prepared to blister his ears with a set down, but the devilish look in his eyes stopped her.

He was gazing at her smugly, knowingly, as if he were very aware of her anger. And highly amused by it.

"I look forward to the challenge of proving my worth, sir, and improving the minds and well-being of my charges."

Mr. Wainwright's eyes narrowed. "Tell me, Miss Sainthill, what exact course of study do you propose for the children, given the differences in their ages, abilities, and interests?"

Mr. Wainwright fired off a rapid series of questions. He seemed determined to rattle her and she was equally determined to remain calm. After a few minutes, Harriet could tell he was becoming annoyed at her curt answers, yet if he persisted in being so boorish she was not about to alter her attitude.

They might have continued this sharp volley of words interminably, with neither giving ground, but Mr. Wainwright broke the stalemate with one wholly inappropriate question.

" 'Tis surprising that a woman of your strong convictions is not happily married and rearing a dozen children of her own." He regarded her solemnly for a long moment. "Why have you not married?"

Harriet opened her mouth to reply, but no sound emerged.

" 'Tis obvious you are a gently reared lady, endowed with charm and grace, possessing a handsome face and figure. I would think a woman like you would be fairly drowning in marriage proposals. Are all the men in England blind? Or merely witless?"

"Pardon?"

He dipped his head closer. She could feel the warmth of his breath brush her cheek, could smell the ale and oatcakes he had just consumed. Surprisingly it was not an unpleasant odor, but rather an earthy, vibrant reminder that he was a flesh and blood male. An extremely attractive flesh and blood male.

"To leave a woman of your spirit, your vitality unattached," he whispered. "Why, it borders on criminal."

Harriet could hardly contain her shocked amazement. It was not just his words, but the sultry way they were spoken. The man could tread the boards of Drury Lane with those glib lines! She had cursed herself silently earlier for letting him get the better of her, but this was simply too much to let slip by.

Paying particular attention to her posture and facial expression, Harriet turned to Mr. Wainwright and asked in a cold voice, "Are you flirting with me?"

Chapter Six

The edges of Nathaniel's mouth curved into a wicked grin. At last! It had taken the better part of an hour and a good deal of cunning, but he had finally broken through Miss Sainthill's composure. It had been more difficult than he expected and her reaction was not precisely what he had hoped. Given his knowledge of her background, Nathaniel assumed once she realized what he was doing she would blister his ears with a scathing set down and storm from the room.

Her belongings would be quickly gathered and packed and she would be gone from the castle within the hour. Exactly as he intended. Yet here she still sat, with nary a hint of emotion in her hazel eyes as they stared unwaveringly into his own. Apparently there was far more depth to Miss Sainthill than he had realized. How intriguing.

"Are you flirting with me?" she repeated.

"Am I?" he asked, deliberately lowering his voice to a husky whisper.

Nathaniel angled a penetrating look at her and bestowed his most heart-wrenching smile. Now that he knew she would not turn tail and run so quickly, he allowed himself to speak freely. Lord Avery had never in his life met a woman who was immune to charm and flirtation; he waited for her eyes to lower in a coy gesture of understanding. Instead they remained focused on his.

"I believe you are flirting with me, sir." Miss Saint-hill drew herself away from him. "Why?"

"I would think the answer is obvious," he said, moving his head closer to hers. "You are a thoroughly charming woman."

Even as he spoke the words, Nathaniel knew there was more than a grain of truth in them. Beneath the severe hairstyle and the dull, serviceable gown she was a charming woman. Not pretty in the conventional sense, but vibrant and attractive in her own unique way. Her face had character as well as a hint of beauty and her figure was endowed with generous breasts and rounded hips.

Lord Avery decided she was the type of woman whose looks would be enhanced with age and maturity. As he gazed at her strong features, his eyes kept drifting to her mouth, where her slightly parted lips revealed even white teeth. Nathaniel felt a most unexpected stirring of sexual desire.

"Charming? You think that I am charming?" Miss Sainthill cast him a dubious look and then she snorted, making the most unladylike noise he had ever heard.

Oddly, he found the gesture endearing.

"I do not like females who simper and giggle, who smile and fawn over my every word," Nathaniel said. "I like maturity and intelligence in a woman."

"Now, I find that rather difficult to believe." Her lips compressed in an almost imperceptible expression of annoyance. "I am very much aware of the feminine charms men truly do admire and my lack of them. Perhaps there are situations when a governess is easy prey to a handsome, glib employer, but I can assure you I am not, nor have I ever been, such a foolishly gullible woman."

"Pity." Nathaniel let out an exaggerated sigh. He was enjoying himself immensely, he realized, yet he had quite lost sight of his original goal. In order to ensure the safety of the children Miss Sainthill must leave the castle. At once.

He wondered what she would do if he leaned forward and kissed her? Slap his face? Or relax her lips and participate? The temptation to find out was nearly too much to control, yet some small vestige of honor held him back. No matter how dire the circumstances, Lord Avery did not press his attentions on an unwilling female.

But would she really be unwilling?

"Mr. Wainwright, I think it is imperative that we establish an understanding of the boundaries of my position." Miss Sainthill's eyes narrowed dangerously. "I am in your home as a paid employee, charged with the responsibility of caring for your three wards. I am not here for your amusement or your mockery or your sport. Is that clear?"

Nathaniel was surprised to feel a sharp pang of disappointment at her words. This had all started as a harmless little game, an attempt to remove her from the household quickly and with a minimal amount of fuss. He had not really expected, nor sought, a brief dalliance with this woman. Had he?

Lord Avery rubbed his chin and stared with unseeing eyes at the mullioned windows on the far side of the room. Though he had enjoyed this brief, one-sided flirtation, he did feel some guilt. Along with the obvious disbelief, there had been an edge of vulnerability in her voice, reminding him of her past.

She had been jilted by her fiancé, suffering the ultimate humiliation in front of a society that was seldom forgiving or understanding. It must have been extremely difficult to endure, especially for a woman who possessed so much pride.

He wanted to tell her that her fiancé had been a fool, had not deserved her regard or affection, if she had in truth bestowed those gifts upon him. But Nathaniel was not supposed to know anything of her past, so he could offer no opinion.

"You do not approve of any form of light flirtation, Miss Sainthill? I have found it to be an effective way of discovering what truly lies beneath a cool façade."

She looked at him warily.

"However, in deference to your wishes I shall attempt to restrain my impudence," he said. "Though it will be difficult."

There was a long silence. She seemed unconvinced and Nathaniel accepted that it was probably for the best. Perhaps she would regain some confidence in her feminine appeal if she was forced to leave her position due to the lecherous intentions of her employer. It was as good a reason as any to get her to depart.

She lifted her chin and he braced himself. "Then we are agreed that our relationship will never be more than strictly business?"

"Not unless you have a change of heart," Nathaniel could not resist adding, surprised by her acquiescence. He must seem to her either more sincere in his conversation than he thought or she was more desperate to keep this job than he had considered.

"I shall do the job I was hired for, Mr. Wainwright, and I fully expect you to behave as a proper, respectful employer." A smile quivered at her lips. "Since it is my first day, I believe it would benefit the children if we spent some time together. It might make the transition smoother if you introduced me, but if you prefer I can accomplish the task on my own. I merely require someone to escort me to the nursery."

This was the opening that Nathaniel knew he needed to put the final seal on her leaving. Yet he waited until she lifted the tankard of ale to her lips before speaking. "Well, therein lies the rub, Miss Sainthill. The children are not currently in residence at Hillsdale Castle. And to be perfectly honest, I am unsure precisely when they will arrive."

Harriet's first inclination was to explode with anger. Thankfully, her mouth was full of sour tasting ale, making it impossible to yell, and swallow, at the same time. But that moment's hesitation gave her the split second of time she needed to harness her reaction.

He had been playing games with her all morning. First attempting to frighten her in the hallway, then taking on a tyrannical demeanor, and finally trying to act the role of seducer. As if she would ever succumb to such blatantly false flattery!

She was not the sort of woman that men found beautiful or desirable. Her younger sister had always attracted a large number of male admirers. Elizabeth was sweet and innocent and lovely—the direct opposite of Harriet.

She thought her firm and frosty reaction to his ridiculous flattery had settled things between them, but apparently Mr. Wainwright still had a few more tricks to play. The smug expression on his hand-some face told her he was waiting for her reaction to this latest bit of news. Well, he was going to be rather disappointed.

"Actually, you failed to mention that the children are not here, Mr. Wainwright. A most interesting omission."

Calling forth her inner strength and all the training she had ever had in her lifetime, Harriet settled back in her chair. She lifted her napkin to her mouth and daintily wiped the corners.

Then she pushed back the chair, scraping it loudly on the stone floor, and stood. With great effort she managed a frigid smile.

"Since I have no charges to look after, I presume the rest of my day is free to enjoy as I wish?"

She stared hard at him until he nodded ever-so-slightly.

"Excellent. Then I believe I shall retire to my chamber. I would like luncheon served in my room at two o'clock. Will you be so kind as to make the arrangements for me?"

Again a slight nod of that dark head.

"You are too kind, sir. I will see you at dinner, Mr. Wainwright. Is it served at eight o'clock?"

"Six-thirty."

"Ah, yes, you keep true country hours here at Hillsdale Castle. How quaint. I shall see you at six-thirty. Sharp."

Then she sailed from the room with unhurried dignity. Though the temptation was great, Harriet did not glance back as she turned down the hall and away from the dining room.

Her anger and indignation propelled her feet forward and her excellent innate sense of direction brought her to the correct bedchamber. Harriet entered her room and was relieved to find it empty.

Kate must have risen and gone in search of some breakfast. A lopsided smile twisted Harriet's lips. Lord only knew what the maid would find to eat in the kitchen of this odd household if the best of the food was reserved for the master.

Harriet let out a long sigh and leaned against one of the wooden posts on her massive bed for support. It took her several minutes to realize how badly she was shaking from her encounter with her mysterious employer. She was unsure if she wanted to laugh or cry or start smashing items on the floor. Probably some of all three.

What a coil! This experience had turned out to be something beyond her wildest imaginings. She had come to what she perceived as a crossroad in her life and had boldly taken a risk.

She had foolishly convinced herself that somehow she would find what she sought if she struck out on her own. She had deliberately ignored the advice of her family, had clung stubbornly to asserting her independence. She had taken this job in good faith, intending to work hard and to the best of her abilities.

Harriet believed it would give her a purpose, a sense of self-worth that had been missing ever since Julian had abandoned her. Instead she had found herself in an untamed, disordered place awash in layers of mysteries that made little sense.

Harriet expelled another breath of frustration and silently cursed her own stupidity. It would be difficult to return to her brother's home so soon after leaving. Cowed, defeated, a failure. Yet she had no choice. She could hardly remain in this strange place when there were no children for her to instruct.

It was too late to strike out today. Besides, the horses and servants required at least one complete day of rest before undertaking the arduous journey back to England. Yet when the sky began to lighten tomorrow, Harriet and her entourage would be packed and ready to go.

Spinning about, Harriet stalked to her portmanteau and searched for her reticule. She rummaged through the small bag and pulled out her letter of employment, along with the letter of reference the vicar had written on her behalf. Though addressed to Mr. Wainwright, Harriet felt nary a twinge of guilt as she broke the seal and read the contents.

The vicar had given a glowing recommendation of her character, her sense of duty and responsibility and her knowledge of propriety and proper behavior. Harriet privately thought it made her sound rather dull and rigid, but she supposed those would be considered keen assets for a governess. Mr. Wainwright would have most likely been impressed, if he had bothered to ask for her references.

Next she read the letter of employment. It was all there, spelled out most clearly. A governess was required by Mr. Wainwright of Hillsdale Castle to care for his three orphaned wards, two girls and one boy. In addition to the basic course of study which included reading, arithmetic and penmanship, lessons in drawing, embroidery, and deportment were to be provided.

Since no governess was currently installed, it was necessary that she start her duties immediately. Terms of employment included a generous weekly salary of two pounds plus a half day off each month.

Harriet replaced the letters and stared out the window in brooding silence. She was suddenly exhausted, feeling drained of emotion and energy. The long days of her weary journey combined with the sleepless night hit her full force. Though unmade and messy, the large bed looked very inviting.

She made her way to the other side of the room and crawled beneath the linens. The room was gray and dreary, but the steady pelting of raindrops against the window provided a rhythmic lullaby. Within minutes, Harriet fell fast asleep.

The sound of chewing woke her. Jolted awake, her heart thudded and she sat up quickly, clutching the counterpane to her chest. She half expected to see the beastly hound Brutus prowling about the chamber gnawing on some of her belongings, but instead found Kate reclining in a stuffed chair consuming what Harriet assumed was the luncheon she had requested Mr. Wainwright have sent to the chamber.

"Good afternoon, Kate."

The maid paled and guiltily dropped the piece of cheese she held. "Hello, Miss Harriet. Did you have a good nap?"

"Yes. My head at last feels clear." Harriet rubbed her eyes and climbed out of the bed. "What time is it?"

"Half past the hour of two. I started unpacking your garments, but I didn't know where you wanted to put them. And I didn't want to awaken you. I had a feeling you badly needed this rest."

"I did. Thank you for your consideration," Harriet said dryly as she inspected the remaining contents of the luncheon tray.

At least this meal was recognizable. She cut a generous wedge of cheese and took a small bite. The sharp tang that burst upon her tongue as she chewed tasted marvelous. Harriet eagerly reached for a second piece, along with a thick slice of dark bread. There were some dried apples, a dish of stewed cucumbers, and a gooseberry tart resting on a chipped plate.

Once she began eating, Harriet did not stop until she had consumed every morsel. Rested and full, she pushed herself away from the empty tray. Now that her most pressing physical needs had been met, Harriet's naturally determined spirits began to rise.

The memory of her morning encounter with Mr. Wainwright still rankled, but for some reason she did not feel quite as powerless. She knew of course it would be impossible to remain here but she most definitely did not want to leave meekly and mildly, without any fuss or bother.

She had been deceived, brought here under false pretenses and she intended to depart making Mr. Wainwright regret ever trying to make a fool out of her, or any other woman. Harriet had learned from his actions this morning that he was an accomplished flirt and she planned to turn that weakness against him, to teach him a lesson he would not soon forget.

She also intended to take a memory for herself from this dismal, unsettling experience. For all his irritating habits—and they were numerous—Mr. Wainwright was still a favorably handsome and appealing gentleman. Though Harriet would like to have stated otherwise, she knew in her heart she was not immune to his charm.

She knew also that she was not a person made for wild, passionate emotions. Still, a part of her yearned to be spontaneous and daring and uninhibited. To disregard strict propriety, to allow herself to experience an evening in the company of a dashing man as a *woman*, not a *lady*.

It would be a challenge to spar with him again. Harriet was unsure if she could equal him in guile and strategy, but she felt she was his match in intelligence and pride.

Well, such a daring feat would require a great deal of preparation. Harriet rested her elbow on the chair back in front of her and lay her cheek in her hand. She would need to look pretty tonight, a difficult task in the best of circumstances. Yet, with the right gown, a flattering hairstyle and the shimmering glow of candlelight, it might be possible to transform herself into a woman of vast appeal.

Heavens, Mr. Wainwright had shown an interest in her person while dressed in this hideous gray gown. Lord only knew how he would react when she was garbed in silk and lace.

Harriet glanced over at the porcelain jug and basin set in the washstand in the corner of the room and wrinkled her nose in distaste. "I will need to do more than spatter cold water over my face to prepare for tonight. I want a proper bath."

Kate's eyes filled with doubt. "I can't imagine how you will manage such a feat in this place. Why, the stables back home are cleaner than most of the rooms in this castle. And all the servants I saw today look as though they would break out in a rash if they ever got near a bar of soap and tub filled with water."

"Well, there must be a copper tub somewhere in the castle, because Mr. Wainwright appeared quite clean."

Harriet folded her hands in front of her and waited. After a few moments Kate shrugged her shoulders and ambled out of the room, muttering with each step. Close to an hour later, the maid returned with two scrawny lads carrying an awkward-sized tub.

Under Kate's watchful eye the tub was filled with hot water. Once the lads had left, Harriet quickly removed her gown and undergarments and donned a warm wrapper. While Kate built up the fire in the hearth, Harriet added several drops of lavender oil to the tub, then inhaled deeply as the pungent, spicy scent wafted through the room.

"You'd best hurry before the water cools," Kate admonished.

Though the chamber still held a slight chill, Harriet allowed Kate to remove her wrapper. She dipped a toe into the glistening water, then cautiously stepped into the tub, sinking down slowly. It felt heavenly.

"I believe I shall just lie here and soak for a few minutes," Harriet said. "Would you please find my green silk gown? If we drape it by the fire, the worst of the wrinkles should let out."

"The green silk?" Kate's eyebrows raised. "Isn't that a mite fancy?"

"Not for tonight."

"Is there to be a ball? Or a dinner party? Or some other form of entertainment?"

"The green silk, Kate," Harriet insisted, giving no further explanation.

As Kate grumbled and stalked away, Harriet swirled a coarse cloth into the water and began to wash. She was glad her sister had insisted she pack several cakes of her favorite lavender soap, for the familiar smell relaxed and comforted her.

Within minutes, the dirt and grime of the past few days fell away, leaving Harriet feeling not only clean, but renewed. She stayed in the tub until the chilling water forced her to reluctantly abandon her bath. Before she left, Harriet quickly scrubbed her hair with the lavender soap, then held tightly to the sides of the tub as Kate poured a bucket of clean, and rather cold, water atop her head.

Once the suds were washed away, Kate handed

her a warmed towel. Harriet wrapped it securely around her body as she stepped from the tub. Hopping about on her toes to ward off the chill, Harriet rushed to be near the fire while she dried herself off.

Gracious, it was cold in this place! Even standing so near the fire she shivered, but Harriet admitted it might be from nerves or excitement, not just the temperature. She quickly donned her undergarments, a fresh chemise and clean stockings, then used the now damp towel to rub the remaining water out of her hair.

Kate brushed out the tangles and draped the long tresses over the back of a chair. The warmth of the fire aided in the drying. Harriet sat in reflective thought while she waited, working hard to ensure that common sense and a regard for propriety would not prevail and force her to rethink her daring plans for the evening.

"Come and sit near the window so I can arrange your hair," Kate instructed. "I need the light, as pitiful as it may be, or else I'll make a total muddle of it."

Though the maid protested, Harriet insisted that Kate dress her hair in an elaborate style, pinning up most of the long tresses in a topknot. One ripple of long curls was left free, cascading over her right shoulder.

The style was unique, and Harriet knew it showed off one of her better features by drawing attention to the exposed column of her neck. It also gave her the courage to forgo any jewelry, since it covered a portion of her bare bosom.

Harriet had been having second thoughts about her gown selection, but when Kate lifted it over her head and fastened it securely, Harriet knew she had made the right choice.

The dress was of the latest style and probably the prettiest garment she had ever owned. Fashioned of watered green silk, the gown boasted sleeves embroidered in gold thread, a high waist and a low, square-cut neckline edged with ivory lace.

The modiste had used all of her considerable skill to fit the gown closely to Harriet's form, and the skirt draped perfectly in both the front and back. The color brought out the green flecks in her hazel eyes and the delicate whiteness of her skin and the gold embroidered threads made the dress shimmer and glow each time she moved.

As she gazed at herself in the small mirror, Harriet actually felt pretty. Especially since she was not standing beside her beautiful younger sister.

Though she was ready, Harriet forced herself to wait until the clock chimed six-thirty before leaving the room. Arriving late would irritate Mr. Wainwright and catch him off-balance. She had every intention of controlling as many aspects of the evening as possible, but she was smart enough to realize that would not be an easy task. Keeping Mr. Wainwright puzzled was one way to give herself an advantage she knew she would need.

When she was at last ready to leave, Harriet snatched up a lantern. One final glance in the mirror boosted her confidence, confirming she truly did look lovely.

"Have a care, Miss Harriet," Kate warned.

Harriet nodded, taking the sage advice seriously. She made her way through the gloomy hallway to the dining room without taking one false turn. The rustling of her petticoats was a comforting sound, for as usual, Harriet encountered no one.

It seemed odd that such a large dwelling would not house an equally large staff. Then again, the overall unkempt condition of the castle attested to the fact that it was badly neglected. Harriet's anticipation built as she neared her destination, yet she paused a moment to gather all her bravado before taking the last steps into the dining hall.

Mr. Wainwright stood at the far end of the room beside the roaring fire. He was dressed less formally than she in a coat of deep burgundy, a stark white shirt with a low collar and simply tied cravat, a single-breasted gray silk waistcoat and gray trousers.

A goblet of red wine dangled from his fingers and Harriet could not help but notice that his hands, though strong and manly, were also elegant and refined.

The effect of his handsome, striking appearance was marred however, for he turned to glower at her the moment she moved towards him. "You are late, Miss Sainthill."

"Am I?"

She gave an unconcerned shrug and settled herself in a chair at the long table. He huffed again, in annoyance she assumed, and moved to join her. Harriet waited until Mr. Wainwright had seated himself and turned his full attention her way before deliberately letting the shawl slip from her shoulders.

Both of his dark brows shot upward. "Though I must confess that is a lovely gown, won't you feel chilled in such a skimpy garment?"

Harriet caught the note of censure in his voice and bit the inside of her cheek to keep from smiling. "Thanks to that blazing fire, I feel quite comfortable. And I have my shawl to protect me from the draft." She extended her hand and touched his sleeve lightly. "Oh, and thank you for the compliment. I am pleased that you admire my dress."

He stiffened at her touch. Harriet's entire being tingled with wayward excitement. This time she did allow a slight smile to emerge. Deciding the only way to stay in control was to face him, eye to eye, she lifted her chin and kept her gaze steady.

Mr. Wainwright reacted by dropping his stare, but not before she could read the puzzlement in his eyes. Splendid. Pleased with the start of the evening, Harriet reached for the empty crystal goblet set before her and held it towards him.

He raised his hand and a servant stepped forward to fill the glass. It was then Harriet noticed there was a second servant, standing in the back of the room, craning his neck to have a look at her. She resisted the impulse to wave in his direction.

Aware that Mr. Wainwright's eyes were trained upon her, Harriet took a judicious sip of the wine then carefully set her glass down. She noted the linen cloth covering the table, the delicate china plates, the rows of polished silver flatware. Apparently dinner was going to be a far more civilized meal than breakfast.

"Did you have a pleasant day, Miss Sainthill?" Mr. Wainwright asked as the first course was served.

"I had hoped to go exploring in some of the chambers of this fascinating place, but alas, I needed to tend to other matters." Harriet waited until he had eaten several spoonfuls of soup before trying it herself. After three swallows she could still not identify what she was eating, but the hot broth felt warm in her stomach and had a mild flavor. "Please, tell me some of the history of this noble castle. Has it been in your family for countless generations?"

"No."

"Oh. Is it a recently acquired purchase?"

His eyes narrowed. "I do not own the castle."

"You are a tenant here?"

"I lease the property."

"You live out here by choice?" Though she was

striving to keep her voice low and sultry, there was no way Harriet could disguise the surprise she was feeling at this latest revelation.

He shrugged and resumed eating. "I take it you object to the location?"

" 'Tis rather remote and uncivilized."

"I like it."

"Yes, it somehow suits you. Well, now I understand why you have no trace of a Scottish brogue in your speech. Where did you grow up?"

He put down his spoon and turned to her with a look of pure annoyance. "What possible interest could it be to you where I was raised?"

Harriet leaned toward him. She resisted the urge to flutter her eyelashes, presuming she would look like a demented ingenue. "I find everything about a handsome, dashing man such as yourself to be of supreme interest."

He sputtered so much the flame on the candle set near the edge of the table flickered. Harriet made a move to thump his back to help him swallow but the look he gave her changed her mind.

"You stated most emphatically this morning that our relationship would never be more than strictly business, Miss Sainthill," he said hoarsely.

Harriet gave him a provocative, knowing half-smile and daintily wiped the corners of her mouth with her napkin. "True, yet I never said what sort of business, did I, Mr. Wainwright?"

She had timed her remarks perfectly to coincide with the removal of the soup plates. Mr. Wainwright raised his eyes in question, but said nothing in front of the servant, as Harriet had hoped. The only hint of his growing agitation was the drumming of his fingers on the table near his wine glass.

Changing tactics when the fish course was unveiled, Harriet concentrated hard on introducing neutral, innocuous topics. She held her breath as she waited to see if Mr. Wainwright would allow her to take the lead. After an obvious hesitation and a clear glower of warning, he answered her question about the dreary weather, and followed by making a remark that spring was his favorite season.

By the time the game birds were served, they had achieved a natural, mundane flow of conversation. After the culinary success of the first two courses, Harriet was anxious to try the next, even though her stomach was fluttering with nervous energy.

But the birds were not up to the standards of the previous dishes. They must have been a hasty, last minute addition for the skin was barely golden and Harriet could see that the juices running onto the plate were pink.

"At least it is not burnt," Mr. Wainwright said with a wry grimace as he studied his plate.

"A small reason to give thanks." Harriet poked the bird with her fork. "You know, my nursemaid always told me I would get worms if I ate under-cooked fowl. Do you think she was being truthful?"

"I'm not sure, but it certainly isn't a theory I would be anxious to test."

"Perhaps we should make Mrs. Mullins eat it first, then wait to see if there are any ill effects."

"Or I could let the dogs in and we could slip a bird under the table," he suggested. "They would not turn up their noses at such a feast."

"For shame, sir, to subject your poor dogs to worms," Harriet scolded in a mocking tone.

They shared a laugh, but when their eyes met, Harriet's heart skipped a beat. Mr. Wainwright's vibrant, masculine beauty was almost irresistible and this shared joviality had somehow created a connection between them. Harriet felt herself being drawn to him, as hungry, erotic, unthinkable emotions suddenly rolled through her. For the first time in her memory, she felt her body *yearn*.

She cleared her throat, avoiding his gaze, doing her best to hide her reaction. Yet she sensed that he knew very well what was in her thoughts.

He signaled for the fowl to be removed and the spell was momentarily broken. Harriet tried to settle back into a normal rhythm of conversation, but her thoughts were jumbled and disoriented.

"You have a most unusual expression on your face, Miss Sainthill," he said calmly. " 'Tis as though you have just realized it can be dangerous for a woman to be alone with a man such as myself."

Harriet released a long breath, then suddenly her mood became almost giddy. Perhaps the result of feeling too much emotion? Or maybe it was the wine? "I believe the amount of danger depends entirely upon the woman, Mr. Wainwright."

"Indeed." His eyes had darkened as deep as thunderclouds and in their stormy depths she saw an honest, intense, sensual longing she never believed would be cast her way.

The look he gave her made her feel light-headed. Her pulse began a steady, primitive drumming. This was a man who was made for temptation, who could rob a lady of speech, of sense, of judgment.

Yet as she struggled for sanity, Harriet admitted one final, secret truth to herself. Sometime, before the evening ended, she intended to steal a kiss, a real kiss, from this enigmatic man.

Chapter Seven

Nathaniel took a thoughtful sip of wine, allowing the full-bodied taste to linger on his tongue, though in truth he barely noticed what he was drinking. But it was a distraction and prevented him from doing what he really wanted.

Which was to kiss Miss Harriet Sainthill. To lean forward and capture her lips with his own. To allow his tongue to stroke her bottom lip, to plunder and taste the sweetness of her mouth, to succumb to the lust that suddenly burned deep and bright within him.

To bed her. To allow his hands, and lips, to rove up and down her bare torso, to suckle her breast, to stroke her tender womanly flesh. To penetrate her body and fill the air with the raw musk of sex and sweat and honest passion.

To have her spread beneath him, spent, sated, exhausted. And smiling.

The woman who appeared at his dinner table this evening was not the same rain-soaked creature who had arrived last night, nor the prim and strait-laced female who had sparred with him over breakfast. And it was far more than the sophisticated coiffure and the fashionable gown that had transformed her.

It was her flirtatious and sultry attitude, her suggestive remarks and that come-hither playfulness that kept him off balance. Her satiny skin glowed pale and fine in the candlelight, her soft luscious lips were ripe for tasting and despite his best efforts Nathaniel was unwillingly captivated by her sensuous, hypnotic stare.

He doubted she had any real sexual experience with men, for there was an air of purity about her that no amount of passionate stares could disguise. On the other hand, she was far beyond the age of a virginal debutante and she had been engaged for several years to a rogue, a man well-known for his prowess with women. Perhaps some of that untapped wantonness had been set free.

A bloody dangerous thought, indeed.

Outside the rain began again, pelting the windows with its fury. Lord Avery knew the governess had left word with her coachman to be ready to depart at first light. He was pleased when he initially heard the news, but now he found himself hoping this dreadful weather would keep her at the castle. For another day. And another night.

"Creamed peas, Mr. Wainwright?"

Startled from his musing, Nathaniel looked up. Miss Sainthill held out a bowl filled with the vegetables floating in a thick sauce. She must have taken the dish from one of the servants, for there was no one near the table.

"Would you care for some?" she said softly, glancing at him from beneath half-lowered lashes.

Lord Avery was impressed. He had never heard

such a suggestive innuendo placed on so mundane a question. *This must have been how Adam felt, when Eve procured an apple and offered him a bite.*

"Thank you, no," he replied pleasantly. "I do not like peas in any form. Probably because my governess always forced me to eat them as a child."

"But peas are good for you," she scolded, with a slight laugh.

Nathaniel lifted his eyebrows. "My dear Miss Sainthill, upon reaching adulthood I have long gravitated toward those things that are clearly *not* good for me."

A smile curved her lips. "How delicious."

Nathaniel nearly choked on the small piece of beef he was chewing. When she gazed at him like that he had to struggle for control. Somehow, and he was totally unsure when this had occurred, their roles had become reversed. Miraculously it was now she who pursued him. But why the sudden change of heart?

A cold chill ran through him. Had she discovered the truth? Did she know his real identity, was she aware of the reason for his exile here in the wilds of Scotland?

Pensively, Lord Avery made a great pretense of cutting another piece of beef. He was just being fanciful. Miss Sainthill had proven herself to be a forthright woman. If she suspected something was amiss, she would have confronted him immediately.

Unless she was waiting for the right moment? Perhaps that was the reason for this sudden change in her manner and appearance? Nathaniel's stomach clenched as a rush of wary mistrust overtook him.

"This morning you were ready to box my ears over a mild flirtation, Miss Sainthill. Yet tonight you seem to have undergone a complete transformation," he said. "Can you explain this rather sudden change?"

"I do not know what you mean," she replied calmly. Her face betrayed nothing, though a hint of something that might have been guilt flickered in her eyes.

"Your gown, your smiles, your sultry glances. I am a grown man, yet never in all of my thirty-three years has any female directed an inquiry to me concerning creamed peas in such a naughty murmur."

She laughed softly. "I did not realize you have led such a sheltered life, Mr. Wainwright."

"Far from it."

"Good." She smiled again, presenting a picture of brash confidence. "This morning you told me I was charming. Perhaps I now believe you were being sincere."

"Try again."

She regarded him with simmering amusement, never flinching from his hard stare. In fact, he could see his own reflection in the depths of her eyes. But then her expression grew thoughtful, almost serious.

"Do you have any idea what it is like to live your life according to the expectations of others?" she asked. "To always be the sensible one, the practical one, the boring, responsible one?"

"I have an inkling."

"Well, sir, I have had a lifetime." She drew in a breath. "I was the eldest sister in a motherless household. At a far too early age the servants looked to me for guidance and direction, since my father had little interest in the condition of his home or the antics of his children.

"He doted on his first-born son and heir and

pointedly ignored the rest of us. My brother, Griffin, the second son, left England the moment he reached maturity, but I was female and thus denied the chance to shape my own fate."

"What would you have done, given the opportunity?"

"I don't know." Her fingers closed over the stem of her wineglass. "Perhaps I would have gone to sea, like my brother, or maybe bought a commission in the army. Or I could have taken an extended grand tour, traveling the continent and studying art."

"You have artistic aspirations?"

"Not really." She straightened her spine and lifted her chin. Nathaniel was fascinated by the way she controlled the emotion in her voice. "From what I have seen and heard, artistic talent is not a prerequisite for those men who live such a life."

Lord Avery thought back to the wild nights of drinking, carousing, and women he enjoyed during his European grand tour and conceded she had a point. He stared at her profile as she took a small sip of her wine and realized he had been completely wrong about Miss Sainthill.

Her reputation as a stickler for all things proper and correct was not born out of a righteous sense of superiority but a result of her childhood. It had shaped the woman she became, yet had not completely destroyed her spirit of curiosity and adventure. Perhaps even the selection of a fiancé who was wild and reckless was her way of trying to cheat the role that destiny had chosen for her.

"So that is what tonight is all about? An opportunity to be spontaneous instead of measured?"

"Partly." She lifted her wineglass, but did not take another sip. "I will admit that I would like to know how it feels to throw off the restraints that bind me. I have thought about it often, yet never dared act upon it." She laughed, giving him a look of soft reproach. "I think you are a bad influence on me, Mr. Wainwright."

"I find that impossible to believe. You hardly strike me as a person whose opinion is easily swayed or influenced." He waited until the servants had cleared away their dishes before speaking. "Perhaps my company has merely encouraged you to be more open and honest about your true feelings. 'Tis a somewhat humbling revelation, is it not, to discover that deep down we are all human, possessing the same needs, the same desires?"

She tried to hide her widening smile, but failed. "Ah, so it is only society's morals and standards that prevent the inappropriate sparks between men and women from flaring into flames?"

"One cannot deny that it is society which deems these natural inclinations inappropriate." Nathaniel dipped his spoon into his trifle dessert. "Yet these artificial rules cannot always stem the tide of human behavior."

"Or control a clever, determined man who is willing to rationalize his actions when it suits his purpose."

"Trust me, Miss Sainthill, true passion is an emotion that lacks any rational thought." Nathaniel grimaced slightly, surprised at the strong burst of lust that pulsed through him. How odd to find this banter so stimulating. Had he been so long without the company of a woman that mere conversation could get his blood up? "Have you no faith in your gender? Are women so easily duped into shameless behavior by a handsome face and a clever tongue?"

"Are they, Mr. Wainwright?" She lowered her

lashes provocatively. "I suspect you are more qualified to answer that question."

He shook his head with a smirk. "I know enough not to speak of other women when in the company of a lady."

She shifted, and her knee brushed against his thigh. Although their clothing offered a proper barrier, his body reacted with typical male fervor. He could sense a prickle of sensation moving across her skin. Knowing she too felt this vibrant attraction brought a groan of frustration charging to the surface, but Nathaniel swallowed it back.

"Though men may claim to have the more difficult role, women often find themselves on tenuous ground when establishing a relationship," she continued. "It takes hard work to walk that narrow line to avoid a fall from grace. Fortunately we have a great advantage over men."

"You are trained to be ladies?"

"No, we possess in abundance what men lack." She paused. "Common sense."

Nathaniel laughed and after a moment Miss Sainthill joined him. A delectable dimple creased one cheek and he had a mad impulse to lean forward and place his lips upon it. Sitting so close he could smell the lavender scent on her skin. It encircled him like an enticing cloud, stimulating his senses.

The sound of silverware clinking on china drew Lord Avery's attention. The intimate nature of their conversation had created an illusion of privacy, but they were not alone. There were servants present. Servants with perfectly good hearing who were already very curious about him.

Nathaniel glanced down at his plate, surprised to find it nearly empty. Trifle was his favorite dessert, yet he could barely recall tasting a spoonful of it.

"Would you care to adjourn to the library?" he asked. "I instructed Mrs. Mullins to have a fire lit so the room would be comfortable."

He failed to mention there was a cozy sofa in the library, perfectly designed for a couple to share. Sequestered inside, seated side by side with their arms and thighs pressed together, they could continue this discussion at their leisure.

He waited, holding his breath like a green lad, hoping she would agree to at least enter his lair. But his hopes were dashed when she rose to her feet and shook her head. "I believe it would be best if I retire to my chamber."

Before he could stop himself, Lord Avery found himself asking, "May I escort you?"

He could tell the question startled her. Her eyes widened with surprise and the muscles around her lips tightened as she considered the request. "You may walk me to my room if you answer one question."

He nodded.

"Do you truly have three wards who are in need of a governess?"

"Yes."

"Then where are they? Why are they not here, living with you?"

Nathaniel's gut clenched. He was so tempted to tell her. Not the complete truth, of course. But a modified version of it. Yet he knew the risk was too great.

"That makes three questions, Miss Sainthill," he said gently.

He fully expected her to stare reproachfully at him, pivot on her heel and stalk away. Instead she gave a small shrug of acceptance and gracefully extended her arm. Nathaniel reached out boldly and took her hand, lacing his fingers in hers.

Though dressed formally, she had not worn gloves to dinner. The feel of her warm flesh pressed against his hand shot a bolt of desire straight to his groin. He could not tell if she was experiencing similar feelings, though there was a slight blush of color in her cheeks.

They strolled the halls in companionable silence. It was better not to speak, Nathaniel decided, for his tongue felt paralyzed by the promise of what might happen when they reached her door. A kiss, for a certainty, and more than one.

Beyond that—who knew?

Normally he was a patient man. But these were hardly normal circumstances. The lack of time to woo her had somehow caused his desire to heighten to unrealistic proportions. Younger, prettier, more agreeable women had not been able to so capture his attention or stimulate his desire. For reasons he could not entirely explain, this woman tickled his fancy more than any other.

"I cannot help but marvel at the size of this castle. And though I have walked these halls several times, I've yet to encounter a soul," Miss Sainthill commented as they neared her door. "Where do all the servants hide?"

"As far away from Mrs. Mullins as they can," Lord Avery replied in a mocking tone.

The sparkle of laughter in her eyes drove him to action. Taking advantage of her good humor, Nathaniel stopped abruptly, turning her until her back was against the wall. She inhaled sharply, but made no move to escape his embrace. Encouraged, he moved closer.

When Mr. Wainwright took her chin in his hand and tilted her head slightly, Harriet's breathing came fast. But when he bent his head and placed his mouth on her lips, the dim, gloomy hallway was suddenly whirling with color.

He brought his mouth down softly at first. A taste, a tease, a nibble. Harriet was surprised by this gentle exploration that made her senses swim. Lust always held a titillating, secret interest in her mind, yet she had never completely experienced it.

Until now. And it was impossible to resist the raw longing and emotions this magical kiss brought forth. She responded in a wholly inappropriate manner by clutching his lapels and pulling him closer. He deepened the kiss, coaxing her mouth open. His tongue thrust at hers and she answered with her own, amazed at the depths of feeling and passion he could arouse.

Her blood pulsed rapidly through her veins. Her breasts tingled and she pressed her thighs together, trying to ease the sudden ache. As she allowed herself to be cradled in his strong arms, Harriet gave herself over completely to the experience of giving and receiving pleasure.

She could feel his muscled hardness and body heat, could smell his musky cologne, could hear his harsh breathing, could taste his passion. *It felt so good,* she admitted with a sigh. *In an uncontrolled, unfamiliar way.*

Their hips rocked together. He kissed her temple, her cheek, her jaw. He bit her earlobe, then sucked it gently between his teeth. Harriet tipped her head, allowing him easier access and he kissed her neck, nuzzling it softly.

Then he went very still. He leaned forward, resting his forehead against hers. His chest heaved against her breasts, rubbing them, creating an unbearable, restless friction.

"Where is your famous female common sense now, Miss Sainthill?" he whispered raggedly.

His words brought her sharply back to her senses. There was certainly madness connected to this wild reckless behavior, but she could no longer allow herself to indulge. Reluctantly, Harriet pulled herself out of his arms. " 'Twas gone for a fleeting instant, but thankfully it has returned."

"Thankfully?" His voice turned husky. "Shall I chase it away and rekindle our passion? I promise the bliss we will achieve, the delights we will share, the fulfillment we will reach shall make it well worthwhile."

He reached for her again, but she stepped away. Though this attraction held her in its dizzying power, Harriet knew her head must rule her actions. "Good bye, Mr. Wainwright." She let out an audible sigh. "I suspect it will come as no surprise to you that I have decided to terminate my very brief employment. My servants and I will be leaving in the morning."

"Then stay with me tonight."

He ran his fingertips along the line of her jaw, adjusting her head so she was forced to look into his eyes. His stare was hot, filled with hunger and raw need, yet oddly earnest. Humbling amazement unfurled within her as she realized he was the first man to be so open and honest about his passion. *For her.*

This was not an act or a ploy. He truly did find her desirable, for the smile that crept across his handsome face was pure sin.

Her heartbeat roared in her ears. For an instant Harriet feared she did not have the strength to resist. Slowly, she lifted her hand and caressed his clean-shaven cheek. She stared intensely at him for a long moment, desperately struggling to keep the temptation she felt from her face.

And oh, how she was tempted.

With the two most important male relationships of her life, Harriet always felt she had been striving to reach for something beyond her grasp. Her father's love and attention. Her fiancé's love and attention.

Mr. Wainwright's proposition should have left her bristling with embarrassment and outrage. Instead it made her feel beautiful. Womanly. For once she was not reaching towards a man who was turning away. For once someone she found desirable was reaching for *her.*

'Tis long past the time that you did something daring in your life, Harriet thought. Yet while the yearning hit her hard and deep, she could not lose sight of the fact that there were limits that all women had to place on their actions. And consequences.

"Good-bye, Mr. Wainwright." Her voice was breathy, but determined.

He suddenly jerked his head and kissed the hand she still held against his cheek. "You have broken my heart, Miss Sainthill."

His attempt at humor eased some of the tension. As she turned away, Harriet could feel his burning gaze on her body. She knew it would only take one slight gesture of encouragement to bring him near. It was a heady, womanly power she never believed she would have the privilege of possessing.

Pity, this was not the right time to use it.

She fumbled slightly with the door handle before slipping inside. She shut the door quickly, practically in Mr. Wainwright's face, then turned and pressed her back to the solid wood.

Nervously smoothing her hair and righting her

gown, Harriet waited to hear his footsteps fade away. The sound was a long time in coming and when she did hear it, a deep sigh of pure loneliness escaped. For the first time in her life, Harriet loudly cursed her rigid, moral conscience and innate common sense.

Though it was not late, the snores from the corner of the room told Harriet that Kate was already fast asleep. Harriet did not bother lighting any candles, fearing it might awaken Kate. Given the unsettled nature of her emotional state, she was in no mood to answer any of the maid's questions about the evening.

It was a struggle to remove the green silk gown without aid, and difficult to negotiate the dark room, but Harriet managed. She folded each of her garments carefully as she undressed, then carried the pile to her open portmanteau. Kate had already packed most of Harriet's garments, so it was a tight fit, but Harriet managed to get the rest of her clothes inside.

Before fastening the portmanteau closed, Harriet's fingers brushed against the soft silk gown that rested on top. She sighed, knowing any time she wore this garment she would remember this night. And this man.

Kate had laid out her nightgown on the bed, so there was no need to go searching through the luggage. Harriet pulled it over her head, taking note of its shapeless, unflattering design. Made of simple white cotton, it had long sleeves, a high neckline that brushed against the bottom of her chin, and a hem that swirled about her ankles.

The only touch of color on the entire garment was a small design of pink and blue embroidered flowers along the cuff of each sleeve. It was hardly the garment a seductress would wear to entice a man, yet she wondered how Mr. Wainwright would react if he saw her in it.

Stop it! Harriet nearly screamed the words out loud. This carnal speculation was pure folly. She had made her decision regarding Mr. Wainwright and there was no going back.

Rushing to finish her preparations for bed, Harriet stalked to the washstand and poured cold water from the chipped pitcher into the basin. She splashed her face liberally, then patted it dry. Next she removed the pins from her hair, wincing as a few caught in the long curls and pulled at her scalp.

She brushed her hair slowly, but found no comfort in this normally soothing ritual. Disgusted, she plaited her hair into two neat braids and secured the ends with plain ribbons. Feeling more like herself, Harriet at last climbed under the covers and pulled the heavy blanket to her chin.

As the minutes slowly ticked by she listened to the steady rain and waited with open eyes for the morning to arrive.

There was no change in the weather at daybreak. Steady rain continued to pelt the windows and the gloomy sky darkened the room. For a fleeting instant Harriet wished she had the choice of turning over and snuggling under the covers, but she knew that was not to be. They needed to get on the road as soon as possible, for it was no doubt full of puddles and mud already and travel today would be slow.

The meager fire had long since gone cold in the hearth and Harriet dreaded leaving the warmth of her bed. She sat up, drew her knees to her chest and wrapped her arms around them, all the while keeping the blankets tucked snugly around her.

Her final morning at Hillsdale Castle. The pang of regret she felt at leaving was a confusing emotion. It was the only course of action she could take and yet the thought of leaving this mysterious place with so many unanswered questions crowding her mind left her feeling unsettled.

Harriet stole a glance around the room, surprised to spy Kate still abed, apparently sleeping soundly. The maid was usually up long before Harriet awoke. The older woman had done nothing but complain since setting foot inside this household, so Harriet assumed when she woke this morning she would find Kate sitting on the luggage, fully dressed, with her bonnet tied and her gloves on, eager for the journey back to England to begin.

Knowing the roads would be treacherous and uncomfortable, Harriet decided to let the maid enjoy a little more rest. Harriet stretched out her legs, moving them restlessly beneath the covers as she debated where to eat her morning meal. When Kate awoke, should she tell the maid to fetch a tray from the kitchen? Or would it be better to brave the dining room for a last shared meal with her former employer?

What would Mr. Wainwright do if she did not appear for breakfast? Would he seek her out one final time? Would there be an opportunity for a lingering, *improper* good-bye? Would that be wise?

Angered at her indecisive vacillations, Harriet threw back the covers and jumped from the bed. Her bare feet on the frigid stone floor jolted her awake. She wrapped her arms tightly around herself to ward off the cold, then set about laying a fire. Pleased with the flickering flames, she made a brief inspection of the luggage, conceding that Kate might be a meddlesome pest, but she was an excellent maid.

"Kate, 'tis time to rise," Harriet called out. "There is still much to be done before we can depart."

Harriet poured the last remaining drops of cold water from the pitcher and tried to wash her face. Realizing she would need more water, preferably hot, to complete her toilette, Harriet turned toward her maid.

"Kate, please, we have much to accomplish. You must get out of bed."

Harriet waited impatiently, the empty pitcher dangling from her hand, but the elderly maid never lifted her head off the pillow.

Concerned, Harriet moved closer. Kate shifted restlessly on the mattress, making odd, guttural sounds. Her face seemed unnaturally pale and her teeth chattered even while she slept. Harriet reached out and placed a hand upon the maid's forehead. It felt hot and feverish.

Kate reacted to the contact by moaning loudly and kicking the bedcovers off her body. Good Lord! The maid was gravely ill. Fearing the worst, Harriet rushed from the room to find aid.

Chapter Eight

Harriet arrived at the dining room panting and out of breath. To her utter dismay, she discovered the room was empty, with no sign of Mr. Wainwright or his breakfast. He had either eaten already and was gone or had yet to begin his day. She was too early or too late.

Chest heaving with frustration, Harriet scurried toward the back of the room, looking for a second exit and finding none. Whirling around, she hurried out the same door she had entered, then paused. She lifted her chin, drew in a deep breath and then another.

Where to now? Forcing her mind to concentrate, Harriet was barely aware of the odors wafting through the air until she took another deep breath. *Food!* If she could smell it, then someone must be cooking it. Without hesitation Harriet let her nose lead her down a long hallway, hoping she would discover the source, and the cook, quickly.

She did. It was a cavernous room, both wide and

long with high arched stone ceilings, several fireplaces, cooking pots, two stoves and four long trestle tables. Dried herbs hung from the ceiling, baskets of vegetables sat in the corner, freshly killed game covered a small bench. As she crossed the kitchen threshold, all her questions about seeing barely any servants in the castle were immediately answered.

The room was fairly crawling with people, whose station as servants was easily ascertained by their dress, if not their manner. They were sitting about in cozy repast, eating and drinking heartily, talking and joking amongst themselves. There was a festive, almost party atmosphere in the room. A startling contrast to the gloomy, lifeless feeling that permeated the rest of the dwelling.

Harriet's sudden, unannounced appearance caused little reaction in the kitchen, as everyone was too engrossed in their own conversations to take much notice of her. Fortunately, there was one face in the group that she recognized.

"Mrs. Mullins. Oh, thank goodness. You must send for the physician immediately." Harriet took several long strides across the stone floor, moving closer to the housekeeper. "My maid is ill and needs care."

Mrs. Mullins turned slowly. Her gaze moved from Harriet's face to her feet and back again before delivering a cut worthy of the most aristocratic dowager. "Are yer daft, lass? Runnin' aboot the castle in yer nightclothes as if the dev'l hisself wer on yer heels? What's wrong with ye?"

"I need help!" Harriet's agitated state only enhanced the difficulty of understanding the housekeeper's thick brogue. Harriet shifted restlessly, returning tenfold the look of pinched disapproval she was receiving.

As the standoff continued, the conversation

around them buzzed for a few minutes, then grew softer and softer until it finally fell silent. Harriet knew without looking around that every eye in the room was now trained upon her. She felt a prickle of unease rush up her spine at nearly the same instant she noticed an icy draft swirling around her ankles.

Harriet glanced down. Good Lord! It was no wonder that everyone was staring at her as if she were some sort of lunatic. Her feet were bare, her braided hair was rumpled and unkempt and she was standing in the middle of a crowded kitchen dressed only in her nightgown, without even a wrapper to cover and preserve an ounce of her dignity.

In her haste to summon help for her maid, Harriet had run from the room wearing her nightgown! Her embarrassment frizzled under her skin, but she could not afford the luxury of indulging it. Kate was ill and needed help. Harriet tugged at her sleeves, knowing that while her attire was outrageously inappropriate, it also covered her completely, certainly far better than the daring gown she had worn to dinner last night.

Head high, she turned again to Mrs. Mullins. "A physician must be summoned at once."

The housekeeper's lip curled, but the servant was interrupted before she could make any further remarks. By the arrival of Mr. Wainwright. Apparently one of the other servants had the presence of mind to fetch his master.

"What is the matter?"

Both women turned at the same time. Harriet felt Mr. Wainwright's gaze upon her, but he made no comment about her attire, and she was grateful for his restraint. She put a hand to her whirling head, blinked, refocused. "Please, you must come at once. 'Tis Kate."

He met her eyes. "Kate?"

"My maid. She's burning up with fever. I fear she is dangerously ill and in need of immediate medical attention."

Mr. Wainwright reached for her, closing his fingers firmly about her wrist. "I appreciate your concern, but more often than not what appears to be a serious illness is nothing more than a mild cold. There is no need to start a panic."

Harriet opened her mouth to haughtily declare that she well knew the difference between a serious fever and a simple cold, but the gentle pressure of his fingers on her arm stopped her. She paused, read the caution in his eyes, then took a moment to glance around the room. When she saw the crowd of anxious faces staring intently at her, Harriet understood Mr. Wainwright's silent warning.

"My apologies for the overset," she said in a deliberately loud voice, seeking to be heard. Then she dropped her chin, leaned closer and whispered, "Kate is gravely ill. Please, you must find help at once."

"I'll take care of it."

"Thank you."

Harriet turned on her heel and strode away quickly, praying that the firelight was too dim to illuminate her limbs through the cotton of her nightgown.

Once back in her bedchamber, she checked on Kate, who was still in a feverish, delirious state. Then Harriet quickly dressed, putting on her traveling clothes since they were the most easily accessible garments. Though she knew she would not be starting her journey home today.

Needing to keep herself occupied, Harriet set about organizing the clutter in the room. She briefly considered unpacking, but felt guilty at undoing all of Kate's hard work. After all, who knew when the maid would be up to tackling such a big job again.

A knock at the door interrupted Harriet's disturbed thoughts. Though she would have preferred to see the doctor, she was not displeased to find Mr. Wainwright.

"I've sent Douglas for the physician, but it will probably take several hours for him to arrive," Mr. Wainwright said. "He lives a fair distance away and this storm will hamper his progress."

"I had not really expected him to be here quickly. Though I did hope." A worried frown creased her brow. "I think Kate will be more comfortable in the bed, but I cannot move her on my own."

"I'll do it." He crossed the room and knelt by the thick pallet where the maid tossed restlessly. As he glanced down, an expression of alarm crossed his handsome features.

Harriet rushed forward. "Is it Kate? Has she worsened?"

Mr. Wainwright shrugged his shoulders helplessly. "Since this is the first that I have seen of her, I can make no comparison. But she is very pale and burning with fever."

Harriet lay her palm on Kate's forehead. "Her skin is warmer to the touch, but I cannot tell if it is the fever or the warmth of the fire."

"Your idea to move her is a good one. Let's put her on the bed," Mr. Wainwright said.

Harriet pulled back the bed curtains, ignoring the cloud of dust, knowing the heavy cloth would serve to keep out the draft. She drew down the covers, angry that she had not thought to set a warming pan in the bed to chase away the chill.

With a single grunt, Mr. Wainwright lifted the

maid up in his arms. He hesitated for a moment, balancing his burden, then carefully carried her across the room. The minute she was in position, Harriet covered her with several blankets.

The maid looked pale and lifeless stretched out in the large bed. Harriet's heart constricted in panic. " 'Tis very serious, isn't it?" she whispered.

"It could be," Mr. Wainwright admitted. "I've only seen fever this extreme one other time."

"What happened?"

"The patient died."

Harriet held back her gasp. She was stricken by the torment that laced through his voice, and she could not help but wonder who this mysterious person was that could cause Mr. Wainwright such emotional agony.

"Miss Sainthill, forgive me." He rested one hand on her shoulder. "I did not mean to suggest that Kate will meet a similar fate."

"I know. I appreciate your honesty. I feel so helpless." Tight-lipped, Harriet gulped back a tide of emotion.

"All we can do now is wait for the doctor and pray that he has the skills to cure her," Mr. Wainwright said. "Is there anything we should do in the meantime?"

"I don't know. Give her some tea, perhaps? It seems to me that anytime anyone is feeling poorly, tea is prescribed."

"I'll have some sent up immediately." He walked to the door. Harriet remained at Kate's bedside. "I'll bring the physician here the moment he arrives. If you have need of me, I'll be in the library."

Harriet nodded her thanks. The remainder of the morning passed in a blur. She waited, paced and waited. The servants, fearful of the dreadful disease the Sassenach woman carried, refused to enter the bedchamber. They left trays with the supplies she requested outside the bedchamber door, scurrying away before Harriet even caught a glimpse of them.

When she wasn't pacing, she sat at Kate's bedside, bathing the older woman's face with cold cloths. It seemed to calm her, but only for a short time. All too soon she would again thrash and moan in delirium.

At last the physician arrived. As promised, Mr. Wainwright escorted him into the bedchamber and introduced him as Mr. MacLeod. He was a portly fellow with gray whiskers and kind eyes. He had not even bothered to shed his mud-spattered hat or travel-stained cloak. Harriet felt bolstered by this show of medical dedication.

"Mr. Wainwright explained that one of yer servants has taken ill," the doctor said. "What seems to be the trouble?"

"Fever, chills, delirium. One moment she is shivering and begging for more blankets and the next she is kicking about and throwing them off, complaining of the heat." Harriet sighed and rubbed a finger between her brows. "It seems to have gotten worse over the morning hours."

"Hmmm." The doctor nodded gravely and removed his hat and cloak.

Mr. Wainwright appeared at Harriet's side. "Are you all right?"

"It is just my head. It hurts dreadfully."

He wrinkled his brow and gave her a peculiar look. "Do you think you might have caught Kate's fever?"

"Me? I'm never sick." Harriet rubbed her temples vigorously, attempting to soothe the persistent aching, but ceased when she noticed Mr. Wainwright staring at her. "I'm fine. Just very tired. I barely slept last night. I'm certain that is the source of my headache."

"Nevertheless, it might be best if Mr. MacLeod examines you when he is finished tending to your maid."

Harriet waved her hand, dismissing the notion as frivolous, yet she could not as easily dismiss the warm feeling of delightful astonishment that engulfed her over his concern. No man had ever shown her such caring.

"Well, now, let's set about makin' ye better, my good woman." Mr. MacLeod took a few steps towards the bed, stumbled and nearly fell on top of his patient.

"He's drunk!" Harriet exclaimed with indignity, as the strong odor of spirits made her move away.

Mr. MacLeod turned his head and gave her a sheepish shrug. "I was hopin' ye wouldn't notice."

"Not notice!"

"No need to fear, lass. I'm a trained physician, a graduate of Edinburgh College of Surgeons. Well, a near graduate." With concentrated effort, the doctor regained his feet. His mustache quivered as his lips curved into a friendly smile. "I know plenty about treatin' the sick. Been doin' it for nigh on twenty years. And I am rather proud to report that many of my patients have recovered most splendidly."

"Mr. Wainwright, may I have a word with you? Please!" Harriet moved to the shadows, though she doubted it mattered if the doctor overheard the conversation. "I asked you for help, and this is what you deliver?"

A frown formed on Mr. Wainwright's face. "He is hardly my first choice, but unfortunately he is the only person with any medical training in the area. I'm afraid it is Mr. MacLeod or no one."

"He looks perfectly capable of killing her," Harriet retorted.

Mr. Wainwright sighed and ran a hand through his already rumpled hair. "We both know she is very ill and in urgent need of medical assistance. Do you want him to take a look at her or not? Or would you prefer to try and nurse her on your own? Kate is your servant, this must be your decision."

Harriet thought a moment. "He may examine her, under my supervision. But I will not allow him to administer any sort of treatment until he explains, to my satisfaction, what he intends to do."

Mr. Wainwright nodded, then turned to the doctor. "You may proceed, Mr. MacLeod, but I caution you to exercise great care."

Head down, the doctor retrieved his satchel from the floor and set it on the edge of the bed. Harriet watched as he withdrew bottles from his bag. He uncorked them, sniffed, then set several of them in a cluster on the bedside table. "I shall need a bowl, water, clean cloths and a bottle of yer best Scotch whiskey."

"I could barely get Kate to take a few sips of weak tea earlier this morning," Harriet said. "I'm sure she cannot tolerate strong spirits."

The doctor turned and smiled pleasantly. "Quite right. A patient in her frail condition should only be given small amounts of plain liquids, along with the proper medicines." He broadened his smile, then winked. "The whiskey is fer me. To steady my nerves."

If the situation were not so grave, Harriet might have burst out laughing. "Let me assure you, Mr. MacLeod, that not a drop of spirits will cross your lips until my maid is hale and hearty."

The physician seemed hurt by her remarks. He

shuffled closer to the bed like a sulky child and proceeded to lean over the mattress and examine his patient. When he finished, he mixed together a vile-smelling concoction of herbs in the bowl that Mr. Wainwright provided, then added a dash of water.

"The patient must swallow at least two large spoonfuls every four hours," Mr. MacLeod announced.

"What's in it?" Harriet asked.

"A special blend of medicine that will aid in her sleep, clear her lungs, and reduce her fever."

"Sounds miraculous," Mr. Wainwright said sarcastically.

The doctor was not offended. Quite the opposite in fact. He smiled and nodded his head in modest recognition of what he clearly perceived as praise.

"If it does only half of what he claims, it will be of great help." Harriet rested her hands on her hips. "However, in order to ease my fears, Mr. Mac-Leod, I require that you ingest a dose of this miraculous elixir before it is given to my maid."

"I beg yer pardon?" The doctor covered his mouth in obvious horror.

Harriet allowed herself a slight smile, pleased that she had managed to penetrate his whiskey-soaked brain. "You must swallow the medicine before being allowed to administer it to Kate."

"But I'm not ill."

Harriet merely shrugged. Mr. MacLeod stared at her for several long moments, as if weighing her resolve. Then with a shrug of defeat, he swiftly downed a mouthful of the medicine. His face contorted comically, but the doctor not only swallowed it, he kept it down.

Satisfied there was nothing in the concoction that would harm Kate, Harriet nodded her approval. It took all three of them to get the proper dose of medicine poured down the older woman's throat. When it was done, Harriet slumped against the headboard, silently wondering how she would manage to properly care for Kate throughout the long day.

But she had to do it. After a few parting words of instructions, Mr. MacLeod left. All day and throughout the night Harriet nursed the older woman. She tried her best to dose her with medicine and fill her with fluids. She bathed Kate's head with cool cloths when she threw off the blankets, and she piled the quilts higher when Kate's teeth would chatter and she shivered.

Mr. MacLeod made a second call the following morning and confirmed Harriet's worst fear. Kate had the influenza and was not responding to the medication. A new mixture of medicines was prescribed, but Harriet's hope for recovery was fading.

Exhausted, discouraged, and frightened, Harriet redoubled her efforts. Kate would not die! Though Harriet had never felt a particular bond with the servant, the thought of losing someone who was her responsibility pulled at Harriet's soul.

A knock at the door signaled that dinner had arrived. Wearily Harriet retrieved the tray, almost hoping she would catch a glimpse of the servant who had left it. She had seen no one other than Mr. MacLeod and Mr. Wainwright in nearly two days and their visits had been brief.

Kate was twisting restlessly on the bed. Harriet closed the door and set aside the tray. She would eat later, when Kate was more settled, improved.

Harriet piled two blankets on top of the shivering maid, tucking both sides tightly beneath the mattress to keep her from thrashing about and injuring herself. The maid began talking, babbling a string of delirious mumblings that were impossible to understand.

"All will be well, Kate," Harriet declared. She spoke constantly to the maid, partially in hopes that the sound of another voice might calm the older woman, but Harriet also used it as a device to keep herself awake. "Would you like a sip of cool water? It should feel good on your parched lips and throat."

Harriet lifted Kate into a sitting position and brought the cup up to the older woman's lips, but the maid struck out, twisting and turning, knocking the water out of Harriet's hand.

"All right then, no water just yet. Perhaps later."

Harriet straightened, brushing the droplets from her dress. Fortunately the water had fallen on her and not the bed. It would have been impossible to change wet sheets with Kate in such an agitated state and the servants afraid to enter the room.

She would have had to call Mr. Wainwright to assist her. The idea of asking for his help was not a repugnant one, for she realized he would have done this without question or complaint.

Harriet could hear movement outside her door, the sound of footsteps approaching. "How is Kate?" Mr. Wainwright asked as he entered the room.

Harriet shrugged. "No worse than earlier this morning. I've given her two doses of the newest medicine but it seems to have had little effect."

He joined her at the bedside, his expression silent and austere as he stared down at the sick woman. "I am certain you are doing an excellent job of caring for her, but you need to rest now, Miss Sainthill," he said. "I've had a bedchamber down the hall cleaned and aired for you so you may sleep in comfort and privacy."

"I cannot leave her. She is too frail and helpless." Harriet stretched onto her toes and arched her back, attempting to ease the tightness in her muscles. "I'll rest when her fever breaks."

"That could take hours, even days. You'll be of no use to anyone if you are worn to a frazzle."

Harriet shook her head in protest. "I'm fine."

"Stop blaming yourself. Her illness is not your fault."

"How did you—" Harriet clamped her lips tightly, then sighed. "She is my servant and my responsibility. I should never have taken such an elderly maid on this arduous journey. And I should never have allowed her to sleep on the pallet. 'Tis too near the damp, cold stone floor. I'm sure that chill has caused this fever."

"I highly doubt it. I slept in far more barbaric conditions when I first arrived at the castle and never once fell ill." He tilted his head and squinted slightly. "That's not entirely true. I have experienced a bit of soreness from using some long dormant muscles, but that has been my only physical discomfort."

Ah, and what splendid muscles they are, sir. Do you wish me to soothe and massage away any lingering aches? Harriet blinked and shook her head, realizing that she was far more exhausted than she thought, if she was allowing these thoughts to invade her consciousness. At least she still possessed the wit not to say them aloud.

"Since you refuse to leave, I will stay and care for Kate while you sleep on one of the chairs," Mr. Wainwright decided.

" 'Tis highly improper for you to be in a bedchamber, behind closed doors with me for any significant length of time," Harriet responded automatically.

"I thought you weren't going to care about proprieties any longer, Miss Sainthill. Harriet." He smiled for the first time since this ordeal began and she was struck anew by how handsome he was—and kind.

"I have not given you leave to address me by my first name," she retorted with a raised brow.

"I have taken the liberty." A hint of a roguish leer surfaced. "After all, we are going to be sleeping together."

"Hardly!" A rush of heat surged into Harriet's cheeks.

"Be sensible, Harriet. I've already tried bribing some of the younger maids into helping care for Kate, but they are all too frightened of catching this illness. I suppose I could order them, but it doesn't seem fair. To them or Kate."

Harriet sighed heavily. "You're right. It is highly doubtful she would receive proper care from someone who is afraid to be in the same room with her."

"Precisely. Please, lie down for a few hours before we have two patients to worry about." His eyes took on a teasing glint. "Besides, 'tis a trifle late to be worrying about the propriety of our situation. Especially since I've already seen you in your nightclothes."

Her heart did an immediate leap as he flashed that seductive smile at her. Feeling that she needed to preserve some control over the situation, Harriet shot him a reproachful glare, though it seemed to have little effect.

Deciding she was too tired to argue, Harriet allowed him to drape his arms across her shoulders and lead her to an overstuffed chair. She sat down and tucked her legs up, then rolled onto her side and curled into a ball, dragging the blankets he provided over her shoulder.

"Since you are so insistent, I will rest for a few hours," Harriet said wearily. "But you must promise that you will wake me if Kate worsens or calls for me."

"I will." He handed her a fluffy feather pillow.

The moment her head settled into the softness, Harriet let her muscles relax and felt her lids get heavy. The last thing she remembered was the trustworthy expression on his handsome face and the feeling of warmth and safety that invaded her tired bones.

The sound of snoring woke her. There was a deep snort, followed by a snuffle and another snort. It was both an annoying and familiar sound, but Harriet's foggy head could not determine why this noise was such a comfort.

She opened her eyes. The room was bathed in sunlight, the first she had seen since arriving in Scotland. Mr. Wainwright was sprawled inelegantly in the chair by Kate's bedside. He had removed his coat and cravat, opened his shirt at the neck and rolled the sleeves to his elbows.

Most surprising of all was the sight of his stocking feet, propped on the edge of the bed. It seemed ridiculously intimate for him to be so casually attired and her heart fluttered oddly at the notion. Harriet shifted her head, her eyes seeking out Kate. 'Twas the maid that created the snoring sounds. Simmering with hope, Harriet stood and hurried to the bed.

Kate still lay on her back, but her face was less

distressed, more relaxed. Anxiously, Harriet placed her hand upon the maid's forehead. It was slightly clammy, but mercifully cool to the touch.

Harriet didn't say anything, but Mr. Wainwright must have sensed she was near because he opened his eyes and stared straight at her.

"Good news," Harriet reported with a smile. "Kate is no longer feverish."

"Yes, I know. Her fever broke early this morning." He removed his feet from the edge of the bed and leaned forward. "Though I cannot claim to have Mr. MacLeod's experience, I believe she has somehow survived the worst and will make a full recovery."

Then he reached up with one hand, encircled the back of Harriet's neck, pulled her into his lap and captured her lips in a searing, commanding kiss.

Chapter Nine

Nathaniel felt her inner gasp, her initial shock as his surprising move took her breath away. But this was a celebration, a victory over an illness that had seemed poised to win, and he was determined to enjoy every moment of it. His hand drifted to Harriet's cheek and he stroked it softly, caressing her gently. She sighed, parting her lips so he could slip his tongue through and taste the warm recesses of her mouth. Heat surged through his body at her ardent response.

"It feels good to cheat death, does it not?" he asked, nuzzling the soft skin below her ear.

"Wonderful," she sighed. She made a sound in the back of her throat, a sensual purr of excitement. "Nearly as wonderful as this." She lifted her face and pressed her lips against his in a gesture of trusting welcome.

Nathaniel immersed himself completely in the sensations her kisses created, nibbling at her bottom lip, stroking her tongue, molding his body into her softness. Driven by mutual need, it took little coaxing for her lips to cling to his, briefly part, then join again.

Nathaniel felt Harriet's yearning rise to meet his own and it filled him with such an expanded sense of rightness. There was something unique about this woman that captured more than his lust—though it did a fine job of that—it captured his imagination and compelled some inner basic instinct to seize and take and claim. Her.

Deepening his kisses, Nathaniel allowed his hand to feather a light touch along her throat and neck. Harriet reacted with a moan and moved closer. Unable to resist, Nathaniel released the top buttons of her gown and thrust his hand inside, cupping her firm breasts, teasing his thumb across their stiffening crests.

She pulled away from his lips and released a shuddering cry. Nathaniel's arms held her steady. How he longed to fit his aching loins between the sweetness of her thighs, to lower his head until his mouth covered her nipple, to suck it gently, roughly, thoroughly until she caught on fire. To introduce her to fierce urgency and intoxicating release.

Of their own will his hands roamed over her back and waist and hips. A frisson of lust raced across his skin. Desire for her blinded him to reason. He forgot they sat within a few feet of her sick maid. He remembered only the feelings she evoked, the desperate need, the promise of true fulfillment, which lay so close within his grasp.

"We must stop," she admonished, though there was little conviction in her tone.

"In a moment."

He lifted his hand, wet the tip of his index finger, then returned to her hardened nipple. Her breathing altered and deepened as she stretched herself forward, arching to get closer. He moved his finger slowly in a circle and she began thrusting against his hand, making whimpering noises deep in the back of her throat.

"Please," she cried. "If you do not stop soon, Kate will awaken and see us."

"Is she so innocent, your maid? Will she be scandalized by our love-play?"

"The shock will most likely send her into heart failure and we shall have even bigger problems than those we have finally conquered."

Nathaniel smiled, despite the painful discomfort of his arousal. Somewhere during this harrowing ordeal their relationship had become closer, which included the comfort of lighthearted teasing. That pleased him.

Nathaniel looked down at Harriet's face and studied her eyes. Awakening desire rimmed the circle of her irises. He could read the amusement in them—and the regret? Or did he just wish to see amusement there, for his body was screaming for release and his soul, his soul was searching for something he could not yet fully understand.

The urge to take her lips again waxed strong, but he shook aside the impulse, knowing this was not the right time or place. Harriet turned and tried to rise from his lap, but Nathaniel found he could not let go. Just a few more minutes, he told himself.

"Wait," he whispered in her ear. "You don't want to startle Kate and awaken her abruptly by making a lot of noise. Or let her see your bodice gaping open with my hand pressed inside."

Harriet shifted and looked at him with awareness and understanding glistening in her eyes. Slowly he removed his hand and placed it on his thigh. She straightened her shoulders and brought her bodice back to its correct position. He watched, feeling a strong sense of regret as her nimble fingers methodically refastened the row of buttons he had taken such delight in releasing.

But when she leaned forward to lift herself from his lap, Nathaniel discovered he was not yet ready to let her go. Sliding his hand around the front of her waist, he pulled her tightly back against him. The tempting curves of her soft body drove him mad. He wanted only to run his hands over her, but he feared she would stiffen and pull away.

A shudder rocked him as her bottom pressed against his jutting erection. He splayed his palm over the flatness of her stomach, anchoring her against him, wishing he had the right to reach further down and stroke between her legs. With his other hand he swept aside the tendrils of hair that covered her neck and placed a sensual kiss. Her thighs clamped together and he smiled. Her body too was taut with need and desire.

Kate, finally rousing from her illness, groaned loudly and the spell was broken. Reluctantly Nathaniel released Harriet. She stumbled awkwardly to her feet, pushing away his hand when he reached out to steady her. But when she turned to look at him, her eyes twinkled.

Harriet moved to the foot of the bed and adjusted the coverlet. "How are you feeling, Kate?"

"Like Wellington's troops have marched over my old, weary bones," the maid grumbled. Her eyelids slowly opened. "What's wrong with me?"

"You've been sick with fever and chills," Harriet answered. "Wait, don't try to sit up. If you move too fast you'll make yourself dizzy."

Harriet fluffed the pillows and arranged them behind Kate's back. The maid attempted to lift herself onto her elbows. "Have I truly been so poorly?"

"The fever raged for several days," Harriet explained, encouraging the older woman to lie back.

"Fortunately for all of us, Miss Sainthill has proven herself to be an excellent nurse," Nathaniel said.

Kate looked startled. "You, Miss? It was you who cared for me?"

"Yes, me. With a bit of help from Mr. Wainwright and the local physician." Harriet filled a cup with water. She slid her arms behind Kate's shoulder to lift her, then held the cup to Kate's lips. The maid drank greedily, then sank back against her pillows as if she were exhausted. "I can hardly wait for you to meet your doctor, Mr. MacLeod," Harriet added. "He is quite the character."

"More of a quack," Nathaniel rumbled. "Though he miraculously saved you, Kate, so I suppose we have no cause to criticize."

The older woman turned her head, squinted, then blinked. "Is my mind playing tricks on me or is that weak sunshine I see creeping through the windows?"

"It is sunshine," Harriet replied with a laugh. "'Tis difficult to believe we are still in Scotland, heh, Kate?"

The maid smiled and nodded. Harriet plucked at the blanket and adjusted the pillows once again. Her attention was fully focused on her patient, allowing Nathaniel to observe her at his leisure. She wore a dark green gown buttoned up to the neck, but it was fitted in such a way as to display her trim waist and amply curving breasts.

Even though she had had too little sleep and too much worry in the past few days, she looked pretty. Tendrils of her rich, dark hair tumbled about her shoulders and brushed her cheek. Her lips held a hint of rosy color, no doubt from the kisses they had just shared.

Though he regretted the horrible ordeal she had been forced to endure, he was glad that Harriet had not departed as planned, was pleased that she had remained under his roof and in his company for a few more days. Now that Kate was recovering, Harriet would soon leave. But not for several days, or perhaps even a week.

The distinct sound of a stomach growling rose above the women's conversation. "Hunger is a good sign," Nathaniel commented. "Kate is clearly improving if she is ready to eat again."

Harriet cleared her throat. "Kate has fallen back to sleep. That was my stomach rumbling."

Though he suspected she was more than a little embarrassed; after all, ladies did not acknowledge or draw attention to bodily functions when in the presence of a gentleman, Harriet refused to blush or avert her eyes from his.

"I'll go down to the kitchen," he volunteered.

"There is no need to bother. I see that my dinner tray from yesterday remains untouched. That will suffice."

Harriet drew back the curtains before taking her seat at the small table. Sunlight rayed into the room, relieving some of the gloom and illuminating the dust motes that swirled in the air. Only when Nathaniel saw her eat nearly every morsel did he realize she must be famished, for the majority of Mrs. Mullins's dishes were barely tolerable, even when eaten fresh.

"Would you like more?" Nathaniel asked. "If you can manage to wait a few minutes, I'll have some hot food prepared."

Harriet shook her head. "I've already eaten more than I should. Hot food would have been nice, though the pasties were filled mostly with potatoes and cabbage and tasted no worse after sitting about through the night."

Nathaniel wrinkled his nose. "Lord, if I ate more than one potato and cabbage pastie it would sink to my stomach like a stone."

Harriet set her folded napkin beside her plate and rose from the table. "You are not supposed to notice how much I eat, Mr. Wainwright. Instead, you should be making flattering comments about how my dainty appetite resembles a bird's."

"And so it does." Nathaniel also stood. "However, the bird in this instance is a vulture."

She reacted to the telltale laughter in his voice as he had hoped. Yet, their shared, intimate smile distracted Nathaniel for a moment.

There was so much contradiction and complexity to this woman! The primness, the rigidity, the grave dignity were all there in abundance, yet she also possessed a wicked sense of humor, especially about herself. He had known far too many eminently respectable ladies, and while initially Harriet appeared the very embodiment of respectibility, Nathaniel had discovered she was, indeed, very different from the self-proclaimed paragons of virtue.

She had selflessly nursed a servant through a life-threatening illness at the risk of her own health. She was cool in nature and composure, but far from frigid. She possessed a stubborn streak, a trait always deemed unacceptable in a true lady, yet in Harriet's case it was tempered with the intelligence needed to properly manage it.

On the surface, she was not the type of woman who immediately inspired soaring passions. If they had met in society, as equals, he would have immediately judged her to be a dull, sour, prim woman and dismissed her from his thoughts and attention.

That reaction was as much a reflection of his own expectations as it was an insensitive response to her inability to fulfill some artificial requirements of society regarding beauty, demeanor, and age. Nathaniel was not proud to admit this, yet perhaps this knowledge would prevent him from making a similar misjudgment in the future.

"Since it appears that Kate will no longer require round-the-clock attention, we should move your belongings into a different bedchamber," Nathaniel suggested. "As you may recall, I had one prepared for you yesterday, but you were disinclined to use it."

"You prepared a chamber for me?"

"Well, naturally I did not do the actual work."

"Naturally."

Nathaniel didn't know whether to smile or frown. "I'm sure it isn't up to your exacting standards, but the maids were able to brush down the cobwebs, get rid of the dust and put clean linens on the bed."

"It sounds like a vast improvement over my original quarters," Harriet commented.

Nathaniel struggled to keep his face impassive as guilt knifed through him. Though, at the time, his actions seemed valid, Nathaniel now felt that deliberately allowing Harriet to be placed in such inappropriate conditions had been rather heavy-handed.

"Would you like to inspect the room first?" he asked, not wanting her to question his sincerity.

"That is hardly necessary. If you would kindly carry my portmanteau to the new chamber I will unpack after Mr. MacLeod has seen Kate. I expect him within the hour."

"Excellent. I shall want a full report when the physician is finished. Meet me downstairs in the library after he leaves. And bring your cloak and bonnet."

She nodded and he reached for her portmanteau. It was heavier than it looked, but his masculine pride would not allow him to notice the burden.

In less than an hour, Harriet appeared before him, holding her cloak and bonnet, as he had requested. Smiling with delight, Nathaniel took the cloak from her hand and settled it around her shoulders. He waited patiently while she tied the ribbons of her bonnet, then offered his arm.

"Where are we going?" she asked.

"To the garden, to enjoy some fresh air."

Nathaniel guided her through a large door into a sheltered courtyard. Even though spring had scarcely arrived in the Highlands, there were spears of green leaves pushing through the soil, alongside untamed beds of rose bushes. Even in its dormant state it was obvious that the garden, like everything else at the castle, had been long neglected.

It was overgrown and wild, with rambling patches of heather and lavender over-running the north side of the property, yet the promise of colorful blooms and vibrant beauty remained. With some care and attention, this could once again be a place of fragrant splendor.

The main gravel path was still intact and they followed it to the end. At the edge of the garden there was a surprise—a steep drop down a rocky hill, barren except for a few hardy shrubs stubbornly clinging to its side.

"Ah, so there is the village!" Harriet exclaimed as she leaned forward.

Stretching for miles below was a river valley, the sound of flowing water reaching the garden courtyard set so high upon the craggy hills. Wild, rugged and beautiful, the valley was surrounded on all sides by rising cliffs, towering majestically over the treasure it held within its circle.

There was little green in the patchwork of rolling farmland below, but clearly some of the fields had recently been plowed. Clusters of farm buildings and small cottages sprang up sporadically, and grazing sheep dotted the pastoral landscape.

"I feel as though we have taken a step back in time," Nathaniel remarked. "It seems so quaint and untouched."

She gave him a quizzical stare. "It very much resembles an English village, though it is untamed and rugged, and lacks the neat hedgerows English farmers take such great pride in maintaining."

"I've lived most of my life in London, with only brief visits to rural areas," he replied, without thinking. "This all looks, and smells, the same as England to me."

Nathaniel nearly cursed out loud the moment the words left his lips. *Idiot!* he muttered fiercely to himself. Somehow the delight of Harriet's company and the awe-inspiring beauty of nature was enough to loosen his tongue and reveal personal history that could compromise his secret.

He waited for her reaction, but if she felt any curiosity at his words she gave no sign, nor made any comment. They gazed at the valley for several minutes. Harriet seemed enthralled by the splendor of nature's beauty but the joy of the moment had lessened considerably for Nathaniel.

When the lurching flash of panic subsided, Nathaniel took a deep breath and lifted his eyes skyward. A thick band of clouds drifted across the sky, eventually obscuring the sun.

"Without the sun, the bite of the wind really chills the flesh," Harriet said.

"Shall we return to the house?"

"I would like to stay outside for a little longer." She arranged her skirt and drew her cloak tighter around her waist. "But please don't let me keep you out in the cold. I can easily find my way back."

Nathaniel surveyed the garden. He spied a rustic bench positioned near the stone outer wall of the castle. Deciding it could provide an adequate buffer from the wind, Nathaniel led Harriet there and waited for her to sit down.

He considered taking his place beside her, sitting as close as he dared, with their thighs touching. That would certainly warm her, and him, considerably. Instead, he set one booted foot on the hard seat and rested his arm upon the raised leg. When he leaned forward, his face was only inches from hers.

She raised her brow at him, but did not move away.

"What was Mr. MacLeod's verdict after examining Kate? Was he pleased with her condition?" Nathaniel asked.

"He claims she will make a full recovery, we hope within the week."

Nathaniel's lip quirked. "How much stock should we place in Mr. MacLeod's opinion? Illness of this sort can be unpredictable. It is possible for a sudden relapse to occur, especially for someone of Kate's years."

Harriet's smile was philosophical. "Despite his less than stellar first impression, Mr. MacLeod has proven his worth. I cannot judge him too harshly, even if he only *nearly* graduated from Edinburgh College of Surgeons."

They both laughed.

"Besides," Harriet continued, "you must remember that if you ever become ill, Mr. MacLeod will be the one summoned to tend to you. I suggest you remain on good terms with him."

Nathaniel felt himself shudder. He had never considered that he might actually need Mr. MacLeod's services for himself. Or Heaven forbid, the children. What if one of the children had suddenly gotten sick? He glanced at the sky and tried to halt the thunderbolt of fear that seized him.

How could he possibly cope, on his own, with a sick child? A seriously ill child? The servants had refused to help Kate, fearing they too would fall ill. Would they refuse to help a suffering child? Then what would he do?

The very idea of anything dire happening to Robert's innocent offspring sent a chill of fear straight to Nathaniel's heart. As he had been doing far too often these past few days, he questioned the soundness of his judgment in forwarding the plan to obtain guardianship. In order for it to succeed, the children must remain hidden until he reached an agreement with his uncle. And Hillsdale Castle was the perfect place to hide.

Yet its very isolation engendered an entirely different set of challenges to overcome, as Kate's sudden illness had so starkly proved. Still, the alternative for the children was a joyless, shallow life with his uncle. Would that be any better?

"Your advice concerning Mr. MacLeod is sound," Nathaniel admitted. "I will take it to heart, and do my best to remain on friendly terms with the doctor."

"I think I can safely report that Kate is also trying to be friendly toward him. Though their acquaintance has been brief, it is my opinion that she is quite smitten."

"With Mr. MacLeod? You must be joking!"

Harriet lifted her shoulders in a quick shrug.

"When he left the room to fetch additional herbs and medicines from his carriage, Kate insisted that I help her change into a fresh nightgown before he returned and brush out her hair so it wouldn't look so flat and messy."

"Truly?"

"Oh, yes. She was very clear and powerful in her request, which gave me further proof that she is recovering nicely." Speculation flared in Harriet's eyes. "But what was even more telling was Mr. MacLeod's puffed-out chest and exceedingly solicitous manner when he returned and witnessed her transformation. I think he might return her interest."

"At their age?"

Harriet studied his eyes and then smiled. "My nurse was very fond of Irish sayings. Among her favorites was the expression, *for every sock there's an old shoe.* I believe this situation certainly proves that truth."

And what of our situation? Are we too an old sock and shoe? Nathaniel blinked, not knowing where those thoughts had sprung from nor why they both distressed and intrigued him. He was not the man for Harriet Sainthill, though there had been persistent glimmers of feelings over these past few days that she might be the woman for him.

Yet what chance did he have to woo her? He was lying to her about nearly everything, including his identity. She was a woman who had suffered deceit at the hands of her fiancé. Her reaction, if she ever learned the truth, would be extreme, and he could not fault her. Even if there were a chance, she would never be able to forgive him for his deception.

"Since Kate will need more time to recuperate, I am afraid we will be forced to rely on your generosity for a few more days." Harriet peered at him from beneath the brim of her bonnet. "I hope that will not be inconvenient?"

"I can think of few things that would bring me greater pleasure than your company." It was a routine response, worthy of any self-respecting rake, yet Nathaniel realized he meant every word of it. To punctuate the point, he lifted his hand and ran the back of his finger down one side of her cheek to her chin. It felt like velvet. "The only greater pleasure, of course, would be to kiss you," he whispered.

"That would be most unwise," she said primly. "We have already shared an inappropriate embrace and several kisses today."

"Is that the rule, then? One per day?"

She looked like she wanted to smile, but instead she set her brow together in a taut line. "The rule, as you are very aware, is *none* per day."

Taking advantage of his upright position, he leaned in closer and dipped his head a little lower. "Alas, I have never been very good about following the rules."

This time she did laugh. "That comes as no surprise to me, I assure you. However, it is clear that one of us must keep a level head. If you won't, then I must."

Nathaniel knew he could have pressed the matter. And won. Instead he abruptly lowered his foot to the ground and straightened his spine. Then he caught hold of her hand, raised it to his lips and placed a kiss in her palm. She curled her hand in his and he held her fist tightly for a moment longer before releasing his grip.

"It will be as you wish, dear Harriet. For now."

Chapter Ten

The door opened, closed, and the latch clicked into place. Duncan McTate, ensconced in the privacy of his study, lifted his gaze from the boring stack of correspondence he had been reading and paused to greet his uninvited guest. But no one was visible.

A childish, high-pitched giggle, followed by a whispered hush filled the room.

"I sure hope 'tis the kind fairies that have come to pay me a visit and bring me special sweets and not the old sea monster who haunts the loch that has come here in search of his dinner," Duncan said loudly.

"Monster?" a small voice squeaked.

"Shhh, he's just trying to trick us. Be quiet."

"Ah, more noise, but I still canna see a thing," Duncan said, in the same loud tone. "And I canna be sure if it is friend or foe or maybe even three devilish children who have invaded my lair. I must investigate."

Duncan pushed away from his desk and leaned

back in his chair. He waited for the telltale sounds of scuffling feet to determine exactly where the children were hiding. Once he heard it, he moved.

Crouching on all fours, he slowly circled the thick wooden base of his desk and headed toward the long damask draperies that covered the windows. And hid, no doubt, the children. Since his aim was not to frighten them, he made comical noises to alert them he was nearby.

Duncan could feel the tension and excitement ripple though the air as the anticipation of discovery grew.

Then suddenly the door swung open. Again.

"Och, m'lord, ye've scared me silly." The maid who walked into the room stopped abruptly, shot him a shocked look, then curtseyed several times. "Beggin' yer pardon. I see I've disturbed ye."

Sighing, Duncan raised himself back on his haunches. "What do you want, Maggie?"

"I . . . um . . . I . . . was told to fetch the wee ones. Have they come in here, by chance?"

"No."

His answer was greeted with excited giggles from behind the curtains, followed by more exhortations to be quiet. Maggie's eyes widened. She stepped forward, but Duncan held up a staying hand. He pointed towards the curtain and smiled, hoping the young maid would join in his merriment.

But her eyes widened further in puzzlement. Fearing she would spoil the game, he gestured for her to leave. She took a deep swallow and obeyed his command, but not before casting several concerned looks over her shoulder as she left.

Duncan was annoyed. Perhaps it was not the most dignified position for the laird to be found in, crouched on all fours in the center of his study, but when had he become so stern and unyielding that his servants would be amazed to find him engaging in a bit of lighthearted play? Was that really such a shocking discovery?

Granted, he wasn't a jovial, laughing sort of man. Nor was he the type who normally welcomed disorder or chaos of any kind. The household staff was very much aware of that fact, yet the unexpected arrival of the children had turned his well-run house into something of a circus.

When he had agreed to house this trio, he never imagined they could so completely disrupt a well-developed household schedule and create so much confusion, change, and noise. But surprisingly Duncan had not minded the sounds these three had brought to his house.

It gave the house the life and joy that had long since been missing. An inner voice mocked this sudden acceptance of familial bliss, but the practical side of Duncan's nature decided he was enjoying the children so much because he knew the arrangement was only temporary. They were staying with him in town only until Nathaniel had ensured all was ready for them at Hillsdale Castle in the Highlands.

And, given that it had been nearly ten years since Duncan had last set foot in his northernmost property, he knew it would take Nathaniel plenty of time to make everything acceptable.

While they waited here in Edinburgh, there was no reason not to enjoy himself and bring a bit of fun into the children's lives. They had suffered greatly these past few months. They deserved to experience some carefree childhood days again.

Dismissing the maid from his thoughts, Duncan turned back to the game. The movement behind the green damask let him know the children had not taken advantage of his distraction to find another hiding place.

Resuming his crawling position, Duncan inched forward slowly. He could see three pairs of small slippered feet poking out from beneath the heavy fabric. With a cry of glee, he reached out and strongly grasped the closest limb.

An ear-splitting squeal of excitement tore through the room as his hapless victim tried desperately to escape.

"I've caught you now," Duncan cried, tugging gently.

"He's got me! Help!" the child screeched, kicking out with both legs, trying unsuccessfully to dislodge the hold on his ankle.

"Don't worry, we'll set you free."

Two sets of hands joined the fray, but those delicate fingers could not dislodge his grip. All three were still concealed behind the curtains. Only the foot and ankle of Duncan's prisoner was revealed, but he knew he had caught young Gregory.

Realizing a different tack was needed, Gregory's sisters yanked hard on a section of the drapes, trying to use it as leverage to free their brother. Impressed with their cleverness, Duncan glanced upward, hoping the rods were strong enough to support this abuse.

"I'll never let you go," he cried, heightening the excitement of the game. "In fact, you feel like such a tasty little morsel, I believe I will eat you for my dinner."

His pronouncement was met with a gale of laughter.

"We already ate our dinner," a young girlish voice said. "Is Uncle Duncan still hungry?"

"He is only teasing," a second voice clarified.

"Oh. Now what should we do?"

"We attack!"

It was a brilliant suggestion, a strategy of boldness worthy of any of Wellington's generals. Without any additional warning, the children wheeled around and leaped toward him. He tried to back up, but being caught unawares and positioned on his knees made it difficult to maneuver. He lost his grip on his prisoner, who quickly turned and joined the assault. Within seconds they surrounded him and Duncan toppled over onto his back.

The trio took instant advantage of this vulnerable position and fell on top of him. Laughing, Duncan seized the chance to engulf all three of them in a large hug. They resisted for a moment, squirming and fidgeting, then collapsed against him.

Struggling to regain his breath, Duncan sat up. The children clustered around him, their faces shining with delight. They were dressed in their nightclothes and robes. Duncan grinned ruefully, deciding he should probably not have been rough-housing with them so near to bedtime.

Hell, he probably shouldn't have been rough-housing with them at all, especially the girls. He should be treating them like proper young ladies. But they weren't ladies. They were little girls, who seemed to crave the physical activity and release even more than their younger brother at times.

They had all been silent and reserved when they first arrived, but the younger two had soon reacted to the pleasant atmosphere of Duncan's home and the affectionate fussing of the staff. The eldest, Phoebe, had taken longer to let down her guard, probably because she realized more than her brother and sister that something was terribly odd about their situation.

It was obvious however that she was worried about not seeing her uncle. She never asked directly where Nathaniel was or when he would return for them, but Duncan could tell that while she liked him, she really only completely trusted Nathaniel.

To ease the child's fears, Duncan began mentioning Nathaniel in casual conversation every day, speculating what the other man was doing in the far north, explaining how much fun and adventure the children would have when they joined Nathaniel. Eventually he was able to coax a few smiles from Phoebe and ease away the furrow that usually creased her brow.

It was with no small amount of pride that Duncan conceded there wasn't a woman, young or old, that could resist the charm of The McTate when he applied himself. As if proving that very point, Jeanne Marie scrambled into his lap and nestled her head against his shoulder.

"It was fun to play, but I got scared when you said you were going to eat Gregory," Jeanne Marie announced. "Gregory was scared, too."

"I was not!"

Duncan smoothed a hand over the boy's hair. "There's nothing wrong with being scared of something bigger than you are, lad. But Goodness, I would never have eaten Gregory! If I gobbled him up, I know I'd get a bellyache."

"A big bellyache," Jeanne Marie said with a chuckle.

"It was a good game," Duncan commented. "But next time we should play in a larger area, where there are more places to hide."

All three heads bobbed enthusiastically. "Maybe we can play this game with Uncle Nathaniel too," Phoebe said. "When we go live with him."

Duncan gave the girl a gentle smile. "I'm sure Uncle Nathaniel would like that very much."

Her lighthearted grin touched his heart. Yet as much as he enjoyed having this trio in his house, he knew it would be best for them to be with Nathaniel. Soon.

"It was a contest, not a game," Jeanne Marie explained. "We had to see which of us could hide without being caught. Gregory lost."

"I won," Gregory protested. "The winner was the first one who got caught. That was me."

"You lost," Jeanne Marie said, sticking out her tongue to emphasize the point.

"I won!" Gregory crossed his arms over his chest and lowered his chin. A faint pout touched the corners of his face. Duncan had to hide his smile. The boy was a male tyrant in the making, determined to have his own way in everything. In retrospect, an excellent temperament for an English duke.

It had not taken long for Duncan to realize that Gregory hated to lose at anything. At first, his sisters had deferred to his wishes, but these past few days had seen a change in their attitudes. They were not so quick to grant him his every wish now.

Duncan supposed the change was partly due to his attitude toward the boy. As the adult, he felt it was his obligation to teach the lad to redouble his effort to win, rather than trying to change the rules to suit himself.

A tough lesson for a four-year-old to comprehend.

Duncan worried that he might be a bit too hard on the lad. He tried to remember what it felt like to have the freedom of being young and wild, not having a care in the world. But he could not. Childhood was a luxury that had never been offered to the laird of the clan, and the heir to the English earldom. Like young Gregory, Duncan's father had died young: After that, the responsibilities and obligations of his birth and title had been emphasized even more.

A rather daunting lesson for an eight-year-old to learn.

"You played fair Gregory and put up a good fight." Duncan said, and chucked the boy under the chin, trying to coax a smile. "Of course, it did take all three of you to defeat me."

"Next time we're going to win faster," Gregory promised.

There was a tap on the door, and it opened just wide enough to allow the housekeeper to poke her head around it.

"Praise be, I've found ye at last," she said, glancing reproachfully at Duncan. " 'Tis long past time you were in bed, children. Your nursemaids are waiting. Now hurry along."

"We don't want to go to bed. Can't we stay up longer?" Jeanne Marie asked. All three turned pleading eyes toward Duncan.

The laird grimaced. It was very difficult to refuse them anything, especially when it was so easily within his power to grant their wish. And it really wasn't that late. "Well, perhaps—"

"Off to bed," the housekeeper interrupted. "Ye'll not be fit company for man nor beast if you don't get yer full night's sleep."

The children turned again to Duncan in mute appeal, but the stern look on the housekeeper's face warned the laird not to counter her edict.

"Proper rest is important for growing children," Duncan said. "And if you get to sleep right now, you'll be ready for a ride with me first thing in the morning."

"Before breakfast?" Jeanne Marie asked.

Duncan, never fond of early rising, managed a rueful grin. "Before breakfast. I know how much you like being on your ponies."

"We had wonderful horses back home in London," Phoebe said quietly. "Do you think Lord

Bridwell is making sure they are being fed and taken out for exercise while we are away?"

"Of course," Duncan replied cheerfully, hoping that Nathaniel's villainous uncle, Lord Bridwell, had no idea the children were so attached to their ponies. For if he did, Duncan suspected the older man would probably have the poor creatures destroyed. "But it is my fat ponies who will be in need of a good gallop tomorrow morning."

"Before breakfast," Jeanne Marie reiterated.

Duncan nodded and all three children smiled.

The housekeeper ushered them out the door, then turned to him. "If this is a taste of yer discipline, I'll be needing to warn the staff we're in for a rough time. I can see ye're going to be impossible when yer own bairns come along, spoilin' them rotten and grantin' their every whim."

Duncan noted while her tone was scolding, her eyes were filled with affection. Having children had always been a vague thought lingering in the back of his mind, residing no doubt near the similar idea of one day acquiring a wife. Yet these ideal dreams were part of a very distant future.

Duncan slowly stood and smoothed his coat. He glanced at the stack of abandoned correspondence on his desk, and decided there was nothing that could not wait until morning. After his ride. And after breakfast.

He would retire to the private sitting room adjacent to his bedchamber and enjoy some fine claret, a good smoke, and a few chapters of a new book. Meeting the butler in the foyer, Duncan instructed him to dismiss the footman for the evening.

"Ye're staying in again, m'lord?"

Duncan merely lifted his brow. The servant blushed and lowered his gaze, as if realizing the impudence of questioning the laird's actions. The butler bowed, then left, his footsteps echoing on the marble floor.

Though Duncan had been annoyed by the butler's remark, he could not fault the man for his surprise. Duncan's social life had suffered drastically since the children arrived. Normally, he was a much sought after guest in the tight circle that made up Edinburgh society.

It was not something he enjoyed over much, but ever-conscious of his duty, Duncan made brief appearances at all the necessary functions. He also made the rounds at the gentlemen's clubs and gaming establishments when the mood suited him. Society here could not compare to the hurried and frantic pace of London Society, but there were distractions in the Scottish capital for men of wealth and power, such as he.

The one thing he did miss, however, was female companionship. He had not visited his mistress once since the children arrived, fearing that her luscious, sensual body would be too much of a distraction, and keep him too long away from home.

Anna had a fiery temper to match her passionate nature and she was no doubt made furious by the lack of attention. He had sent several bouquets of her favorite flowers, along with a charming note, but Duncan knew from experience it would take an expensive gem to turn her frowns and pouts into a welcoming embrace.

Although there were servants aplenty to perform the task, Duncan carefully walked through each of the downstairs rooms, checking and re-checking every window and door. Duncan took his temporary position as guardian and protector very seriously, even though he doubted Nathaniel's uncle,

Lord Bridwell, had any idea where the children were being hidden.

For his own sanity, Duncan needed to ensure there would be no surprise threat in the middle of the night, no chance that any harm would come to those three young innocents. Once he was confident the house was properly secure, Duncan went upstairs to bid the children a final goodnight.

His first stop was Gregory's room, but, as usual, Duncan was too late. As he approached the bed, the nursemaid sitting quietly in the corner smiled and shook her head. Gregory was already sleeping. It seemed that the minute the child's head hit the pillow he was asleep.

Smiling, Duncan gazed at the innocent face. In slumber, Gregory's features took on an almost baby-like quality, reminding him of how young, helpless and dependent was this child that he had vowed to protect.

He next entered the chamber the girls now occupied. Since he wanted the children housed near him, the girls were placed in the room that had been his mother's. The chamber reflected the status and taste of its previous occupant. Expensive wallpaper adorned the walls, thick rugs covered the polished oak floors, and the massive bed was covered in satin and rich brocade.

Upon waking the first morning, young Jeanne Marie had solemnly reported the large, soft bed had "swallowed her up." But she liked the pretty figurines and silk tasselled pillows, and as long as her sister Phoebe slept beside her, the younger girl was content to stay in this room.

The girls, unlike their slumbering brother, were waiting patiently for his arrival. With their nurse-maid looking on, they solemnly recited their bed-time prayers. As always, Duncan was humbled to hear himself included, even if he was placed *after* the girls' ponies left behind in London.

He kissed each girl on the forehead, and helped them slide beneath the covers. They settled their heads on their pillows and fixed their eyes on him. Duncan squirmed a bit under such innocent trust, worried anew with the responsibility of keeping them safe.

"Sleep well, wee ones. May your dreams be filled with sweetness."

As he spoke the words, Duncan knew their sleep would not be as restful as their brother's. The nursemaid who watched over the girls reported they often whimpered and cried out during the night, clearly troubled by nightmares.

Duncan wished that Nathaniel were here. Not that his bachelor friend could do any better, but these children were his flesh and blood. They asked for him every day. They needed him.

Duncan entered his room and dismissed his valet. He stood, folded his hands behind his back and broodingly gazed into the fire. In less than a week's time he would bring the children north, to Hillsdale Castle. He hoped that Nathaniel had managed to prepare everything properly and that the new governess either had arrived, or would do so shortly.

Duncan knew he should feel a sense of relief that his responsibility would soon be ending. He should be pleased that his household would once again be well-organized, his social life proper, his love-life fulfilled.

Yet instead all he felt was a confusing sense of lethargy and loss.

Lord Bridwell tried in vain to rein in his temper. For the past fifteen minutes, he had been listening

Take A Trip Into A Timeless World of Passion and Adventure with Kensington Choice Historical Romances! —Absolutely FREE!

Enjoy the passion and adventure of another time with Kensington Choice Historical Romances. They are the finest novels of their kind, written by today's best-selling romance authors. Each Kensington Choice Historical Romance transports you to distant lands in a bygone age. Experience the adventure and share the delight as proud men and spirited women discover the wonder and passion of true love.

Get 4 FREE Books!

We created our convenient Home Subscription Service so you'll be sure to have the hottest new romances delivered each month right to your doorstep—usually before they are available in book stores. Just to show you how convenient the Zebra Home Subscription Service is, we would like to send you 4 FREE Kensington Choice Historical Romances. The books are worth up to $24.96, but you only pay $1.99 for shipping and handling. There's no obligation to buy additional books—ever!

Save Up To 30% With Home Delivery!

Accept your FREE books and each month we'll deliver 4 brand new titles as soon as they are published. They'll be yours to examine FREE for 10 days. Then if you decide to keep the books, you'll pay the preferred subscriber's price (up to 30% off the cover price!), plus shipping and handling. Remember, you are under no obligation to buy any of these books at any time! If you are not delighted with them, simply return them and owe nothing. But if you enjoy Kensington Choice Historical Romances as much as we think you will, pay the special preferred subscriber rate and save over $8.00 off the cover price!

We have **4 FREE BOOKS** for you as your introduction to
KENSINGTON CHOICE!
To get your FREE BOOKS, worth up to $24.96, mail the card below or call TOLL-FREE 1-800-770-1963.
Visit our website at www.kensingtonbooks.com.

Get 4 FREE Kensington Choice Historical Romances!

💙 **YES!** Please send me my 4 FREE KENSINGTON CHOICE HISTORICAL ROMANCES (without obligation to purchase other books). I only pay $1.99 for shipping and handling. Unless you hear from me after I receive my 4 FREE BOOKS, you may send me 4 new novels—as soon as they are published—to preview each month FREE for 10 days. If I am not satisfied, I may return them and owe nothing. Otherwise, I will pay the money-saving preferred subscriber's price (over $8.00 off the cover price), plus shipping and handling. I may return any shipment within 10 days and owe nothing, and I may cancel any time I wish. In any case the 4 FREE books will be mine to keep.

Name _____

Address _____ Apt. _____

City _____ State _____ Zip _____

Telephone (___) _____

Signature _____

(If under 18, parent or guardian must sign)

Offer limited to one per household and not to current subscribers. Terms, offer and prices subject to change. Orders subject to acceptance by Kensington Choice Book Club.
Offer Valid in the U.S. only.

KN074A

4 FREE

Kensington
Choice
Historical
Romances
*(worth up to
$24.96)
are waiting
for you to
claim them!*

*See details
inside…*

ıll..ıl..llıl...llıl.ıl..ıl..ıl..ıl..llıl..l..llıl.ıll...l

KENSINGTON CHOICE
Zebra Home Subscription Service, Inc.
P.O. Box 5214
Clifton NJ 07015-5214

to a progress report filled with no progress at all, only excuses and evasions.

"You have yet again nothing substantial to report?" he finally asked, letting both his ire and his exasperation show themselves. "Is that truly possible? Why did you even bother to come to see me today? Bloody hell, Brockhurst, if you are an example of the best the famed Bow Street Runners have to offer, I can only shudder to think what sort of mess the others would have created if I had hired them to perform such a simple task."

Jerome Brockhurst, a seasoned and experienced detective, lifted his chin and returned the hard stare. "The task is hardly simple, my lord. Your nephew and wards appear to have vanished. London is a large city, especially for someone with deep pockets. There is also some evidence to suggest that Lord Avery has departed from Town, which widens the area to be searched considerably."

Lord Bridwell's temper rose a notch. "I expect results, not excuses. You have been in my employ for over a fortnight and have yet to discover any trace of the missing children or my nephew."

Mr. Brockhurst's mouth turned down. "I am not entirely convinced that your nephew is responsible for the children's disappearance. Perhaps that is the reason my investigation has yielded no results."

For a moment, doubt nibbled at Lord Bridwell. Ever since he had learned that the children had disappeared, he had assumed Nathaniel had taken them and refused to allow Brockhurst to pursue another course of investigation. He was convinced that if Lord Avery could be located, the children would be found. Could he be wrong?

"There has been no demand for ransom," Lord Bridwell exclaimed. "My nephew would call each day and visit the brats, yet the moment they disappeared he ceased calling. I've made a few inquiries of my own and no one can recall seeing him about Town for two solid weeks. That cannot be a mere coincidence."

"Lord Avery told several of his friends he was not leaving London until the spring," Mr. Brockhurst said. "That could have merely been a ruse, if indeed your nephew is involved in this affair, especially since there was some general confusion as to his exact destination. Most of the gentlemen I spoke with were under the impression he was traveling north."

"Lies! If he said north, you should be looking south. Do I have to tell you how do to everything?"

Brockhurst's posture stiffened. "I have several men making discreet inquiries in the north. But we must be prepared with an alternative strategy if Lord Avery is found and the children are not with him."

"Who else would want them?"

Brockhurst frowned. "This city is filled with all manner of people, my lord. The girls are rather young, but I've been told they are very pretty children."

"And the boy? He is little more than an infant. Of what use would he be to anyone?"

A red flush stained Brockhurst's cheeks. "Perversion in all forms thrives among men. I've seen more than my share of it in my line of work."

Lord Bridwell tried to feel an appropriate degree of horror at the thought of the children meeting such a dire fate. Yet he could not summon the necessary emotion to care. Unless the boy was dead. If so, his claim to the dukedom would be clear and with his nephew away from Town, Lord Bridwell could begin legal proceedings immediately. But first he needed solid proof.

"Have you searched the morgues?"

"Normally it is among my first stops, however you were adamant that your nephew had taken the children, so I have not put any of my resources in that direction."

"Then do so at once."

Brockhurst cast him a curious look. "The extra cost?"

"Damn, the cost! They must be found. Dead or alive. Do I make myself clearly understood?"

Brockhurst bobbed his head. "I've been going over the facts very carefully and there is a doubt concerning exactly when the children disappeared. No one seems to know with any certainty. When did you last see them?"

Lord Bridwell gripped the edge of his desk and glared at the runner. He didn't like Brockhurst. The man didn't show the proper deference or respect to his betters. Nor was he in awe of the aristocracy. If he had his way, Lord Bridwell would not even have hired the man, but he was reputed to be the best and Bridwell was in desperate need of his skills.

He fixed a disdainful eye on Brockhurst. "I have already explained that I rarely had contact with my great-nieces and great-nephew. Therefore, I can be of limited assistance. The servants would know best. I have ordered them to cooperate fully with you."

"Your staff has been most forthcoming in my interviews with them, however many of them are new to the household and know little about the children," Mr. Brockhurst said.

Lord Bridwell heaved an annoyed sigh. "Ask the housekeeper, Mrs. Hutchinson. She has been on staff here as long as I can remember. She doted on those children, yet her reaction to their disappearance has been most telling. While initially upset, she has said very little these past few days. She must know something."

"I have questioned Mrs. Hutchinson on three separate occasions," Brockhurst replied. "She knows nothing."

"Are you certain?"

"I am very good at telling when people are lying."

Lord Bridwell rested one elbow on the arm of his chair and set his chin upon his closed fist. "If the housekeeper suspected that someone besides my nephew had taken those brats she would be up in arms. Hell, she'd probably be scouring the streets herself searching for them."

"Her loyalty speaks well of her character."

"Her loyalty is only useful if it is pledged to me!" Lord Bridwell pursed his lips in a disapproving manner. "Mrs. Hutchinson's acceptance of this situation is further proof in my mind that my nephew has taken them away."

Brockhurst shook his head slowly. "I still contend she knows nothing of this matter. She's either the best liar in the world or an accomplished actress."

Lord Bridwell let out a loud curse. "She is neither, Brockhurst. She does not possess the wit to sustain an elaborate deception for any length of time. Though apparently she has been able to easily outsmart you."

He glared at the runner, challenging Brockhurst to dispute the insult. Brockhurst looked sharply at him, but said nothing.

"What news from the local employment agencies?" Lord Bridwell asked. "If my nephew has taken the brats, he would need someone to look after them."

Brockhurst consulted his notes. "I have checked the most reputable agencies, and no one matching Lord Avery's needs has hired any nursemaids or a governess."

Lord Bridwell snorted. "Then make inquiries at

those establishments that are less stringent about experience and references. My nephew is very particular about the brats, but he would have needed help with this stunt."

Brockhurst made a few notations on his pad. "Is there anything else?"

"Do not return until you have something of significance to report," Lord Bridwell commanded, in a voice heavy with sarcasm.

The Bow Street Runner was shown the door. Once he was alone, Lord Bridwell felt the bluster drained out of him. He poured himself a glass of claret, sat at his desk and brooded.

The matter had to be resolved. Quickly. He was already having difficulty getting at some of the ducal funds. He could not press for complete legal guardianship, fearing it might become known that the children were no longer in his possession.

He had underestimated his nephew, never imagining he would go to such lengths. Lord Bridwell was not completely convinced his nephew's motivation was purely the welfare of those brats. There was far too much money at stake to make that claim.

Yet there was no denying the feat had been daring and effective and a bloody nuisance, too. The more he thought of it, the more Lord Bridwell's gut churned with the familiar mingling of anger and fear. Anger, at being so easily duped. Fear, that he might not win this all-important contest.

Seething with frustration, Lord Bridwell banged his fist sharply on the desk, causing the goblet to tip over and shatter. Cursing loudly, he rang for a servant to clean up the mess. Armed with a clean goblet and a fresh bottle of wine, he spent the remainder of the afternoon barricaded in his study, plotting his revenge.

Chapter Eleven

It was the strangest week of Harriet's life. She began each day caring for Kate, an odd reversal of roles for the mistress to care for the maid. It was necessary however, because even though she posed no great risk to anyone else's health, the castle staff had no interest in being near the sick Sassenach woman.

Fortunately, Kate was rapidly improving. Each day she required less assistance and was eager for Harriet to leave so she could "rest." Harriet soon realized this was merely an excuse to be alone when Mr. MacLeod arrived. He visited his patient daily, staying longer each time. She joked privately that Kate was improving through sheer force of will, just to become a testament to Mr. MacLeod's skill as a healer.

Once Kate was comfortably settled for the day, Harriet was free to do as she pleased. Initially time hung heavy, for Harriet was not used to being idle. And while she greatly enjoyed reading, the meager selection of books in the dusty, grimy library were mainly historical tomes.

Deciding to treat this unexpected free time as a holiday, Harriet set about exploring the castle. Though she found it forbidding and mysterious, there was something mystical about the towering battlements and ancient keep that drew her to them.

She explored each afternoon on her own, amazed and fascinated by what she discovered. The drum towers on each corner around a high curtain wall held great appeal, so they were her first destination. Harriet assumed she would have to brave the elements and walk the narrow parapets to reach the top interior of each tower, but purely by accident she found a hidden passage and circular staircase leading to the inside of the first tower.

She climbed the little-used stairway carefully and stepped inside the round tower. It was like being transported back through time. There was a hard stone floor, whitewashed domed walls, and narrow slit windows without glass designed to allow a skilled archer to shoot through it and defend his position.

Set beneath one of these windows was an elegant carved trunk. Her hands itched to explore the contents, but it was locked and no key was in evidence. Hoping there would be time to return on another day, with a tool capable of forcing the lock, Harriet proceeded to the next tower.

Here she found remnants of a weaving room for the castle. Harriet closed her eyes and tried to imagine how the room had appeared several hundred years ago when it was bustling with activity and gossip as the women worked their skillful magic on the hand looms.

The third tower room was empty and the crumbling masonry in one part served as a grim reminder that the castle was very old and not in the best repair. Yet it was in the fourth and final tower where Harriet made her most amazing discovery.

Resting prominently in the center of the room were the effigies of a medieval knight and his lady. The edge of the tomb depicted in carved stone the main pursuits of a lord of his time—the hunt, the land, the battles. A Highland claymore was also inscribed, beautifully depicted with its characteristic cross guard with four ring quillons.

Harriet knew that the two-handed sword known as the claymore was often the weapon of choice for a Highlander. It exemplified the arrogance and recklessness of these mighty warriors, who disdained the protection of a shield in order to wield this lethal weapon with both hands.

There was a coat of arms on the edge of the lady's tomb with the chilling motto *"Virtue flourishes with wounding."* After realizing she had found no evidence of a chapel elsewhere, this no longer seemed such an unusual resting place for this noble pair, for it was the perfect reflection of a military society and religious piety.

Invigorated by her success, Harriet bolstered her courage and next descended to the depths of the castle. She both hoped and feared to find some long forgotten dungeon but instead happened upon a barrel-vaulted storage basement. It contained all the necessary equipment to operate a malt whiskey distillery and judging by the smell that permeated the room, Harriet decided it was very much operational.

As much as she had enjoyed her forays into the interior of Hillsdale Castle, the following day Harriet was pleased to accept Mr. Wainwright's invitation for a late morning ride. The weather was still brisk but sunny, and for once not a cloud appeared in the endless blue sky.

There were two horses saddled and ready when Harriet arrived in the stableyard. Though it was not strictly necessary, it certainly would have been proper to have a groom accompany them. Apparently that was not to be the case on this ride.

Harriet smiled briefly, silently applauding Mr. Wainwright's skill at maneuvering this private time together, by arranging for them to be free of any servant's inquisitive stares. Her body fairly tingled at the possibilities.

"Good morning." Mr. Wainwright looked so delighted to see her that for a moment Harriet felt giddy. She dipped her head in uncharacteristic embarrassment and stroked her mare's velvet nose.

She was inwardly glad that she was wearing her sapphire blue riding habit, complete with a whimsical hat adorned with a jaunty feather. The trimly fitted coat was comfortable and showed her figure to its advantage. Though Harriet scoffed at other women who continually fussed over their appearance, she admitted to herself that she possessed just enough feminine vanity to want Mr. Wainwright to remember her looking her best.

" 'Tis a fine morning to go exploring," Harriet said as she checked the straps of her saddle and gathered the reins to one side. "I look forward to seeing more of this rugged countryside."

There was no mounting block. Harriet cast an expectant glance at the stable hand but Mr. Wainwright waved the lad off. With a mysterious smile, he cupped his hands for her booted foot and gave her a leg up.

Harriet adjusted her position in the saddle and arranged her skirts, while Mr. Wainwright swung up, unassisted, onto his own mount. She was pleased to note that both horses were prime animals, sleek and young and full of energy.

Mr. Wainwright led the way. The stable lad, with a disgruntled expression on his face, opened the gate for them.

"We shall return for a late luncheon. Please make sure Mrs. Mullins is informed of our plans," Mr. Wainwright commanded.

The young man nodded his head. Though he made a brief attempt to doff his cap, the half-hearted gesture did little to conceal his exasperation with them.

"Was it something I said?" Mr. Wainwright asked as they cleared the stableyard.

Harriet shrugged. "We are outsiders, Mr. Wainwright. English. Though I do not understand their continued dislike and mistrust of us, I have no cause to criticize their forthright manner. I confess that I have often been accused of being blunt to the point of rudeness."

"But must he narrow his eyes at me as if we are bound on some mischief? Or something far more dire?"

Harriet smiled. "I can tell you are not familiar with the pitfalls of unpopularity." Though in truth she wondered why a man with his arrogance and confidence would care about the opinion of a servant. "Being tolerated is something I have often experienced. The situation here is no exception, though it seems more intense because the Scots do not endeavor to hide their feelings, even if they are servants. I swear there have been times when Mrs. Mullins regards me as if I am a particularly unpleasant insect."

He frowned thoughtfully. "Does it bother you?"

"I am used to such reactions." Harriet grinned mockingly. "And I usually can't understand what

Mrs. Mullins is saying most of the time, so I am probably missing the majority of her direct insults."

"All I know is that the Scots are a far different breed of servant from the ones I am accustomed to having around."

"Why didn't you bring your own people with you?"

"There wasn't adequate time to make the proper arrangements," Mr. Wainwright explained. "Besides, the price of the lease included a fully staffed establishment."

"Perhaps you can negotiate a partial refund," Harriet remarked.

"Clearly you have had no financial dealings with a Scotsman," Mr. Wainwright countered, reining in his horse as they came to an open field.

Harriet pulled alongside him. It was a flat, inviting landscape of hard-packed earth not yet tilled for the season. The horses, as if sensing what was about to come, pawed at the ground anxiously.

Harriet tightened her grip on the reins, crouched low and bent forward. "Shall we?" With no other warning than those softly spoken words, she dug her spurs into her horse's side and took off.

She heard Mr. Wainwright's delighted laugh, but dared not glance behind to see him, knowing it would waste her ill-gotten start. Earlier she had admired his command of his horse and excellent form and knew he was a skilled rider. Their horses appeared equally matched in strength, but Mr. Wainwright's mount was larger and therefore had greater stamina. Harriet knew if she had any hope of winning this impromptu race it would have to be a short one.

The ground was flying beneath the horse's hooves, the cold whipping at her cheeks, the feather in her riding hat bobbing wildly. Basking in the excitement and exhilaration, Harriet felt more alive at that moment than she had in months, perhaps years.

A gate came into sight, marking the end of the field and beginning of the woods. It was the natural finish line and both riders knew it. Harriet could sense her opponent drawing closer and soon the horses were galloping neck and neck. She urged her horse on, crouching lower, realizing with just a few yards to go she would win.

Harriet barely contained her shout of excitement as she reached the gate a few seconds before Mr. Wainwright. Her feelings of euphoria unleashed an avalanche of emotions. She raised her arm in triumph and began to laugh, unable to remember ever feeling such unencumbered joy, coupled with a sense of well-being.

While she did not completely understand how a silly race could create the depth of these emotions, Harriet knew that somehow these feelings were directly related to the man who had shared the experience with her. With him, everything seemed more intense, no matter what the activity.

Mr. Wainwright looked across at her, a smile in his eyes. "You won."

"Did I?"

"Such coy surprise, Harriet?" He lifted his brow in a mischievous expression. "Of course the race was unfairly played."

"Spoken like a totally trounced man." Harriet grinned. She turned her horse, walking the animal slowly so it could cool down. Mr. Wainwright did the same with his mount.

"I know of a trail that leads up the hill to a small summit," he informed her. " 'Tis a picturesque spot. Follow me."

Harriet fell into place beside him as if it were the most natural thing in the world. They trotted along in companionable silence, enjoying the rustling of the leaves, the sway of the tree branches, and the brightness of the sunshine.

The increasingly loud sound of water let Harriet know they were nearing a stream. It came into view quickly as the denseness of the trees lessened. The water flowed down the side of a jagged cliff, almost like a waterfall. It was surrounded by lush, green undergrowth, mossy rocks and a score of wild flowers just on the verge of blooming.

"Let's stop here," Mr. Wainwright suggested. "I'm sure the horses are thirsty."

Harriet nodded and dismounted. The animals had more than earned a rest and she was enjoying being outside, even in such cool weather. Mr. Wainwright moved closer, clasping her waist with a strong grip, Harriet assumed to steady her, though in truth her feet were already firmly planted on the ground.

Until he dipped his head and kissed her.

She closed her eyes and savored the sensations. The wonderful feeling of his arms tight and possessive around her back and waist, his warm, hard body pressed so intimately against her softness, the intoxicating smell of earthy woods mixing with his cologne.

He parted his lips over hers and licked at the seam with his tongue. She granted him entrance and kissed him back, angling her head and touching his tongue with her own. She nearly jumped, as every part of her body sizzled with awareness. Desire, low and deep in her belly, began to ache and throb.

The kiss deepened, became more frantic and frenzied. Every inch of Harriet's body came alive. His grip tightened for a moment and he feathered kisses on her cheeks, her eyes, her temples. He lifted his head and she could feel him looking down at her. Slowly she opened her eyes. His features were slightly distorted and yet she still thought he was the most attractive, appealing man she had ever known. Harriet's flesh tingled and for a split-second she swore she felt her heart move.

"I've been thinking of this kiss from the moment you appeared in the stableyard," he said in a husky tone. "And when you won our race I nearly lost my seat with the urge to seize you and pull you into my lap. My concentration has been so lacking for the past hour that just before we stopped I nearly led my horse into a ravine."

Harriet gave a shaky laugh. "Now that you have kissed me, am I exorcised from your system, sir?"

"Just the opposite, as you well know. One taste has merely whet my appetite for more. But alas, this is neither the time nor the place."

He turned from her and walked away. She was glad of the physical distance, for she needed the space to regain her composure. Harriet watched him pace for several moments near the edge of the rushing water. She opened her mouth, then caught herself just before calling out a caution to be careful of his footing.

He did not need her warning. He was a man very much in control of himself and his surroundings. As he stood high atop a rounded boulder, an image came to her mind of the first time she had seen him, standing in the entrance hall of the castle—powerful, mysterious, and menacing. He had frightened her almost beyond speech at that initial meeting, but she had faced him down, albeit not with her usual bravado.

When she thought about that first encounter later that night, Harriet worried that her courage had nearly failed her because her fiancé's betrayal had changed her utterly. It had damaged her spirit, stolen her confidence, wreaked havoc with her already fragile sense of self-worth.

Here in the wilds of Scotland she had rediscovered those missing pieces. She had somehow regained the essential parts that had been hurt and beaten down. But she had also discovered something else, something that she never knew existed.

A female vulnerability. It was at times a disconcerting thought that for some unknown reason this man possessed the power to make her feel the fragility of her womanhood. Even more disturbing was the notion that occasionally she had come to *like* that feeling.

"Such a serious, thoughtful expression, Harriet. Are you longing for more of my kisses?"

"I am remembering my past."

"With regret?"

"Sometimes I feel my past is composed solely of regrets." She sighed softly. "And horrible mistakes."

The words, once spoken, could not be called back. She turned her back on him, staring out into the woods, hoping he would take the hint that she did not wish to further elaborate.

But of course, he did not. She heard his booted feet crunching the dried leaves, felt him standing beside her, a formidable male presence.

"Who hurt you, Harriet?"

"Julian. My fiancé." She whispered, wondering if saying the words softly would ease the pain. She crossed her arms tightly over her chest and hunched her shoulders.

"What happened?"

She nearly groaned. *What had happened, exactly? Were there truly words to explain it all?* She had been abandoned in the midst of a great scandal, but that humiliation was not the root of her pain. "There is no easy or simple answer to your question. Julian and I became engaged at the end of my third Season. He was a soldier, serving with Wellington, so I knew it might be a long engagement. It didn't matter. I was so proud of him, but more significantly I was so proud of myself for wringing a marriage proposal from one of the Season's most elusive bachelors.

"He was a handsome man, popular in Society, though I quickly learned he did not possess the kind of friends who would stand by and support him through a difficult time. He left for the Continent a week after our engagement was announced. I wrote to him diligently for years, though I rarely received any letters in return.

"I made excuses for his lack of regard, his lack of consideration. I comforted myself with the notion that someday he would return and then, at last, I would be his wife and we could begin our life together."

"Did he fail to return?"

She let out a hollow laugh. "Oh, no, he came back. It was a disaster. I should have broken it off when it became apparent he wanted no part of honoring the commitment he had made to me. But I was too proud and too frightened of being alone. In the end my poor judgment of his character led others into grave danger."

"It was not your fault that he acted without honor."

Agitated, Harriet lifted her hand and rubbed her brow. "It was my responsibility. Deep in my heart of hearts, I knew what sort of man Julian was and yet I ignored it, I told myself it wasn't true. I made him out to be a far better man than he was because I so desperately *needed* him to love me.

And the most laughable truth of all was that he never did. I doubt he even liked me."

Mr. Wainwright turned her shoulder so she faced him. She took a deep breath, wondering if he understood how guilty and humiliated she felt. "Dear Harriet. It is hardly a sin to wish to be loved."

He enveloped her in his arms. The embrace lacked the usual sensuality and passion that seemed to flair so easily between them. Instead it was a gesture of comfort. Harriet had not realized how badly she craved this show of kindness and support until it was so selflessly offered.

She felt a sob rise up from her throat, but valiantly fought it back, clenching her jaw tightly until it ached. Julian had already taken far too many of her tears. He no longer warranted any of her time or emotions.

"What an idiot you must think I am," she muttered. "A weak, spineless woman who embraced the foolish notion that, miraculously, love changes everything."

His broad chest rumbled and moved and she realized he was laughing. She lifted her head and stared at him, her cheeks hot.

"I have never in my life met a less fragile woman than you, dear Harriet. And we both know you are far too clever by half, so there is no need to berate yourself for seeking what we all crave. Someone who will love us. Completely and unconditionally."

He went very still and searched her eyes with his own. Harriet licked her lips and swallowed, wishing a breeze would flutter by, for she felt very overheated.

"Is that what you wish? To find someone who will love you?" Harriet whispered, hearing her own labored breathing as she waited for his answer.

"Certainly. A future alone is barren and empty. A future with a wife to love and children to spoil has meaning and substance."

Harriet was so stunned by his answer she nearly lost her balance. So many men felt that marriage compromised not only their freedom, but their sanity. As for love—well, far too many males often considered that a very unnecessary emotion.

Harriet's fingers stole up his chest, and across his shoulders. She lifted a hand and pushed aside a lock of hair that had fallen over his forehead. The intensity of his stare never wavered, giving further credence to the sincerity of his words, but it was the expression on his handsome features that made her heart turn over.

"I wish you luck in your search for love and happiness," Harriet said solemnly. "I believe you will not find it too arduous a task."

For an instant, Harriet felt overwhelmed by bitter regret. More than anything, she longed to be that woman. The wife who was loved, the woman who gave birth to the children who would be spoiled. His wife, his children.

But she knew it could never be.

Dinner that night was a strained affair. The intimacy they had shared in the afternoon had suddenly disappeared and they treated each other with unfailing politeness that made everything they did seem awkward and unnatural. Conversation was as sparse and mundane as the food they were served.

When the meal finally ended, Harriet suffered a moment of panic, worried that he would not volunteer to walk her to her bedchamber door, as he had done every night. She had decided this afternoon on the long, silent ride back to the castle, that she would leave in the morning. Kate was well enough to travel—there was no reason to linger.

She had not informed Mr. Wainwright of her decision, yet for some strange reason she believed he knew, especially when he so hesitatingly asked if she would like his escort to her chamber.

Her stomach was in knots as they made the all too familiar walk. Harriet struggled not to think beyond the moment. When they reached her door they stopped and turned at the exact same moment, facing each other. For a second he appeared ready to kiss her. But he did not.

Instead he reached out and took a stray lock of her hair between his thumb and forefinger. "The stable master informs me that your coach and driver are planning to depart early tomorrow morning."

"There is no reason to remain. Kate is fully recovered, though she may claim otherwise." Harriet studied a mark on the wall over his left shoulder with abject curiosity. "This afternoon Kate tried to tell me she was in grave danger of having a relapse, but I know that was merely an excuse to stay near Mr. MacLeod."

"So you will also be leaving?"

Harriet nodded, not trusting her voice.

"If I ask you to stay, to wait until the children arrive, would you do so?"

"I cannot."

He gently cupped her shoulders with his hands and brushed his lips against hers, holding her deliberately away from his body. "I should like to think we are parting as friends."

"Of course."

"Then, just once, I would like to hear you call me by my Christian name."

Harriet pulled in a deep breath. For some reason his simple request brought her alarmingly close to tears. "Good night, Nathaniel."

"Good night, Harriet. Sleep well."

She clasped her hands together, lacing her fingers and gripping them so hard they turned white. It was the only way she knew to prevent herself from reaching for him and making an utter fool of herself. She wondered what else she could say, how she could somehow magically make things different between them. But there were no words.

Her sleep that night was tormented. Her thoughts centered on how she could have done things differently, could have changed the ending to this most bizarre chapter of her life. But the restless hours of sleep brought no answers.

Nathaniel's fingers slowly curled around the doorknob to Harriet's bedchamber. He hesitated, a part of him knowing this was wrong. Yet circumstances compelled him to twist the knob and push the door open.

He was hoping she was a light sleeper, that the noise he made would rouse her from slumber. It did not. He raised the candlestick he carried in one hand, thinking that perhaps the light would disturb her rest. It didn't.

Straining to see through the shadows he could barely discern her shape beneath the heavy coverlet. He could summon one of the female servants to wake her, but he was under the distinct impression that most of them returned to the village each night.

He knew Mrs. Mullins had rooms at the castle, but Harriet had already joked that she could barely understand the housekeeper's thick burr. It hardly seemed fair to summon her.

Nathaniel took a deep breath, and moved closer. All the various conventions he and Harriet had flouted this week were overshadowed by the vast impropriety of this moment. A gentleman never entered the bedchamber of an unmarried female in the middle of the night. Especially not the bedchamber of a woman in his employ.

He soothed his conscience by telling himself these were exceptional circumstances. Besides, he technically wasn't alone with Harriet. There were three young chaperons following closely on his heels.

Nathaniel approached the bed. Harriet was sleeping on her back. She had not braided her hair and the dark strands were fanned out in wanton abandon on the pillow. The sight held him momentarily spellbound and he cursed the sudden quickening in his loins.

Nathaniel took a deep, steadying breath, unintentionally inhaling her delicate fragrance. The scent only sharpened his desire. He felt like shouting out his frustrations, hoping it might startle Harriet awake, but that would most likely frighten the children.

His breathing unsteady, Nathaniel loomed over the massive bed. His hand reached out—

"Nathaniel, please we must stop. Oh, please do not test me," she cried suddenly, thrashing her legs beneath the coverlet. "I fear I don't have the strength to resist you." She turned on her side, burrowed her head in the pillow and sighed in her sleep.

Nathaniel moved back from the bed. His face burst into a wide grin. The little minx. She was dreaming of him! If the situation had not been so dire he would have crawled in beside her and slowly brought her to wakefulness, slowly kissing the edges of her delicious mouth, gently stroking the tender flesh of her bare breasts, and then delving into her moist, yearning womanhood.

"Uncle Nathaniel?" whispered a childish voice.

Lord Avery took a stumbling step away from the bed, feeling as if he had been caught in an act of pure debauchery. "Yes, Jeanne Marie?"

"Is this our room? Mine and Phoebe's? Because if it is, I don't want to stay in the bed with that strange lady. She talks while she is sleeping."

Nathaniel managed to hold back his laughter.

"You and Phoebe shall have your own bedchamber, right near mine," Nathaniel replied. "And Gregory will be in the chamber next to your own."

"Do you talk while you sleep?" Jeanne Marie asked solemnly.

"No." Nathaniel regarded his young niece with a teasing grin. "I whistle. And sometimes I sing."

His remark brought the hoped for smile to the child's face. Then, with his focus once more centered on the task at hand, Nathaniel reached out and shook Harriet's shoulder.

"Wake up, Harriet," he said. "We need you."

Chapter Twelve

Harriet stirred, opened, then shut her eyes. Her sleep-laden brain struggled to awake and understand. There was a soft, glowing brightness in her room, yet she knew it could not be morning. There were voices, too. Deep masculine tones mixed with sweet high-pitched chords.

Slowly, Harriet again opened her eyes. She carefully sat upright in her bed and drew the covers to her chin. It was dim. It was cold. It was raining. And Nathaniel was in her bedchamber.

His sculpted features and sensual mouth looked especially appealing in the shadowy intimacy of her chamber. He was dressed informally in a black waistcoat, white shirt, dark breeches and boots, with no coat or cravat. He was staring at her with such an intent expression that her heart gave an unsteady jolt.

It was like her dreams, her fantasies. He had come to her room, had come to her bed. His lithe, muscular body emanated a raw, masculine vitality that overwhelmed her senses. It was enticing, intoxicating. The thought of what was to come dazzled her spirit. It was what she had wished for, had yearned for, had finally dared to dream about—the promise of physical and emotional fulfillment shared between them.

But he wasn't alone. He had brought others with him. Children. There were children. His three young wards? Was it possible? They stood beside her bed, gazing up at her, from tallest to shortest in a neat little row, lined up like steps on a stairs. Harriet blinked, then reached for the flint she kept on her bedside table. She struck it and lit the candle that was also kept nearby.

With the aid of additional light, Harriet was better able to examine her uninvited, unknown guests. They gazed at her with unwavering regard, with wary, lost expressions on their young faces. It was enough to make her heart turn over in her chest.

They were a handsome trio, similar in looks, though their coloring varied from delicate blond to dark hair and blue to brown eyes. Though she knew their ages to be nine, seven, and four they looked far younger, far more defenseless. Harriet's throat tightened at the somber picture they made and for a long moment there was only the sound of the beating rain echoing through the bedchamber.

"I am sorry to have disturbed your sleep, but the children are here and we have a problem that needs your assistance," Nathaniel said.

"They have arrived *now?*" Harriet at last croaked. "In the middle of the night? In the middle of a storm?"

Nathaniel made no attempt to hide his grimace. "It seems to be the preferred form for visitors to Hillsdale Castle. If memory serves, that is exactly how you arrived."

Harriet looked at him in alarm as she remembered that stormy night. "Where is Brutus?"

"I have already taken care of the hound. He is locked in my bedchamber, no doubt chewing on my best pair of boots."

"Good." Harriet let out a breath. "That should keep him entertained for a few hours."

"Who is Brutus?" the boy asked, as he wiped his nose on a grimy sleeve.

"He is one of the castle dogs," Nathaniel explained. "You may meet him in the morning, if you like."

"After the beast has eaten a large breakfast," Harriet muttered under her breath.

"I like dogs," the younger girl announced. "Especially when they sit in your lap and let you cuddle and kiss them."

"Brutus is a very large dog. Why, I bet he could put *you* in his lap," Harriet said with a slight smile. "But I'm sure he will like a pat on the head and a good rub behind the ears. We shall wait until he knows you better before you start giving him kisses. Your—"

Harriet glanced up at Mr. Wainwright in complete confusion.

"Uncle Nathaniel," he supplied softly.

Harriet nodded. "Your Uncle Nathaniel will supervise an introduction to Brutus sometime in the morning. After you are well-rested."

"We slept in the carriage. We don't need to rest anymore," the boy declared in a belligerent tone.

"Carriages can be very uncomfortable," Harriet said, wondering how far they had come on this journey. "Won't it feel good to stretch out in a big, comfortable bed, with a deep, soft mattress?"

"No." To emphasize the point, the little boy shook his head, his dark hair flopping into his eyes.

"We really aren't very tired," the older girl said hesitantly, glancing at her sister.

The younger girl seemed to get the unspoken message, for she straightened her shoulders and declared loudly, "I was sleeping for a very long time. And I don't like squishy beds."

Ah, so that was the way of things. Harriet was glad they were showing a solidarity of spirit, though she would have preferred if they wait until a more reasonable hour to be defiant about going to bed.

Mr. Wainwright let out a distressed sigh and ran his fingers through his already ruffled hair. "If they aren't sleepy, we can't send them to bed. Perhaps they—"

"If the children do not wish to go to sleep, they may sit in the front parlor until morning," Harriet interrupted, hardly believing what a push-over Nathaniel was with these three young scamps. "Though I doubt there is a fire lit, so the room will be very cold. Perhaps we can find a spare blanket to chase away the chill. You could all share it. Snuggling together might aid in keeping away the worst of the cold. And we will also need to search for a few candles, though they will most likely sputter and go out, leaving you in total darkness. It will be hours before dawn arrives."

"I don't like the dark," the younger girl whispered.

"Neither do I." Harriet reached out and smoothed her hand over the child's shoulder. "If you go to bed, I shall make certain to leave a candle burning where you can see it all night. And we'll check to make sure the mattress isn't squishy. Would that be all right?"

The child's face relaxed. "Yes."

"I don't need a candle. I'm not a baby."

"Of course you aren't. You are a big strong boy.

I have a nephew who is nearly the same age, so I know a great deal about boys."

The little boy's brows knit together, as if he were trying to decide if this was a good or a bad thing.

Nathaniel's gaze swung in her direction. "Then it is agreed the children shall go to bed. However, there was some sort of mishap with the luggage coach. It broke a wheel early this evening and had to be left behind. In the confusion, the children's bags were not transferred to their traveling coach. They have no nightclothes."

"A problem easily remedied," Harriet replied. She threw back the covers and rose from the bed. "I need a minute to locate my robe and slippers. Then we can get the children settled for the night. Have you woken any of the other servants?"

Harriet received no answer. Her back was towards Nathaniel and the children. If she hadn't heard their breathing, she might have thought they had left. She shrugged into her robe and turned around to face them. The three children were observing her movements with innocent curiosity, but Nathaniel was looking at her with such frank sexual interest it sent a shiver down Harriet's spine.

He cleared his throat. "As far as I know, the household is asleep. I answered the front door myself when the children arrived."

Harriet steeled her shoulders, willing herself to composure. Having him in her bedchamber in the middle of the night was far too close to her disturbing, erotic dream. Thank goodness for the three young chaperons.

"Mrs. Mullins will have to be roused so that rooms can be prepared. I'll not have the children sleeping among dust and cobwebs," Harriet said.

"Their rooms have been ready for several days," Nathaniel said.

Harriet glanced at him in suspicion. "Is there clean linen? Freshly washed drapes? Properly cleaned rugs? No musty odors?"

"The rooms are in excellent condition. I inspected them myself."

"Oh." Harriet fidgeted with the belt of her robe. "How about food? Have the children eaten? Are they hungry?"

"Apparently all they have been doing is eating," Nathaniel replied wryly. "And not the type of food conducive to the swaying motion of coach travel."

The older girl nodded her head. "Gregory got sick. They stopped the coach and Uncle Duncan was trying to get him out when it happened. A lot of it went on Uncle Duncan's shiny black boots."

"It smelled horrible," the younger girl declared. "We played near a stream and threw rocks in the water while the servants cleaned it up." She wrinkled her nose. "But they didn't get rid of the smell, so at the next inn we got a new carriage."

"Goodness, that was quite an adventure." Harriet smiled briefly at the trio, then turned to Nathaniel. "Is Duncan your brother?"

Nathaniel looked blank for a moment, then his eyes strickened with alarm. "N-no. The children address us both as uncle out of affection and regard, not because of any familial relationship."

Harriet's gaze narrowed. Though his answer seemed forthright, there was something about Nathaniel's expression that rang false. It was as though he were trying to hide something from her.

"It may seem silly given the circumstances, but I would very much like to be properly introduced to your wards," Harriet said.

"Of course." Nathaniel moved to stand behind them. "Children, this is Miss Sainthill."

The girls both executed a polite curtsey and Gregory managed a quick bow. Harriet was charmed.

"This is Phoebe," Nathaniel continued, placing his hand gently on the older girl's head. His hand touched the younger girl next and she snuggled close to his arm. "This is Jeanne Marie. And this, is Gregory."

The little boy jerked back, then darted his body side to side, making a game of avoiding his guardian's touch. Nathaniel chuckled, pursuing the child until he captured him in a hug that had them both laughing.

"I am very pleased to meet you all," Harriet said. "Even if it is the middle of the night." She gave them what she hoped was a friendly smile and then announced, "We had best go and find your new bedchamber so you can settle in for a nice rest."

Not surprisingly there were groans of protest from all three youngsters, but the adults were not swayed. Nathaniel led the way, gripping a candelabrum held high. The children followed and Harriet brought up the rear.

As they headed along the dark passage to the opposite side of the castle the ghostly echo of a low moan filled the air. The sound sent goosebumps skittering up Harriet's arms. She glanced ahead anxiously to see if the children had a similar reaction, but those three pair of feet never missed a step.

They entered a room in a section of the castle that Harriet had not explored, knowing this was where Nathaniel's bedchamber was located. The room was well lit, with several candelabra burning brightly. It was also occupied by a man who was unknown to her. He was crouched in front of the hearth obviously trying to light a fire. He appeared to be having very little success, for the room was cold.

Harriet was surprised to see him, since Nathaniel had said no other servants were awake.

"Devil take it, I had no idea the place was in such a disgraceful state," the man muttered. "What a poor friend you must think me, Nathaniel, to send you off to such a crumbling old keep. We need to take the children back to Edinburgh as soon as possible. They must be kept safe. 'Tis too late to begin the journey tonight, but we—"

The stranger ceased speaking abruptly when he noticed her. He rose slowly to his feet, seeming to half fill the room. "Oh, hello. And who do we have here?" he asked, with a charming, roguish smile on his face.

The timbre of his voice was low and cultured, with just a faint trace of a Scottish burr. He spoke like a gentleman, yet his wolfish appraisal made Harriet feel the need to check the top button of her nightgown and tighten the closure of her robe.

"Good evening, sir. I am Miss Sainthill," Harriet replied in a frosty tone, inclining her head slightly.

He stared at her for a moment before bowing. "Duncan McTate, at your service."

"McTate? I know that name."

He smiled again, revealing himself to be an especially handsome specimen of a man. "I imagine you've met several McTates during your stay. This is my castle and my clan, and many of these good people cling to the tradition of taking the laird's name as their own."

Harriet's eyes locked with his and in that instant she felt a jolt of recognition. "The Scottish warrior in the portrait gallery," she said in quiet amazement. " 'Tis most remarkable. The resemblance between you and him is quite marked."

McTate's eyes filled with an amusement that was almost tender. "I've always fancied myself a fighter, a valiant defender of home and hearth. I vaguely remember those portraits from my visits here when I was a lad, no bigger than young Gregory. You must stroll with me in the gallery tomorrow, Miss Sainthill, and show me which of those handsome lads shares my good looks."

Harriet nearly grinned, but caught herself. Living at Hillsdale Castle must have addled her brain, for she had never before succumbed to such blatant charm. It was a point of pride that she had always possessed a low tolerance for this type of drivel. Yet somehow Duncan McTate had charmed his way past her defenses.

Frowning fiercely, Nathaniel stepped between them. "If you two are through, perhaps we can turn our attention to the children. Or have you forgotten about them already?"

Harriet blinked at Nathaniel's curt tone. McTate met his look with a steady gaze. "I hadn't realized I was poaching on your territory. Forgive me. Yet I'm pleased that living in this fine Scottish environment, breathing the crisp Highland air, has opened your eyes to the value of a good woman."

Nathaniel's brows crashed together in an ominous line. "As usual McTate, you have completely misread the situation, but what else can one expect from such a great Scottish lout."

"Ah, so she's not a good woman?"

"She is far more than a good woman," Nathaniel declared.

"I knew it." The Scotsman slapped his knee.

"How can you claim to know anything?" Nathaniel cried. "You just met her!"

" 'Tis clear to anyone with a lick of sense in their skull that she's a lady. Possessing brains and spirit, not to mention handsome looks."

And she is also standing right in front of you, Harriet wanted to shout out, but she held her tongue and instead followed this exchange with mounting interest, noting the easy, familiar way the men bantered and teased each other. Clearly they were much more than landlord and tenant. They were obviously close friends of long standing. And the children addressed them both as uncle. What was the real connection that all of them shared?

McTate? McTate? A tangle of confusion raced through Harriet's mind as she tried to remember where else she had heard that name.

"The vicar," she blurted out. "You are the McTate who is a distant cousin of the vicar back home! It was through his recommendation that I came here as governess."

At her interruption both men ceased their bickering and turned towards her. "Yes, the vicar is a cousin and I claim the relationship, even if it is on my mother's English side," McTate said. "I'll have to remember to think of him more kindly in the future. He chose well, far better than I dared to hope."

"He did not choose me, sir, " Harriet insisted. "I went to him looking for assistance and he recommended me for the position. It was my decision to take the job."

"Initially," Nathaniel added. He took a step toward her and spoke in a tone only the two of them could hear. "Are you staying?"

Lifting her chin she declared stoically, "For the moment."

"Splendid."

Harriet allowed her eyes to meet Nathaniel's

and they shared a brief moment of camaraderie. Then she turned her attention back to her duties.

"The children are starting to look very sleepy. Where is their nursemaid?" Harriet asked.

McTate frowned and shook his head. "There was a misunderstanding and she was unintentionally moved to the luggage coach during our last stop. When that vehicle broke down, she was mistakenly left behind."

"No nightclothes and no nursemaid. Now I understand why you woke me in the middle of the night," Harriet said with a small sigh. Disheartened but far from daunted, she took a deep breath and started doing what came naturally. Organizing and ordering.

"I will prepare the girls for bed and stay here with them for the remainder of the night, but first Gregory needs to be sorted out."

"I would gladly offer one of my shirts for him to sleep in, but it is far too large," Nathaniel said.

"Gregory can sleep in his small clothes," Harriet decided. "Though he claims not to be a baby, he is still only four and I'd rather not leave him entirely on his own tonight. The castle produces some odd sounds that might frighten him. Can one of you sleep in his room?"

"If you prepare him for bed, we can handle the rest," Nathaniel replied.

"Excellent."

As Harriet moved to take Gregory to his room, the little boy suddenly complained of being too tired to walk that far. Without asking, Nathaniel patiently scooped the lad up in his arms and carried him. The sight of those tousled curls resting so serenely on Nathaniel's broad shoulder brought an odd rush of emotion to Harriet's throat.

She followed the pair into the next chamber. As

Nathaniel carefully lowered Gregory to the mattress, the little boy stirred. He threw his arms around Nathaniel's neck and held him tight. "I missed you. And Phoebe worried that you had forgotten about us. It was fun staying with Uncle Duncan, but it is better here with you."

Guilt flashed in Nathaniel's eyes before he recovered himself. "Thoughts of you and your sisters stayed in my heart each and every day. Uncle Duncan is a fine man and I trusted him with my greatest treasures—you, Jeanne Marie, and Phoebe.

"But you must always remember, Gregory, that we are of the same blood and share a bond that can never be broken or forgotten. No matter how far or how long we are away from each other. Do you understand?"

"I think so."

Gregory let out a loud yawn. Nathaniel stepped away from the bed, allowing Harriet to move toward it. His face was guarded and Harriet wondered if she had misheard the remarks he had made to the boy. *We are of the same blood? What in the world could that possibly mean?*

The child was very tired and Harriet had no trouble preparing him for bed and tucking him beneath the covers. She bade Nathaniel and McTate, who had also come to the bedchamber to look at the boy, a good night.

Telling herself she must have imagined the guarded, shuttered expression that appeared suddenly on Nathaniel's face when he gazed at her, Harriet returned to the other chamber. She assisted the girls, who by this time were far too tired to offer any sort of protest. When they were snuggled beneath the covers, Harriet gratefully sank into an overstuffed chair near the fireplace.

She waited patiently for the steady, rhythmic

breathing that would let her know the girls were sleeping. It began, but suddenly stopped. She glanced over and saw they were both looking toward the door, their faces flushed with delight.

Nathaniel was standing in the doorway. "I did not have a chance to say good night."

He crossed the room and sat on the edge of the bed. The girls moved close to him, their bent heads nearly touching as they scrambled to get nearer. Harriet heard whispered snippets of conversation, but could make no sense of the words.

After a hug and a gentle kiss on each brow, Nathaniel turned and left, sparing Harriet barely a glance. She set her head back against the chair and closed her eyes. Her thoughts and emotions were a jumble of confusion, yet one fact remained clear. She had no doubt that her decision to stay at the castle and care for these children was somehow going to have a deep and lasting effect on her life.

"What news from London?" Nathaniel asked in a soft voice.

"There's no need to whisper," McTate replied, as he stretched his longs legs before the roaring fire. "Naturally we cannot shout, but conversation at a civilized level should be all right. The boy sleeps like a log."

"Just like his father," Nathaniel said with a slight smile. "I always teased Robert that it would take a cavalry charge in the middle of his bedchamber to rouse him from sleep."

"At least you know the lad comes by it honestly."

"He does." Yet at the mention of his brother, a deep wave of emotion tore through Nathaniel. He could not help but wonder what Robert, a man of honor and principle, would think of this turn of events. Kidnapping the children, removing them from London, hiding them in the wilds of the Highlands in an ancient medieval castle.

Would his brother have approved of these extreme measures? Or would he think them rash and unnecessary? Even dangerous?

"Stop looking so infernally worried," McTate said, breaking into Nathaniel's thoughts. "I think you, nay, *we*, have managed to pull it off."

Nathaniel regarded his friend with cautious optimism. "You have heard no news of the children's disappearance? No rumors? No gossip?"

"Not a peep." McTate grinned merrily. "While in Edinburgh I spent most evenings at home, but I made a point of attending several afternoon events expressly for the purpose of hearing the London gossip."

"And?" Nathaniel prompted, leaning forward in his chair.

"And your assumptions about how your uncle would react to our intervention appear to be correct. As far as I can tell, Lord Bridwell has not set up a hue and cry about the missing children."

Nathaniel felt the tension gradually drain from his body. "Are you certain?"

"Yes." McTate cleared his throat. "Before I brought the children here, I had the distinct displeasure of meeting Lady Treadmont at an excruciatingly boring musical afternoon party. She had just returned from London the previous day because she felt it was her duty to be home for the birth of her first grandchild. She is precisely the sort of gossiping old biddy known for her wagging tongue who would relish the honor of spreading such a juicy tale.

"Three young, innocent, newly orphaned English aristocratic children, kidnapped. One of whom is a duke. Lady Treadmont would be the most sought-after guest of the year, as she told and retold this amazing tale. But all she could drone on about was the new fashions, the miserable weather, and some old news that was the sensation of last Season about a pitiful woman on the brink of spinsterhood who was scandalously jilted and abandoned by her roguish fiancé.

"I therefore conclude if Lady Treadmont has heard nothing about the children, Lord Bridwell is most assuredly keeping this matter to himself."

"Did she perchance name this poor, unfortunate woman?" Nathaniel asked.

"What woman?"

"The jilted spinster."

"I don't remember." McTate frowned and draped his hands over the arms of his chair. "Why should you care about some pitiful female? Isn't Bridwell your main concern?"

"He is." Nathaniel cupped one hand over his suddenly pounding head. "However, I have a fair suspicion that this abandoned bride so eagerly gossiped about is my new governess."

"What!" McTate practically shot out of his chair. "That idiot cousin of mine! He doesn't have the sense God gave a goose. I knew my English relations were good for nothing, and this proves it. How could he possibly recommend such a tainted creature for a respectable position?"

"Not an hour ago you were singing her praises," Nathaniel said.

"I was only saying that to get a rise out of you," McTate admitted. "Especially because you seemed so protective of her. Though my initial impression of her was very favorable and you know I have excellent instincts."

"When it comes to making judgments on the

character of men," Nathaniel retorted. "With women, you tend to think with your cock."

"Doesn't every man?"

"Much to their eventual regret."

"A confession, Nathaniel?"

"You are crossing the line, old friend," Nathaniel said softly. His feelings about Harriet were complex and complicated and he wasn't about to discuss them with anyone. "My relationship with Miss Sainthill is none of your business."

"I choose to make it my business," McTate replied heatedly. "Employing a woman who was embroiled in the most shocking scandal of the Season is not the best way to impress a magistrate."

"Neither is kidnapping, yet I have also done that. Or rather, *we* have also done that."

There was a tense moment of silence. Then McTate broke into a grin. "Aye, we snatched the bairns right out from under old Bridwell's nose."

Nathaniel returned the grin. "So we did. Now tell me, how have the children been getting on these past few weeks?"

Lord Avery listened carefully as the Scotsman gave his account, ending with the tale of their journey north.

"Bloody hell, you should have seen us." McTate let out a soft chuckle. "Stopped by the side of the road like a broken down gypsy caravan. The children racing around merrily, thinking it was all a great lark, me with the most foul-smelling puke running down the side of my favorite pair of boots, and the nursemaid weeping pitifully because she thought it was her fault the boy got sick and she was afraid I was going to give her the sack. If you were there, you'd have been laughing your arse off, that's for certain."

Lord Avery's expression lightened. "It sounds vastly entertaining."

"Entertaining! It reeked of melodrama, like a badly written play. I suppose the only thing more astonishing was realizing I was in the middle of it all."

"You have been brought low, my friend," Nathaniel said in mock sympathy. "Though I am sorry for having to put you through such a scrape, I am forever grateful for your assistance."

McTate waved his hand dismissively. "Don't give it another thought. I was honored to be of service."

"Nevertheless, I appreciate all your help. It seems as though I got the better end of the deal, coming to the castle to set it to rights. Though I'll admit I didn't feel that way the first few days."

"God, it is a sight, isn't it?" McTate let out an exaggerated sigh. "Shows you what tricks the mind can play. I have fond memories of visiting this old keep as a boy. Exploring the ancient rooms, riding like a demon in the open fields, sneaking away on warm summer afternoons to swim in the lake. I ran wild, with little supervision or discipline. To me it was always the perfect spot to escape. I suppose I never noticed the crumbling stones, overgrown gardens, and mountains of dust and cobwebs."

"Oh, I'm sure you noticed. You just didn't mind it."

"Perhaps." McTate got to his feet. "I'm for bed. Since you are staying in here with Gregory, I will take your chamber."

"Wise decision." Nathaniel grinned at his friend. "The cobwebs and dust are gone from my room, but alas I cannot say the same is true in the other bedchambers."

Once he was alone, Nathaniel reclined his head and took stock of the situation, telling himself he felt reassured that all was going according to plan. The children were safely away from his uncle, seemingly none the worse for wear. Hiding out here would give him additional time to formulate his next move as well as agitate his opponent.

Harriet had decided to stay. That brought an edge of doubt to Nathaniel's sense of confidence. He was unsure if it was the wisest decision to allow her to become part of his household. She was an intelligent and perceptive woman. It would not take her long to realize something was very wrong with Mr. Wainwright, the wool merchant, and his three wards.

But what other choice did he have? None whatsoever. Tonight was a prime example of how ill-equipped he was to properly care for the children on his own. Their welfare was his key concern. He must have a capable governess to take charge of them.

Nathaniel tightened his jaw. There was one alternative. He could send Harriet away and hire a Scottish woman to take charge of Phoebe, Jeanne Marie, and Gregory. Perhaps that was the more cautious, prudent course to take.

Yet the truth was, he did not want Harriet to leave. As he thought of her, Nathaniel felt his chest constrict with the wild mix of emotions she always inspired in him. For the time being, he would stay the course as it was plotted, ever alert to any signs of danger.

And pray he was not taking any unnecessary risk that would prove costly in the end.

Chapter Thirteen

"Why don't you let me stay? Please. I can be of great help to you, Miss Harriet." Kate, her voice low and pleading, hung her head out the carriage window that she had moments ago been bundled inside, and begged unashamedly.

"Have a safe journey," Harriet called out. She nodded to John Coachman, indicating that he should leave. The servant touched the rim of his hat, then picked up the carriage reins. "Now Kate, don't forget to deliver all my letters to the family. Especially those meant for my sister Elizabeth."

"Please, Miss. I really want to stay!"

The carriage lurched forward, the wheels crunching loudly on the stones. For an instant, doubt assailed Harriet. She could use all the help she could muster and while not the most pleasant of companions, Kate had proved to be a competent maid. And she was a familiar face in this hostile and alien environment.

The older woman leaned farther out the window

and made an impatient gesture with her hand. Harriet steeled herself to remain motionless, knowing it would be utterly ridiculous to call the servant back.

Harriet was a governess in this household. She was not entitled to, nor did she require, a personal maid. Even in these unusual circumstance, Harriet could not see her way clear to making an exception. Still, she did feel a jolt of remorse when the carriage turned at the bend in the road and disappeared from sight.

Her only assured route of escape was now cut off.

"Miss Sainthill! What are you doing out here all alone on such a windy, cold morning?"

Harriet whirled about, poised with a ready answer, yet for a moment she was robbed of her voice. Duncan McTate approached, his long, muscular legs making short work of the distance across the courtyard. His long, *bare*, muscular legs.

Saints above, it had to be near freezing outside and the man was walking about half-dressed, with parts of his limbs exposed to the elements. He quickly drew closer, looking broader and taller than he had last night and far more imposing.

Which seemed ridiculous since the daft man was wearing a skirt.

Though she tried to act as if nothing was out of the ordinary, Harriet knew her eyes must be flaring wide as saucers as she got her first close-up view of a man dressed in a kilt. Hand-knit wool stockings gathered at the knee, a sporran tied about his waist and a kilt that allowed for ample glimpses of his muscled thighs and bare knees.

"Good morning, Mr. McTate," she finally managed.

"You're staring at my legs, lass, and looking more

than a bit flabbergasted. Have you never seen a true Scotsman wearing the plaid?"

"Ah, no, I haven't," Harriet said in what she hoped was a casual voice. " 'Tis a most unusual sight. Especially since I thought it was illegal to wear such attire."

"Bloody English." McTate gave a harsh laugh. "It takes more than an Act of Parliament to crush a man's heritage. Especially a proud Scot."

Harriet made a pensive noise in the back of her throat. "I imagine you are safe enough from the arm of English law up here. And your countrymen no doubt applaud your commitment to keeping the old traditions alive."

"Not entirely. If a tartan-clad Highlander appeared in a Lowland town a few years ago, he would have been locked up, if not shot on sight. The Highlanders have long been regarded as barbarous thieves by Lowland Scots."

"I cannot imagine why," Harriet remarked dryly.

McTate cocked one of his arrogant eyebrows. Too late, Harriet realized she had insulted the man and his heritage. Thankfully he decided to ignore it.

" 'Tis true that since the battle of Culloden the tartan was associated with revolt and lawlessness," McTate explained. "But the loyal service of Scottish regiments in the Colonial conflicts and the war with Napoleon have won them the right to once again wear the traditional garb of their forefathers. Even some of the English have taken to wearing such outfits when visiting our fair land."

Harriet choked back a laugh. "I've yet to see Mr. Wainwright succumb to that temptation."

"You sound disappointed." McTate's nostrils flared with amusement. "There's no need to feel as if you are missing anything of grave importance.

Truth be told, my legs are far more impressive than Wainwright's."

Harriet turned her head up sharply. McTate gave her a thoroughly wicked smile, then winked. The gesture immediately put Harriet's back up. McTate was boyish, charming, and exceedingly handsome. And he knew it.

"I can assure you, Mr. McTate, I have no interest in Mr. Wainwright's limbs. Bare or otherwise."

"Odd. That's not what I hear."

Harriet's eyes narrowed at the insolent remark. Had the servants been gossiping? Or even worse, had Mr. Wainwright said something? That thought brought an acid taste to Harriet's mouth. She stared hard at the Scotsman and soon realized he was trying much too hard to look innocent. Suspicion ignited inside her.

"I see you enjoy fishing, Mr. McTate," Harriet said flatly. "Might I suggest you try your luck at the river near the mountain's edge? You are certainly apt to catch more there than here."

"Och, righteous indignation. Another sure sign that I've hit a nerve of truth." He smirked knowingly at her, as if he knew of her annoyance and was amused by it.

There were a few moments of terse silence. Harriet was not about to let her temper get the best of her, and yet she knew she could not let this pass. Even if there were more than a grain of truth in McTate's words.

"Well, if you are in the mood to be truthful, Mr. McTate, perhaps you could tell me more about your friendship with Mr. Wainwright. Are you two in business together? Or is your acquaintance of longer standing? And what of his wards? They call you uncle, yet Mr. Wainwright reported you are not a relation."

McTate stared at her with undisguised admiration. "There is no better defense than a strong offense, as any army general will attest." Though he smiled at her, something that fleetingly looked like guilt twisted in his rugged face. "I think the wisest course would be for me to call a truce. It seems only fair that we are both allowed our little secrets."

His words offered Harriet limited comfort, for they merely confirmed what she had always suspected. All was not as it seemed to be with Mr. Wainwright and the children. She briefly considered pressing McTate for information, but she realized that would be futile. Though he teased and joked about his friend, there was no doubting his loyalty to Mr. Wainwright. She would learn nothing from the Scotsman.

"A truce." She thrust out her hand.

He took it instantly and held it far longer than was proper. The rogue. "I am delighted we were able to come to such a civilized agreement, Miss Sainthill. I make it a point never to be at odds with beautiful young women."

"Our truce extends to your glib tongue, Mr. McTate," Harriet said with a stern warning in her voice. "I am neither young nor beautiful, as we are both well aware."

"You are an exceedingly handsome woman," he replied, with a smile weaving through his silky tones. "Your genuine modesty lends you an inner beauty and charm that is unique and tantalizing to any man with eyes in his head."

Despite her attempts to quell it, a burst of laughter bubbled up and escaped from Harriet's lips. It was strange how such a heated exchange had lifted her spirits. "Duncan McTate, you are by far the most shameless man I have ever met."

"Stop flattering me, lass, or you'll put me to the blush."

Harriet tilted her chin to an impertinent angle. "Any man who has the nerve to be seen in public with a large portion of his limbs exposed has no right to any blushes."

"Hmm, 'tis not only the exposed limbs but the draft that brings the color to a man's face—and other unmentionable parts of the anatomy."

Harriet felt her spine begin to stiffen, then caught sight of McTate's devilish expression. It was clear from his sparkling eyes that Duncan McTate was simply unable to resist the opportunity to shake a female's composure. And he very nearly succeeded with those final remarks. She decided she had no choice but to let the comment pass with nary a reaction. For the sake of her newly established truce. And her sanity.

"Have you breakfasted yet this morning?" Harriet asked.

"No, and I am feeling rather hungry now that you mention it."

She cleared her throat. "Mrs. Mullins sets a most unusual table. I've learned during my brief stay that most of the items are best eaten hot. Shall we?"

They strolled with an almost practiced elegance across the courtyard. Harriet nodded her thanks demurely when Mr. McTate held the door for her, the glee of anticipation rising. When they entered the dining room Harriet knew she must be grinning like a well fed cat, for she could hardly wait to see McTate's reaction after he took his first large bite of Mrs. Mullins's breakfast fare.

* * *

Harriet anxiously checked her timepiece again. The children were over a half hour late. Nathaniel and McTate had taken them on an exploratory journey through the oldest section of the castle, promising faithfully to return in time for a few afternoon lessons. But they were long overdue and Harriet had started to worry.

Making up her mind to take action rather than sit and wait, Harriet bounded out of the library and wove her way through the maze of hallways at the far edge of the castle. This was unknown territory to her. The wooden beams and stonework in this section were the most ancient she had encountered, making her wonder again exactly how many centuries this dwelling had stood on this spot.

She slowed her gait and walked carefully along the uneven floor, glad that the highly placed narrow windows allowed shafts of sunlight to illuminate the way. This would not be a place one would wish to fall and injure a limb, for it could be days before someone thought to search the area.

The folds of her gray skirt rustled softly around her ankles. Now that the children had arrived Harriet had resumed wearing her dull, serviceable gowns, as befitting her position as governess. Though a feminine part of her nature occasionally longed for a more colorful, attractive garment, especially when in the company of her handsome employer, she wore these gowns to remind herself of her proper place in the household. And her employer's life.

When she at last reached the end of the hallway, Harriet came to a formidable door barring her way. It was pitted and weathered with age, but appeared sturdy and strong. Her hand formed a fist and she pounded on it, then laughed at herself when there was no answer. If the men and children had come this way the door would most likely be open. If they had not, then who could possibly be on the other side to admit her?

Harriet debated turning around and retracing her steps, but further inspection revealed the door was not locked. She slowly turned the great iron handle. With a bit of effort and a strong push it swung open.

She paused, her heart pounding with excitement as she stepped through it. On the other side was a giant of a room, with stone walls soaring so high she had to squint to see the heavy wooden beams of the ceiling. The sun streamed through arched windows casting soft rays of light on the long oak banquet table that sat prominently in the middle of the room.

The floor was smooth and even, worn down to an almost glass-like consistency from centuries of treading feet. The faded tapestries hanging on the wall depicted the legendary Highland feats of days long ago. The bravery of bold knights, the chastity of fair maidens, the threat of mythical beasts.

My goodness, I could explore this place for weeks and still be amazed at what I discover, Harriet thought, as she stared, entranced by her surroundings.

The distinctive sound of steel clanging on steel caught her notice and she realized she was not alone. Dipping her head, she peered curiously toward the far end of the room and spied two figures engaged in a spirited bout of swordplay. It took but a moment to determine that it was Nathaniel and McTate.

Realizing the children must be near, she scanned the perimeter of the room and quickly located them. They were perched together on an oversized, heavy wooden chair that was set on a raised dais and pushed against the stone wall. It resembled a medieval throne and was so big that all three could sit comfortably together on the center cushion. Their eyes were riveted on the dueling men and they shouted and called out enthusiastically as the combatants thrust and parried.

Both men were stripped down to their breeches and shirts and were dripping with sweat. They grunted and groaned in mock agony, delighting their young audience with their antics. Yet Harriet could see that they were both skilled swordsmen, taking care to provide excellent entertainment while staying out of harm's way.

The children let out another loud cheer, clapping and hooting wildly. Harriet moved closer to the action, drawn by the metallic clang of the swords and the sight of the two enticing men who wielded them.

McTate was the larger of the two, but that did not automatically give him a greater advantage. Nathaniel was agile and quick on his feet, weaving back and forth to avoid contact, then suddenly moving forward to attack. With an impressive blur of sword movement he drove McTate toward the massive fireplace in the center of the room. The Scotsman expertly deflected his opponent's thrust, but Harriet detected a slight drooping of his left shoulder, a sure sign the Scot was tiring.

Nathaniel, on the other hand, was a whirlwind of motion and strength. His snug breeches hugged the athletic lines of his upper thighs and she could see the strength in those limbs as they moved with graceful precision and dazzling speed.

McTate had changed out of his kilt in favor of more standard dress. His black boots clicked on the stone floor as he moved quickly to avoid defeat. Harriet knew the contest was a friendly competition but there was also male pride riding on the outcome. Neither man was going to go down without an earnest effort to win.

As the dueling pair came closer, Harriet caught a glimpse of Nathaniel's face and she marveled anew at the many different guises he seemed to assume so naturally. Though clearly fixed in concentration, there was also a relaxed, almost boyish enthusiasm on his flushed face. Yet it was the sight of Nathaniel's white shirt clinging to his dampened skin that vividly reminded her there was nothing boyish about him.

Realizing she was openly staring, Harriet tore her gaze away and turned her attention to the children. They smiled and waved excitedly when they spied her. She anxiously motioned for them to stay seated, worried that her unexpected arrival would break the swordsmen's concentration. Though she soon learned her presence was already noted.

"We've got company, children," McTate called out.

"We aren't children," Jeanne Marie protested. "We are princesses."

"And I'm a prince," Gregory added.

"That you are, laddie," McTate answered with a laugh.

Flushed, animated and magnificent, Nathaniel circled around McTate and turned his head in Harriet's direction. "I am the brave knight sent to protect my noble charges from the evil dragon."

"Evil dragon? Are you perchance referring to me, Mr. Wainwright?" Harriet asked.

"I could be." He laughed. "Even you must admit you often look as though you can hardly wait to box my ears."

"That is what a governess does with an unruly

charge," Harriet said. "But what does a dragon do?"

"Uncle Duncan is the dragon," Jeanne Marie said. "He's going to cook us and eat us if he wins."

"Aye, that I will, and such a tasty morsel you will be." The Scotsman bared his teeth and growled. "First I shall nibble on Gregory and for the main course it will be Jeanne Marie. I shall save lovely Phoebe for dessert, for she is the sweetest of the three."

The ridiculous rhyme had the children shrieking with laughter. Even Nathaniel could not hold back his chuckles.

"Have no fear, fair princess, the dragon is about to be disarmed," Nathaniel declared.

He charged forward, caught the center of McTate's blade and flipped the sword out of the Scotsman's hand. It arched high into the air, spinning as it fell, hitting the stone floor with a deafening clang.

"Victory!" Nathaniel said with a smirk.

"We are saved!" Jeanne Marie shouted. Then she draped her arm dramatically across her forehead.

Harriet lifted her hand to her mouth to hide her smile, wondering where in the world the little girl had learned such behavior.

Jeanne Marie eventually recovered from her near-swoon and joined her siblings, who had rushed the victor. Nathaniel stood, hands on hips, his sword dangling, calmly accepting their exuberant praise.

"I let him win, you know," McTate insisted. He came to stand beside Harriet and they both observed Nathaniel. His strong affection for the children was obvious, as was their regard of him. "It would be far too embarrassing to show him up in front of the children. And you."

"That was most generous of you, Mr. McTate,"

Harriet drawled. "And you made it look so authentic. Your skills would most certainly do a Drury Lane actor proud."

"Making excuses for your defeat?" Nathaniel asked. "Or trying to explain how you let yourself get soft and fat while living the life of a lazy town gentleman?"

McTate laughed and massaged the stiff muscles on the back of his neck. "Next you'll accuse me of becoming a dandy and then I'll have to challenge you to another contest."

"Which you will also lose." Nathaniel stepped forward, brushing the sweat off his brow with his forearm. With a smile, he accepted a flask from McTate. Tilting his head back, he took a long swallow, then licked his wet lips in satisfaction.

Harriet watched him with almost mesmerizing interest, wondering why such a simple, normal gesture made her feel like falling weak-kneed into his arms.

"Did you see the duel, Miss Sainthill? Wasn't it marvelous?" Phoebe asked enthusiastically, her eyes sparkling with delight.

"It was a most invigorating contest," Harriet agreed, turning her attention away from the disturbingly fascinating Mr. Wainwright. "We must read through the history books in the library and see what we can learn about rules of combat during medieval times. There were jousts and tournaments and many opportunities for errant knights to earn their fortunes and perhaps even a small parcel of land."

Mr. Wainwright looked sharply at her. "That doesn't sound like a very appropriate lesson for a young girl. Aren't you supposed to be teaching them things like embroidery stitches and how to speak French?"

"I don't want to learn how to sew," Gregory wailed out in protest.

"I did not mean you," Mr. Wainwright clarified.

He cocked his eyebrow at Harriet inquiringly. She stared back at him. She was not about to launch into a defense of her methods of education in front of her charges and the far-too-interested Duncan McTate. Besides, Mr. Wainwright at the very least owed her the courtesy of allowing her to begin teaching his wards before he started criticizing her methods.

They continued to stare at each other, neither giving any ground. It might have lasted for hours had not Jeanne Marie interrupted with a basic call of nature.

"I need to use the privy, Uncle Duncan," Jeanne Marie announced in a loud whisper. "Where is it?"

"Did the knights have a privy? What did they call it?" Gregory asked.

"A garderobe," all three adults answered in unison.

"I daresay, there is probably a garderobe here somewhere," McTate remarked. "It might even still be in use."

"Can we see it?" Gregory asked.

"Do I have to use it?" Jeanne Marie inquired with a worried frown.

"Of course not," Mr. Wainwright answered. He leaned close enough towards Harriet so she could feel the heat of his displeasure. "Miss Sainthill will accompany you to the privy, Jeanne Marie."

Harriet reached out and took the little girl's hand. "And if any of you wish to see it, we will arrange a tour of the garderobe when your Uncle Duncan is available," Harriet countered.

Mr. Wainwright stared at her so hard it made her want to squirm, but Harriet refused to give him the satisfaction of seeing her move a single muscle.

"Reduced to garderobe tour guide," McTate said with an exaggerated sigh. "The laird truly has fallen on hard times."

Phoebe started to giggle. Her infectious laugh soon had her younger brother and sister joining in the frivolity. Even the adults succumbed to the merriment, easing the tension in the room.

"Stop making me laugh!" Jeanne Marie hiccupped, then crossed her legs. Recognizing that the little girl was close to having an embarrassing accident, Harriet whisked her away. Not wanting to be left behind, Phoebe and Gregory quickly fell into step behind them.

"Miss Sainthill appears to be off to a good start," McTate commented the moment the two men were alone. "The children certainly seem to be taking to her."

"It's early going," Nathaniel replied with a wry grin.

"I think she will prove to be a most competent governess. Don't you?"

Nathaniel shoved a hand through his hair. "She is very opinionated. And stubborn."

"Qualities that will stand her in good stead when dealing with three lively youngsters." McTate's jaw began to twitch. "And one surly uncle. You'd best watch your step around her, my friend, or you'll soon find yourself dancing to *her* tune."

Nathaniel flicked a careful glance at the Scotsman. "I can assure you that I will not for one minute make the mistake of underestimating my adversary."

"I have a great deal of difficulty believing you view her as the enemy. Quite the opposite, in truth." McTate gave him a questioning stare. "I find myself wondering what might happen between the two of you after I leave the castle and return to Edinburgh."

Nathaniel hesitated. Harriet was the last thing he wanted to discuss, but he recognized the set of McTate's jaw and knew he had no choice.

"If I were a prickly sort, I'd be taking great offense at your tone, for it seems to imply that you expect me to fall on her like a ravening beast the moment you are gone." Nathaniel pulled a clean rag from the pile they had brought and calmly began to clean his sword blade. "Need I remind you that Miss Sainthill and I have been alone in this castle for nearly a fortnight? When you go, you will be leaving behind three rather keen-eyed chaperons."

"All of whom go to bed at a very early hour." McTate caught the cloth Nathaniel tossed at him and wiped his own blade. "Not that nightfall, or darkness for that matter, are a requirement for lovemaking."

"McTate!"

"Calm down," McTate said, casting a sidelong glance at Nathaniel. "I am merely testing my theory. It seems that whenever the enchanting Miss Sainthill is the subject of our conversation you start to boil with jealousy."

Lord Avery shoved his sword into its scabbard. Jealous? It was an unpalatable and unwelcome thought.

"I cannot have any feelings for her," he said quietly. "She's been hurt most cruelly by her former fiancé, a man who deceived her. If I engage her affections without being honest about my situation, I am no better than he. And she deserves better. Far better."

"Why not tell her the truth?" McTate asked mildly.

It was an intriguing proposition and one Nathaniel had considered, reconsidered, then considered again. Yet something inside him urged caution. "Miss Sainthill can be a damn prickly sort when it comes to observing the proprieties. I certainly admire the fact that she is no milk-and-water miss. She has strong opinions and holds them dearly.

"If I told her that we had kidnapped the children away from their temporary guardian, I'm honestly not sure how she would react. Nor would she be pleased to know I have been lying to her about my identity. We both know I cannot risk her disapproving of my actions. With my luck, she might decide it was her solemn duty to run off to London, and tell my uncle the whole sordid tale."

"Lord! We certainly can't allow that to happen."

"Precisely."

McTate rubbed his chin thoughtfully. "I suppose it is best for you to keep up the charade until things are settled."

Nathaniel shook his head a little sadly. In so many ways it would be a relief to reveal the truth to Harriet. He had come to hate this deception, had begun to worry that Harriet's reaction when she learned the truth would be extreme.

Yet McTate clearly agreed it was the best course, nay the only course, he could follow. Still, knowing he was justified did not help ease Nathaniel's conscience.

Chapter Fourteen

In the distance, the bells from the country parish chimed merrily. Startled, Harriet looked up from her breakfast plate and realized with a flush of guilt that it was Sunday. The Lord's day.

Gracious, how could that have possibly slipped her mind? She normally found the spiritual rejuvenation of a weekly sermon a pleasant duty. The time spent on reflection and retrospection was a cleansing, invigorating effort, especially if the pastor was an inspiring orator.

Given the less than wholesome thoughts she had been experiencing while living under Mr. Wainwright's roof, it might serve her well to spend a morning in church. But it was not only her own salvation that she needed to think of these days. She had the children to consider. A good governess saw not only to the academic but spiritual needs of her charges.

How embarrassing to be such a blatant failure in this regard so early in her tenure as governess!

The house had been at sixes and sevens ever since Duncan McTate had arrived three days ago, but she knew she could not blame the Scotsman for her own failings.

At least Mr. Wainwright would not be able to find fault with her neglect. He obviously had no intention of attending church himself, for he had sat at the table with her not a quarter of an hour ago, dressed for riding.

Mr. McTate had also joined them for breakfast, mentioning that he would be leaving shortly to return to Edinburgh. Harriet had mixed emotions about McTate going away. He was an outrageous flirt and a rakish gentleman, but she had come to enjoy his witty remarks and naughty sense of humor.

The Scotsman's absence from the castle would also afford opportunities for her to once again be alone with Mr. Wainwright. A situation that Harriet knew from experience could prove dangerous to her emotions.

It was almost a relief to have these disturbing thoughts interrupted by the sudden appearance of Mrs. Mullins. The stout housekeeper was flushed and out of breath and Harriet wondered what could have possibly put her in such a state.

"Ye 'ad best come quick, Miss." Mrs. Mullins's voice was gruff, but her eyes held genuine concern. " 'Tis the wee one, cryin' and frettin' and carryin' on so much we dunna na' what tae do."

Harriet gave the housekeeper a puzzled frown, understanding just enough of Mrs. Mullins's thick brogue to know that one of the children needed her.

"Who is it? Who needs my help?"

"The littlest lass. Cryin' like her heart was broke, puir mite."

Harriet's own heart gave a sudden lurch as she

sprang to her feet and hurried from the room. Sounds of sobbing greeted her as she opened the girls' bedchamber door.

Both girls were in the room, huddled close together. Jeanne Marie was wedged into a corner, curled into a tight ball, sobbing pitifully. Phoebe knelt beside her sister, trying unsuccessfully to offer the younger child some comfort. Yet it seemed that the more Phoebe patted her sister's shoulder, the louder Jeanne Marie wailed.

The sounds were so loud and so dramatic Harriet at first suspected the child was exaggerating the extent of her distress. She had learned over the past few days that Jeanne Marie had a flare for dramatics. The noises she was currently making, which in some ways resembled a wounded animal, were extreme.

"Whatever is the matter?" Harriet inquired in a gentle voice as she entered the room. "Are you hurt? Or in pain?"

Phoebe turned at the sound of her voice. Harriet could see silent tears leaking from the older girl's eyes and running unchecked down her cheeks. "I tried and tried, but I can't make her stop."

Her protective attitude and sense of responsibility cut straight to Harriet's heart. The older sister struggling to bear the burdens of her younger siblings. It so resembled Harriet's own childhood that a flash of pain shot through her. Determined that no youngster should suffer as she had, Harriet hugged Phoebe tightly, offering comfort, hoping to convey her support.

She removed a clean handkerchief from the pocket of her gown and tenderly wiped Phoebe's face. The little girl gave a shuddering sigh and moved closer, clearly relieved to have an adult take charge of the situation.

Harriet next tried to get closer to Jeanne Marie, but the child flinched and let out a sniffling wail of desperation the moment she moved toward her. Harriet backed away, deciding it might be better to let the girl tire herself out before approaching her again.

"Did you do something to upset Jeanne Marie?" Harriet asked the now quiet Phoebe. "Or perhaps Gregory is responsible for making her cry?"

Phoebe's eyes widened. "Oh, no. Jeanne Marie is crying because of Lady Julienne."

Harriet's brows rose in puzzlement. Who in the world was Lady Julienne? Someone from the children's past? Yet what could this lady have possibly done to bring on such an outpouring of emotion this morning?

The questions crowded her mind, but Harriet knew they would have to wait until the child regained control of herself before she would discover any answers.

Gradually Jeanne Marie's sobs began to lessen. Harriet approached her cautiously, ever alert to the possibility of a fresh frenzy of tears. But the crying jag had clearly exhausted the little girl and she made no protest when Harriet smoothed the hair out of her face, then sat on the floor and gathered her in her lap.

Harriet insisted that Phoebe sit next to them and the child clambered to get close. For a few moments all three snuggled together, too emotionally spent to even speak.

Finally, Harriet cleared her throat. "Phoebe has told me that Lady Julienne upset you, Jeanne Marie. Can you tell me what happened?"

Jeanne Marie pulled away from Harriet's shoulder and gave her a brooding stare.

"I miss her. I love her and I want her to be with

me and it makes me very, very sad because she is not." Jeanne Marie's face contorted, but she was able to hold back her sobs. Either that, or else there were no tears left for the little girl to release.

Harriet nodded her head. Though it was an extreme reaction, it was understandable that Jeanne Marie would be upset over being separated from someone who obviously meant a great deal to her.

"Well, I'll bet that Lady Julienne is missing you just as much as you are missing her," Harriet remarked. "If you like, I will help you write a letter. You can tell her all about Hillsdale Castle and I'm sure when she replies, she will tell you everything that she has been doing. Would that make you feel better?"

Harriet thought it seemed like a reasonable offer. Yet both children were gazing at her with equally astonished expressions prompting Harriet to ask, "Who exactly is Lady Julienne? Is she a relative? A friend of the family?"

"Lady Julienne is Jeanne Marie's favorite doll," Phoebe answered.

"My very favorite!" Jeanne Marie insisted, rubbing her tear-damp eyes. "And I want her with me!"

Harriet bit her lip hard to keep from laughing—at herself. She had assumed Lady Julienne was a person. Whoever would have thought a missing toy could bring on such a reaction?

"A doll?" Harriet's mouth firmed. It would be a devastating blow to the child if she treated her very real distress with anything less than a serious attitude. "What happened to Lady Julienne? Why was she not brought on the journey to Hillsdale Castle with you?"

The room became almost uncomfortably silent. Jeanne Marie dug her head in Harriet's shoulder.

Phoebe bit her lip in agitation, then turned her head away, refusing to meet Harriet's eyes.

"Where is she?" Harriet asked.

"She got left behind," Phoebe finally admitted.

"At your Uncle Duncan's house in Edinburgh?"

"No at our other—"

"Jeanne Marie!" Phoebe's nervous interruption startled her younger sister.

Jeanne Marie's breath caught and she looked stricken. "We aren't supposed to talk about our other house. Ever."

"Then we shall not," Harriet replied cheerfully. She hated seeing the fear in the children's eyes, hated knowing they were bound to keep secrets about their past. But why?

"We didn't notice that Lady Julienne wasn't with us until it was too late to go back for her," Phoebe said.

"I didn't cry then, cause I was being a very brave girl," Jeanne Marie said. "But I'm tired of being brave. I want my doll."

"I know." Harriet hugged the child tighter and kissed the top of her head. "I am sure you were a very brave girl, indeed. And I know you feel very sad and are missing Lady Julienne. But perhaps we can find another doll to take her place." Harriet felt Jeanne Marie stiffen in her arms and hastily added, "For the time being. Eventually we will figure out a way to bring Lady Julienne to Scotland."

Phoebe gave her a doubtful look. "Uncle Duncan has already tried giving Jeanne Marie a new doll." She stood and walked to the trunk that had been placed near the window.

The luggage coach containing the children's belongings had arrived a day after they had come to the castle. Harriet had supervised the nursemaid's unpacking of her new charges' clothing, but had not gone through all of their things, so the contents of this particular trunk were unknown to her.

She rose with curiosity to see what Phoebe was so anxious to show her. It was a struggle, but with Harriet's assistance the trunk lid was lifted. Harriet tried, but could not contain her gasp of surprise as she looked inside. The trunk was of a good size, designed to hold a substantial number of garments. But there were no clothes packed away. Instead, it was filled to the brim with dolls.

Small, medium, large, and even larger. With hair of gold, of brown, of black, of red. Dressed as ladies, dressed as servants, dressed as queens, dressed as characters from fairy tales. A Scottish lass with a smart red plaid, an English miss with a beautiful silk ball gown, a pretty country shepherdess with a straw bonnet. Harriet had never before seen so many exquisitely crafted dolls in one place.

"Gracious!" She blew out her breath and turned toward Jeanne Marie who was still sulking in the corner. "Many girls do not even own a single doll, while others feel privileged to have one. I have never known a child who possessed an entire trunk-full."

"Uncle Duncan's housekeeper said he had bought every doll in the city," Phoebe reported solemnly.

"I believe he must have," Harriet concurred. "Is there not one doll among all of these that pleases you, Jeanne Marie?"

The younger girl shook her head belligerently and turned her face to the wall.

Phoebe leaned close and whispered in Harriet's ear. "Lady Julienne was a gift from Mama. She said the doll looked like Jeanne Marie and it has been her very favorite ever since."

Harriet's lips pursed in understanding. This put a whole new wrinkle on the problem. Not only was the toy a familiar comfort, it was a tangible link to the child's mother. Suddenly, Jeanne Marie's emotional outburst did not seem so unreasonable.

"It does seem a waste for all these beautiful dolls to go unloved," Harriet remarked, hoping that Jeanne Marie would at least show an interest. She knew Lady Julienne could never be replaced, but perhaps there was a substitute that could afford the child some comfort.

"It is sad to think of them locked up in this old trunk. Maybe there are other girls who would like to have a doll," Phoebe suggested. "Do you know any, Miss Sainthill?"

"I don't. But Mrs. Mullins might. We could ask her. I'm sure she is acquainted with most of the families in the village."

"You can give the dolls away," Jeanne Marie offered, finally becoming interested in the conversation. She abandoned her position against the wall and peered into the trunk. "I don't mind if other girls play with my dolls. They can even keep them. I just want Lady Julienne."

"Then let's sort through the trunk and arrange the dolls by size," Harriet suggested. Though she knew it was a long shot, Harriet reasoned if Jeanne Marie spent time examining each of the toys she might yet find one that appealed to her.

The females were so intent on their task they did not hear the heavy footsteps approaching. Without warning the half open heavy oak door was pushed so hard it swung around and struck the wall behind it.

Harriet gasped and placed herself protectively in front of the girls, then lifted startled eyes to the intruder. To her relief, she beheld Mr. Wainwright, his expression grim, his garments slightly disheveled, stalking back and forth in the doorway.

"Is everything all right?" His breath came out in great gasping gulps. "Mrs. Mullins sent one of the lads to fetch me. I was riding in the south woods. She said one of the girls was very upset. Who is it? Is she ill? Or injured?"

"Everything is fine, Mr. Wainwright." The corners of Harriet's mouth strained to form a comforting smile, but her heart was still racing from the shock of his sudden, abrupt appearance. "Jeanne Marie was rather distressed, but I believe I have managed to sort out the problem."

"Thank God." Closing his eyes, he rested one hand on the door frame. "Mrs. Mullins was so distraught. I've never seem her like that, babbling on and on, making no sense. I thought . . ." his voice trailed off in unspoken fear.

He took a long breath, then ran his hand through his already ruffled hair. It stuck out at odd angles and should have made him look ridiculous, yet Harriet thought she had never seen him look more handsome.

The girls had turned their attention back to the trunk filled with dolls, but Harriet feared their uncle's obvious distress might upset them.

"Come, take a minute to catch your breath," Harriet said. She grasped Mr. Wainwright's arm and propelled him to the opposite side of the chamber, out of the girls' range of hearing.

"I suppose I overreacted a bit," he said with a sheepish grin.

"Nonsense. It is never wrong to show care and concern for those you love."

Nathaniel shrugged. He seemed embarrassed by his reaction, but Harriet thought his concern endearing. Encouraged by his attitude, Harriet decided this would be the perfect time to bring up the matter of Jeanne Marie's missing doll.

"I need your assistance on a most important matter," she began. "It seems that somehow when the children moved Jeanne Marie's doll was forgotten." Harriet turned and gazed fondly at the little girls. "That was why she was crying so much this morning. She misses the toy dreadfully."

"A doll?"

"Yes. She calls it Lady Julienne."

Mr. Wainwright was instantly on guard. "I remember she used to cling to a tattered rag doll. It might be the same toy, though I assumed it had ended up on the trash heap."

"My goodness, I hope not," Harriet exclaimed. "Jeanne Marie loves that toy and Phoebe just explained it was a gift from their mother, so it has even more significance for the child."

Harriet noticed his jaw was twitching and his face seemed to pale slightly at this news.

"The girls mentioned it was left behind by mistake," Harriet continued. "I imagine it would be easy enough to have it sent here. Though I suppose it will take some time for it to arrive."

"No! It cannot be sent here."

Harriet took a half-step back, surprised at his vehement, almost growling tone.

"I really do not—"

"I said no," he interrupted. "If Jeanne Marie is upset, I shall buy her another doll to replace the one that is lost."

Harriet smiled sourly and placed her hand on her hip. "Mr. McTate has already tried that approach, as that trunk filled to nearly overflowing with dolls will attest. It has not worked. I know it might sound trite, but you must understand the special significance of this particular toy. For Jeanne Marie it is simply irreplaceable."

Mr. Wainwright shoved his hand through his

hair again. "I do not want the child spoiled beyond reason. Besides, you said it would take a long time for the doll to arrive here in Scotland. We might be gone when it at last reaches Hillsdale Castle."

"We are leaving here? Just when the children have finally arrived? Why have you waited until now to tell me this news?"

Scorn curled Mr. Wainwright's lips. "I am not in the habit of consulting my employees when making decisions, Miss Sainthill."

Harriet felt her entire body go rigid as the barb hit its mark. With just one sentence he had rather neatly reminded her of her place in his household. And in his life. She tore her gaze from his and stared blindly toward the opposite side of the room where the girls were gathered.

"I certainly understand how you would be far too busy to focus your attention on such a trivial matter as a child's toy, therefore I am more than willing to cope with solving this problem," Harriet said quietly. "All I require is some basic information. The address of the children's former home and the name of a servant who would be able to assist me. A nursemaid or nanny or even the housekeeper will suffice."

"You are far exceeding your authority, Miss Sainthill." He shot her a strained look, his eyes cold and hard. "I absolutely forbid you to take any action on this matter."

He stormed away before she had a chance to offer any objections.

His words had cast a pall over the room. Harriet could barely contain her astonishment, and her hurt. She had watched him closely as he spoke, weighing all his reactions, listening intently to his words. Questions tormented her. There was something he was not telling her. Harriet was certain of it. But what? Something that had to do with the children's past, but it also seemed mixed together with his true relationship to them.

Harriet only knew they were his wards. And they were orphans. She did not know the particulars of the connection between them all and while she had been curious, she did agree it was not her business to meddle in the affairs of her employer. But now she felt she was unable to do her job without knowing at least *some* of their background.

Discouraged, she rejoined the girls, who thankfully were unaware of the tension between their governess and guardian. On the verge of dropping the matter entirely, Harriet watched the sisters with a careful eye, wishing there was some way she could help.

"Lady Julienne's dress is also blue," Jeanne Marie said in a sorrowful tone as she held up a doll clothed in a blue gown. "It is her favorite color. Mine, too."

Though she did not begin to cry, Harriet could not fail to notice the shadow of sadness that darkened the child's eyes. A small, warm hand grabbed Harriet's. She tugged at it gently, encouraging Jeanne Marie to climb into her lap. When the child complied, Harriet rubbed her cheek against the little girl's soft curls and held her tight.

Jeanne Marie let out a few shuddering breaths, then took a deep, quivering sigh. It was that sorrowful, emotional sigh that forced Harriet's decision.

"Your Uncle Nathaniel was just telling me about your old house," Harriet said in a patently cheerful tone. "The one you lived in before you went to Uncle Duncan's. He said it was much smaller than the castle, but I'm not sure that's right. What do you think?"

Both Phoebe and Jeanne Marie gazed at her in wide-eyed innocence. "Uncle Nathaniel told you about our London house?" Phoebe asked.

Harriet nodded slightly. *London. She would never have guessed they had once lived in Town.* Her stomach gave a sickening lurch. She knew in her heart it was wrong to manipulate the children in an effort to gain information, but if she had any hope of getting Jeanne Marie's doll she would need some help. Since Mr. Wainwright was not forthcoming, that left the children as her only source.

"Yes, the London house. What can you tell me about it?"

"It was very grand," Phoebe said in a wistful voice.

"And had lots of stairs," Jeanne Marie added helpfully.

"I've been to London several times." Harriet leaned her back against the wall. "Why, I might have even ridden right by it. By any chance, do you remember the address or the name of the street?"

Jeanne Marie squirmed to place herself in a more comfortable position. "I know. It was in Grosvenor Square," she said, resting her cheek against Harriet's arm.

Harriet had difficulty hiding her astonishment. Grosvenor Square was among the most exclusive addresses in town, an area where only the very wealthy nobility lived.

"It was a very wonderful place," Phoebe said. "We miss it."

"And our ponies. We miss them too," Jeanne Marie sniffed.

"I miss Mrs. Hutchinson," Phoebe said. "She was always kind to us and never raised her voice, even when Gregory was naughty and the other servants were mad at him."

"Was she your nanny?"

"No, she is our housekeeper."

"She always made sure Cook baked our favorite cakes and cooked only the things we liked to eat for our dinner." Jeanne Marie's face darkened. "And when the other servants were mean to us, she would yell at them."

"Well, she certainly sounds like a wonderful person," Harriet replied, her mind spinning with confusion. "Did Uncle Nathaniel live at the house too?"

"When he was a boy." Phoebe ran her hands through the long blond curls of the doll perched in her lap. "May I get a brush so I can properly arrange her hair?"

Harriet nodded. "And bring some pins and ribbons so we can tie the curls atop her head."

"I know where the pins are," Jeanne Marie shouted. She scrambled out of Harriet's lap and raced her sister across the room.

Harriet tossed her head back against the wall with a loud thump and thought about the information the children had given her. Yet this little discussion had created more questions than answers. A posh London address, servants that were mean to them, the place where Nathaniel had lived as a boy. What did it all mean?

The girls soon returned with an armload of supplies. Harriet was glad the distraction of dressing the doll's hair had eased Jeanne Marie's sorrow and she turned her attention towards helping those small fingers braid and twist and pin an elaborate coiffure. But her mind could not entirely abandon what she had just discovered.

Harriet believed she had sufficient information to mail a letter and request that Jeanne Marie's doll be sent to Hillsdale Castle. The problem was, she could not decide if that was the best course of action, given these most peculiar circumstances.

Nathaniel stood silently at the open library door, the hamper filled with picnic goodies he had Mrs. Mullins make for him dangling from one arm. As he gazed at the children, each bent studiously over their work, he found himself impressed with the order Harriet had created.

Since the castle lacked a proper school room, she had commandeered a section of the library, fitting it with proper sized furniture and the necessary supplies to accommodate her young students. Sunlight crept through the curtains, brightening the whole room, making it an even more cheerful environment.

Harriet circled her students slowly, answering questions, bending down to make corrections on their slates, smiling with encouragement as they struggled with a complicated problem. The sunlight illuminated the shine in her hair and the glow of her cheeks. She had the most incredible complexion of any woman he had ever known, pure as snow and soft to the touch.

Nathaniel cleared his throat loudly. Three small heads instantly popped up.

"Uncle Nathaniel!" The children immediately clamored out of their chairs and swarmed toward him. Nathaniel smiled, enjoying both their greeting and attention. If only their governess would look at him with one-tenth of their enthusiasm, then he could truly enjoy this sunny day.

Her back was to the doorway, but he had seen her stiffen when the children called out his name. Slowly she turned to face him. His gaze flickered to hers and he smiled. She nodded her head fractionally, not looking at all pleased to see him.

Nathaniel grimaced. Harriet had been decidedly cool to him since the incident over the doll and in all honesty he couldn't blame her. She had come to him with a problem concerning one of the children and he had acted like an autocratic ass. Instead of trying to aid her, he had bullied and belittled her. For a woman of Harriet's pride he knew that must surely be a devastating blow.

Yet he felt he had no choice. He had panicked utterly when she spoke of contacting someone to send the doll. It was tantamount to sending a road map to his uncle and a beacon to light the way to the missing children.

Nathaniel was also angry with himself. He felt that he and McTate had done a superior job when snatching the children. They had left London with only the clothes on their backs, but he had trunks of new garments waiting for them in Edinburgh. He thought he had been so careful, so thorough and it was a blow to discover he had indeed been shamefully neglectful.

He knew how much Jeanne Marie loved her doll. He should have somehow made certain it was brought along. This lack of foresight was causing the child deep distress and had placed a barrier of misunderstanding between him and Harriet.

"What's in the basket, Uncle Nathaniel?" Gregory asked, stretching on his toes in an attempt to peer inside.

Lord Avery lifted the basket higher and smiled mysteriously. All three children joined in the game, but it was Phoebe, the oldest and the tallest who got a good look at the contents.

"A picnic!" she exclaimed. "Oh, I do love picnics."

"Is it for us?" Jeanne Marie asked.

"It could be, if your governess allows it."

Phoebe turned to Harriet. "I have nearly finished my assignments. Please say that we may go, Miss Sainthill."

"There is one other condition." Nathaniel smiled pleasantly. "Miss Sainthill must join us."

A strained silence filled the room. "It really won't be any fun for us if you don't come along," Nathaniel added gently.

"Please!" Gregory shouted, hopping up and down excitedly on one foot. "Say yes!"

Harriet managed a pained smile. She obviously knew she was being shamelessly manipulated. "All right, I suppose I can come."

Everyone scrambled to find coats and bonnets and put on proper walking shoes. As soon as they were ready, they set out, packed together tightly in an open rig, with Nathaniel at the reins. He was disappointed that Harriet had managed to put the children between them on the front bench, for he would have enjoyed pressing his thigh against hers and watching the charming surge of color rise in her cheek.

Still, the midday sun felt warm on his hatless head and the children were laughing and fidgeting, eager for an adventure. He was determined to make this a memorable afternoon. For all of them.

When the road ended, Nathaniel tethered the mount to a tree, hefted the picnic basket from the carriage and led his little troop up the mountain. He chose a spot high on a hill overlooking the castle that afforded a view of the stone cottages and green pastures spotted with sheep in the valley.

"Does this meet with your approval?" he asked Harriet, charmed by the way the faint breeze ruffled a few stands of hair that had escaped from their pins.

"It is lovely."

She helped him spread the blanket, then laid out the simple feast. Harriet, he noticed, ate only the fruit, cheese, and crusty bread, leaving the meat pies for him and the children to devour. Fresh air inspired everyone's appetites, or else they were finally becoming used to Mrs. Mullins's cooking. In short order the majority of food was gone.

The children sprawled lazily on the blanket, their expressions an identical dreamlike state. If they did not get moving soon, they would all be asleep, himself included.

His eyes half opened, Nathaniel noticed Harriet reach into the pocket of her cloak and pull something out.

"Who wants to play?"

The children were roused from their near slumber by the sound of the shuffling deck.

"Cards?" Nathaniel rolled over and sat up. "Will there be wagering too?"

"Why not?" Harriet glanced around the area near the blanket. "You may each gather a small pile of fifteen stones. That will be your stake."

They all scrambled to find the best stones. Jeanne Marie wanted only white rocks and Gregory wanted only very large rocks but eventually it was all sorted out. The children listened carefully as Harriet explained the simple rules.

Soon they were all laughing and joking as the piles in front of them got bigger, then smaller.

"You have a most unique approach to education," Nathaniel said as he lost a round to Gregory. "I am not entirely sure that I approve."

Harriet shrugged. " 'Tis a painless way to teach addition and subtraction and far more interesting than trying to memorize and recite countless mathematical tables."

They played several more hands, but the children began to lose interest when Nathaniel started to win every game.

"You're cheating," Harriet said.

"Prove it." He favored her with a wicked smile that she pointedly ignored. "The stream is straight ahead through that small gathering of trees. I've brought gear for fishing, but first we need to find a good spot."

"I'll go look," Phoebe offered.

"Me, too!"

"And me!"

The children were gone in an instant, talking excitedly. Nathaniel gave a satisfied smile, then leaned back against a tree trunk and laced his hands behind his head. "Alone at last."

"With our chaperons very close. As is proper."

Harriet gave him a stiff, quelling glare that made no secret of her feelings. Nathaniel nearly laughed out loud. Her feisty spirit never failed to ignite his passion and he became suddenly conscious of how much he desired her. Of how much he wanted her— breathless and hungry and thrashing beneath him.

These wanton thoughts were rudely interrupted by the sound of rustling trees. Nathaniel glanced up just as all three children came crashing towards the blanket.

"That was quick," he said wryly.

"We found the most wonderful place to fish," Phoebe exclaimed. "There is sun and shade and even rocks for us to sit on."

"Excellent. You'd best hurry back to save our spot. I shall be along in a few minutes with the gear we need to make our poles."

The girls rushed off, but Gregory stayed behind. He toed his foot in the dirt and kicked at the pebble he had dislodged. Nathaniel suspected the boy wasn't very enamored with the notion of having to sit silently while waiting for the fish to bite.

"I wish Brutus could have come with us," Gregory said with a pout. " 'Tis always more fun when he is here."

"So, you prefer the company of a mangy old hound to being with me?" Nathaniel dove towards the child and tumbled him gently to the blanket. The little boy squealed with delight and launched himself at Nathaniel's chest. They wrestled for several minutes, laughing and crying out, until they were both out of breath.

Nathaniel pulled himself into a sitting position, then settled the little boy on his knees so they faced one another.

"Would you care to try your luck at a bit of fishing, Miss Sainthill?" Nathaniel turned towards her. Gregory imitated his uncle, pressing his soft cheek next to the rough stubble of the older man.

Nathaniel heard Harriet's breath seize. Her eyes fluttered from his face to Gregory's, then back to his. She made a peculiar sound in the back of her throat, then started slowly backing away from them.

"Excuse me, I think I hear the girls calling." She ran from the clearing, tearing leaves from the small shrubs in her haste to get away.

Puzzled, Nathaniel gathered up the fishing gear, took Gregory by the hand and followed her.

Chapter Fifteen

Harriet picked her way blindly down the path. Behind her, she could hear Nathaniel and Gregory's voices as they gradually closed the distance between them. She gritted her teeth and moved faster, her mind playing and re-playing what she had just seen.

Those two faces pressed cheek to cheek. One small, round and innocent, the other lean, handsome and strong. But the resemblance was so marked, so true, she was amazed at herself for not noticing it sooner.

It was all suddenly, startlingly clear. The secrecy surrounding the children's past. Servants who occasionally treated them with disrespect. Nathaniel's cryptic remark to the boy, reminding the child that *we are of the same blood and share a bond that can never be broken or forgotten.*

They were Nathaniel's children. And since he was not openly claiming them as such, they must be illegitimate. What a shock! Base-born and therefore needing to be brought to this remote area of Scotland, away from London, away from the scrutiny of the public eye. Or perhaps even hidden from Nathaniel's family. Hidden from his wife.

Nausea churned in Harriet's stomach at the thought. She clasped her hand over her mouth and swallowed the bile. The pain in her side forced her to slow her stride. For a moment Harriet thought she might collapse. She leaned her shoulder against a large tree trunk and held herself erect, forcing in deep gulps of air.

"Ah, there you are," a cheerful male voice called out. "Is everything all right? You seemed to be in a bit of distress when you left us."

Turning toward Nathaniel, Harriet felt nothing but pain. She had trusted him, had allowed herself to care for him. Hell, if she were completely honest with herself she would admit that she was in love with him.

She, who had so steadfastly avoided love after her last disastrous experience. Harriet bit the inside of her cheek, cursing herself as she felt the hot, urgent tears well up behind her eyes. She was twice a fool to have allowed this to happen.

He continued to approach. She stared into his face, searching for signs of the truth, knowing she would not find them. The air around her seemed too thick to breathe. She needed time to get herself under control, time to think and absorb what she had just discovered. She was terrified of what she would say to him, terrified of what she might reveal.

"Your face is rather pale. Are you ill? Do you need assistance?"

The concern in his voice sounded so genuine, but Harriet refused to become susceptible to it. "I just need a few minutes of privacy." Harriet painstakingly gathered her composure. "To answer the call of nature."

It was a fairly crass statement for a lady to make to a gentleman, but Harriet was beyond caring. And it produced the desired effect. Nathaniel inclined his head, grabbed young Gregory by the hand, and scurried off.

She forged ahead through the dense trees, walking toward the sound of rushing water. Fearing she might be seen by the children who were waiting by the stream, Harriet moved in the opposite direction. She followed a sharp bend in the river, finally coming to rest when she had found a large boulder to hide behind.

She knelt in the damp earth, linked her fingers together and scooped a handful of water up to her face. It cooled some of the heat from her cheeks, but could not wash away her shock. Or her pain. Removing the linen handkerchief from her pocket, she dipped it in the clear water, then pressed the damp cloth to her temples.

Harriet knew logically that she had no right to feel so deeply, horribly wounded. She was the governess, for pity's sake, not an affronted wife. What had she expected? Just because he had pursued her, most likely because he was bored and she was available, was he required to share his secrets?

It was partially her fault for placing such importance on their relationship. She thought of herself as his equal. She believed that he respected her, valued her opinion. And when he took her in his arms, it seemed that nothing existed in the world except the two of them.

Yet he did not feel he could trust her with this truth about the children. His children. Her charges.

Was that wrong of him? It certainly *felt* wrong, but a small voice inside her head cautioned her against being unreasonable. Nathaniel had not blatantly lied to her. He had rather deliberately kept the truth from her, but that was not the same thing.

Besides, what gave her the right to cast aspersions on his character? Her own brother had an illegitimate child. But Nathaniel had three. *Three!*

One child could be explained as an impulsive act of passion. That was largely the case with her dear nephew, Georgie. But three children constituted a relationship of long standing. A commitment of emotions, a bond of significant duration, a love of sizable proportion.

That speculation brought even more pain to Harriet's bruised heart. Far more disturbing than thinking Nathaniel was an immoral, jaded man was knowing that he had cared for and loved a woman enough to have three children with her.

Yet he had refused to marry her. Or maybe he had already been married. To someone else!

Harriet crossed and uncrossed her arms. This was ridiculous. Her speculations about the children's mother and her relationship with Nathaniel were limited to Harriet's rather vivid imagination. If she wanted to know the truth, she would have to ask him, and then convince him to be honest with his answers.

It was time to return. She had already been away from them for a long time. Fearful if she did not appear soon, Nathaniel might feel compelled to come searching for her, Harriet rose to her feet. She gave her face a final wipe with the wet cloth and tucked a stray hair behind her ear. She had removed her bonnet when the picnic began and in her haste to escape must have left it on the blanket.

Glancing down, she absently brushed at the mud from the river that had caked on her gown, then laughed at herself for even noticing her appearance. Harriet walked slowly on the winding path, each step a reluctant move towards the stark reality she was having difficulty accepting.

She soon spied the happy little group through the trees. Nathaniel was cutting down a young sapling, obviously to use as a fishing pole. Phoebe already held one in her hand and Jeanne Marie was waiting expectantly beside her sister. Though Harriet was not yet close enough to hear their conversation, whatever Nathaniel was saying had put smiles on the girls' faces.

For a brief, stark instant she wondered if the children knew the truth about their *Uncle* Nathaniel. Probably not. It would mean so much to them, knowing they had a father who loved them.

"Have you caught anything yet, children?" Harriet asked. She pushed her feet, which felt like lead weights, forward and attempted to smile.

"We haven't started," Gregory complained. "Uncle Nathaniel is still making our fishing poles."

"I am working as fast as I can, boy," Nathaniel grumbled good naturedly. He turned towards Harriet and smiled. "Would you care to fish, Miss Sainthill?"

The sound of his voice echoed through her. She was never very good at pretending, at putting on the social niceties merely because it was expected. But there were innocent bystanders present. This was hardly the time to make a scene.

"I prefer to watch," she replied primly.

"Good. That means less work for me." He tilted his head towards the children and winked.

"Oh, do hurry, please," Jeanne Marie entreated. "If we don't start soon all the fish will run away."

Nathaniel laughed, but he increased his efforts and in short order had all three children set along a quiet stretch of the river. Harriet noticed he did not prepare a pole for himself, but instead moved from one child to the next, making sure they had all the assistance and attention they needed.

Harriet walked to a spot beneath the shade of a tree and watched him openly, trying to see beyond the façade, beyond the face that he put forth to the world.

He was natural and at ease with the children. Baiting their hooks, casting the lines, securing a safe spot away from the river's edge to sit and wait for the fish to bite. He showed them how to hold the pole so their arms would not tire so quickly and gently admonished Jeanne Marie of the necessity for quiet so the fish would not be frightened away.

"I think I've caught something." Phoebe's voice, edged with nervous excitement, broke through the required silence.

She jerked her pole skyward, pulling the line out of the water. Dancing on the end was a fish, its silver streaks winking brightly in the sunlight, on the verge of escaping its fate.

Both adults moved forward at the same time. Nathaniel reached the child first. His arm shot out and he hauled the line in just as the fish fell from the hook. It landed on the water's edge, but a swift kick from his booted foot put it in a soft pile of pine needles.

"Well done, Phoebe." Nathaniel proudly displayed the fish for all to admire. "Here's one for tonight's supper table."

The children all applauded. At her sister's encouragement, Phoebe took a brief bow, then returned to her spot. Her eyes sparkled with excitement and her cheeks were flushed with pride.

Above her head, Harriet's eyes met Nathaniel's.

His were warm, intimate and cheerful. She felt anew the knife of betrayal and turned away. She turned to once again place some physical distance between them, but in her haste to flee she did not notice the tree root in the middle of the path. Her feet stumbled and she tripped over the gnarled wood.

Catching her arm, Nathaniel kept her on her feet, but once she was steadied, he did not withdraw his touch. Harriet's arm prickled at the contact. She was suddenly aware of every heartbeat, every breath of air that coursed through her body. And his.

"Is anything wrong?" he asked. "You seem distracted."

Harriet didn't trust herself to speak, so she remained silent. Nathaniel raised his eyebrows, but all Harriet could manage was a tight, closed-lipped nod of dismissal.

Oblivious to the undercurrents, the children turned their attention back to the stream and the schools of fish they believed were waiting to be caught. Even Gregory managed to stay in place for an impressive ten minutes. When his fidgeting became too distracting, Nathaniel set him to the task of digging up worms, a job the little boy took to most enthusiastically.

Harriet remained beneath her tree, tapping her toe impatiently against a rock. It was sheer torture for her to sit here and say *nothing*, while these questions swirled about in her brain. Yet she forced herself to be calm. The air was warm, the sound of the water babbling in the stream restful, the merry spirits and excitement of the children infectious.

It all seemed so natural, so ordinary. Still, it could not distract Harriet from her pain.

"I've caught one!" Jeanne Marie shrieked. The

little girl yanked on her pole, imitating her sister's actions, but when her hook came into view there was nothing to be seen. "Drat! That nasty old fish got away."

Jeanne Marie sighed with exaggerated tragedy, and attempted a swoon on the rocks, which nearly landed her in the cold river.

Harriet found herself scrutinizing the gesture. Maybe the children's mother had been an actress? That would certainly explain Jeanne Marie's flair for dramatics. And why Nathaniel would not marry the woman.

Actresses were known to live by a different code, a different set of rules. They did not feel it was a betrayal of their family or their upbringing to enter into such an arrangement with a wealthy man.

Yet, how much had the poor female sacrificed for her love? 'Twas often said that a man cherished his mistress while he tolerated his wife. Was that the case here? Had Nathaniel taken a proper, acceptable wife and then lavished all his attention and affection on his mistress?

Had they shared a love that crossed the barriers of class, a love that was so pure it survived without the legal bonds of matrimony, without the honor of wedded security? Was that why he now showed such great concern and regard for his children even if he did not publicly acknowledge them as his own?

"I am tired of fishing and I'm tired of digging for worms," Gregory announced suddenly. He picked up a sizable rock and tossed it into the river. "Let's do something funner."

"More card games?" Jeanne Marie asked, as she quickly abandoned her pole and scrambled down from the rock where she had been waiting, unsuccessfully, to catch a fish.

Phoebe caught the tip of her sister's pole just before it slid into the rushing river. "I don't want to play cards. 'Tis no fun if Uncle Nathaniel wins every hand."

All three turned to stare accusingly at Nathaniel. He struggled manfully to hide a grin. "How about a race? The first one back to our picnic blanket wins."

He didn't have to suggest it twice. In the blink of an eye, all three children had disappeared down the path, shoving and laughing and running as hard as they could.

Caught off guard, Harriet scrambled to follow them, but Nathaniel grabbed her arm and held her back.

"A word please, Miss Sainthill."

"The children—"

"Will be perfectly fine on their own for a few minutes."

Harriet did not like the commanding look he was giving her. Earlier he had ceased questioning her mood and seemed to accept it. That apparently had changed and Harriet was not about to listen to a lecture on her attitude or answer any questions about it. So instead she straightened her spine and went on the attack.

"Will you answer a question, Mr. Wainwright?"

"Certainly."

Harriet wasted no time. "Will you promise, nay, will you swear that your answer is the solemn truth, that you are being honest and forthright, no matter how you imagine I will react?"

Nathaniel jerked his head up. "I shall endeavor to try," he said slowly. He rubbed his palm on his breeches, looking decidedly uncomfortable.

Harriet straightened and looked him directly in the eye. "Are you married?"

His reply was a choking sound of pure astonishment.

Harriet did not know what to make of that reaction. Astonishment at the question or was it amazement at being confronted with the truth? She waited, but he did not answer.

"Do I really need to repeat the question?"

"No." The harsh answer echoed through the tree tops. "And no." The muscles around his lips tightened. "No, you do not need to repeat the question and a most emphatic no to that same unbelievable question. I do not have a wife, nor have I ever been married." His voice grew pensive. "And I cannot, for the life of me, imagine what possessed you to ask me such a ridiculous, inappropriate question."

Harriet glared at him for a long, angry moment, then lifted her chin. "No, I don't suppose you would."

She took advantage of his momentary shock to hurry away before he had a chance to say another word.

Though she greatly feared a chance encounter with Nathaniel, Harriet knew it was important that she look in on the girls before retiring to her own chamber, especially since the young nursemaid who slept in the girls' room had reported they suffered from nightmares and were often restless during the night.

Tonight, all appeared calm when Harriet entered the room. The nursemaid was dozing quietly on her pallet near the fireplace and Phoebe and Jeanne Marie were in the large bed, tucked safely beneath a warm coverlet.

Harriet made her way across the room to examine the burning candle she had instructed be left lit each night. Confident that the taper was long enough to last until dawn and the flame was not near any of the bedcurtains, Harriet turned to leave. Yet as she began to walk away she heard the sheets rustle.

Approaching the bed, Harriet saw Jeanne Marie's legs moving and noticed that her head was jerking from side to side. The child was also making incoherent mumblings and uttering short, painful little cries.

Distressed to realize the child was having a nightmare, Harriet came closer. As the little girl's thrashing grew increasingly agitated, small beads of sweat began to form on her forehead.

"Wake up, Jeanne Marie." Harriet cradled the sweet face in her hands, rousing the child from the demons of her nightmares.

Her arms flayed out, then Jeanne Marie's red-rimmed eyes opened. Pale and frightened, the child stared at her. "Miss Sainthill?"

"I am here," Harriet answered, sitting on the edge of the bed. "There is no need to be frightened."

"I had a bad dream." The little girl's mouth worked as if she were trying very hard not to cry.

"Would you like to tell me about it?"

"No."

Harriet brought out her handkerchief and dabbed at the moisture on the child's forehead. "Were you dreaming of fishes? Sometimes when something new and exciting happens during the day, we dream about it at night."

Jeanne Marie shook her head. "I like fishes, even though I didn't catch any. They wouldn't make me feel sad."

"Something made you feel sad?"

"Yes, sad." Jeanne Marie's brow wrinkled into a frown. "And lonely."

"Really?" Harriet began combing the little girl's hair with her fingers. "Even with Phoebe and Gregory and me and your Uncle Nathaniel around, you still feel lonely?"

"Uh, huh. I was missing someone very special," Jeanne Marie yawned, nuzzling herself closer to Harriet. "I was missing my Mama."

Harriet felt her pain and understood from her own experience how difficult it was to lose a mother at such an early, impressionable age. "It is sometimes frightening when we no longer see and talk with and just hug and kiss those special people we love so much. But that does not mean the love we felt for them and the love they had for us is gone. We carry it always, deep inside our hearts."

"Uncle Nathaniel says Mama still loves us very much." Jeanne Marie's face contorted into a frown of incomprehension. "But why did she go away? Why did she die?"

A sharp pain pierced Harriet's chest. "I don't know. All I can tell you is that someday you will begin to feel a bit better about it."

"Really?"

"I promise." Harriet settled her hand between the child's shoulder blades and rubbed lightly back and forth.

"Lady Julienne always helps me feel safe."

"I know." Harriet sighed. The missing doll was certainly contributing to the anxiety the child was feeling. "I can make no promises, but perhaps there is a way for Lady Julienne to come to Scotland. Do you think she would enjoy living here in this large, old castle?"

Jeanne Marie took a quavering breath. "Can she

stay in my room? I don't have such terrible dreams when Lady Julienne is with me."

"Where else would she stay?" Harriet smiled. "Certainly not with your Uncle Nathaniel."

The child attempted an answering grin. It tore at Harriet's heart to see how brave she was despite her real distress. "Will it take a long time?"

"Probably. I know you remember it was a long journey when you came to Scotland. And you must understand that I cannot be certain Lady Julienne will be able to make this very long trip. I can only promise to try my best to get her here."

The gratitude that shone in Jeanne Marie's eyes gave Harriet a start of guilt. She truly would do all that she could to bring the child's toy here, but there were no guarantees. Perhaps it was a mistake to tell the little girl of her plans, for she might be worse off if the plan failed.

Yet Harriet knew from experience it was important to have hope. And she really would do everything she could to make sure that somehow that doll was put back where it belonged—in Jeanne Marie's arms.

"It probably would be best if you don't mention anything about this to anyone else," Harriet suggested.

"May I tell Phoebe?"

"Well, only Phoebe. After all, she too is a girl and will understand such an important matter." Harriet let out an exaggerated yawn. "Time for sleep. Scrunch down under the covers so I can tuck you in nice and tight."

The child followed her instructions without protest. "Will you stay until I go to sleep?"

"If you wish."

"Thank you. I do believe you are the finest governess I have ever known," Jeanne Marie whispered solemnly. Then she turned over and cuddled next to her sleeping sister.

High praise indeed, from a child who at the very most had known perhaps one or two others in that position. Still Harriet knew the words came directly from Jeanne Marie's heart and they touched her deeply. She swallowed hard and got to her feet.

Stepping into the shadows of the chamber, Harriet waited until the quiet, even breaths told her the little girl was deep in slumber.

The moment she arrived back at her room, Harriet lit several candles and pulled out a leaf of her private writing paper. It took her a long time to compose the letter to Mrs. Hutchinson, housekeeper of a grand mansion in Grosvenor Square. She wanted to convey a sense of urgency and importance, but it was difficult to strike the right balance when discussing a child's toy.

Yet Harriet was hopeful that the children's fond memories of the housekeeper illustrated an accurate account of her character. When she was finally satisfied with the missive, Harriet sanded the page and sealed the letter.

Early the following morning she sought out one of the stable lads, remembering the boy had mentioned he had a brother who had recently joined the army. The young soldier would be leaving for his post in a few days, passing through London before making the journey to the continent. It would take weeks, perhaps even a month for a letter to reach England from this remote area, but if this soldier was willing to take the letter for her, it could arrive in record time.

Harriet forced herself to ignore the stab of guilt as she handed over the missive and several coins to the eager young recruit. The boy seemed to be an honest, sensible lad and Harriet believed he would indeed deliver the letter personally.

Knowing she was going directly against the orders of her employer made this a more difficult task, but Harriet had never been the type of woman who took the easy, expected path when making decisions. Right or wrong, she often had only the courage of her convictions to give her the necessary strength to face down censure and adversity.

She was not acting on a whim or out of defiance or spite. Jeanne Marie was hurting and Harriet saw a way to ease that suffering.

Still, she could not fully suppress the nagging feeling that she was somehow betraying the trust Nathaniel had placed in her by so blatantly ignoring his command to let the matter of the missing doll drop. Harriet could only hope that when Jeanne Marie was united with her beloved toy, that feeling would disappear.

Chapter Sixteen

The next week was tense and the week following that put Harriet's nerves even further on edge, for she found herself spending a good deal of her time eluding her employer. Yet it seemed that the more she tried to retreat, the more determined he seemed to seek her out. Perhaps it was the challenge of the chase. Or the fact that she was the only gentlewoman with whom he had any contact.

Whatever the reason it created an awkward situation. She knew very well that when he chose to be, Mr. Wainwright could be a most charming man. He was also too darn attractive for his own good. And her peace of mind.

It took continuing effort, but Harriet did succeed in keeping her distance from him. She never allowed herself to be alone with him, fearing she would remember the closeness they once shared, fearing she would once again long for those things a responsible, respectable governess would *never* even imagine when thinking of her employer.

As was proper, it was the children who became Harriet's main concern. It took a few attempts, but eventually she was able to establish a daily routine that provided a good balance between lessons and leisure. The youngsters' abilities were as varied as their ages, but they proved to be eager students, with quick minds and inquisitive natures. She was pleased with their progress, however, Harriet often worried about the future they would one day face.

Illegitimate children were not welcomed into the better families and Harriet feared the girls would have a difficult time making an advantageous match. No matter how genteelly raised, Society and the landed gentry would not look favorably upon those born on the wrong side of the blanket. The wealthy merchant class had an even stricter moral code, so a generous dowry would make little difference to them.

Gregory would have a slightly easier time, as men often do. He would have an opportunity to establish himself in business or perhaps even own a small parcel of land. Yet many doors would remain closed to him due to the circumstances of his birth.

Harriet was not one to bemoan the unfairness of fate, however she knew in her heart that if given the opportunity she would eagerly express her opinion to Mr. Wainwright on the consequences of bringing three innocent souls into the world when he had no intention of giving them his name.

She therefore redoubled her efforts to prepare the children to face the world. If she could give them a sense of self-worth, a thick skin, and a positive outlook, they would be far better equipped to face the many challenges in life that awaited them.

Harriet began taking all her meals with the children. She thought it best to spend as much time with her charges as possible and this arrangement also had the added benefit of separating her from Mr. Wainwright. He, however, quickly put his foot down and insisted that the children and their governess join him each evening for dinner.

It was a highly unusual request and Harriet assumed that after one disastrous meal the invitation would be rescinded. But Mr. Wainwright appeared only mildly distressed when the children spilled their drinks, refused to eat anything remotely resembling a vegetable, and had heated discussions on a variety of topics ill-suited for the dinner table. Harriet made a few, gentle corrections during the first meal, but since her objective was to discourage spending this time with Mr. Wainwright, she quickly gave the children free rein in their behavior and expressing their opinions.

It did not produce the desired effect. More often than not, Mr. Wainwright was amused by the youngsters' antics. She would feel his gaze upon her, knowing he was trying to catch her eye, to share the humor of the moment. Harriet stubbornly kept her attention focused on her plate or her charges, never once directing her gaze toward the head of the table where Mr. Wainwright sat.

Her one relief was that the young trio seemed unaware that anything was amiss. They began to look forward to the evening meal, thriving in an environment where they were encouraged to relax and enjoy themselves. They competed unabashedly for Mr. Wainwright's attention, but he showed no overt favoritism to any of them, treating the children as if each one was the most important one.

These dinners were difficult, but Harriet soon discovered that nights were hardest of all. Either she would lie awake for hours, eventually drifting off to a fitful sleep in the very early morning, or she would immediately fall asleep upon entering her bed, wake up, and then toss and turn restlessly through the wee hours of the morning.

Realizing it was useless to stay in bed when she could not sleep, Harriet began leaving her bedchamber and wandering down to the library in the middle of the night. She would work on her lessons, browse through a book or just relax in front of a warm fire. There was something calming and strangely soothing about being awake and in the center of the castle while the rest of its occupants slept. At least it made her sleepless nights more tolerable.

Tonight had been especially long. No sleep at all had come, so Harriet left her bed, donned her robe, put on her slippers and lit a candle. She made her way quickly through the long corridors, down the stairs to the second floor, then turned the corner.

Nathaniel suddenly appeared at the end of the hallway. Harriet choked back a gasp of surprise. Apparently she wasn't the only one who had difficulty sleeping at night. He was dressed in the same scarlet red dressing gown he had worn on the night she arrived at the castle. The vibrant color of the garment emphasized his dark, sculptured features and broad shoulders. He looked fierce and menacing and disturbingly handsome.

The moment she spied him, Harriet came to an abrupt halt. Thinking fast, she blew out her candle, then waited in the darkness, her ears alert to the slightest sound. She prayed he had not seen her. All remained quiet for several long minutes and Harriet dared to breathe a small sigh of relief. Using her right hand, she felt along the stone wall and carefully began to ease her way backwards.

A burst of light fell on her path. He knew she was there! Harriet turned, moving her feet as quickly as she could, her mind intent only on flight.

"Running away again, Miss Sainthill?"

The challenge in his voice brought her to a dead stop. Harriet slowly pivoted on her heel to face him.

"I was not running, I was walking. Back to my chamber. 'Tis rather late."

"Yes, it is late." He gave her a critical eye. "Since you are in your nightclothes, I assume you could not sleep. Were you headed toward the library, perchance?"

Harriet did not answer, knowing she should not be surprised that he was aware of her late night activities.

"If the library was indeed your destination, pray, do not let me chase you away."

It was very difficult, but Harriet managed to ignore the barb. She crossed her arms under her chest and placed a stern frown upon her face. "I am not in danger of being chased away by you or anyone else."

Mr. Wainwright pulled a grim face. "Then why do you run in the opposite direction every time I find myself within a few feet of you?"

"I am not running away," Harriet insisted. "I have responsibilities and duties that require an enormous amount of my time and attention."

"You are chillingly distant whenever we converse."

"Nonsense." Harriet shivered involuntarily as a cold draft whirled around her ankles. "I am merely too busy to engage in idle chatter."

"The hallway is drafty and cold," he said. "There is a warm fire in the library. Let us continue our discussion in comfort."

Biting back a retort, Harriet regarded him cautiously. It might be better if they did clear the air between them. Yet, did she dare risk being alone with him? "I prefer the door to remain open," she said as she preceded him into the library.

He raised his eyebrows, but Harriet would not be deterred. Above all, she could not allow the physical bond that seemed to ignite between them whenever they were alone to take hold. The library was cozy enough without the added privacy of a closed door.

"Will you have a seat?" he offered cordially.

"I do not care—"

"Sit down." He made an impatient sound. "Please."

Her cheeks heated. She had forgotten what a large man he was, how formidable he could be, especially when he wanted something.

She thrust herself into the nearest seat, realizing too late it was a couch. Mr. Wainwright took immediate advantage of her mistake by seating himself beside her. The couch was small and narrow. He pressed against her arm and thigh, causing the chills she had been feeling to change to heat.

The air around them hummed. She briefly considered moving herself to a chair on the far side of the room, but that seemed to give too much importance to the fact they were seated so closely.

"It appears that I have done something to deeply offend you, Harriet. I would like to offer an explanation or an apology, yet in truth, I know not what I have done."

She looked at the fire, wondering why he had finally decided to say something. "I am merely the lowly governess, sir. My opinions and feelings are of no consequence to you."

To her chagrin, instead of being angered or put out by her response, he laughed. "Hell, I must have really put my foot in it this time if you are using your best governess tone with me."

His joviality stung. "How lovely that I can provide some much needed amusement for you, Mr. Wainwright."

His expression quickly sobered. "You have deliberately placed a wall between us, Harriet. I thought we were friends."

"We are nothing but employer and employee, sir," she stated dully.

"My God, woman, we are far more than that," he replied harshly.

"If we were, then you would not feel compelled to keep the truth about my charges from me."

"I do not understand what you mean."

Harriet narrowed her eyes and stared at him, then determined he was trying much too hard to look innocent. "Reality is not always pleasant, but as adults we must face the consequences of our actions." She stood on her feet and walked towards the open door. "You have tried to hide the truth from me, but I have eyes in my head and a perfectly functioning brain. I know your secret, Nathaniel."

There, she had said it. Inexplicable tears began to sting the back of her eyelids. Harriet balled her hand into a fist and pressed it hard to her lips to keep the sobs at bay. Until that moment she had not realized how deeply she had been hurt by his duplicity, how betrayed she felt by his lack of trust.

Nathaniel scrambled off the couch and blocked the doorway. "What did you say?"

She lifted her chin defiantly. "I have figured out what you were so determined to hide from me. I know your secret."

"You cannot!" He slammed the door so hard that a book fell off the shelf and crashed to the carpet.

Harriet let out a hollow laugh. Even now he would lie to her, deny the truth? "It does not take a scholar to see the true relationship between you and the children. Why, 'tis plain as the nose on your face. Or should I say the eyes in your head? You are certainly entitled to your privacy, but when your pride or whatever it is unnecessarily causes the suffering of an innocent child I will not stand idly by and allow that to happen."

His eyes darkened. His breath came in short puffs and then he moved towards her, so quickly she had no time to react. With a snarl of barely controlled rage, Nathaniel grabbed her shoulders roughly and pinned her with his body against the wall. "Bloody hell, Harriet, you are making no sense. What have you done?"

Her heart pounded in her throat. Though she told herself he would not harm her, she was very much aware of his superior physical strength. "I have followed my conscience, sir."

"I do not know what that means!" His voice was raw and rasping. "Tell me exactly what you have done."

A long, awful silence hung over them. "I wrote a letter to Mrs. Hutchinson and asked her to send Jeanne Marie's doll to Hillsdale Castle. I also enclosed directions and a small draft to cover the cost of sending the toy."

Harriet felt Nathaniel's entire body jolt. Slowly, his hands fell away, though his eyes seemed to be burning through her. With shaking hands she adjusted her robe and the nightgown beneath it. She could still feel the imprint of his fingers, the hard muscled length of him pressing her back against the wall.

His loss of control had frightened her. Not because she feared any physical danger to her person. Oh, no. His reaction let her know that something awful had happened. A niggling worm of doubt and fear began to build within her.

"I expressly forbade you to contact anyone from the children's past. Why would you do such a thing?" The tension stretched taut. "If you know my secret, you know that the children must remain hidden or else I am in danger of losing them."

Harriet let out an exasperated groan. "But they are your children. You have the right to take them wherever you wish."

He released a long breath and admitted, "No, I do not. I am not their legal guardian. At least not yet."

"Of course you are, you are their father."

"Their father!" The words exploded out of Nathaniel. "Bloody hell, is that what you believe?"

"That is what I know. Your resemblance to Gregory is marked. 'Tis obvious that he is your son."

He looked completely taken aback. "Gregory is not my child, though I wish to God he were, for then I would not be in this mess." Frustration shone in his dark eyes. "Tell me again about the letter."

He looked so righteously indignant it caused Harriet's stomach to twist uneasily. *Gregory was not his son?* "Jeanne Marie is utterly miserable without her doll. I assumed you did not wish to contact the household because you were ashamed of her illegitimate birth, so I wrote the housekeeper a note and arranged for the letter to be delivered to London."

"How did you know about London? And Mrs. Hutchinson?"

Harriet swallowed thickly. She was not proud of how she had obtained the information. Haltingly she told him the rest, including how she had arranged for a quick delivery of the missive through the stable lad's brother.

"All my careful plans destroyed with a simple letter about a doll." He leaned back against the door and rubbed his hand over his face. "Phoebe, Jeanne Marie, and Gregory are the children of the legitimate marriage between my older brother, Robert and his wife, Bernadette. They both died earlier this year after contracting influenza. I know that Robert wanted me to raise his children, but no codicil had been added to his will.

"My claim for guardianship is being contested by my uncle and he managed to get himself appointed temporary guardian. Since he is only interested in their fortune and their power, I took the children from London, without his knowledge or consent and hid them in Scotland. For their protection."

"Their power? What power can children possess that would interest an adult?"

His gaze became distant. "We are not a merchant family. Gregory is a duke. The eighth Duke of Claridge, to be precise."

Harriet let out an ironic laugh. The lies went even deeper than she thought, though she had always suspected Nathaniel was not who he claimed. "I always had difficulty believing you were a wool merchant."

"I am Nathaniel Bennet, Baron of Avery. Amazingly our paths never crossed in Society, though I knew all about you." He executed a deep mocking bow. "I should have recognized trouble when I saw it, and had the sense to send you packing the moment you crossed this threshold, dripping with rain and filled with a spirit no typical governess would ever display. My better judgment urged me to do so, and fool that I am, I ignored my own intuition."

Harriet froze in confusion, her face draining of all color. "You knew who I was?"

He responded with an arrogant snort. "Didn't everyone? The infamous Miss Harriet Sainthill. The talk, and scandal, of the Season."

His mocking tone cut her sharply. She went utterly still, as a searing pain burst through her chest. Humiliation and betrayal threatened to crush her spirit, but Harriet struggled to think beyond the swirling emotions. He was angry and lashing out. And she was hardly blameless in this situation. Her rash, headstrong actions had put the children in danger and ruined Nathaniel's plans to keep his family safe. *But she had not known!*

She owed him an apology. She understood the importance of family, the instinct to protect those you loved. Yet it would take her a few moments to gather her thoughts, to somehow formulate the words. Harriet stared down at her fingers, twisting her hands restlessly against the front of her robe. Finally, she was ready to speak.

But when she looked up, he was gone.

Nathaniel felt a light sweat break out on his face as he stormed down the hall. He knew he could not have stayed one moment longer in that library without saying something far more hurtful to Harriet. For a few moments, shock, anger, and utter frustration had taken control of his tongue and he had needed to strike back.

All his careful planning and cautious execution, gone in an instant. Ruined by a woman who thought she knew better than he, who was determined to see her own way in everything and damn the consequences to everyone else.

True, it was not entirely her fault. She had jumped to some fairly outrageous conclusions, and by using those as the basis of making her decisions had ruined everything. His natural children! What kind of amoral creature did she believe him to be?

But it was not her erroneous conclusions that upset Nathaniel so much. It was knowing that she had deliberately ignored his command to let the matter of the doll drop, that she had willingly disobeyed his orders. He had underestimated her will, had not realized that underneath she was such a terribly managing and stubborn female. And his lack of judgment had cost them all.

Given the circumstances, Nathaniel knew his initial explosion of anger was justified, yet when he remembered Harriet's pale face, staring so accusingly at him with those soul searching eyes, he felt sick down to the depths of his own soul. For the person he was most angry with, and disappointed in, was himself.

He believed he had been so careful, so clever, when in truth, he had made a total muddle of it all. He had placed the children's safety in jeopardy and hurt the feelings of a woman who was only guilty of caring too much and having too much character to let an injustice go unanswered.

Cursing loudly, Nathaniel entered his room and slammed the bedchamber door, wondering how in God's name he was going to fix this mess.

Once back in her chamber, Harriet was uncertain how long she sat in reflected solitude. Her body felt tired and lethargic while her mind refused to allow itself any rest, any break from the myriad recriminations that kept rolling through her thoughts.

She forced herself to climb into her bed. Her motions were automatic, as if her body were somehow detached from her mind. She lay on her back, pulled the covers to her chin and stared at the ceiling.

Her eyes stung, her chest hurt. Harriet could feel the emotions choking her throat. She squeezed her eyes tightly shut, trying to release the pain, but the tears would not come.

Frustrated, she clenched her hands into fists and punched at her pillows. The gesture only served to render her breathless. The pain did not ease at all.

Harriet realized she would never sleep until she spoke with Nathaniel, until she had a chance to explain herself and make him understand her mistake was an honest one.

Throwing off the covers, she leaped from the bed and put on her robe. Crouching low, she searched for her slippers, but could not locate them. Deciding it was not worth wasting the time, she left the room in bare feet.

The cold stone floor barely penetrated her troubled mind. She was focused completely on the meeting to come. When she arrived at the other side of the castle, Harriet could see a light shining from beneath Nathaniel's door. She hesitated, debating if she should knock, then realized it might be best not to bother in case Nathaniel refused her entry. Instead, she pushed the door open and boldly walked inside.

A low growl sounded. Harriet looked to the area near the hearth and saw a great black mass of fur rise from the floor.

"Hello, Brutus," she said calmly.

At her friendly greeting, the hound stretched out his back legs, then came padding across the room, tail wagging. She gave him a good rub behind the ears and was rewarded with several warm, wet licks on her hand.

Nathaniel stalked to the door and held it open wider. "Out!"

Oh, no, Harriet thought in dismay, he won't even give me a chance to explain. She lifted her eyes beseechingly, then belatedly realized he was speaking to the dog.

Nathaniel repeated the command. Brutus slowly moved forward. Head down, with a sulking posture and a mournful look, Brutus left the room. As he slunk past his master, Harriet thought she heard Nathaniel mutter something under his breath. It sounded like a single word. *Traitor.*

Nathaniel had removed his scarlet robe and was dressed in a shirt, cravat, waistcoat, and jacket. Faint, silver moonlight filtered through the room, adding illumination to the few lit candles. In this setting Lord Avery looked every inch the haughty, arrogant, superior aristocrat, and Harriet marveled at herself for not seeing it sooner. Or perhaps she had known, but did not want to admit it.

He was exactly the type of man she feared most, an opinionated male with a backbone of steel and a true heart. How impossibly ironic that she had fallen in love with him and, despite the deceit and the hurtful exchange of words, she loved him still.

"I would ask only that you please listen to me," Harriet began. "I know I have made a total muck of things and I know how angry you are, but you must know that I meant no harm.

"I am rash and stubborn and once I set my mind on a course 'tis almost impossible for me to stray from it. 'Tis a failing, I know, and I promise I have learned a most valuable lesson. Never again will I be so quick to rush to judgment and action."

Harriet instinctively reached for his hand. He allowed it, but his fingers rested cold and unresponsive in hers.

"I love the children and I acted on that love. I could not bear to see Jeanne Marie so distressed and upset, especially when I felt it was so easily within my power to alleviate her suffering."

Harriet scanned Nathaniel's face for any sign he was listening to her, at least attempting to understand. His expression was stoic, his eyes hard, but at least he had not tossed her from the room like poor Brutus. Harriet forced herself to continue.

"I know now that I should have consulted you before writing—"

"And who knows what I would have told you?

Certainly not the truth." He frowned, then lifted her hand to his face and gently brushed his lips across her knuckles. "We share the blame equally, Harriet. My wariness and distrust and continuing uncertainty are also responsible for this mess. I was wrong to be so harsh with you earlier. My words were cruel and unforgiving, yet I humbly beg your pardon."

Harriet drew in a breath and tried to refocus her mind. He released her hand, then he smiled at her and Harriet felt her heart begin to melt.

"It is true that I did recognize you when you first arrived at the castle," he explained. "My first thought was that you must leave. Not because of any ludicrous scandal, but because you had the reputation of being an intelligent woman and I feared you would discover the truth.

"Later, I found myself drawn to you. Your character, your strength, your alluring female charms." His expression grew soft, tender. "Alas, I found I could not entertain the idea of you leaving me. Ever."

His eyes had never looked so dark. She felt as though she was drowning in their intensity. "Truly?"

"Lord, yes." He framed her jaw, bent his head and captured her lips in a searing kiss. Long and lingering. Fully and completely. The pressure of his mouth against hers made Harriet feel so dizzy it was a wonder she could remain standing.

Reluctantly they drew apart. They exchanged glances, knowing this would need to wait until a few more things were settled.

"What are you going to do?" Harriet asked, taking a deep breath to steady her heartbeat. "How will you protect the children from your uncle?"

"I will take them to Edinburgh. They will be safe under Duncan's care until I can plot my next move."

Harriet nodded, agreeing it was a sensible solution. "I'm coming with you."

"No. Under the circumstances, I think it is best if you return to your brother's house in England."

"I will not be left behind," she retorted, her temper rising.

"Harriet, I do not do this to punish you. This is a messy situation. My uncle is a vicious man. Trust me, you do not wish to be involved."

"I am already involved."

Nathaniel dropped his head back with a vexed groan. "You are, aren't you?" He straightened his shoulders, kissed the tip of her nose, then smiled. "And I am a selfish bastard for feeling glad of it. Dearest Harriet."

A knot of fear buried so deep inside her began to slowly unravel and flow away. He was not rejecting her, he was not about to abandon her because she was less than perfect. He accepted, and cared, and dared she hope, perhaps even loved her.

Well, there was only one way to be certain. She was going to have to call upon her much vaunted courage and expose the secrets of her own heart.

Taking a deep breath, Harriet shut the door softly behind her and deliberately turned the key. The lock clicked into place and at the sound, a shiver of sexual anticipation raced down her spine. Then, with a pounding heart and a sultry smile, Miss Harriet Sainthill turned eagerly to embrace her destiny.

Chapter Seventeen

She moved forward, invitingly drawing herself nearer. Nathaniel went very still and searched her eyes with his own. "Harriet."

His voice was a warning that she appeared not to heed. She continued to walk toward him slowly, her lush form silhouetted in the firelight.

"I want this, Nathaniel. Truly."

"But it is wrong."

She stopped walking for an instant and tilted her head to look at him, startled, as if he was making no sense.

"It cannot be wrong when I feel down to my soul that it is right. So very right."

"Harriet, you know my situation is tenuous. I cannot give you what you need. What you deserve."

She gave a sultry laugh. "That is not what you have told me in the past."

Nathaniel had the grace to blush. "That was before."

"Before what? Before I decided I wanted you in my bed?"

"No before—" he stopped abruptly, knowing he could not yet say the words to her. Not when his future was so uncertain. Not when he could offer her nothing beyond a few pleasure-filled nights.

She sensed his confusion. "Are you not a rake, my lord?"

Nathaniel's jaw tightened. "What does that have to do with anything?"

"Why, I have often heard there are advantages to bedding a rake. Perhaps I would like to know if that is true."

A sting of anger rose up in him. "Is that all I am to you? Convenient bedsport?"

She laughed. "What do you think?"

Bloody hell, he was acting like a lovestruck fool! This vulnerable rush of emotion was the most disconcerting feeling he had ever experienced. But he also knew it was among the most honest of emotions because it spoke to the depth of true love he felt for Harriet.

Startled at the strength of his feelings, he turned his head away. She caught his hand and pressed it to her cheek. "Is it really so awful?" she whispered.

Nathaniel's mouth thinned. He brushed her cheek with the back of his fingers, then bent until his face was even with hers. She was gazing back at him with all the longing she seemed to feel inside. His lips were within a breath of touching hers.

She moved forward. When their lips met he knew that one kiss would never be enough to satisfy him, and that one night with her in his bed would only cause him to yearn for more.

Despite his resolve to remain detached, excitement stirred in his stomach and quickened his blood. The kiss ended as he almost savagely pulled away. Nathaniel's gaze traveled over her body. The robe and nightgown she wore could never be construed as sensuous garments, but standing so close to the firelight rendered them nearly transparent.

He could clearly see the outline of the firm, uplifted breasts that seemed made for his mouth, the long, slender legs that would perfectly wrap around his waist, the nest of dark curls so delicate and sweet at the apex of her thighs. She was curved and round and lushly inviting. Her flesh was like pure alabaster beneath the garments. Heat and vitality and passion seemed to radiate from her.

How he longed to skim his hands over that sleek, cool flesh. To touch her where she ached and wanted. Where he would make her skin flush and her loins burn. As his did.

She angled her head, rose unsteadily up on her toes and brushed her lips over his for another kiss. The rush of sensation nearly brought him to his knees. But this was wrong, wrong!

His body tensed. "Stop."

"I cannot." She gave him another sweet, tender kiss on the lips. "Nor do I want to."

His answer was a groan.

Harriet's hands slid beneath the fabric of his coat, up to his shoulders, her touch as soft as silk. "May I help you remove your coat, my lord?"

Nathaniel dragged the sharp air into his lungs and slowly blew it out again. She smelled of soap and lavender and something uniquely her own. The warmth of her body and scent enveloped him as she pressed herself closer and pulled the coat over his arms.

A melting heat unfurled low in his gut and desire flooded every part of his body. The primitive drive to possess her increased, for knowing that she wanted him so intensely somehow made his own need even stronger.

"The waistcoat comes next," she whispered, her trembling fingers fumbling with the buttons.

Her efforts were awkward, but she was determined, and soon that garment joined his coat on the floor. The realization that she was willing to give herself to him, set his brain afire. Nathaniel touched her face, tilting her chin so that their eyes would meet.

"I can make no promises," he rasped, needing her to know the truth, even if it risked an abrupt end to this moment. He made a weak attempt to pull away from her.

"I understand. All that matters is that you want me."

"That was never in doubt."

She softly kissed his mouth, then brushed her lips along his jaw. When she reached his throat, she bit it playfully, then licked the spot where she had sunk her teeth.

Her kisses, the feel of her soft, round breasts pressed so tightly against his chest was such a tempting distraction. For a moment Nathaniel let himself experience the bliss. Then he dragged himself away.

"This isn't right, it isn't honorable. Being a mistress isn't good enough for you, Harriet. You deserve much more than I can give you. Marriage, respectability, a proper place in society. Perhaps someday it will be possible, but now it is not."

She smiled, shrugged philosophically and attempted to loosen his cravat. "I'll not lie to you. All those things used to matter to me a great deal, but that is no longer the case. For me, marriage is of limited importance. I do not need that sanction of society to express my heart. I love you, Nathaniel, and this feels very right to me."

She loved him? How was that possible? After all he had done, he hardly deserved such a precious gift. Yet deep inside he dared to hope that it could be true.

"Harriet—"

"Nathaniel." Her bosom heaved as she took a long breath. "I will not be your mistress. I will not come to your bed in return for your money and your protection." She gave him a long, earnest searching stare that made the hair on the back of his head rise. "I will not be your mistress. But I will be your lover. Most gladly. Most willingly."

His cock pulsed violently. But even more amazingly, his heart filled with love. A part of him knew he had no right to accept this gift. Harriet was unique. She deserved far more than he could pledge to her at this moment in time.

As if sensing his reluctance, and his weakening resolve, she pressed herself even closer. Chest to chest. Groin to groin. He swore he could already taste the passion on her skin. Her eyes, and her body, let him know she would hold nothing back, she would give him everything. And more.

"I shall be your most willing, seductive, sensual lover. Please, don't turn me away, Nathaniel."

Her voice was vulnerable, pleading. She stared at him with open emotion. Her flesh felt hot beneath the layers of her robe and nightgown. Nathaniel struggled to think beyond the moment, but it was impossible. Somehow tomorrow would take care of itself. Tonight he was going to satisfy the uninhibited expectation in her eyes, and love her as she deserved. With supreme intensity that would shatter every last vestige of control. Both hers and his.

His arms reached out and caught her up in a tight embrace. His hands splayed firmly over her back, pressing her to him, pulling her close. He kissed her deeply, one hand cradling her head, holding her still as he ravished her senses.

She was a tall woman, but she felt so delicate, so fragile in his embrace. Yet when she moaned enthusiastically and pressed her breasts and belly against him, Nathaniel knew she was all woman. He rolled his hips into hers, lifting her feminine mound against his hardness, deliberately tormenting her with the heat and hardness of his erection.

The need to caress her bare skin became a quest. He pulled at the tie that closed her robe, then pushed it off her shoulders. Nerveless fingers made quick work of the tiny row of buttons on her nightgown. She shuddered slightly as he tugged firmly on the neckline, easing one breast out. He shaped the weight of it in his hand.

"You are so beautiful, Harriet," he whispered, admiring the creamy pale flesh and taut dusky pink nipples.

He heard her soft gasp of anticipation as he bent his head and then she cried out with pleasure the moment he fastened his mouth over that pert nipple. Her body surged forward, arching against him. He suckled for a long time, first tender and gentle, then rough and hungry.

He placed his hand on her thigh and rucked up her nightgown. She was deliciously bare beneath the garment and his hands told him what his eyes could not see. Her flesh was warm and delicate, smooth perfection waiting for his touch.

Nathaniel settled his hand on her taut stomach, rubbing in smooth circles. Harriet moaned, arching against his hand. She opened her mouth and kissed him as though she would consume him, moving her hips restlessly. His fingers gradually arrived where she needed them most. He touched her curls, running one finger down through them and felt her shiver. His touch was tender and light as he spread those plump inner lips searching for the tender peak hidden by the protective folds.

She flinched with pleasure and cried out as he rubbed his finger over the sensitive nub. "Quiet, my sweet." He nipped the lobe of her ear, sinking his teeth into the tender flesh. "You don't want to wake the household, do you?"

Her answer was an incoherent mumble of passion. Nathaniel smiled, delighted at her response. Now that she was slick with moisture it was easy to press his middle finger deep inside her. Using his thumb he teased and swirled at the core of her womanhood, holding her upright as she bucked and jerked. With delicate precision he pulled out, then slid in, deeper with every stroke, until her body relaxed even further, allowing him to touch the fragile barrier of her virginity.

He knew it was there. Knew that she had known no other man. Yet feeling the proof, knowing with absolute certainty that he would be the one to show her the depths of her passion unleashed something inside him voracious and feral and powerful.

Long ago she had loved another man. But that was over and now, now she loved him. And she was about to express that love in the most basic and trusting manner—by giving herself to him. Nathaniel worried briefly if he was worthy of it, yet when he looked to the feelings in his heart he knew he would guard that trust, and her love, for the rest of his life.

The need to lay claim to her, to brand her as his own slammed into him hard. *Mine! She will belong to me and to no other man!*

He stroked her a few more times, entering then retreating until her appetite peaked and his male pride was shining for having brought her to such wanton delight. Deciding it was time to heighten her pleasure even more, Nathaniel abruptly pulled away.

"Why did you stop?" Her voice was breathless, almost desperate.

"For this," he whispered mysteriously, sinking to his knees. He lifted her nightgown above her hips and pressed himself forward.

The unexpected caress made her shriek. Nathaniel smiled at her reaction. Her shock was endearing and incredibly arousing. She tried to back away from him, pushing deliberately at his shoulders, but he splayed his palm firmly across her naked buttocks and held her in place.

Nathaniel again set his lips to her curls. Harriet trembled violently, trying to shift her hips as he softly laved her delicate flesh. Determined, he continued the assault, applying the full expertise of his tongue until her hands were frantically clutching his hair and pulling him closer.

He knew it would take but a few more moments to bring her to a shuddering climax, but he wanted to wait, wanted to put himself deep within her warmth when she achieved that final bliss.

"I need you on the bed," he muttered. Scooping her up in his arms, he deposited her in the middle of his bed, literally sweeping her off her feet.

She was delightfully tousled, her thick dark hair falling over her brow and shoulders. Her lips were swollen from his kisses, her cheeks glistening and flushed in the flickering light. She looked sinful and innocent all in the same moment, with her modest nightgown gaping open and her breasts spilling forward, their tips soft and rosy.

He quickly pulled off his untied cravat, then hurled his shirt to the floor. Thankfully he had not bothered to put on his boots. Nathaniel easily tore off his breeches and small clothes. His erection sprang free, throbbing for release.

As he approached the bed, Nathaniel's nostrils filled with the perfume of female desire. He grew harder, feeling powerful and strong in the face of his own passion. He sucked in slow breaths of air, trying to will his rigid body to stay in control so he could savor every touch, every caress.

"How strange." Harriet licked her lips in a quick, nervous motion. "I thought you would appear vulnerable in your nakedness, but instead you seem even more powerful."

She reached for him and they touched each other with heated desperation. Her nightgown was a barrier that was quickly dispensed. She splayed her palm on his chest, and Nathaniel felt the tension coil in his spine as she bent her head and eagerly kissed his nipple.

Her hot, wet, open mouth blazed a trail of fire down his body, causing him to jerk. It was almost too much mindless pleasure to endure! He knew it was important for her to feel this sense of feminine power, to explore and experience, to feel comfortable and familiar with his body, yet it was torture that brought his pleasure to an almost uncomfortable level.

Nathaniel knew he was not strong enough to let her continue, for his control grew more brittle by the second. When her questing fingers circled his penis, he clenched his jaw. When her thumb stroked down the length and then flicked over the aching head he groaned. But when her lips slid teasingly along his swollen flesh and she took him deep in her mouth, he practically flew off the bed.

"Almighty Christ, where did you learn a trick like that?"

"I am merely imitating your actions." Harriet lifted her head. "Did I do it wrong?"

Nathaniel dragged in a huge breath and flipped her on her back. "You did it most deliciously right, Harriet, but I have other things I'd like to try first."

"You do?"

One look at her lovely face, glowing with excitement and anticipation and Nathaniel knew he could no longer hold back the fierce desire which had completely possessed him.

"I have saved the best until I felt you were ready." He kissed her hard on her lips, then raised his knee and pushed it between hers, parting her thighs, spreading her legs so he could settle between them. Nathaniel braced above her, supporting his weight on his forearms, trapping her gaze with his own. "You are mine," he declared, thrusting powerfully.

He heard her sharp intake of breath, but it did not slow him down. He thrust again and felt the fleeting resistance of her maidenhead give way. She was wet with desire, hot with wanting, yet impossibly tight.

He bent his head and touched his lips to hers. She blinked, then let out a long, shuddering breath. Her breasts swelled against his chest and the ache inside him increased. Nathaniel raised himself above her, then thrust forward. Harriet gasped, then instinctively relaxed as he deepened the penetration. He had never been an overly patient man and he wanted and needed her too desperately to hold himself back.

He breathed a throaty endearment into her ear, telling her how good she tasted. His words seemed to distract her from the temporary discomfort.

Harriet's fists closed tightly around the muscles of his upper arm, just as her inner flesh accepted the pulsing length of his shaft.

He filled her with deep, heavy surges. She made a sound of surprise and clung to him, her eyes widening.

"Hook your legs around my waist and draw yourself closer," he whispered. "Then relax your body and let me do the work."

Harriet's movements were awkward and disjointed and Nathaniel was unsure she had heard his demand. He pushed his hips hard against hers. Her head thrashed and she whimpered as her body rose with his.

"Show me," Harriet cried out in frustration. Nathaniel grabbed her knees, dragged her body closer, and guided her legs around him.

The room was soon filled with the sounds of their labored breathing and low moans. Flexing his hips, Nathaniel thrust harder. Harriet let out a choked whimper and surged towards him. She called out his name and he knew she had reached her pleasure. He held himself perfectly still, cherishing the exquisite moment, feeling her quiver around him, the hot spasms pulling him deeper into her warmth.

Nathaniel knew his own passion was close to a blinding culmination, but he wanted to hold it off, to savor this moment of sheer perfection. He squeezed his eyes shut and tried to hold back the fierce desire which seemed to possess him, but it was impossible.

Moaning, he buried his face in the curve of her neck. Clutching her hips, he entered her again with long, decisive, possessive thrusts. Shuddering violently, Nathaniel spent himself inside her, his seed spurting forth, claiming her in the most basic way.

He held himself in place even after the spasms had passed, treasuring the incredible sensation. A feeling of rightness settled over him. Never before had an interlude with a woman created such intense emotions, such physical perfection. And she was only a novice! Who knew what heights they would reach once he had an opportunity to tutor her.

They were both breathing in long gasps, labored, heavy and erratic. Nathaniel flipped himself onto his back, and instantly felt bereft. He hauled Harriet into the crook of his neck and nuzzled her cheek. A great wave of protectiveness flowed over him and he felt the need to protect her always, to provide physical and emotional comfort whenever she was in need.

He dozed briefly, exhaustion overtaking him. When he awoke, Harriet's body was curled around his. Turning Harriet's face towards him, Nathaniel smoothed the hair back from her forehead. She opened her eyes, then lowered her gaze and stifled a yawn.

"Tired?" he asked.

She shook her head, lifted her head and stared at him with a soft, contented gaze. He liked the drowsy, well-pleasured smile that curved her lips. Liked it even more, knowing he was the one who put it there.

"Are you all right?" he asked.

"It hurt a bit more than I expected." She rifled her fingers through the mat of dark hair on his chest " 'Tis a curious sensation, having part of someone else's body inside your own."

Nathaniel smiled. Leave it to Harriet to discuss

the physical aspects of their union first, setting aside the emotional and spiritual connection. Since his brain was too mellow to function he would allow it. At present.

"Any regrets?" he asked.

She shifted her position and her lips brushed his ear. Then she caught his earlobe between her teeth and suckled gently.

"Dare I assume that means you are content?"

"You may," she replied with a laugh.

There was a protracted pause. Nathaniel placed his hand between her thighs. Thanks to her playful petting, he was rapidly developing another erection. "How do you feel? Are you terribly sore?"

She buried her head in his shoulder, but not before he saw the telltale flush of red in her cheeks. "How shockingly intimate we have become in so short a time," she said primly. Lifting her head, she flashed him a wicked wink, then began to nibble on his chest. "I find I rather like it."

Propping herself up on one arm, Harriet studied her handsome lover with unabashed delight. The shadow of his beard gave him a ruthless look, but she knew his masculine power was tempered by a good and gentle heart. His chest was moving with regular rhythm, but she felt too energized to join him in sleep.

Harriet moved her legs restlessly, hoping the action might disturb his rest. Yet with the movement she felt her body ache in places she never imagined could ache. It didn't matter. These strange sensations had brought her boundless joy, for they proved she was a thoroughly loved woman.

It was late, or rather early in the morning. She

knew she should let him sleep, but it was somehow impossible to keep her hands from touching him. Anywhere. Everywhere. She ran her fingertips lightly across Nathaniel's nose. It twitched. Charmed, she did it again, then blew a wisp of breath strong enough to ruffle the hair that had fallen over his forehead.

"Stop it," a deep voice admonished.

"Oh, you're awake. Wonderful."

Nathaniel's' eyes opened. "And why aren't you sound asleep? You should be faint with exhaustion after all that rigorous exercise."

"Well, I am not."

"Should I feel insulted?" Humor lit his gaze.

"I don't know." She tilted her head and gave him a saucy stare. "You are, after all, my first lover, so I can make no comparison. Perhaps a younger man would be a more suitable choice for my passionate nature."

"There will be no other in your bed, save me, and don't you dare to forget it." As if to emphasis the point, Nathaniel gripped her firmly around the waist.

Her heart leapt at his declaration. Yet she knew there were far more important matters that needed to be settled before they could devote their complete attention to their ripening relationship.

"Now that I have truly ruined everything, how do you suggest we escape from the Highlands without getting caught?"

Nathaniel's lips brushed against her forehead. "You haven't ruined things, Harriet. You have just managed to make life a wee bit more challenging."

"Do not joke about this Nathaniel. I am upset enough without you making me feel worse."

He lifted his head off the pillow. "We both agreed

that casting blame would serve no useful purpose. And I do share the responsibility."

"Yes, but not equally."

"Fine. This time you win the prize for being the bigger fool. I daresay next time it will be me."

Harriet stretched out her legs, curling her toes. She knew she bore the brunt of guilt, but Nathaniel was right. Whining over it was just a waste of time. "We cannot let your uncle find the children. I agree our best chance is with Duncan in Edinburgh, yet I hesitate to leave the castle. Perhaps it would be better to hide out here than risk getting caught on the road?"

Nathaniel sighed and ran his hand lightly down her back. "Hillsdale Castle is very isolated. I have no wish to confront my uncle or a gang of Bow Street Runners without a lot of witnesses. I think my original plan of seeking refuge with Duncan is the best decision. In fact, if at all possible we should leave today."

"I too have been thinking about the journey," Harriet said. Nathaniel's hand strayed to the top of her breast and began to inch its way toward her nipple. Harriet's pulse sped up and she lost her thoughts. Grabbing his wrist, she pulled his hand off her bosom and placed it on her shoulder. "We should travel to Edinburgh disguised as a family. A prosperous merchant, his wife, and three children. It might make our trail harder for the runners to follow."

"It might."

Nathaniel started the swirling rhythm again, this time with the tip of his finger on a delicate spot behind her ear. Harriet swallowed hard and tried to force her brain to concentrate. "The children and I have been studying Scottish history and it has given me a rather radical idea."

"I've never known you to have any other kind."

Harriet frowned, deciding to let that comment pass. Besides, his talented hands were once again on the move, heading down her side towards the top of her thighs. "The children have been especially taken with any stories of courage and bravery. We recently read an account of Flora MacDonald, a great Scottish heroine. Apparently she saved the young Pretender's life after the defeat at Culloden by dressing him as her maid. In spite of the enormous reward of 30,000 pounds, no Highlander betrayed the prince."

"Such is the loyalty of the Scots," Nathaniel remarked. "For one of their own."

"Well, I think we should borrow from their example of dressing a man as a maid."

Nathaniel's hand ceased all movement. "You want me to dress as a maid?"

Harriet burst out laughing. "Lord, now that would be a sight! I believe I would pay 30,000 pounds to see you in an apron and mobcap."

"Even for the safety of the children, there is no way that I—"

"Oh, calm down." She giggled once more. "If there are runners scouring the countryside, they will be looking for someone traveling with two girls and one young boy. However, if we take a page from Scottish history and dress Gregory in a simple gown, we can pose as a merchant family traveling with their three daughters. If we are unlucky enough to encounter anyone searching for us, it might render us beyond their notice."

"Dress Gregory as a girl? Won't that scar him for life?"

Harriet wrinkled her brow. "Well, McTate wears a skirt and he seems none the worse for wear."

"Be serious."

"I am." Harriet lifted her gaze to his. "You can talk as much as you like about sharing the blame for this mess, but I do feel a keen sense of responsibility and I need to do everything within my power to set it to rights."

"Then we shall try this plan." Nathaniel turned his head and glanced out the window. " 'Tis dark outside, but dawn cannot be far away. Will it take you long to be ready?"

"We will need a few hours to prepare Gregory's new wardrobe. I am certain I can fashion one or two of Jeanne Marie's simpler gowns to fit him." Harriet grimaced. "Of course the real challenge will be convincing him to wear the dress."

"We might have to bribe him," Nathaniel agreed. "Do you think he would accept a bank draft?"

Harriet let out a loud giggle and punched Nathaniel playfully on the chest. He grabbed her arm and held her so she could not land another blow. They tussled briefly on the bed and Harriet soon found herself pinned beneath her lover.

His eyes heated to darkness. He began nibbling, then lightly sucking the tips of her fingers. The strange action made her feel restless and was stirring up excitement in the oddest places.

Her breath hissed from between her teeth. "What are you doing?"

She caught a glimpse of his sly grin of triumph just before he rolled her onto her back and covered her with his body. "We have hours till dawn," he said. "Let's make the most of it."

Chapter Eighteen

Jerome Brockhurst did not particularly like horses nor riding on horseback for an extended period of time. As a Bow Street Runner, his normal territory encompassed the streets of London and his normal mode of transportation was on foot or if the distance was far and time of the essence, a hired hackney.

He was familiar and comfortable with London's back streets and rookeries, the criminal haunts and seedier areas that teemed with swarms of people packed into ramshackle buildings. He relied on a network of informants and a brotherhood of fellow runners to solve his cases and apprehend the criminals responsible for those crimes.

Aside from taking pride in a job well done, Jerome often felt a great deal of personal satisfaction from setting certain wrongs to right, of ensuring that justice and fair play prevailed at the end of the day. It was part of the reason he became a runner in the first place and part of the reason why he continued in this dangerous profession.

He had been selected personally by the chief magistrate to handle Lord Bridwell's unusual case and from the beginning there had been many elements that had troubled him. Cases involving young children were rare, events of kidnapping by a relative even more of an oddity. Jerome knew there were important facts about this incident that Lord Bridwell was desperately trying to hide and that had hindered the runner's progress and heightened his suspicions.

He had been instructed by Lord Bridwell to keep a close eye on the household servants, particularly the housekeeper, Mrs. Hutchinson. Jerome did so with extreme reluctance, feeling it was a waste of time to pester the woman. Yet amazingly a clue was uncovered when purely by chance, he intercepted a letter addressed to the housekeeper.

Jerome was honest enough to admit it was more a result of fate than skill that he even saw the letter. He was leaving Lord Bridwell's home at the exact moment a young soldier, with a thick Scottish burr, mistakenly came to the front door asking for Mrs. Hutchinson. Before the lad could be directed to the servants' entrance, Jerome had accepted the letter, read it, reported its contents to Lord Bridwell and informed his lordship he would start preparations for the journey north immediately.

Jerome's initial suspicion was that the letter might be a hoax, some form of trickery designed to put any investigators off the scent, but further conversation with the housekeeper confirmed the existence of the much beloved doll mentioned in the correspondence. Additionally, the runner had discovered papers within the mansion that shed new light on the intricacies of the case.

So armed with this knowledge, and an even further commitment to see justice done, Jerome set out for the Highlands. He had been riding for days, as his sore backside would attest, and was heartily sick of fresh air, large mountains and suspicious villagers.

Still, he pressed on. Time was of the essence and there were no guarantees the children would be at the castle when he finally arrived. Lord Avery had proven himself to be a clever foe, though clearly he had made a very wrong choice when employing a governess.

On this day, an early start and sunny skies had done little to lift Jerome's spirits. By day's end he was even more discouraged, for he had not traveled as many miles as he had planned. Yet it would be foolish and unsafe to travel these unknown roads at night. Fortunately an inn came into sight in the bottom of the valley, nestled beside a small lake. Welcoming lights gleamed in the windows and smoke curled in great billowing clouds from the chimneys.

The scent of freshly cooked meat and other culinary aromas drifted through the evening air. Jerome licked his lips hungrily, hoping there would be room for him in this quaint establishment.

He guided his horse cautiously into the graveled yard and swung down from the saddle. A lad hurried over to attend him.

"Hallo, sir. Are ye 'ere fer a meal or will ye be stayin' the night?"

"I need a bed and my horse badly needs rest." Jerome replied. He unfastened one of the saddlebags and removed the satchel that contained his personal items and a few clean clothes. He flipped the lad a coin, instructing him to feed the horse a substantial dinner and settle the animal comfortably in a stall for the night.

A pleasant commotion greeted Jerome when he

entered the inn through the brightly painted yellow door. The taproom was crowded, most likely with local men eager for a night of companionship and hearty ale. As a lone male traveler he attracted little attention, until he opened his mouth. Though he tried to keep his tone low when inquiring after a room, his broad English accent attracted the notice of many.

The noise of conversation dimmed and several guests craned their necks to have a look at him. Jerome straightened himself up to his full height and frowned at the staring men. It took a few tense seconds for them to give up the intimidation game and turn their attention back to their drinks, dinner, and conversation.

Jerome took his time making arrangements for his room, hoping to engage the innkeeper in conversation. He had learned over the years it was far easier to solicit information when the individual you were questioning had no idea the information was of value.

However, the runner soon discovered the barrel-chested Scot who owned the inn was not the type to engage in idle chatter.

"Who did ye say ye were lookin' fer?" the innkeeper asked in a suspicious tone.

"Ah well, there's the rub," Jerome replied. "I'm hoping to find Lord Avery, but you know how queer the aristocracy can be at times. He might not be using his title on this journey. But he wouldn't be difficult to spot, since he's traveling with three young children, two girls and a lad."

Casually Jerome slid twice the price of the room across the worn oak counter. The innkeeper's eye lit up and he reached eagerly for the coins, but the runner quickly snatched them back.

"Have you seen them?"

The innkeeper darted a look in Jerome's direction. "What's this feller done?"

"Nothing." Jerome could feel the innkeeper watching him very closely. "I have news I know Lord Avery will be eager to receive. A great-aunt has remembered him most kindly in her will." He smiled and patted the breast coat of his pocket. "In addition to the modest wage I'm earning for this job, I'm hoping his lordship will reward the man who brings him word of his sudden good fortune."

Understanding creased the innkeeper's brow, then he scowled. "No, I hadna seen him nor the wee bairns."

Jerome nodded and pushed the coins back across the counter. All of them. Since he needed the rest he intended to sleep soundly tonight. There was no sense in putting his neck in jeopardy by annoying the innkeeper. Besides, Lord Bridwell was paying all the expenses for this journey.

Craving privacy, Jerome had his meal sent to his room. It was delivered by a buxom tavern wench who was clearly disappointed when he thanked her politely and sent her away, even after she went to the trouble of thrusting her breasts nearly in his face to show her interest. Jerome held no illusions about his masculine appeal—he assumed the woman had heard about his payment to the innkeeper and was hoping to supplement her income.

He quickly ate the surprisingly tasty meal of beefsteak, pigeon pie, potatoes, and stewed cucumber, washing it all down with a half bottle of tolerable wine. His belly full, Jerome made good use of the water provided in the washstand to scrub away the day's grime.

He packed away his soiled garments and pulled out a clean shirt for tomorrow's journey, knowing it would be important to leave at first light. It was such a great relief to be off his horse for a few hours that he barely noticed the lumpy mattress and less than pristine sheets when he crawled into the bed.

For safety's sake, Jerome slept with the papers he carried beneath his pillow, uneasy with the thought of having them out of his possession. This was among the more interesting and challenging cases he had ever undertaken, and as his eyes drifted closed the runner could not help but wonder how Lord Avery would react when he arrived on the doorstep of Hillsdale Castle.

"I won't wear it. It's for girls."

"Come on, Gregory, it will be fun," Nathaniel cajoled with an encouraging grin. "If you put the frock on we can go down to the kitchen and play a trick on Mrs. Mullins. She'll never guess that it is you."

For a few seconds the child seemed to be considering the notion. Then his eyes darkened and he shook his head emphatically. "No! I won't do it!"

Harriet pinched the bridge of her nose and pondered the best way to handle the situation. On one hand, she could not blame the child for feeling awkward about putting on the gown, yet the disguise would certainly be of benefit to all of them. On the other, it seemed cruel to force him. And while the disguise would be a help, it certainly wasn't a necessity. Perhaps if Gregory understood the gravity of the situation it would be easier to obtain his cooperation, but neither Harriet nor Nathaniel were about to frighten the child with the truth.

"Do you remember the daring story we read

about Bonnie Prince Charlie and his escape from Culloden?" Harriet asked.

Gregory wrinkled his brow. "The lady saved him."

"Exactly. But the prince was very brave and very clever. He dressed up like a maid to fool the men who were chasing him and thus avoided being captured. Don't you think it would be fun to be like him?"

"Will everyone else dress up?"

"Ah, no, not today," Nathaniel replied. "Perhaps later."

"After we arrive at Uncle Duncan's house in Edinburgh," Harriet added, not wanting to mislead the child into thinking the following day they would all be wearing odd clothing.

"I don't want to play this game and act like that Scottish man," Gregory decided. "Uncle Nathaniel tells me all the time that I am an English gentleman."

"That's right, you are," Harriet said. "I bet you never even knew there was another Prince Charles who was said to have escaped right beneath the nose of Cromwell's troops dressed as a lady."

"He later became king," Nathaniel interjected. "Of England."

"Was he the one that got his head chopped off?" Phoebe asked.

"No, that was his father, King Charles I," Harriet answered distractedly.

Nathaniel made a disgusted noise in the back of his throat. "My God, what are you teaching these children?"

"The truth." Harriet shushed him with a hard look and turned her attention back to Gregory. The gown she had altered for the little boy to wear was extremely plain, with no lace or ribbons or bows. She held it up to show him, explaining how easy it would be to put on.

"Give it a try, Gregory." She smiled hopefully. "You'll be just like the princes."

A shadow crossed his face. "But I'm not a prince. I'm a duke."

Nathaniel let out an exasperated groan. "He can be amazingly stubborn at times."

"It must be a family trait," Harriet muttered, then shook her head. "Clearly the child has made up his mind. I don't think we should force him."

"I agree." Nathaniel regarded his nieces for a moment, stroking his chin thoughtfully. "Maybe it would be easier to dress the girls as lads. They are far more cooperative than Gregory and traveling with three young sons would still lend us some type of disguise."

Harriet worried her bottom lip. She had already wasted an hour this morning altering the gown for Gregory. If they were to pose as a merchant family, the clothes the children wore must be of good quality. "We have no appropriate male clothing to alter for the girls and no time to make new garments."

"Maybe we can purchase something in the village?" Nathaniel suggested.

"I have not ventured into town, nor seen any of the shops, yet I doubt there are any ready-made clothes to buy that would suit our purposes."

"Then I'll ask Mrs. Mullins if she has any ideas."

Harriet frowned skeptically. "Housekeeper, chief cook, and now clothes merchant. Is there anything Mrs. Mullins cannot do?"

"Speak so we understand her?" Nathaniel quipped.

When they entered the kitchen, Mrs. Mullins rose from her chair and set her knitting basket on the floor. She listened carefully to their most unusual request, her shrewd eyes contorting with curiosity. But the housekeeper did not ask why they needed the garments and within the hour provided exactly what was needed: two changes of clothing for each girl.

"Wherever did you find these?" Harriet asked in amazement as she examined the garments.

"I dinna have tae ask twice," Mrs. Mullins replied proudly. "Many village families were eager tae lend a hand, 'specially when they knew it was fer the young lasses who were so generous in sharin' their dolls. We dinna forget a kindness."

"We thank you most sincerely, Mrs. Mullins. And please express our gratitude to those who were so willing to aid us in our time of need."

Unlike their brother, Phoebe and Jeanne Marie were excited to try on the outfits. They pranced and paraded in front of Harriet, mimicking Gregory's, Nathaniel's, and even Duncan McTate's proud male stance. Their antics put a much needed smile on Harriet's face, but she cautioned the girls repeatedly it would be best if they kept quietly in the background whenever they encountered other travelers.

They left the castle far later than originally planned, but the weather was clear and it seemed prudent to take advantage of the dry roads rather than wait until morning. Harriet, a nursemaid, and the three children rode in the coach while Nathaniel traveled beside them, mounted on a fine bay mare.

As the coach rumbled across the wooden drawbridge, Harriet turned for one final look at the ancient castle. It glimmered in the brilliant sunshine, a solid tower of strength and pride. Harriet felt a strange tug at her heart, realizing she was going to miss living within those ancient walls. Given the vagaries of life, she wondered fleetingly if she would ever have an opportunity to set eyes on it again.

* * *

Harriet was pleased with the inn Nathaniel selected. It was small, yet large enough to give them anonymity, and most important, clean. The innkeeper and his wife were friendly and seemed genuinely happy to have them as guests, especially when Nathaniel provided a generous tip for bringing in the luggage, fetching hot water for washing, and providing a hot meal in one of the two private dining rooms.

Harriet was nervous about Phoebe and Jeanne Marie making their first public appearance dressed as boys, but as Nathaniel had predicted no one so much as glanced in their direction when they were guided through the public rooms to the private dining room.

All three youngsters were glad to be released from the confining interior of the coach and provided their usual lively dinner conversation. Observing their antics made Harriet's heart swell with emotion. The mutual affection between the children and their uncle was glaringly obvious and it had deepened and strengthened in the weeks they had been together.

Silently, Harriet renewed her vow to do all that she was able to ensure that Nathaniel was appointed the children's legal guardian. For while the children did indeed have a great need of him, he too needed those youngsters.

When dinner was over, Harriet and Nathaniel hustled the trio through the tap room and up the stairs to the rooms that had been secured for the night. Nathaniel had expressed delight when he had seen their accommodations. Their rooms were at the back of the inn, which meant they would be quieter, though this establishment did not have the amount of traffic a city or even a crowded village would generate.

Apparently the key appeal was the configuration of the rooms. They were connected by an interior door, but the second, slightly smaller room had no separate access to the hallway. Nathaniel immediately decided the children would sleep in the smaller room. If there was danger of any sort, the intruder would have to go through him to reach them.

As they prepared for bed Harriet bustled between the two rooms. The hot water in the pitcher that so pleased her was not met with the same enthusiasm by the children. There was a disagreement about which bed the trio would share and a general complaint that the air smelled of vinegar. They were not impressed when Harriet insisted that was a sign of cleanliness and one they should look for in future whenever staying at an inn.

"Well, I believe I have finally settled them down for the night, though I would not be surprised if one of them needs a drink of water or a trip to the privy soon," Harriet said as she walked into the larger room to bid Nathaniel good night.

He was pacing with restless energy. He had stripped to his shirtsleeves, but still wore his black riding boots and snug breeches. The aura of male power and strength permeated the chamber, for his presence seemed to fill the room.

"I've been waiting for you." Nathaniel smiled warmly at her, his mouth tilting in a sexy, inviting manner. A shiver of pure sensation rolled down her spine, yet Harriet did her best to hide her reaction and cautiously back away from him.

"I intend to sleep in the other room with the children," she said.

"And leave me here all alone?" He strode towards her then stopped, his booted feet apart, his hands at his back. "The bed looks very comfortable and is certainly large enough for two." His voice was low and husky and dripping with illicit temptation.

Harriet ruthlessly tamped down the impulse to fling herself in his arms. "Really, Nathaniel, what would the nursemaid think if I spend the night with you?"

"That I am irresistible?"

Harriet rolled her eyes. "Servants who don't respect you will not follow orders nor work with diligence," she said primly. "Besides, if the children have need of me during the night, I must be close at hand."

"What of my needs?" He captured her in a loose embrace and pressed his lips to her neck.

Harriet turned her head. "Your needs will have to wait."

"Hmm, sometimes I really dislike how you are always so damn responsible." He cushioned his words with a gentle caress of her cheek. "Yet I am forced to agree it is safer for us all if I remain undistracted for the night and you, Miss Sainthill, are a most devilish distraction."

Soothed by his teasing comment, Harriet grinned. Though she could not fault him for his honesty when remarking on her sense of duty, it was an aspect of her character that she could only temper, but never change. Thankfully it appeared that Nathaniel had decided he was going to cope with it. And her.

Harriet watched the candlelight flicker over his handsome face and felt herself flush with heat. His desire for her was evident in his expression and the hardness of his body and it still amazed her that he felt this strongly toward her.

She felt almost light-headed remembering the sight of his bare chest and rippling muscles, recalling with delight the intimacies they had shared, the heights of passion and pleasure they had achieved. A tangle of erotic images kept playing through her mind, filling her senses to overflowing.

It was difficult to keep her hands to herself. She wanted so badly to kiss him, to fondle and caress, to tease and excite. She pulled away, yet the primal urge was so strong, Harriet could not resist the opportunity to rub herself playfully against him as she walked past on her way to her room.

Nathaniel's armed snaked out quick as a flash. Holding only the back of her neck, he drew her towards him. Harriet laughed softly, allowing her common sense to flee for just a moment. She closed her eyes, savoring the satiny warmth of his mouth against hers. Time slowed as a pulsing urgency sprang throughout her body. He was like a drug she craved, an addiction she could not control, for he freed her spirit and allowed the love in her heart to flow unrestrained.

She gave herself permission to indulge for a few mindless moments, pressing herself closer so that their bodies melded together. "You must not kiss me," she mumbled, twisting her head and burrowing it into his shoulder.

"Why?"

" 'Cause it is sheer torture when you stop."

He laughed, hugging her tight. Then he moved his hands to the front, cupped her breasts and began to slowly, erotically knead them. The nipples hardened. Harriet could scarcely breathe. She raised her head from his shoulder. Passion darkened his eyes. Passion, hunger, and love.

"Ah, sweetheart, don't you know our fates are forever entwined?" he whispered. "That it will always be torture for me whenever we are separated?"

Something quivered inside of Harriet. His words brought her joy, but there was an edge of fear creeping into her consciousness that she could not ignore. Their future was so uncertain, their chance at happiness fleeting. Though she fervently hoped otherwise, she knew these few nights might be all they would ever have together.

Harriet clung to Nathaniel. This tangible bond they shared completed the person she was, made her stronger, more confident. The physical pleasure he could so easily create was raw and intense and it spread like wildfire through every inch of her body. But the emotions he evoked were solid and lasting and even more miraculous.

He maneuvered her to the far side of the room. Harriet waited expectantly to be tossed onto the bed and was surprised to instead feel the solid hardness of the wall against her shoulder blades.

He pressed his full length against her. Harriet wet her lips, staring at him. As if sensing her desire, Nathaniel dipped his head and kissed her thoroughly, his tongue delving deeply, his hips rotating in a slow, grinding motion that made her shiver with pleasure.

Beneath her gown, Harriet felt her breasts tighten and tingle. The familiar restless ache began along her inner thighs and up into her belly. The yearning and need to give of herself and in turn be filled by him caught and held her heart.

"We must stop," Harriet whispered. Yet even as she spoke the words her hands slid down his shirt front, around his waist and beneath his coat. She stroked his muscled back, then reached lower, grasping his tight buttocks through his breeches.

He groaned and pressed her harder against the wall. Harriet leaned her head back and sighed with contentment as he wove a trail of kisses down the curve of her neck. Her chest rose and fell rapidly, her body trembled against his.

Because she was unable to do otherwise, Harriet surrendered to the madness. She knew no other man would ever make her feel this way, would make her shudder and want and need. Only him.

"Is there a lock on the door that connects this room to the children's chamber?" she asked in a raspy, unsteady voice.

"Yes, and I turned the key the moment you entered the room."

She inhaled slowly, then lifted her head and stared at his handsome face. His eyes were sensual and heavy-lidded, his smile tender and loving. Harriet felt her body grow wet with anticipation and need.

"I'm so desperately in love with you," she whispered, almost in awe of the depth of her feelings.

"I hardly deserve such an incredible gift," he replied solemnly. "But I'm not fool enough to turn away from it."

His hands moved caressingly up and down her back. Harriet arched her hips forward and settled her belly against the thickness of his arousal. Then she moved and she felt his penis flex, growing even harder.

Between her own legs the dampness and pressure grew. It brought on a restless ache that he seemed to know of, for he thrust his hand beneath her gown and his clever fingers quickly found the slit in her drawers. She parted her legs so he could touch her more completely, caress the spot where she ached and needed him most.

"This is how I want you," Nathaniel whispered. "Burning with desire for me. Needing me. Craving me."

His fingers circled her moist cleft, then thrust

inside the warmth. The heat of his touch ignited fiery sparks in her blood. Harriet trembled so much she could only remain upright by clinging tightly to Nathaniel's broad shoulders.

He stroked her until she was panting and tossing her head, until she was nearly out of her mind. Then she felt his rigid flesh probing her body and she knew he meant to take her there, standing against the wall. Her legs convulsed around his waist and she opened her body wider.

"Now," she gasped loudly. "I want it now."

He sank into her and Harriet joyfully clenched her muscles around the thick hardness inside her. The intense pleasure made them both shudder.

Nathaniel thrust harder and Harriet rocked forward against him, eager to meet the heat of his straining body, eager to surrender to his possession. His breath sounded harsh in the stillness of the room, while her own voice was a whimper of feminine need. Harriet wrapped her arms around Nathaniel's broad shoulders and held on tightly, arching her spine, opening herself wider so he could press deeper into her body.

It was an exquisite sensation, this urgency that built so quickly yet could be sustained for as long as Nathaniel desired. She felt him reach down between their bodies. His touch was clever and knowing, circling and teasing the most sensitive part of her flesh. He drew heat and fire from her and she shattered, shuddering under the force of his thrusts and the unbearable pleasure of his caress.

His orgasm quickly followed hers. A moan burst from between his clenched lips. Harriet felt the hot rush of seed spurt into her in a powerful stream. The muscles in his neck corded as he drove into her one final time, until the last drop of his passion was spent.

Nathaniel fell against her, gasping for breath. They clung to each other in the aftermath, pulses still racing. Gradually Harriet realized her feet were once again on the floor. Yet when she tested the strength of her legs, she found she could not yet stand unassisted.

Harriet rested her head against the base of Nathaniel's throat and listened to the frenzied beating of his heart. It was such an utterly perfect moment. She had opened herself up to this man physically and emotionally and he had accepted her completely. A lethargic sense of peace and contentment settled over her.

It was difficult to leave. The bed looked so inviting and Nathaniel looked even more irresistible. Her hunger had been sated, but she knew it was a momentary satisfaction, knew that she would soon be craving his touch. But as Nathaniel had so glaringly pointed out earlier, Harriet also knew her duty.

She straightened her clothing as best she could, then smoothed back her ruffled hair. Nathaniel reached for her but she slid out of his embrace, not allowing herself to be tempted.

"Good night," she whispered.

With a final farewell kiss, Harriet slipped quietly into the other room. Everyone was sound asleep, including the nursemaid. Harriet gave a quick look upon the children, then stripped down to her chemise and curled contently in her bed, feeling safe and loved and surprisingly happy.

Chapter Nineteen

It was chaotic in the morning and no simple task getting the children dressed and fed and ready to face another day of traveling. To obtain their co-operation, Harriet promised if the weather held they could each take a turn riding on horseback with their uncle. This promised treat of escaping the confines of the carriage held great appeal and put all three children on their best behavior.

All the rushing and organizing left Harriet a bit frazzled and she did not listen closely to Nathaniel's instructions. Misunderstanding his orders, she arrived too early in the inn's yard. Their carriage had not been brought out and neither Nathaniel nor the male servants were in evidence.

Harriet felt conspicuously exposed standing in the open yard, the bright morning sunshine beating down on her bonnet, but the children were happy to be outdoors. The girls especially seemed to enjoy the freedom of movement their male attire provided. Since there was a greater chance of getting into mischief and revealing their disguise inside the inn, Harriet decided to stay, figuring that Nathaniel was no doubt in the stable at this very moment, seeing to his mount and supervising the harnessing of the coach horses.

"You're it!" Gregory called out merrily. He poked his sister in the ribs and scurried behind Harriet, clutching on to her skirts.

Jeanne Marie giggled and lunged forward, attempting to retaliate. Gregory skillfully evaded her tag, so Jeanne Marie took the easier choice and tagged Phoebe. The older girl smiled and reached for her brother. Gregory pulled away and the game began in earnest.

Harriet allowed it to continue for a few minutes. "Enough!"

Recognizing her tone, the children stopped. Harriet nervously touched the cap on Phoebe's head to make certain it was secure and admonished both Jeanne Marie and Gregory to stay close by her side and away from any of the horses being brought into the yard.

"Jane, please walk down to the stable and look for Mr. Wainwright. Inform him that we are ready to leave," Harriet instructed the nursemaid. She knew it was partially her own over-active imagination, but Harriet felt edgy and anxious without Nathaniel. The sooner she and the children were safely settled inside the carriage, the better.

Jane, an affable, middle-aged widow, curtseyed slightly and left on her errand. Harriet took a deep breath and gathered the children close. She glanced about the yard, relieved to see that everyone seemed focused on their own business.

Yet Harriet still remained vigilant, her eyes darting about the yard every few minutes, alert to danger and also anxious for a glimpse of Nathaniel.

Her attention however was soon caught by the figure of a man standing several yards away. She assumed he had been a guest at the inn and was waiting for either his carriage or mount to be brought around.

Yet after five minutes Harriet knew it was not her nerves or imagination. The stranger was definitely regarding her and the children with keen interest.

Harriet's heartbeat quickened. The hairs on the nape of her neck prickled slightly, the classic warning sign of danger, yet she could hardly claim the man was acting in a threatening manner. She supposed it was a rather uncommon sight to find a gentlewoman and her three young children standing alone and unescorted in the yard of an inn. Perhaps the man was merely curious about them.

As Harriet tried to calm her thrashing pulse, her gaze accidently met the stranger's. He nodded and smiled at her in a polite manner. Harriet bit her lip to control her gasp. An over-reaction to such an innocuous gesture would certainly draw more curious eyes.

"I'm relieved to see it is such a fine day for traveling."

The low rumble of the stranger's voice startled her and Harriet stiffened slightly. He had moved closer and stood but a few feet away. A touch of nausea attacked her stomach. Her first instinct was to grab the children and run for the stable, her second was to open her mouth and scream at the top of her voice.

"Yes, 'tis a lovely day," Harriet replied, proud of the steadiness of her voice. She inclined her head marginally, so as not to appear terribly rude, but also turned her shoulder in a dismissive gesture to discourage any further discourse. *Where was Nathaniel?*

"I imagine the children are quite a handful in the carriage. Boys don't take kindly to being cooped up for long periods of time. Do you have a long distance to go?"

An edge of annoyance momentarily pushed aside Harriet's fear. The man certainly had no right to be so bold and daring merely because she had acknowledged his presence. It was highly improper for him to approach her and try to engage her in conversation and Harriet was miffed by his lack of manners.

His clothing was of good quality, his accent English. He seemed to be a man who would certainly understand the proprieties, yet he chose not to follow them. Well, she was finished with allowing males to take those sorts of liberties!

"Excuse me, I see my husband and our coachman approaching."

"But that's not our—"

Harriet pulled Jeanne Marie against her side, effectively muffling the rest of the child's words. "Come along, boys," she said, warning them with her eyes to be cautious.

The children meekly fell into place and Harriet guided them across the yard. As they walked away, she noted the stranger pointedly looking down at her ringless finger. Harriet instinctively clenched her gloveless hands and told herself it meant nothing, she had hardly given herself away as an imposter. Not all married women wore rings.

She moved across the yard at a steady pace, her back straight, chin up, her hands grasping the coats of all three children. She knew the stranger was watching her closely, so she neither quickened nor slowed her pace, but kept her stride even and purposeful.

A coach and four pulled directly into their path,

slowing as it prepared to make the turn out of the yard and into the road. Forced to stop, Harriet tapped her foot impatiently as she waited, not daring to turn around and see if the stranger was following. *What could possibly be keeping Nathaniel?*

Jerome Brockhurst watched the woman and her three young children with a jaundice eye. There was something not quite right about them, yet he could not put his finger on anything that specifically justified his suspicion.

She was clearly nervous, but there were any number of things that could account for that behavior. Women often exhibited oversensitive nerves when traveling. He probably should not have spoken to her, though he hardly looked like a villainous thug intent on doing her harm.

When she first entered the yard she had been attended by a female servant who had later been sent on an errand, presumably to find out why their carriage was not here. Perhaps she was upset because the start of the day's journey had been delayed. Yet her level of agitation seemed disproportionate to her circumstances. Deciding to test his theory further, Jerome stopped a young groom and asked in a deliberately loud voice.

"I'm searching for a friend of mine and was wondering if he has come this way. By any chance, have you recently seen an English gentleman? He'd most likely be traveling by private coach since he'd have three children with him, two girls and a little boy."

The groom shook his head, but Jerome hardly noticed. He was far more interested in seeing the woman's reaction. She stiffened slightly, then

seemed to force herself to relax. Jerome's already
heightened senses went on alert.

He began walking towards her. She must have
sensed his approach for she turned and glanced at
him over her shoulder. He smiled pleasantly and
tipped his hat. She gave him a haughty glare and
he noticed her arms reaching down protectively
around her children.

Inspired, Jerome shouted, "Miss Sainthill, please
wait!"

The name seemed to hang in the air, echoing
through the bustling yard. The woman jerked at
the sound of his voice, turned her head, then gasped
in horror as if realizing she had just acknowledged
her identity. She held the children in front of her
body. The moment the coach moved out of the
way, she pushed them forward. She shouted something to them, but a second carriage rumbled into
the yard and Jerome could not understand her
command.

He tried to get closer, tried to warn her not to
run away, but he wasn't quick enough.

"Nathaniel, help!"

Jerome turned in anticipation, anxious for his
first sighting of Lord Avery. Then a fist shot out of
nowhere and caught him square on the jaw. He
tilted backward and hit the ground with a re-
sounding thud.

Harriet had never been more relieved to see
anyone in her life. She fell forward, practically col-
lapsing into Nathaniel's arms. He caught her against
his chest, and held her close. Harriet concentrated
on taking long, deep breaths, amazed that her
trembling was even greater now that the incident
was over.

Nathaniel shifted his position and slid a supportive arm around her waist, his eyes anxiously searching her person. "Are you all right?"

"I think so."

"My God, what happened? Did that man assault you?"

"No." Harriet shivered with suppressed emotion. Her eyes darted frantically about the yard. "Where are the children?"

"In the carriage with Jane." Nathaniel brushed his hand gently across her cheek. "My heart nearly ceased beating when they came charging into the stable. Then I heard you scream for help. Are you certain you are unharmed?"

"Yes, I'm merely frightened. And angry."

"Angry?"

"At myself." Harriet glared down at the man sprawled in the dirt. "I walked so neatly into his trap. He must have suspected my identity, but like a dolt I confirmed his suspicions by reacting to my name."

"Well, he's hardly a threat now. He's out cold." Nathaniel removed a handkerchief from his pocket and handed it to Harriet. She pressed the clean cloth to her upper lip, surprised to realize it was moist with perspiration.

"He had an English accent," Harriet said.

"He must be a runner, hired by my uncle to find us," Nathaniel decided.

"Which isn't very difficult, thanks to my letter and explicit directions," Harriet said wryly.

" 'ere now, what's the trouble?" The burly innkeeper marched out into the yard, leading a small army of curious spectators. "We'll have no brawlin' at my place, even if you do take it outside. It frightens the women and chases away the customers."

"This stranger accosted my wife," Nathaniel told the innkeeper and the gathering crowd. "Apparently he mistook her identity and when she pointed out the error he refused to believe her."

The innkeeper looked aghast at hearing the news. "Why the blighter! I've never heard of anything like that happenin' 'round here. We run a quality, safe establishment, always have, always will."

"I am certain this is an isolated incident," Nathaniel declared. "Clearly the man is deranged."

Harriet saw the nods of agreement from the crowd and drew a sigh of relief. All eyes turned to the runner, who lay meek and motionless on the ground. She caught Nathaniel's gaze and understood his silent message to try to slip away as the crowd debated the appropriate punishment for the attacker.

Harriet almost felt sorry for the runner when one woman suggested that hanging was too good for the likes of him and another man offered to beat some manners into him. Only one level head voiced the suggestion of calling the local magistrate, but that idea was quickly overruled. Everyone else seemed to favor a more physical retaliation.

"Please, do not make any more of a fuss. It will upset the children." Harriet lifted the handkerchief and held it to her mouth. "I know I'll feel better once I am in our coach, with my wee ones gathered around me."

"Of course ye would, puir dear," the innkeeper's wife agreed, elbowing her way through the crowd. She patted Harriet's shoulder with solicitous female comfort. Then she turned to the crowd and bellowed, "Make way fer the lady."

She linked her arm with Harriet's and parted the crowd. Flanked by the innkeeper's wife and Nathaniel, Harriet was escorted to the coach. She thanked the woman profusely for her kindness and understanding, then stepped inside.

The children fell on her like eager puppies, alternating questions and hugs with equal fervor. Gregory's eyes were round as saucers and he was nearly bouncing with excitement.

"We saw the whole thing," he stated eagerly. "Uncle Nathaniel planted one right on that man's jaw and *twack* he fell over. I even heard the noise when he fell down. It was marvelous."

Harriet sighed. "While I was certainly relieved to have your uncle's assistance, only under the most dire of circumstances does a gentleman resort to fisticuffs in public, Gregory."

"Did the man hurt you, Miss Sainthill?" Phoebe asked anxiously.

"Heavens, no." Harriet hugged the child reassuringly. "He merely startled me. However, the incident was partially my fault and should be a lesson to us all. A respectable lady must never engage in any sort of conversation with a gentleman until she has been properly introduced, especially when she is in a public place."

The girls both nodded their heads in understanding, but Gregory was too enamored with the outcome of the event to listen to any advice. After listening to him retell the story several times, Harriet decided that Gregory would become like most men of his class and enjoy the manly pursuits of sparring, horse racing, shooting, hunting, fishing, boxing, and swordsmanship. Especially with Nathaniel as his guardian.

Gregory's hero worship reached epic proportions by noon. Harriet elected to allow him the first horseback ride with his uncle. She and the girls needed a respite from the little boy's exhilaration, though she hoped the child's constant chatter would not be too taxing on Lord Avery.

She felt rather nervous about stopping for the night, wanting to put as much distance between them and the runner as possible. Nathaniel humored her concern by pushing forward until full darkness. The inn this night was not as clean, but it was not as crowded either. Two rooms were engaged and Harriet insisted Nathaniel sleep in the larger room with the children while she and Jane took the other chamber.

Above all else, the children's safety must come first.

The remaining days of the journey took on a repetitive nature, varied only by the weather, condition of the roads, and the size and quality of the inns where they spent the night. Finally, the weary travelers arrived on the outskirts of Edinburgh. Jane, the nursemaid, once had the privilege of visiting the city and she helpfully pointed out the historic landmarks to a rather curious Harriet.

The city made a most stirring first impression. A walled community dominated in the center by Edinburgh Castle, sitting majestically on its high basaltic rock, with its silhouette of ramparts and rooftops. Harriet enjoyed the beauty of the architecture and the splendor of the churches, though the less than pleasant odors reminded her that she was once again in a bustling, thriving, highly populated city.

After a brief drive down Queen Street, the coach turned onto Charlotte Square, a palace-fronted block of elegant homes that reminded Harriet very much of London. The carriage slowed as they reached the center of the street, yet even before the vehicle came to a complete stop the front entryway of a most elegant home opened and several servants hurried out to assist them.

"Please inform the Laird that Lord Avery has arrived," Nathaniel told the groom who stood at the ready to take charge of his mount.

"Aye."

"Uncle Duncan! Uncle Duncan! Guess what happened to us!" Gregory bolted from the coach, ran up the front steps and disappeared into the house.

Mortified by the child's lack of manners, Harriet scrambled out of the carriage and followed quickly on his heels.

"Are ye lookin' fer the young lad?" A pleasant-faced footman asked when Harriet entered the foyer. "He's gone tae the library searching for the Laird."

Harriet nodded her thanks. She was not about to push herself further into the house, so she waited for Nathaniel and the girls to join her and hoped Gregory was not making a total nuisance of himself. As she waited, Harriet let her gaze drift around, taking note of her surroundings with no small measure of astonishment.

The marble floors were stunning, the crystal chandelier impressive, and the vases of fresh flowers, discreetly placed on several wall tables, a delightful surprise. There was an intricate wrought-iron railing following a winding set of stairs to the next floor. Adorning the large expanse of wall along the staircase was an array of pictures, an eye-pleasing mix of landscapes and portraits.

"Miss Sainthill. This is quite a surprise." An uncharacteristically grim-faced Duncan McTate entered the elegant foyer. Gregory was nowhere in sight.

"I'm sorry we have invaded without prior notice, but there was no time to let you know of our dilemma," Harriet said. She waited for her chance to teasingly scold the Scotsman for taking liberties with his greeting, but he made no move to grasp her hand.

"You are always welcome in any of my homes," Mr. McTate replied formally, executing a stiff bow.

He smiled tightly, without humor and bore an air of distraction that Harriet did not think was entirely owing to their unexpected arrival. *Something was definitely amiss.* A warning knot of caution flickered through her body.

A footstep by the staircase caught Harriet's attention. She looked up, expecting to see Gregory, but it was a gray-haired gentleman who strode purposefully forward. His clothes were of the finest quality, his bearing aristocratic. Harriet smiled hesitantly, assuming he was either a relative or friend of the Laird's.

But then Nathaniel's voice came from the doorway, a low snarl of anger. "Bloody hell, what's he doing here?"

Harriet turned to Nathaniel. His face registered surprise, then anger. The set of his jaw was hard, the expression in his eyes murderous. There was only one individual who could put Nathaniel in such a state and Harriet's blood ran cold as she realized the identity of the mysterious gentleman.

His uncle, Lord Bridwell.

Alarmed, Harriet moved closer to Nathaniel. Her eyes anxiously scanned the open doorway, but Jeanne Marie and Phoebe did not enter the house. She saw them whispering and giggling outside with Jane, then the trio followed one of grooms as he led the carriage away. Relieved the girls would not be seen by the man who was their temporary legal guardian, Harriet turned her attention back to the drama at hand.

Lord Bridwell straightened and took a step forward, his eyes narrowing with malicious triumph. "McTate insisted he knew nothing of your whereabouts, but I knew you'd be turning up here eventually. Are the brats with you or has Brockhurst taken custody of them?"

"My nephew and nieces are none of your concern," Nathaniel insisted hotly, resentment simmering in his every word.

An amused smile curved Lord Bridwell's lips. "That's not what the courts say."

"Courts be damned. The children are mine. They belong with me and while there is breath in my body I will not relinquish them to you!"

Something brittle and dangerous flashed in Lord Bridwell's eyes. Harriet could feel the hostility radiating between the two men. If they each held swords they would in all likelihood be charging each other, swinging with the intent to kill. Though weapons were not necessary for the tension and violence to erupt. Fists would serve just as well.

Hoping to avoid a brawl, Harriet planted herself in front of Nathaniel's adversary. "Good afternoon. I am Harriet Sainthill. You must be Lord Bridwell."

His lordship's rapt gaze fixed on Harriet's face and she struggled to keep her expression neutral.

"Ah, the little governess who likes to write letters. It appears I owe you a debt of gratitude, Miss Sainthill."

Beside her, Nathaniel went rigid.

"You are gravely mistaken, my lord," Harriet replied. "The letter I sent was not meant for you. It was written purely out of concern for one of my charges. In fact, if I was aware of the consequences, I would never have penned the missive."

"Then you would have missed the opportunity

to correct a grave miscarriage of justice." Lord Bridwell's expression hardened. "But I will not condemn you for your part in this fiasco, since I am certain my nephew has lied to you about a great many things. He's rather good at it, you know."

Lord Bridwell's smug, raspy voice grated along Harriet's nerves.

"You know nothing of Lord Avery," she said. "For if you did, you would not spout such nonsense."

"I know he is a kidnapper," Lord Bridwell declared. "And soon the magistrate will also know of his crimes."

Nathaniel looked at his uncle with a speculative gleam. "If you intended to involve the law in our little family squabble, it would have already been done. Your idle threats do not intimidate me, sir."

"They should. I promise you, this is far from over, nephew." Lord Bridwell smiled with chilling certainty and sauntered away.

His departure smoothed away some of the tension that had gripped the room. For a few seconds they all stood in awkward, shocked silence.

Nathaniel finally exploded. "Christ's bones, McTate, how could you let that viper set foot under your roof?"

The Scotsman shrugged. "When he appeared on my doorstep yesterday afternoon, I knew the secret was out. If I sent him away, who knows what he might have done. It seemed wiser to invite him to stay with me. At least if he is here we know he hasn't run to a magistrate and tried to have you arrested."

Though the explanation made perfect sense, Harriet could see that Nathaniel struggled with the reasoning. His attitude was remote. He was regarding McTate cautiously, as if he no longer completely trusted his good friend. Harriet could sympathize with the Scotsman's dilemma for she too had unwittingly betrayed Lord Avery.

"We could all use a bit of rest," Harriet decided. "Perhaps we can make more sense of things in a few hours."

"An excellent suggestion." McTate seized the diversion and shot Nathaniel an unrepentant look. "I have had your usual bedchamber prepared, placed the children in the chamber beside you and Miss Sainthill next to them."

"My uncle?"

"Is on the opposite side of the house."

"Since you are familiar with the residence, will you escort me to my chamber, Lord Avery?" Harriet asked.

"I need to have a private word with the Laird," Nathaniel replied grimly.

With little more than a curt nod, the two men departed. Sighing tiredly, Harriet followed the footman to her room. As she climbed the stairs she could not help but once again be impressed by her elegant surroundings. Duncan McTate's town home was as well appointed, refined, and luxurious as any London establishment she had ever seen. It was such a stark contrast to the ancient, medieval Hillsdale Castle that Harriet could scarcely believe the same individual owned both properties.

Harriet took full advantage of the civilized amenities in her lovely bedchamber and washed away the grime of travel. Then she stretched out on the comfortable bed and closed her eyes, dozing briefly. Refreshed, she left her room an hour later and had taken but a few steps before she was waylaid by a footman.

"His lordship requests your presence in the drawing room, Miss Sainthill."

Harriet nodded and followed the servant, eager to see Nathaniel. But when she entered the drawing room she discovered it was not Lord Avery who awaited her.

"I was not sure you'd have the courage to come."

Lord Bridwell rose stiffly to his feet. His intense gaze honed in on her, but Harriet refused to so much as blink. "I might not have, if you had shown the courage to reveal the summons came from you," Harriet replied tartly.

Lord Bridwell grunted his response. He resumed his seat beside a mahogany table near the window. A shaft of sunlight illuminated his narrow, harsh face. Harriet might have considered him a handsome man if she did not know of his nature.

Harriet took her time settling into a chair. She smoothed her skirt and made a deliberate show of admiring the drawing room's rich, exotic furnishings, silk wallpaper, and gilded ceiling.

"I assume you have called me here to discuss my charges," Harriet said in her most professional, governess tone. "Would you like a detailed report of their progress? They are each apt pupils, showing excellence in various subjects."

Lord Bridwell shifted in his seat. "If you insist."

"Whom shall I speak of first?"

"The boy."

Harriet felt a rush of ill will towards Lord Bridwell. "Yes, the boy. The child you claim to have such a keen regard for, such grave concern for his future, and yet you cannot even recall his name."

There was a slight pause. "Garret."

"Gregory," Harriet said deliberately.

"The young whelp is the eighth Duke of Claridge. He will be known by his family and friends as Claridge and by the rest of society as Your Grace. His Christian name is of no importance."

"He is four years old," Harriet said. "Those of us who love him call him Gregory."

"How disappointing to learn the reports of you were misleading," Lord Bridwell replied with faint hauteur. "I had heard you were a female who disregarded sentiment."

I used to be. Harriet nearly spoke the words out loud, but she would not share such an intimacy with Lord Bridwell. She had been the type of female who was practical and sensible and even rigid. But her weeks at Hillsdale Castle and her love for Nathaniel had softened that part of her personality.

"Enough of this farce." She bolted from her chair. "We both know your interest in the children is purely monetary. Why did you summon me here?"

"I want you to use your influence on my nephew to convince him to give me the children without a legal battle. If you do, I will see that you are handsomely rewarded."

Harriet had fully intended to dislike Lord Bridwell. He had caused no small amount of anguish and suffering to those she loved and those acts of cruelty were difficult to overlook. This suggestion only served to further solidify her initial negative impression.

"Lord Avery is not a man who is easily swayed from his convictions. What makes you think I would have any influence on his decisions?"

"I see the way you look at him, with such care and concern, such deep emotion." Lord Bridwell spat out the words. "He also appears far from indifferent toward you. There are ways a clever woman can manipulate a man, if she is so inclined."

"And if I refuse to help you?"

"Then you will suffer." Lord Bridwell's hand curled into a fist, casting a claw-like shadow on the carpet.

"I am not so easily frightened. Nor is Lord Avery."

"You intend to stand beside him?"

Harriet nodded.

"A most unwise decision. My nephew is foolish, stubborn, and proud. This will be a nasty fight, yet my victory is assured. If you will not help me, at least have the sense to remove yourself from the scandal."

"I am not afraid of gossip."

"No, I do not suppose that you are, especially after last Season." His eyes gleamed with malice. "I am sure you think nothing could possibly be more hurtful or humiliating than the scandal you faced but a few months ago."

Harriet's heart skipped a beat. He was trying to intimidate her, to shake her confidence. "I am only the governess. My character is not at issue."

"Oh, but it could be. And what of my nephew? What will you say if you are called to bear witness to his character? That he lied, employed you under false pretenses, made inappropriate advances towards you? Will you, I wonder, reveal the extent of your involvement with him or will you lie under oath to save your reputation?"

"My relationship with Lord Avery has no relevance in this case," Harriet declared.

"Perhaps. And perhaps not." The corners of Lord Bridwell's mouth turned down. "Moral character is a key element in his case. You cannot deny it will be more difficult for my nephew to prove his worthiness if your involvement in this matter is taken into account."

Harriet lifted her chin. "If that were true, you

would be encouraging me to stay, for it would weaken Lord Avery's position and strengthen your own."

Lord Bridwell sighed. "Whatever you may believe, I am not a cruel man. Though you claim otherwise, I am certain my nephew lied to you. You are an innocent victim in all of this and I would not want you to be further tainted by the scandal to come."

Harriet swallowed hard. "I do not believe you."

Lord Bridwell leaned towards her. "Believe that I will use whatever means necessary to win and that will include dragging what is left of your good name through the mud. I suppose my nephew might be forced to marry you, in an attempt to add an air of respectability to your relationship. Though I believe any magistrate with a lick of sense would see through that ploy. If you have any shred of self-respect, Miss Sainthill, you will gather your belongings and make arrangements to be on the next coach out of the city."

Harriet trembled with anger and humiliation. The brutal frankness of Lord Bridwell's words hit her hard. She had no defense to his arguments. He was as ruthless and formidable as Nathaniel had told her.

"Yes, I think you are right," Harriet whispered. "I need to see about packing. Immediately."

Dignity and strength had always been two of her greatest assets. Harriet now called upon every ounce of that character as she rose from her seat. Without saying another word, she quit the room and marched resolutely up the stairs.

Chapter Twenty

Nathaniel found his uncle in the drawing room, looking smug and satisfied. When he entered the room, Lord Bridwell fixed a disdainful eye on him and Nathaniel returned the glare. He was tired of allowing this man to dictate the particulars of his life. He could hold power over him only if Nathaniel permitted it.

The worry over the fate of the children was Nathaniel's greatest weakness and Lord Bridwell had ruthlessly tried to exploit it. No longer.

Nathaniel knew precisely what he wanted and he had every intention of gaining it. He planted his feet wide and drew himself up to his full height. "I was told Miss Sainthill was in here, but I see you are alone. Has she gone for a walk in the gardens?"

Lord Bridwell raised his eyebrows. It was a forbidding gesture that Nathaniel ignored. "She has gone upstairs to pack her belongings. It took very little effort for me to convince her to leave. I originally thought she held some affection for you, but clearly my impression was mistaken."

The words were chosen carefully with the intention of wounding. Nathaniel's throat constricted. The thought of Harriet leaving brought on a black wave of despair that threatened to overpower him, but Nathaniel would not be drawn away from the true issue. The fate of the children was to be decided here and now and he was not going to be denied his victory.

"Miss Sainthill is my concern, not yours." Nathaniel scanned his uncle's harsh features, seeking some trace of familial sentiment or regard. There was none. "I have given this a great deal of thought. The Highlands are a beautiful place, desolate, harsh, and perfect for reflection." He forced his voice to sound calm, almost bored. "I had considered negotiating with you for custody of the children, essentially buying you off. But I eventually rejected the idea. After all, you might agree to a sum today and decide in a year you wanted more."

Lord Bridwell's expression tightened at the veiled insult, but he made no comment.

Nathaniel continued, "I have many legal options, and a few illegal ones, and I will not cease until I have untangled this mess in my favor. You are an old man sir, and I am a much younger one. My stamina, resources, and dedication are far superior to your own and have grown stronger these past few weeks."

"You are not invincible, nephew. The fact that I so easily located you should be an indication to you of *my* resolve in this matter."

"You found me purely by chance and I can state with certainty that you will never have a second one. Miss Sainthill told you the letter was never meant for your eyes. She acted out of kindness and consideration for the children, two ideals which I am certain you would fail to comprehend. I can find no fault with her behavior."

"You are a highly tolerant employer." Lord Bridwell's lips turned up into a sneer. "She must be an exceptional *governess.*"

Nathaniel felt the fury gathering in his chest. He would endure much from his uncle in order to gain custody of the children, but he could not allow Harriet's honor to be impugned. "There is a Bow Street Runner nursing a sore jaw who had the audacity to approach Miss Sainthill at a posting inn. If you utter one more distasteful remark I will have no difficulty giving you a pair of dark-ringed eyes to match the bruises on the runner's face."

"Threatening me?"

"Hardly. I am merely warning you of the consequences." Nathaniel looked his uncle straight in the eye. "The children belong with me and I will fight you through every court in the land if necessary. I will win. No matter how long it takes or how much money it costs."

Lord Bridwell squirmed slightly in his chair, as if the reality of the situation was just beginning to dawn upon his mind. "You are too hasty with your accusations and your readiness to battle. There is no need for a lot of barristers to get rich over a family disagreement. If we put our minds to it, as civilized men, we should be able to reach an acceptable agreement."

"You are not a civilized man. I am, however, a reasonable one." Nathaniel felt the muscle in his jaw twitch with excitement. Was it possible that he had finally managed to convince his uncle to relent? "My solicitor will draw up the appropriate papers and you will sign them. In recognition of your cooperation you will be awarded modest financial compensation."

"The dukedom is worth a fortune! I'll not be bought off by a mere pittance."

"The amount will be fair. But also non-negotiable."

Nathaniel held his breath as he waited for a response. He had never sat across the gaming tables from his uncle and knew not if he was the type of man willing to wager on the possibility of winning in the distant future or taking the sure thing of the moment. Lord Avery believed he had proven that he would not quietly relinquish his claim. Was it enough to convince the older man to cry off?

Had he underestimated how far his adversary was willing to take this matter? Should he have offered more money, more incentives?

The questions swirled in his brain, but outwardly Nathaniel showed no signs of his inner qualms. Yet his concentration was soon broken by the sound of a loud thump, followed by a shout. It came from an upper floor in the mansion and sounded as if someone was in the middle of an argument.

Lord Avery tried to ignore the noise, but it grew too loud. Worried that one, two, or all three of the children might be involved, Nathaniel had to investigate. Sparing a quick glance at his stone-faced uncle, he quit the drawing room and ascended to the second floor.

He followed the sounds down a short hallway and discovered a servant standing in the open doorway of one of the bedchambers. The shrieks were coming from inside the room. Recognizing the voice, Nathaniel frowned and charged forward.

Upon seeing him, the servant's eyes lit with relief. "Oh sir, please, you must aid me," he cried anxiously. "I am Lord Bridwell's valet and this is his bedchamber. Not ten minutes ago a woman came barreling into the room and began grabbing his lordship's clothing. I tried to stop her, but she screeched like a Bedlamite and then threw his lordship's new coat at me!"

It was then that Nathaniel noticed the man clutched in his hand a coat of blue superfine, guarding the item like a sentry.

"I am acquainted with the lady," Nathaniel told the fidgeting valet. "Perhaps she will tell me what is wrong."

The servant let out an exaggerated sigh and backed away from the doorway. Curious, Nathaniel peered inside the room and discovered Harriet rummaging through the wardrobe. He watched her yank out a pile of clean shirts, stalk across the room and shove them haphazardly into the open portmanteau that was set in the middle of the bed.

"Harriet, what are you doing?"

She glanced up at him briefly, her face taut with suppressed rage. "Your uncle is a horse's arse."

"You'll hear no argument from me on that point."

"First he tried to bribe me, then he insulted me, and finally he tried to frighten me." She dumped a smart pair of riding boots unceremoniously onto the carpet and returned to the wardrobe for a second pair of footwear.

"So you decided to attack his clothing in retaliation?"

Harriet's gaze clouded over. "No, I am merely following his orders. Lord Bridwell insisted that I go upstairs and begin packing and for the first time since I have met him, I agreed with something he said. But instead of packing my belongings, I decided to get *his* ready for a swift departure."

A grin spread across Nathaniel's face. He should have known that Harriet would not be so easily chased away. "Lord Bridwell told me you were leaving."

Harriet paused and stiffened her spine. "He thought he could scare me off, the old coot. But let me tell you, it will take far more than an irritating, tyrannical old bugger like Lord Bridwell to eject me from your life."

A deep sense of relief swept over Nathaniel. For a long moment he just stared at her. She was magnificent in her righteous anger, with her eyes blazing and her bosom heaving. He knew of course that he loved her, but he knew also that he wanted to take care of her, to be her lover, her husband, her partner in all things.

"Harriet, I love you."

Her hand froze in the act of tossing a neat pile of handkerchiefs into the luggage. "What?"

"I said, I love you."

"I know." Harriet's eyes grew soft. "I heard you the first time, but I just wanted to hear you say it again."

She threw the linen handkerchiefs on the floor and came rushing into his arms. Nathaniel enfolded her in his embrace, then lowered his mouth to hers in a kiss that was tender and pure, a promise that at last could be fulfilled.

It felt heavenly to hold her thus, to declare openly that she was his. He realized in that moment that trying to live the rest of his life without Harriet would be impossible. There would be no true, sustained happiness if she were not with him. Love, in its unselfish state, would forever hover elusively beyond his reach.

"Egad, I can't leave the two of you alone for a minute."

Nathaniel reluctantly lifted his head. "Go away, McTate."

"I can't. There's trouble afoot." The laird entered the room and glanced around in confusion. "What happened in here?"

"Harriet is supervising Lord Bridwell's departure," Nathaniel explained. "She has a unique approach to packing."

McTate's eyes lit with humor. "Hmm, remind me never to get that lass truly angry at me."

" 'Tis sound advice that I intend to follow for the rest of my life," Nathaniel replied with a satisfied grin. He gave Harriet a last gentle kiss, then reluctantly turned to McTate. "You said there was trouble?"

"Aye. There's a man here inquiring after you. Says his name is Brockhurst."

Nathaniel frowned. "The name does not sound familiar. Does he claim to know me?"

"No, he insists he has information of grave importance for you. He's English, most likely from London and 'tis my belief he's the runner your uncle hired to find you."

"So naturally you admitted him to the house." Nathaniel exhaled sharply. "I swear McTate, the next thing you'll be telling me is that you've invited the magistrate to dinner!"

The Scotsman shot him an unconcerned glance. "Never fear, I'll not allow him to arrest you. It would be a blot on my otherwise sterling character if it were ever known that I harbored such a dangerous criminal within these walls."

"Duncan McTate!" Harriet's voice trembled with indignation.

"Och, now don't let your feathers get all ruffled, lass. I was merely joking."

Nathaniel, used to the laird's sense of humor, took no offense. "Where is Brockhurst?"

"I had the butler show him to the drawing room."

Nathaniel groaned. "I left my uncle in there barely a half an hour ago. Where are the children?"

"Safe in the nursery having a grand time," McTate replied. "I've got servants posted on all the stairways to the third floor. It would take Wellington's army to get past my men."

Satisfied the children were well taken care of, Nathaniel led the way to the drawing room, his uneasiness growing with each step. Within the room Lord Bridwell and the runner waited in complete silence, the atmosphere brittle with tension.

The grim feelings Nathaniel had experienced earlier strengthened as he faced the two men. A large purple bruise shadowed the runner's jaw and he wore a rumpled coat that needed to be cleaned and pressed. Lord Bridwell's expression seemed more haggard than usual, but Nathaniel though that impression might be more his hopeful imagination than the truth.

"I am Lord Avery. I was told you wanted to speak with me, Brockhurst?"

The runner nodded. "I do, but first, I have something I need to deliver."

Brockhurst reached into his satchel and pulled out a worn, ragged lump of fabric. It received little reaction from the others in the room, but Nathaniel recognized it instantly.

"Lady Julienne," he muttered in astonishment.

"Is it really?" Harriet stepped closer, reaching eagerly for the doll. "Jeanne Marie will be overjoyed. Thank you, Mr. Brockhurst. You have made a little girl very happy."

" 'Tis an honor to be of service, Miss." The runner briskly pulled a second item from the satchel. "In the course of my investigation I discovered this at your family's London residence. The letter is addressed to you, Lord Avery."

Curious, Nathaniel unfolded the parchment. Harriet and McTate crowded close trying to get a look.

"It was written by my brother, Robert, a few days before his death," Nathaniel exclaimed softly as he carefully read the page. "He worries for the future and asks me to care for his children if the fates are so cruel as to take his life."

Nathaniel squeezed his eyes shut as memories of his dear brother filled his mind. The laughter and pranks of childhood, the secrets and fears of boys on the verge of manhood, the solid companionship and trust of men who shared a true regard for each other.

Nathaniel swallowed hard, worried that the ache in his throat would produce the tears he had refused to shed. "Even at the end when he was so dreadfully ill, Robert thought of those he loved. He did not fail me nor his children," Nathaniel said stiffly. "And here stands the proof."

Lord Bridwell's eyes grew round. " 'Tis a forgery," he hissed. "A pathetic attempt to manufacture evidence to support your claim of guardianship."

"A fake letter discovered by a runner in your employ, Uncle? Even I cannot be that clever."

"You could have planted it in the mansion at any time," Lord Bridwell insisted. "There was ample opportunity."

Nathaniel laughed. "To what end? If you discovered it we both know it would have quickly been turned to ash in the fireplace."

With an awkward, nervous motion Lord Bridwell held out his hand. "I demand to read this so-called proof for myself."

"I'll have my solicitor send you a copy the moment I return to London," Nathaniel responded pleasantly as he neatly folded the letter and placed it in his breast coat pocket. Dismissing Lord Bridwell, he turned to the runner. "I owe you a depth of gratitude that will be difficult to repay, Mr. Brockhurst. Along with an apology for that sore jaw."

The runner rubbed his fingers lightly over the bruise. "You certainly caught me with my guard down."

"I have no doubt the element of surprise gave me the greater advantage." Nathaniel held out his hand and the runner shook it. "In appreciation of your efforts, I would like to offer you a bonus."

"No need for any of that, my lord. My reward is a job well done." Mr. Brockhurst leaned close and lowered his voice confidentially, "and, Lord Bridwell has paid me a handsome fee plus all the expenses of my journey to Scotland."

The men shared a private laugh. Then with a final bow and a satisfied expression, the runner left. Lord Bridwell stood in stunned silence for several moments. Nathaniel took advantage of the quiet to issue his final edict.

"Uncle, since your clothes are already packed, I believe this would be a most opportune time for you to depart. Have a safe journey back to England."

The command snapped the older man from his stupor. "You are talking nonsense," he bristled. "I gave my valet no instructions."

"Actually I was the one who handled that particular detail," Harriet replied sweetly.

Lord Bridwell whirled around and glared at her. "You had the audacity to give my servant orders? Without my permission?"

"Goodness, no. I would never be so presumptuous." Harriet pursed her mouth. "Do you not recall, why, less than an hour ago, you suggested I go upstairs to pack? And I have done just that, with one slight alteration. I have packed *your* garments. I so hope you approve of my handling of your belongings. Lord Avery and Mr. McTate thought I was a bit harsh and your valet, well, that poor man might never recover from the incident."

Lord Bridwell opened his mouth, but closed it without uttering another word. After a moment, he seemed to realize he was staring blankly into the air. With a snort of pure disgust he turned away and stormed from the room in a huff, slamming the door behind him for good measure.

"You were magnificent, lass." McTate lifted her up in a giant bear hug and twirled her around twice before setting her back on her feet. "Please tell me you have a sister back home who is waiting for a handsome Scot to come and sweep her off her feet."

Harriet's face paled as she thought of her gentle, fragile sister Elizabeth and the brawny laird. "I do have a sister and she is the most beautiful, most docile creature in the country. Far too delicate to handle a Scottish devil like you, Duncan McTate."

"But I want to meet her!"

"I'm certain she will be at our wedding, but you will only be granted an introduction if you promise to keep your charm to yourself," Nathaniel declared.

A crafty expression crept over the laird's handsome face. "Aye, well, truth be told, there is no need for a wedding, 'cause you are already wed."

"What?" Baffled, both Harriet and Nathaniel stared at the laird.

McTate grinned broadly. "Have you not been traveling about the country telling everyone you are husband and wife?"

Nathaniel nodded. "We have."

"Then it's done." McTate gave Nathaniel a sly nudge. "This is Scotland, my good man, not stuffy old England. If you've proclaimed yourself married in front of witnesses, then indeed you are man and wife."

Harriet felt her jaw lower. "Is he right?"

"Probably." Nathaniel cleared his throat sharply. "But it doesn't matter, because I intend to stand before a priest of the Anglican church with Phoebe, Jeanne Marie, and Gregory, plus all of your family in attendance and marry you properly." Nathaniel turned to Harriet, held her hands between his own and dropped down on one knee. "If you'll have me?"

Harriet almost choked on a bubble of happiness. It was what she had dared to dream and now the reality of it made her giddy with excitement and joy. "Oh, I'll have you, Lord Avery. And I'll keep you, too!"

They were married a month later in the small village church of Harriet's childhood. Her brother, the Viscount Harrowby, gave her away and her sister-in-law, Faith, planned a wedding feast worthy of a princess. All the local gentry had been invited as well as a few select members of London society. Duncan McTate stood up with Nathaniel, and the handsome laird garnered more than his share of attention from the unmarried ladies in attendance.

Even Lord Bridwell had attended the church service, though he declined to stay for the reception. He had not given in gracefully to losing control of the ducal fortune, yet he had no qualms about taking the financial settlement Nathaniel offered in hopes of making peace with his uncle.

Armed with the indisputable proof uncovered by Jerome Brockhurst, Nathaniel's petition for permanent legal guardianship had been swiftly granted. Though he would never publicly admit it,

Lord Bridwell knew he was fortunate to have received anything.

After the ceremony, the guests returned to Hawthorne Castle for the bridal supper. The house was draped with garlands of flowers and the ten course meal was served on the finest china. Harriet felt guilty about the cost of the lavish affair, but her brother and his wife had insisted she be married with all the pomp and circumstance they could muster.

Too excited to eat, Harriet had circulated among the guests, her arm tucked securely in the crook of her new husband's arm. She could not remember a time in her life when she felt such supreme happiness, such hope for a future filled with joy and laughter and children. Her three beloved children by marriage, and she hoped, one day soon, a child from her body to add to the brood.

She was also greatly looking forward to her bridal trip, which would begin in two days. Flouting convention, she had made the arrangements for a month-long respite herself, and she was eager to share her plans with Nathaniel.

Later that night as they snuggled together in their bridal bed, Harriet whispered her surprise in her husband's ear. Amusement flickered across Nathaniel's face. "There are so many exotic places to travel, so many curious sights to see, yet you want to return to Scotland?"

Lazily, she curled her body around his. "The children will be staying here with my brother and Faith and I do not wish to be too far away from them. When I mentioned my idea to Duncan he was more than pleased to offer his much-praised Scottish hospitality."

Nathaniel seemed skeptical. "Are you certain? I

highly doubt Mrs. Mullins's cooking or housekeeping skills have improved."

Harriet laughed. "Not to mention her brogue, though I was beginning to understand her a little better when we left."

"Then why Hillsdale Castle?"

With an impish grin, she twirled her arms around his neck and pressed herself against his hard strength. "Because, my love, that is where this all began!"

ABOUT THE AUTHOR

Adrienne Basso lives with her family in New Jersey. She is the author of five Zebra historical romances set in the Regency period and is currently working on her next historical romance to be published in 2005. Adrienne loves to hear from readers and you may write to her c/o Zebra Books. Please include a self-addressed stamped envelope if you wish a response.

BOOK YOUR PLACE ON OUR WEBSITE AND MAKE THE READING CONNECTION!

We've created a customized website just for our very special readers, where you can get the inside scoop on everything that's going on with Zebra, Pinnacle and Kensington books.

When you come online, you'll have the exciting opportunity to:

- View covers of upcoming books
- Read sample chapters
- Learn about our future publishing schedule (listed by publication month *and author*)
- Find out when your favorite authors will be visiting a city near you
- Search for and order backlist books from our online catalog
- Check out author bios and background information
- Send e-mail to your favorite authors
- Meet the Kensington staff online
- Join us in weekly chats with authors, readers and other guests
- Get writing guidelines
- AND MUCH MORE!

**Visit our website at
http://www.kensingtonbooks.com**